The Gestalt Complete

Book 2 of The Behemoth Gestalt

A Novel In Behemoth's Shadow

Chad W. Knox

ALSO BY CHAD W. KNOX

In The Shadow of Behemoth Universe

The Gestalt Series
Book 0: What Went Before the Gestalt
Book 1: Gathering of the Gestalt
Book 2: The Gestalt Complete
Book 3: War of the Gestalt (in progress)

INTERESTED IN MORE OF THIS
UNIVERSE'S INSANITY? CHECK US OUT
ON FACEBOOK AT
"MUGZ INK BOOKS"

Copyright 2024 Mugz Ink Books LLC

For more information, follow "Mugz Ink Books" on Facebook.

Paperback: ISBN 979-8-9891794-6-6
Hardback: ISBN 979-8-9891794-7-3
E-Book: ISBN 979-8-9891794-8-0

Edited by Moi (sorry)

DEDICATION

Always for Sarah.
(B & V Days are covered; this counts as an anniversary card,
right?)

For Pat M-S,
Your CW are enroute, promise.

CONTENTS

THE GESTALT COMPLETE

ACKNOWLEDGMENTS

To the military healthcare system, thanks for keeping me medicated to the gills so I can get this all out.

Thanks Walt, for reminding me dreamers still have to look after the little things.

Thanks for turning the pages.

Author's Note

Hopefully, Rhi's calmed down enough from Book 0 for me to get some of this down. This story—

NOPE! Still pissed.

Bio-Habitat 00117
Observation Post 36211

CR'EON

Things had become a bit more interesting. The survivors of the initial culling began to cluster and fight back where they could. The fights were what was interesting.

The few organized military units that remained were relatively stagnant in their fighting techniques. While somewhat effective, they were boring to watch.

What really piqued my interest were the fights by the inexperienced. Their struggle constantly created opportunities for ingenuity. The problem was not many of them were good... or entertaining.

Part of my observation post training program said not to get attached during any culling. Most of the time, you'd be disappointed because your attachment would be destroyed. On the rare occasion your attachment survived and was selected for the Chosen Army, you'd still be disappointed as you'd never see them again. Once Chosen, they're whisked away for training and rarely returned to their original Bio-Hab.

So, I watched and waited. The probes Behemoth used were excellent and allowed me to get as close to the action as I wanted. I must admit, I saved a few video clips to add to my collection. While frowned upon, recording Bio-Habs wasn't against regulations. The underground market for these clips was quite active. The most coveted clips were the raw footage of clashes between the AG and DC, not that I'd ever recorded one myself.

I was already opening the report folder when the daily chime sounded. In the past few weeks, I'd begun to look forward to my reports as I finally had something of interest to report! Now, if they would just notice and possibly do something about it.

> This is Cr'eon, Bio-Habitat 00117, with my daily report. No detectible Angel Guard activity. Inhabitants remain unaware of their Bio-Hab containment. The culling protocol continues into the end of the first quarter. The figures of the culled are attached, along with current population densities and locations.

I've included notes on subjects who've survived multiple conflicts. I've flagged them as appropriate for Chosen Army candidate review by Behemoth.

I tried to hold back my excitement as I wasn't allowed to include notes of a personal nature in my reports. Just the facts. But nothing said I couldn't guide my findings.

Verifying the current readings, I returned to my report.

> Bio-Hab failure timeline remains constant. The minor system fluctuations previously observed have begun to cascade. While no system shows signs of malfunction, the pattern of the interference seems to be expanding. I have found no single cause for these fluctuations and continue to observe the affected locations. I have notified next line for assistance in identifying the cause and possible effects if the fluctuations remain unchecked.

I encoded my report and transmitted it quickly so I could get back to recording my clips.

Tolls

JAMES

"You think this is the roadblock the others were telling us about?" Shae glanced at me, her blue eyes flashing.

"More than likely." I took my foot off the gas and allowed the Dilla to slowly coast to a stop. We were at the crest of a hill, a good two klicks shy of the small settlement.

The town was small and straddled the main highway. There were ravines on two sides with bridges crossing them. Cars had been strung around the two sides of the town, which were not protected by the ravines, and across the highway, creating a roadblock. I could just make out what looked like barbed wire strung between the cars. Someone had put up sheet metal at various places, building a poor man's wall.

Shambler bodies littered the fields nearest the wall. A makeshift tower had been constructed, and I could see at least one person manning it with a rifle. There were a few other sentries at the top of the wall, but as I watched, more began to stream out from the houses on either side of the highway.

"Looks like they're using the cars as a protective wall for their town." Glancing at the map again, "There's no way we could maneuver through the river at the bottom of those ravines." I looked up and saw the ravines stretching off towards the horizon in either direction.

"And these guys probably blocked the bridges too," Shae said.

"More than likely," I frowned.

"What do you want to do?" Shae asked.

"If these are the scumbags we're looking for, I want to wipe them out. But, since we're here looking for someone, that wouldn't be very courteous, would it?" I said.

"If these people are the kidnappers, they deserve what they get. Not to mention, we've been told they're 'charging' people to use the road," Shae spat in disgust.

"It's only been what, three months since Z Day and already it's turning into Mad Max out here," I shook my head.

On our way to Houston, we encountered a woman, beaten and bloody, lying in a field next to the road. She was barely conscious but led us to the small town she and her daughter had been abducted from. Apparently, she'd become "too much trouble" for the gang, and they dumped her on the side of the road.

The town had been grateful for her return and thought we were part of the Army, considering the vehicle we were driving. Even once they learned we weren't, they still pleaded with us to try and find the girl. They had a list of several possible culprits in the local area. The fact there were so many gangs in the area it required a list was worrying.

I'd left it up to Pete as we were on his timetable. He'd reluctantly agreed, saying he couldn't live with himself if he looked the other way.

That had been two days ago. We'd taken what intel they could give us and scoured the landscape. Every other lead we'd been given had been a dead-end. This blockade town was the last one the townsfolk knew about.

"That's them alright," Pete said from the back. He'd popped up the "periscope" that contained the optics suite for the Dilla and was scanning the town. "Both vehicles the townsfolk described are parked beside the brown house." He handed us a small tablet that displayed an older single-story house with two vans parked out front.

"I'd consider that a successful recon. Nice work Pete," I nodded as Shae handed him the tablet back. I took another quick look at the landscape, searching for access points.

"We've got company. Two motorcycles are heading our way," Pete said.

"Rescue missions were never frontal assaults," I sighed and wheeled the vehicle around, heading in the opposite direction.

A few kilometers down the road, "They broke off," Pete confirmed via the periscope. The Dilla didn't have a rearview mirror since the cargo compartment at the vehicle's rear was fully enclosed to protect its payload. Aside from the Dilla's side mirrors, Pete and his optics suite were our only "eyes" facing rearward.

"What now?" Shae asked.

"Now, we wait for the Devil's Hour," I frowned as my darker side started to plot.

∞∞Ω∞∞

JAMES

The moon was low in the sky as Shae and I skirted the river's edge, making quick time towards a mark on my map. Thanks to our vampiric abilities, we moved silently over the rocky terrain. We slowed when we could hear the small settlement and became utterly silent.

We crawled slowly up the sloping bank until we could see the dark houses. A few had flickering lights signifying a lantern or candle, while a single generator was running noisily at the far edge of town. We spent several minutes watching and waiting.

No patrols, Shae noted mentally to me.

Didn't think there would be. You see any guards at all? I asked through our mental link.

None. As a matter of fact, I don't see anyone, which is a shame, Shae said.

Why? I asked.

We could ask them where the prisoners are, Shae said, not taking her eyes off the settlement.

I should have thought of that, I said.

Yes, you should have. You're getting soft. Shae grinned.

Yeah. Her words struck a chord with me. I hadn't been following the training regime Rhi had made for me. Real life just kept getting in the way. I felt out of shape, even though my raw abilities still made me better than I'd ever been when I was alive. Shae's touch on my arm drew my attention.

Hey, that was a joke, she soothed. *Let's talk about it later, huh?*

Footfalls made our heads snap around as we saw someone walking away from the houses towards the river further down the bank. We followed silently.

Just as the man unzipped his fly, I snaked my arms around him, one covering the man's mouth, another pinning his arms and lifting him off the ground. Immediately, the man began flailing and grunting. He was nothing compared to my strength, but it still made noise as we moved back down the bank towards the river.

Have you learned nothing? Shae asked as she sliced the man's arm with one of her razor-sharp earrings. The man immediately went quiet and still, her bloodtouch silencing his mind.

Oh yeah. Sorry, old habits, I mumbled, having been schooled twice in the last five minutes.

We'll have to work on that. Now hush, let me work. She was quiet momentarily as she sifted through the man's mind. She stiffened suddenly, and the man's eyes rolled up in his head as his body went limp.

What is it? I asked, lowering the unconscious man to the ground.

There's more than one. She shared the information she'd gleaned from the man with me. This gang had been roaming the surrounding countryside, raping and pillaging as if this were some barbarian movie. They had over a dozen hostages, and nearly everyone was "taking turns" with them.

How do you feel about wholesale slaughter? I asked, my blood starting to boil the same as hers.

Normally, I frown upon it. But, when it comes to rapists and slavers, I make exceptions, Shae said coldly.

I knew about Shae's time as a slave to a pirate captain back in her breathing days. I'd accidentally relived it one night while we were in Bloodtouch. That nightmare was normally a tightly guarded secret with her. She buried it and managed to ignore it, as there weren't many reminders of that sort of thing in modern times. Now, coming face to face with it, something cold and dark inside her awakened.

We took several minutes to go through the man's mind again, noting the locations of guards and trying to decipher if there were still innocents in the gang. There seemed to be a few, but this man was not one of them.

Shae listened as I formed a plan. This was my darker side's territory. While in the service, I'd been trained to do things that were not socially acceptable. I didn't like it. Like Shae, I tried to keep it bottled up until it was needed. Sadly, it was needed more than I liked.

You know I'm pretty much in the against column regarding murder, I said slowly, trying to think of another way around this.

You and I both. But this isn't murder. This is a cancer we're cutting out. If left unchecked, it will grow, attracting more like-minded people. Or worse, converting those who've lost their moral compass, Shae said, her words surprising me.

Of all the dark things in my past, I'd never done them on this scale before. I paused and looked at her. *You don't have to be here,* I said gently.

I'm more than able, Shae said sternly.

I know that luv. But you don't HAVE to be here. I can get this done on my own, I said flatly.

She pretended to think about it a moment. *You're sweet, but you need me.*

Always. I smiled grimly.

I'll be fine. She nodded at my concern for her moral well-being. Then she seemed to stop everything and look at me. *James, we don't have to do this. We could easily sneak in there, grab the hostages and get out.*

Trust me, I thought about it. I paused, collecting my thoughts. *But like you said, this is a cancer. There is no one else to police these things anymore.*

That doesn't mean it's your responsibility, Shae offered.

I could sense Shae was trying to give me a way out, just as I'd tried to give her one. She'd gotten a taste of some of the darker things in my past and was trying to look out for me. I was grateful for her concern, but I could feel the disgust for these monsters coming off her just as much as it was coming from me. I squeezed her hand and nodded. *Let's get to work.*

What about this one? Shae asked.

This one is our top off. We had both fed just before we left the Alamo, but it had been a few days. If we were going to pull off what I had planned, we'd need all the energy we could muster.

We didn't drain him completely; neither of us wanted to risk holding that much blood. There were risks when it came to that sort of thing. When we were done, I made sure he never woke up.

By the time dawn broke, we were done. It had taken longer than I thought it would; it had also been harder. I didn't know if that was a good thing or not.

There had been a few close calls, but our teamwork ensured we had kept each other safe. Thanks to the mental link we shared, we were practically one person sometimes.

We were both filthy from our chore, both in body and mind. We'd had to bloodtouch every person in the town to verify who they were, what they'd done and if we had missed anyone. You couldn't touch that much darkness and not have some of it stain you.

Of the dozen hostages, only eight were still alive, including the girl we'd come looking for. Each of them seemed to be mostly intact mentally, but what they'd been through was obvious.

We packed the survivors into two vans before setting off for the small town we'd come from, meeting up with Pete and the Dilla along the way. The town had been overjoyed with not only the return of the girl but the fact the raiders had been done away with. A few of the surviving hostages asked to stay in the town while the rest took the vans and headed back to where they'd been abducted from.

Shae and I cleaned up and rested the day as the townsfolk cleaned up our clothes for us the best they could.

The townspeople had gone to the roadblock while we rested to loot the place for supplies. They confirmed the few whom we'd let live the previous night appeared to have taken our mental suggestions and fled the area.

But the looks and whispers the townsfolk gave us once they returned showed they were shocked by the massacre they'd found.

We set off again about nightfall, hoping to push through to Houston without getting sidetracked again. Along the way, we stopped at the roadblock and used the Dilla to clear the highway for future travelers.

Ellington Field

JAMES

Back in Austin, I'd managed to tap into a series of relays in order to access the military network. The complexity of Pagoda's military hardware surprised me. It was eye-opening just how much the military had given Pagoda. I'd been able to pull up intel on Pete's mother to discover she was in an evacuation camp located on Ellington Field just southeast of Houston.

Ellington Field was a small Texas Air Guard base that housed units from all branches, NASA, and Homeland Security. The UAVs stationed at the base had been one of the main reasons the military had kept the base open after Z Day. They had reinforced the place and dropped supplies. The last information I could find told me the base was still up and running. I just hoped Pete's mom was still there.

It took us the entire night to cross Houston. We had avoided the highway, as it would have taken us straight through the heart of the massive city. Austin was big, but nothing compared to the size of Houston. I was worried about what might be waiting for us downtown, so we skirted the city's outer ring.

The sun was rising as we approached the gate to Ellington. The typical three meter chain-link fence was covered from the inside with a green tarp-like material that blocked the view onto the base. Some portions had been replaced with sheets of metal, possibly where breaches had occurred. I could see the silhouettes of two HMMWVs just inside the front gate.

A .50 caliber machine gun on top of one of the HMMWVs swung our way as we approached. The gunner was yelling at someone we couldn't see, and suddenly, an airman appeared at the top of the gate. He was in uniform and decked out in full battle rattle.

The Airman started giving us hand signals, telling us to stop. I stopped where we were and looked around. A few more hand signals from the Airman and I started flashing the Dilla's lights, turning on the windshield wipers, turn signals, etc.

Shae watched me curiously. "What are you doing?"

"It's a bomb check," I sounded slightly baffled. "They're ensuring no one's attached a bomb to any of our systems."

"I didn't know the zombies had sappers," Shae shook her head.

After a few more signal checks, the Airman seemed satisfied and opened the gate. We pulled forward into another fenced-off containment area with a second gate. Once inside, the first gate closed, trapping us inside. The Airman approached the vehicle and motioned for us to get out.

The first thing I noticed as I opened the door was how quiet it was. I was so used to certain noises associated with an air base that it made me uneasy not to hear them.

Shae and Pete gathered next to me as the Airman approached.

"IDs, please," The Airman said.

I got a better look at the "kid" now. He looked about 18, had one stripe and was armed with both rifle and pistol. The way the security was being handled reminded me of bases downrange.

I fished out our IDs and handed them to the Airmen, motioning to Pete. "He's a civilian who's been working computer ops for us. He's here to find his family as they were last listed as refugees here." I turned back to the Airmen examining my ID card and watched the kid's eyes widen before glancing back up at me.

As the kid held the card under the handheld scanner, I suddenly remembered why the kid looked like I had just handed him a live grenade. The rank on my ID card had been changed by Travis when we were in San Antonio. I was now a two-star general, according to military records. I just hoped Travis hadn't screwed with it after the incident at Pagoda's compound.

I heard the machine's customary beep and held my breath as the Airman examined my ID card again. I was still holding my breath when the kid scanned Shae's ID and handed both back to me. It wasn't until the Airman snapped a salute that I started breathing again.

"Sorry about that, General. Sir, Airman T...Tucker reports Golf 1 is all secure. Do you request a post-briefing?"

The M2 gunner, who'd been watching us, suddenly stiffened at Amn Tucker's actions.

"That won't be necessary, Airman," I returned the salute and dropped it quickly. "Where can I take this man to find his family?"

"Go straight through the first traffic circle, then turn left at the light. That road will take you straight back to the refugee camp. The guards there can take care of you from there, sir. Would you like me to call an escort?"

"No need, I'm sure we can find it. Thank you," I saluted again, cutting off the Airman's follow-up question by making him return the salute.

"Yes sir," Tucker said.

We returned to the Dilla and started it up as the second gate began opening.

"That was easy," Shae said as we rolled through the gate.

"Don't jinx it!" I said, my own nerves starting to calm down. As we drove. "People get nervous around Generals."

"Why? They're just people," Pete said.

I laughed. "There are not many of them, so it's rare to run across one. And yes, most of the time they're just normal people. The problem is your supervisor and their supervisor, and such love to ping anytime stars are mentioned. So, it trickles downhill."

The Air Base was crowded. Every available space had

equipment, tents, vehicles, or people staged on it. While plenty of uniforms were walking around, there were just as many people in civilian clothes. The tension here was palpable. No one was smiling or talking; instead, their eyes constantly scanned the area for threats. The streets were practically deserted of vehicle traffic.

I followed the directions and approached a large general-purpose tent set up outside a fenced-in area that housed row after row of tents and portable trailers.

"Must be the place," Pete chimed in from the back.

We parked and approached the large tent with a sign out front that said "Administration." More posted signs signaled prohibited weapons, electronic devices, etc. All the standard "no-no's" on a military base.

Inside the tent was a metal detector and a guard sitting at a table beside it. This was another one-striped Airman.

"What can I do for you?" The Airman asked.

I fished my ID out and handed it to the Airman. "We need to find out if you have a certain refugee here."

"Well, the lists are kept with..." He started in a bored tone, then shot to his feet when he saw the rank on the ID card. "I'm sorry sir. Here, come this way please." The Airman led us towards the back.

The metal detectors buzzed as we passed through, but the Airman didn't seem to care as he continued past the partitions and into the next room. A plywood half-wall was set up, with plastic tables behind it holding a pair of computers. Another Airman, this time one with three stripes, was transcribing sheets of paper into one of the computers. A cold cup of coffee sat forgotten next to her.

"Thompson," The Airman started, causing her to look up. "The GENERAL here needs to find someone inside."

Senior Airman Thompson looked confused momentarily, first looking up at me, then back at the first Airman before what he'd said sank in.

"Oh!" She stood up a bit awkwardly. She looked as if she'd been sitting quite a while. "What can I do for you General?"

"Pete?" I ushered Pete up and he started talking with

Thompson.

After a few minutes of computer searching, "I believe this is her." She turned the screen to Pete, whose face lit up.

"That's her!" Pete said.

"OK, let's see. Says here she's in tent 2117. Go through those doors over there and follow it straight back to the twenty-first row of tents. Then it should be the seventeenth tent as you go right. The tents have the numbers stenciled on them, but they tend to fade quickly out here. Let me know if there's anything else I can do for you, sir."

"Actually, can you tell me where the fuel pumps are?" I asked. She gave me directions but said we'd need a fuel key. Since I didn't have one, I'd have to talk to vehicle ops, which was conveniently adjacent to the pumps.

Once in the cantonment area, things got noisy but not loud. It was more like a low murmur constantly in the background. As we passed people, they were talking in soft tones, as if they were in a library or something. No one paid us any attention as we passed through.

The same sense of melancholy seemed to prevail here. Of course, the first time I'd had to live in a tent city, I hadn't been too happy about it either. I couldn't imagine what this was like for civilians who were used to their suburban mcmansions.

Soon enough, we arrived at our destination. I noted the tents continued in both directions for quite a while. I grabbed Pete's arm just as he reached for the tent flap.

"Hold up," I said.

"What?" Pete said, his excitement bubbling over.

"We don't know if this is a female-only tent or not. Shae, can you look please?" I asked.

"Sure," she stepped up and made her way through the tent's layers. A minute later, she emerged with an older woman following slowly behind her.

"Mom!" Pete yelled, startling the woman as he threw his arms around her.

Shae touched my arm and we walked a short distance away, giving Pete and his mother some privacy.

"It's wall to wall in there," Shae said after a minute.

"Usually is in those things," I looked around again. "With the number of people they have here, I don't see how they're keeping this place running. They must have supply drops running constantly."

"Either that or they're running scavenger runs around the clock," Shae nodded. "What now?"

"Well, I want to save Drakes for last. I want to check on my other friends first, if possible."

"I need to check on my family as well," Shae said.

"Yeah...about that," I started.

"Not now, later. Do you have any idea where your other friends are?" Shae asked.

"One's with NASA; that's not too far from here," I said.

"Didn't I see a sign, here on base, for NASA on the way here?" Shae asked.

"I think so," I said, trying to remember.

"Why not check with those guys? Maybe they know something?" Shae said.

"Good idea," I said.

"Have you checked for your other friends in the refugee database?" Shae said.

"Yeah, they weren't in it when we were in Austin."

"Why not check here?" Shae asked.

"You're just chock full of good ideas, aren't you lady?" I grinned.

"That's why they pay me the big bucks," Shae returned my grin.

I told Pete we'd be back in an hour or so and left him and his mom at the tent. Back at the admin tent, SrA Thompson ran all the names I gave her against the database, but none came up. She did tell me where the NASA folks hung out. I thanked her for her help and headed out the door.

We found a group of NASA folks at the first building Thompson had given us. They were all assigned to the ground crew for the two high-altitude birds NASA kept at Ellington Field and didn't have much information about what was happening at Johnson Space Center (JSC). They knew the facility had been overrun; it was just too large to keep secure with the security teams they had. Last they'd heard, a couple of groups of folks had holed up in some of the more secure buildings. Something had happened to coms though and they hadn't heard anything out of the complex in nearly two weeks.

It wasn't very helpful news, but at least I knew someone had survived the initial onslaught of Z Day. I took down the buildings they thought had people still in them and thanked them for their help.

"Where's your family at?" I asked Shae as we were heading for the door.

"Further up North, on the East side," she said.

"That's towards Baytown; we can hit them on the way."

"We heading there now?" Shae looked at me.

"No. I changed my mind. I want to take care of Drakes first," I nodded.

"Oh really, General? You just make all the decisions now?" Shae looked at me.

I stopped, realizing I was doing just that, again. "Sorry, when I get stressed, I fall back on what I know."

"It's OK, General. I know how you top brass types love your power," Shae grinned. "Just so you know that you're still doing it."

"I'll try and stop with the whole giving orders thing. Does going to Drakes first work for you?" I asked.

"Of course. I was going to suggest it anyway," Shae smiled. "But, why the change of heart?" Shae asked.

"If we can get Drakes back up and running, then we have a secured base of operations," I said.

"How secure can it be if it broke down?" Shae asked.

"We don't know what happened. All I know is that if we can get Drakes back up and running, we can send Pete and his mother back home where it's safe. We can focus on the rest once they're out of harm's way."

"Makes sense. It's not like we're on a time limit here," Shae said as we stepped out into the sunlight.

"General Sable," a voice called, bringing us up short. A man wearing Colonel rank in an Air Force uniform stood next to the Dilla with two armed Marines flanking him.

"Yes?" I said, shielding my eyes from the bright sun, which was blinding after the relatively dark building we'd been in.

"I'm COL Sureto, the installation commander here," the man said with just a hint of arrogance.

I blinked my eyes several times, adjusting to the light and stepped closer to the man. When I was a few paces from him, I stopped and waited.

It took a minute, but eventually Sureto reluctantly saluted.

I popped and dropped the salute in one motion. "What can I do for you, Colonel?"

"I heard you were on my base and I came to see if there was anything I could help you with." He then added, "Sir," as an afterthought.

I didn't like where this was going at all.

Be ready, I cautioned Shae mentally.

For what? Shae asked.

I'm not sure. Just keep your guard up, I said.

"Actually yes, Colonel. Can you tell me where I can find the fuel pumps? I need to refill before we head out," I said aloud.

"Leaving already, sir?" Sureto asked.

"Yes, we just needed some Intel and supplies, then we're back on course," I said.

"Where are you headed, sir? Perhaps my boys can be of service?" Sureto asked.

"I appreciate it, Colonel. But for what we're doing, we need to get in and out as quickly as possible," I said.

"In that?" Sureto threw his thumb over his shoulder at the Dilla.

"In a manner of speaking," I smiled.

"That is a good-looking piece of hardware. Haven't seen one so well equipped before." Sureto said.

I gave Colonel a long look, my face deadpan. "Rank still has some privileges."

"Oh yes, it does sir. May I ask what you're doing in Houston, sir?" Sureto said, much too formally.

I smiled, "What's your clearance, Colonel?" I started stressing the rank. "I'm afraid I'm not allowed to discuss operational plans without the proper clearance." I leaned in conspiratorially. "I can tell you it won't interfere with your operations here. Just picking up a few high-value targets, and we'll be out of your pool. Besides, it looks like you have your hands full around here as it is. I should be asking you if there's anything I can do for you." It wasn't an offer.

Sureto took a long time to speak and he was very aloof when he did.

"Oh, things here aren't so bad, sir. Sure, we've had some tight spots, but we keep the birds in the air; that's all that matters," Sureto said.

"True enough. Now, about that fuel?" I asked.

"Sergeant Sothe here will escort you over. You can use his fuel key to tank up. Once you're good, just let him know if you need anything else," Sureto said in a way that I couldn't read from his tone.

"I appreciate the hospitality, Colonel." I got the feeling the Colonel had been afraid I'd been sent here to take over the little kingdom he'd built for himself. Now that Sureto knew we weren't, he just wanted to get me off his base as soon as possible. I had a bad feeling this place would soon turn into another bad Mad Max movie. But I didn't have any proof at the moment, and we honestly didn't have the time.

We can't save everybody, Shae whispered in my mind.

I held out my hand to Sureto, who shook it in turn.

"Anytime," Sureto's smile looked like it should have canary feathers flying out of it. He spun on his heel and returned to his staff car, his one Marine in tow.

"If you'd follow me, General," Sgt Sothe said rather politely.

Well, that wasn't awkward at all, Shae said as we climbed into the Dilla.

Yeah, way too easy as well. I nodded.

I don't see how that could possibly come back and bite us, Shae said sarcastically.

The Dilla, including the spare gas cans, was topped off and ready to go in about thirty minutes. We swung back by and checked on Pete. Things seemed to be going well. We told him we were heading to Drakes to try and rectify that situation and that he should stay here. I warned Pete to stay away from

Sureto and to keep his head down until we got back. Pete said he would, and we shook hands before heading back to the front gate.

Why did that feel like a goodbye? I asked as we headed back to the parking area.

No idea. Shae shrugged, *But it's your turn not to jinx it!*

Drakes - Houston

JAMES

Well James, you were looking for a zombie horde. Seems you finally found one. Shae flipped her hand towards the wide parking lot in front of us. There had to be at least 200 of them shambling around between the two buildings that straddled the lot. *Happy now?*

Ecstatic, I said flatly. *But why are they just hanging out there?*

There weren't many zombies on the streets around us, just one or two, as opposed to the parking lot and our trip here. It seemed every road around Houston was clogged with broken-down cars or wandering ghouls. It had taken some careful driving to keep from damaging the Dilla.

The horde below us now seemed to wander aimlessly inside the parking lot curbs. I singled out one zombie and watched it approach the edge of the parking lot. As it took a step towards the curb, it slowly angled away from it. Each of its next steps angled a little farther away than the last until it was moving parallel to the curb.

"That's damn peculiar," I thought aloud.

What? Shea tried to see what I was looking at.

Watch. Tell me if you see any of them cross the curb leaving the parking lot, I said.

We watched a few minutes. I observed several more "near misses," but not a single shambler exited the parking lot.

Peculiar doesn't cover the half of it. That's where we're going," Shae nodded towards the large concrete building on the left. "Notice anything interesting about it?

One door, no windows, I said.

What about the door? Shae asked.

I picked up the Dilla's tablet and zoomed in on the door. *It's open!*

And? Shae prompted.

As I watched, a shambler came out of it. *Well, shit.*

Oh wait, it gets better, Shae said.

I continued to watch the door as another shambler stumbled out a little while later. A few minutes later, another appeared. I frowned. *How many have they got in there?*

She smiled at me. *Anything else you notice about the door?*

I shook my head, *What am I missing?*

They don't go back in, Shae said.

As I watched, another shambler was heading toward the door and shied away from it at the last moment. The building on the other side of the parking lot looked like its doors had been smashed in, but no shamblers came in or out.

I really don't like this, I murmured. *Do you think if we managed to slip in, they still wouldn't come inside?*

Don't ask me, I only work here. Shae didn't take her eyes off the parking lot as she made the joke. *You're the tactics expert. What do you want to do?*

Take off, nuke the entire site from orbit. I grinned.

Seriously, Shae smirked.

It's the only way to be sure. I didn't take my eyes off the lot as Shae punched me in the side playfully.

Sneaking in would be best if we could find a way to secure the door once inside that would keep the others out. But we don't know how many of them there are inside. We could get sandwiched. I'd love to sit here and snipe them from the roof of the other building, but we don't have enough ammunition. Plus, Goddess knows how many others it would attract, I said.

Being back around Shae now, some of her mannerisms were rubbing off on me. My whole life, I'd like something someone else said and adopt it into my vocabulary. Some were better than others. For instance, my use of the word dude has decreased dramatically recently.

If the invisible fence actually works, we could pick them off from the curb, Shae said.

And if it doesn't... I said.

Hey, I didn't say it was a good plan. What about smashing them with the Dilla like we did on the way up here? Shae said.

Way too many. I grunted at the mention of using the L-ATV to run over the zombies. *While the Dilla is a tough old bird, you get that many bodies wedge up under the fender, and she's gonna get stuck.*

An armadillo is not a bird, Shae mentioned offhand.

I rolled my eyes as I scanned the lot again. *What if we—*

My sentence ended abruptly as a shot rang out, quickly followed by another and another. A second rifle, I guessed by the sound of it, joined the first as they began to snap in tandem.

Where's it coming from? Shae leaned forward to try and see better.

I looked around quickly and cracked the door. *Sounds like it's coming from...*

It's Drakes. Shae pointed at a zombie with a fresh head wound tumbling out of Darkes.

The Dilla roared to life and I put it into motion.

Demolition derby it is. Hold on! The 7-ton monstrosity leaped forward from the small hill overlooking the scene. I dodged around a stalled car and made a hard left turn as I angled to the left side of the building.

Definitely going to lose some paint on this one, I said nervously as I brought the vehicle into a long arc parallel to the front of the building. *Here we go.*

The Dilla bounded over the curb with barely a shudder and waded into the first group of shamblers. The "cattle guard" on the front at least kept the shamblers from striking the engine compartment. The sound of bodies falling beneath the truck would have been stomach-churning if the noise of the truck itself wasn't already deafening.

The driver's side mirror snapped inward on its hinges as it struck the building.

There goes the security deposit, Shae grimaced, bracing herself as we continued to plow through bodies.

Almost there, I said, gritting my teeth.

The door was quickly approaching as the shamblers started noticing the truck roaring through the parking lot. Almost as one, the entire parking lot of zombies turned and followed the truck as we screeched to a stop next to the building's door. I had managed to wedge the Dilla, so there was not enough room for shamblers to approach the door. Both driver-side fenders had dug grooves into the building's cement walls.

I stared out the armored window and could see into Drakes now. It was almost identical to the one in Austin. A large rectangular bar in the middle of the room, ringed by tables and booths. This model also had second-story balconies, as far as I could tell. There were easily two dozen shamblers inside, and that was just in the small angle I could see.

As I killed the engine, I started hearing gunfire again. The shots were almost a drumbeat; they were so steady and constant. This wasn't panic fire, just well-sustained shooting.

Ready? I looked at Shae.

Shouldn't we wait until the gunfire dies down? Shae asked.

Nope, let's move. I pushed open the heavy door and leaned against it as Shae scrambled across my seat to get out of my side. We both drew pistols and started firing from the door.

"One mag only, save the second one," I yelled over the barking of our pistols, completely forgetting I could speak through my mind. It seemed my military training was still my fallback. We slowly carved an entry path.

Front sight, press trigger, reset. Front sight, press trigger, reset. My mantra repeated in my head as I carefully dropped each of my targets with efficient headshots.

Do you mind? Your mantra is very distracting, Shae said, having more difficulty with the pistol.

Sorry, I managed, not realizing I'd been "broadcasting." My gun locked open, empty. I reloaded and holstered just as

Shae's pistol followed suit. We drew machetes and advanced.

I've got right, I said.

I'll take left, Shae said.

"FREINDLIES FREINDLIES FREINDLIES!" I bellowed as we entered the room. I immediately realized how much worse it was inside than I'd seen before. There were shamblers everywhere and no room to maneuver.

Stay close and move towards the bar, I called to Shae as I cut a shambler down with one strike, kicked another in the chest and followed up by lopping the leg off another.

Don't stop, keep moving! I said. We were a blur of motion as we made our way across the room. We looked like a walking wood chipper as blood, gore and body parts flew around us.

It was then I caught sight of the two shooters. They were on top of one of the booth canopies. It looked like they had been trying to make their way across the room towards the stairs when they'd run out of maneuvering room and had to hunker down. The canopy didn't look very stable as it rocked with each gunshot.

The two appeared to be in some sort of military uniform I didn't recognize. It was a simple light gray color with a couple of insignias I couldn't make out. They wore black boots and matching helmets that reminded me of the high-rise comm MITCH helmets I'd seen on operators. They each had some sort of light armor plates on various parts of their bodies.

One was carrying something that looked like a cut-down version of an old M1 carbine, while the other had some sort of long rifle. They were both kneeling, their faces blocked by their rifle scopes. Their gunfire continued as their rifle muzzles swung across the bar slowly, methodically.

We reached the bar and easily leaped to the inside of the rectangle.

Cover the left opening, I said as I went right again. I moved to the break in the bar that allowed people in and out, making quick work of the zombie standing there. I then proceeded to maim and destroy each shambler that stepped up. The bar was nearly chest high, and there were only two openings that zombies could come through. Shae and I were now guarding each one.

Take your time. Use the corpses to build you a nice wall to block off the bar, I said.

This is getting messy, Shae grunted.

You good? I asked.

Oh sure. I'm covered head to toe in vile filth, but I'm OK, Shae said.

I could read the tension underneath her humor. Shae always seemed to keep her cool when the pressure was on. Dealing with all those big wigs back in her courier days, I guessed she got plenty of practice. Even now, she seemed to be keeping a level head even though she was completely out of her element.

We should be good now. I had a pile of corpses two deep and nearly waist-high already. *Just be careful of the bodies slipping in towards you.*

Got it, Shae said shortly.

It was a tedious process. Rhi had been right; dealing with the shamblers was easy. The problem was, it was too easy. I could see how you could get overconfident and sloppy. One mistake could spell disaster if you weren't always on your toes. I had to watch each shambler, waiting for each to get into the right spot before cutting it down. Sometimes, it fell perfectly, sometimes not so much, and I'd have to take a second to position it so I didn't get buried in an avalanche of corpses.

I had a tense moment when my blade became stuck in the vertebrae of one of the shamblers, and it twisted away from me, taking my blade with it.

A gunshot span the zombie back towards me, allowing me to retrieve my blade. It hadn't been a headshot that would have lost me my blade. No, the shooter had planted the shot perfectly into the zombie's shoulder so it would spin back toward me. Whoever the shooter was, they were amazing.

Minutes passed.

How you doing? Shae's "voice" was cool and relaxed in my head now, having settled down to the task. The adrenaline-infused tension from the beginning had drained away as we had established our "defenses" and were now literally waiting for the zombies to make their way to us.

Good luv, you? I replied.

Little bored, Shae said.

I had to chuckle. We were surrounded by a room full of zombies, and she was bored. *Well, don't go showing off, keep it simple, OK?*

If you insist, Shae said.

There was a loud crack as if on cue, and the canopy collapsed, dumping the two shooters into the crowd of zombies that had gathered beneath them.

In unison, Shae and I leaped over the bar and were halfway across the room. Both our pistols were out and blazing away at a speed normally reserved for automatic fire. The zombies between us and the shooters fell as our guns ran dry. We transitioned to hand-to-hand at this point, afraid the blades might cut one of the shooters. We were close.

I still couldn't see the shooters through the shamblers surrounding them. We were about six meters away when I heard a scream ahead of us.

Shae! I barked.

At this point, the world slowed down as Shae and I tapped into our inhuman abilities. The blood I'd topped off on back at the roadblock began to burn hot in my body, fueling me to move faster than a human could track with the naked eye. Arms blurred, hands crushed, knees battered, feet maimed.

From the outside, the walking wood chipper had moved into overdrive as we broke through the shamblers and arrived where the shooters had gone down.

I saw the long gun shooter first. They were down on the ground, a zombie latched onto their arm, trying to bite through the thin plates on their forearm. They were clawing for their sidearm, but I beat them to it.

I ripped the unfamiliar pistol from the holster and dropped the zombie on the shooter's arm. I picked the shooter up with one arm, tossing them over my shoulder and span, the gun spitting flame. Knocking back the surrounding horde, I made some breathing room for us.

I was shocked when the gun continued to fire long after it should have run dry—twenty rounds, twenty-five. Finally, it locked open on the thirtieth round and I tucked it into my belt.

By this time, Shae had recovered the other shooter and supported them with an arm around their waist. It appeared the second shooter had a leg injury and was leaning heavily on Shae. They had their pistol out and cleared a path for us as we made our way back towards the bar.

Just as the gun ran dry, Shae and I gathered the shooters into our arms and leaped the last three meters, landing on the bar. We slid down behind the bar to the relative safety it provided.

"You OK?" I asked as I put my shooter on the ground.

The shooter looked up at me, her crystal blue eyes wide in shock.

"You're arm, are you hurt?" I pulled her arm up and looked at it.

What I'd taken to be thin metal strips was some lightweight polymer. While there were scratches, there weren't any breaks or tear marks in the fabric. I undid the sleeve's Velcro clasp from the gloves and pulled it back to see a soon-to-be bruise forming, but no break in the skin.

I turned to Shae, *How's that one?*

Looks like a twisted ankle from the fall, nothing else, Shae said.

This one's in shock, I said.

Mine's just pissed off, Shae grinned.

I chuckled and stood up to check our surroundings.

"Where the fuck are they coming from?" I said aloud, noting there seemed to be just as many zombies in here as before.

"Back room," The shooter Shae had rescued pointed towards the back of the bar.

The voice sounded familiar, but I didn't have time to contemplate that as I glanced back just in time to see another shambler emerge from the room she'd indicated.

"Well fuck," I looked around at the surrounding horde.

Sandwiched? Shae asked.

We're fucking Manwiched at this point. I looked up and saw the catwalk above. I scanned it and didn't see any shamblers above us.

You see any shamblers up on the second level? I glanced at the stairs. The zombies didn't seem to be paying them any attention.

No, Shae confirmed.

Then we're going up! I looked at the nearest catwalk, running diagonally across the bar. It couldn't be much more than seven meters above us.

I grabbed Shae's wrist, pulled her bracelet off, and tucked it into my pocket. *Give me a lift?*

We climbed onto the center of the bar, kicking bottles out of the way, and she cupped her hands together.

On three, I said.

Wait, she stopped me. *1,2,go or 1,2,3,go.*

Oh, for fucks sake, 1,2,3, go! I said in exasperation.

She heaved me up as I leaped with all my strength. Grabbing the catwalk, I swung myself up. I double-checked to ensure I was alone, then lay down on the catwalk and pulled out Shae's bracelet.

I unwound the 550 chord and did the same with my own bracelet, tying the ends together. I'd never, EVER had to use one of these stupid things. They had always just been in my gear bag for "emergencies." There was always some guy, it was never a girl, who made these emergency bracelets in the barracks and sold them. I'd been pressured into buying these two back then and was now grateful.

Tying a loop in the end, I lowered it down to Shae. She helped the injured ankle shooter up onto the bar and then had her slip her good foot into the loop.

It was nothing for me to pull the first shooter up as she weighed nowhere near the chord's breaking point. Once she could reach the catwalk, she pulled herself the rest of the way up and laid out next to me as I lowered the rope back down.

The second shooter took a bit more coaxing, but Shae got her set up, and I pulled her up. The first shooter grabbed her arms and pulled her up onto the catwalk. A minute later, Shae was up on the catwalk with us.

We all sat catching our breath a moment while I watched the stairs. "They don't seem to like stairs."

"Yeah, we were trying to make it over there when we got

stuck on that stupid canopy," the soldier with an injured ankle said.

My ears were still ringing from the gunfire, but now I could hear the moans and groans from below, making my skin crawl. The shamblers were all stirred up and reaching up towards us. Slowly, I rolled up the bracelet chords and gave Shae back hers.

"What do you want me to do with this? I don't know how to turn it back into a bracelet," Shae said.

"Me neither. Hang onto it, just in case." I looked around. "Anywhere we can get out of this noise for a bit?"

Shae glanced at the far-left wall.

"There were a couple of private party rooms over that way. Should still be there," Shae said.

We made our way over, moving away from the stairs. This caused the horde below to follow us slowly from the ground floor.

Sure enough, there were a couple of doors against the wall.

I tried the first one, and it was locked. The second one popped open easily, and I investigated the darkness beyond. I tried the light switch, but it didn't work. There didn't seem to be anything moving inside, but I shined my small surefire flashlight around just in case.

Several couches dotted the room. In one corner, there was an area with ample pillows and something that looked like beanbags on the floor. Several TVs were on the wall, and a small karaoke machine was in another corner. We moved inside and locked the door behind us. I moved one of the couches up against the door just in case.

The injured ankle shooter pulled a glowstick from a pouch on her vest and cracked it open. A moment later, a green chemical light filled the room. She set it on the table before pulling the other shooter into her lap and holding her firmly.

Careful here, Shae cautioned, looking at me.

"How you two doing?" I knelt next to where they sat on the couch.

"She'll be fine, just a little shaken up from the fall," Twisted ankle said.

"Yeah, not every day you fall into a nest of vipers. How's

your ankle?" I asked.

"It hurts, but I'll survive," she said.

"You should elevate it, get some of the pressure off." I handed her a pillow, and she stretched out on the couch, putting the pillow under her ankle. "Thanks. Where'd you guys come from anyway? I thought we'd cleared all the civvies from the area."

"Passing through, actually," I said.

"Passing through?" She eyed me suspiciously. "Nobody just 'passes through' here anymore," she said as she pulled off her helmet.

It was then I finally got a good look at her face.

"Beth?" I asked in shock.

She leaned away from me, "How do you know my name?"

"You don't recognize me? It's James, James Sable. We worked together in Kuwait when you were on that USO tour. We had the rocket attack and had to bunker down. I rescued Pedro when he got hurt." I could tell she didn't recognize me by the look in her eyes.

"I ended up escorting you for like six weeks after that. I taught you how to shoot a machine gun; you taught me how to do the machine gun trick shot in pool? Nothing? I still owe you $200. Really?" I said in confusion.

"I've never been to Kuwait or did a USO tour. I was supposed to do one once, but I had to cancel it and never got to reschedule," Beth said.

I looked at her dumbfounded. I'd gotten to know her very well over those six weeks and we'd been on a first-name basis ever since. We didn't cross paths very often, her being a top-ten pop artist and me being what I was. But when she had a military or gun question, she'd always call me up, managing to find me no matter where I was on the planet.

Her hair was completely different from the last time I'd seen her, but you couldn't change your eyes; it was definitely the same woman. Besides, when you get that drunk with someone, you don't forget them...usually because—

You slept with this woman? Shae chimed in, more amused than anything. *And she doesn't even remember your name?*

No, we didn't sleep together, I said flatly. *She had a serious boyfriend at the time that she later married. We just kinda got drunk and fooled around.*

And now she doesn't remember you. You must have been terrible. Shae grinned.

Shut up, I said.

Shae smiled, but I was honestly confused.

"What happened?" The other shooter mumbled, seeming to come back to herself.

"There she is," Beth said as her counterpart looked around. "How you feeling poms?"

"Uh, OK, I guess. What happened? Where are we?" The dazed soldier asked.

"We fell, the canopy collapsed, and these folks rescued us. We're upstairs now, safe. Are you hurt?" Beth asked.

"My arm hurts." She rubbed her arm and pulled the sleeve back to expose the quickly growing bruise.

"That was a shambler. But it should just be a bruise, nothing permanent," I added.

The girl looked up, noticing me for the first time. "Who are you?"

"I'm James. That's Shae. We heard your gunfire and thought we'd give y'all a hand," I smiled.

"For what that was worth," Shae chimed in.

"Feeling better now?" I asked, ignoring Shae's comment. *Does she look like she has a concussion to you?* I asked.

I can't see her eyes from here, but the girl is definitely rattled, Shae observed.

Suddenly, the girl's eyes became alert and started looking around frantically. "Where's my gun?"

"It's OK," Beth soothed. "It's downstairs. We'll grab it on the way out to meet back up with the team."

The girl seemed to relax a bit, but she was still obviously anxious.

"I'm Beth," she said to Shae. "This is Rachel."

"You said you were meeting back up with your unit? Are you from Ellington Field?" Shae asked. "We'll be heading back there after this; we can give you a lift if you want."

"Ellington Field? That place fell over a year ago," Beth said.

Shae glanced at me before Beth continued.

"We're with the 9th Regiment, 2nd Battalion, Bravo Team. We got separated from the rest of the team and ended up cornered in this place," Beth said.

I glanced at her uniform; her shoulder patch matched what she said. On her other shoulder, she had a subdued American flag, along with what looked like Corporal stripes. Aside from the stripes and flag, I recognized nothing else on the uniform, not even the style of the clothes.

Then I did a double take. There was a 51st star on her American flag.

What is it? Shae had picked up on my confusion.

None of this is making sense. I don't recognize the uniform or unit. The pistol I've never seen before and the fact Beth doesn't recognize me...none of this adds up, I said with growing frustration.

What do you want to do? Shae asked.

Not a clue, I said honestly.

We still have to figure out how to secure this place, Shae said.

Yeah, and stop the Gauntlet zombie generator in the back room. I frowned.

Oh yeah, forgot about that. Hmmm... Shae thought a moment.

The sound of Velcro ripping drew my attention.

Beth was opening one of her pockets and pulling out a small aid kit. A moment later she was dry swallowing two pills. When she saw me looking she said, "Pain meds."

"Well, for right now, we should get some rest," I nodded. "We appear to be relatively safe here and you're gonna need a bit of time before you can walk on that ankle." I turned to Rachel. "Here. Sorry, I used all the rounds in our escape," I said, handing her the spent pistol.

"Yeah, about that," Beth started, her words starting to slur already. The pills she'd taken were already kicking in. "I didn't see all of your act, but that was some impressive fighting...and jumping."

I nodded, "Yeah, we work out."

"Uh-huh," Beth didn't sound convinced.

"What kind of pistol is that anyway? I've never seen anything like it," I tried to change the subject.

"It's a Sammies M13 pistol," Rachel started, seeming to suddenly come alive at the mention of guns.

"M13? Like the H&K P7 Squeeze-Cock?" I asked.

"Oh no, nothing like that. This baby's American-made, straight out of the beautiful state of Jefferson, not Germany. She uses a modified 5.7x28mm round with micro contact-expanding phosphorus." Rachel's voice became animated.

"Really? I thought I saw some flashes but figured it was just the heat of combat playing tricks on my eyes," I nodded.

"Nope, these babies fry right through a Rotter's brainpan and put him down for good. Don't even need a straight headshot; just get it close, and the chems do the rest." She pulled a magazine from her vest pouch and handed it to me.

Sure enough, each of the tiny rounds had a wicked point on it that was colored purple with a black stripe on it. I had never seen anything like it. "Looks like a specialized dim-tracer."

∞∞Ω∞∞

SHAE

I looked at Beth, "You understand anything they're talking about?" I indicated Rachel and James who were now in a deep discussion.

"Only a little; that's all gun language. But then again, she's been a bit of a gun nut since I met her," Beth smiled as she gazed at Rachel.

"When was that?" I asked as Rachel and James continued to geek out about guns, oblivious to the rest of us.

"Hmm," Beth tapped her lip in thought, her eyes becoming bleary as the pain medication seemed to be kicking in. "Had to have been a year and a half ago or so now. She'd just come out of basic, or at least what passed for basic back then. I'd been with the unit since the beginning, at least...the beginning of the Texas Roughriders. Like everyone else, I was pretty much a mess during the first six months of the infection."

"Really?" I questioned. The outbreak had only been going on for about three months now, but to hear Beth talk, it had been going on for years.

"Yeah, like uh..." Beth started, glancing at James and trying to snap her fingers but they didn't seem to want to work for her.

"James," I provided.

"Yeah, like James there said, I was touring when the big outbreak happened. You know, when all the cities went dark? Anyway, the band had been over in Jacksonville when the shit hit the fan. Luckily...I guess, luckily, my husband and daughter were with me on tour for a change.

"We tried to get back home to California, but they'd stopped all air traffic by the time we realized what was happening. We tried taking the buses back but only made it as far as Shreveport before they broke down, along with the rest of society.

"Eventually, we managed to get our hands on a couple of cars that we thought would get us all the way back. Turns out our luck changed in Abilene..." Beth stopped talking, her voice trailing off.

"You don't have to talk about this; I was just making conversation," I said, but the more Beth talked, the quicker it came out of her.

"No, it's alright." Beth took a deep breath and let it out. "The shrinks told me the more I talked about it, the better," Beth smiled weakly. "We'd been sleeping in the cars, trying to stick together as a group heading back. Someone would stay up and keep an eye open as it had become too dangerous to travel at night.

"It was Jake's turn to keep watch, so Liz and I were in the car. Sometime in the night, Liz woke up and needed to go to the bathroom. She didn't want to wake me, so she quietly slipped out. She'd always been a good sneak," Beth's eyes went distant. "Her screaming woke me up. Then, before I knew it, I could hear Jake screaming as well.

"We'd told her to stay close to us, but she'd wanted privacy to do her business; she was only six. Wherever she'd chosen hadn't been safe. When Jake heard her, he'd rushed into the darkness and straight into the arms of a group of those things."

Rachel and James had stopped talking a while back and were listening quietly now.

"I don't remember much of the rest of that night, or the next couple of months for that matter. Those in our group that survived didn't recover and scattered to the winds. I just wandered afterward, lost out of my mind, until a roughrider unit picked me up in the middle of nowhere.

"They brought me in and got me patched up as best they could. I didn't have anywhere else to go, so I stuck around and eventually enlisted," Beth blinked slowly, bringing herself back to the here and now.

"Been tearing around Texas putting these things back into the ground ever since." Beth looked over at Rachel. "Course, I have to keep this one out of trouble, which is a full-time job in itself."

Rachel hugged her and kissed her briefly. "Goes both ways."

Beth smiled, "I guess so poms," Beth whispered.

"You two finally done geeking out on guns?" I said to James and looked at my watch. "I'd say a couple of hours sleep should give your ankle enough time to stop swelling."

"Sounds good," Rachel said. "We've been up a while. I have no clue how long, but it's been a while."

"Plus, these drugs are kicking my ass," Beth grinned.

I smiled. "I'll keep an eye out; you guys rest up." I moved over to sit on the couch that was blocking the door. *Give them some space and go pretend to sleep,* I sent to James.

James moved over to the large floor pillows before stretching out and closing his eyes.

You catch all that? I asked James as the two girls rearranged two couches so they could lie down side by side.

I wish I hadn't. Have you heard of the Roughriders before? James asked.

Only from the Spanish-American War, I said.

The way Beth talked, the zombies have been here for over two years, James said.

What? You think she's from the future or something? I scoffed.

We're locked up inside a building with magic portals to other cities and surrounded by the walking dead. I'm not ruling anything out. But no, I don't think they're from the future, James said.

Then what? Another dimension? I asked, only half-jokingly.

Parallel planet, maybe? James said seriously. *Somewhere, the apocalypse started earlier. It would explain all the inconsistencies. *

Just because a girl doesn't remember a drunken make-out session with you doesn't mean she's from another planet, I chided.

It was more than once, James said defensively.

Oh, now I'm jealous. I grinned inwardly. *You remember the State of Jefferson?*

Never heard of it. James almost shook his head but remembered he was supposed to be pretending to sleep.

Southern Oregon and Northern California wanted to break away from their states and form the State of Jefferson, I started in my best teacher voice.

When the hell did that happen? I said.

Never did. After years of trying, they finally got the signatures and political clout to get it up to the bigwigs for a vote. But the man behind it died, and Pearl Harbor happened right after...so it quietly died in all the chaos, I said.

But she said the gun was manufactured there, James said.

Yup. I sighed.

The other planet theory would also explain why zombies keep pouring out from downstairs. Maybe they came through one of Drakes portals on their side and somehow ended up here. But in the process, it left the "door" open, and all the shamblers followed them through? James said.

They are like lemmings. I confessed.

Yup. Listen, are you good for a while? I really am a bit tired. James yawned.

You OK? I asked. I could sense he was tired, but there was something else there.

Yeah, just...tired, James sighed.

OK. Get some rest, I said, my voice tinged with concern.

Wake me up if something changes, James said.

Sure thing, I said.

A few minutes passed before James spoke again. *Shae?*

Yes?

How do you keep doing that? he asked.

Doing what? I asked.

Getting people to talk to you so easily. I remember when we first met. I was an introverted recluse. You had me blabbering away like a chatterbox in no time. Do vampires have some sort of charm ability you haven't told me about or something? James asked.

It's called people skills, James. It's not hard. You just have to practice talking to people, I scolded.

That sounds like too much work, James mumbled.

I sighed, *Just go to sleep already.*

Yeah, people skills. Riiiiiight, James said as he drifted off.

Rhi's Folly

[Really? Rhi's folly? Like any of this is my fault. No, it's your fault; it should be YOUR folly, not mine. --Rhi]

RHI

So yeah, he's finally getting back to me again. You remember me, the girl that got left behind to babysit the new human vampire lord while they ran off and had adventures and shit? Yeah, can you tell how happy I am about that?

Oh, SPOILER ALERT, you're going to be with me for a while, so get yourself a drink, something to nibble on and settle in. This is going to be a ride, fair warning.

Last we saw our fearless heroine; she was being cornered in the bedroom by a ruthless blood-worker who threatened her virtue. Can you tell how that one turned out just by the fact I didn't with the "W" word? I still have no idea how she does it. One minute, you're holding your own, perfectly fine; the next, you're naked and spread-eagle on the bed.

In the two weeks after Pagoda's demise there were a lot of changes.

First was teaching this Mark character even the most fundamental aspects of running a household. Sure, he was pretty enough to play the part, but he didn't have the ruthlessness sometimes called for in our politics. Luckily, he had me to take care of that for him. Don't get me wrong, he's a nice guy and all but rarely do nice guys last long in my world.

At Mark's command, a few vampires were sent out to recover family members in the local area. I had to admit it was a good idea but I was too busy to go myself and ended up missing out on all the fun.

The ordinary humans (ords) of the Alamo compound (really James, the Alamo?) Anyway, they elected a governor, not so much to rule over them as to be the liaison between the humans and vampires. The guy seemed OK, a little greasy for my taste, but he had the charisma to pull it off. I kept my eye on him, but he seemed OK. Especially after a bloodtouch verified he wasn't a scumbag.

An interesting side note from filing through the guy's mind: I discovered the ords of the compound actually considered the vampires of the compound "disabled." As in, we needed special care and attention more so than humans did. Seriously? No idea where that idea came from. Probably the same folks who wouldn't wear a mask during a pandemic because they thought it was all a government conspiracy.

We started training the ords in the day-to-day operations of the compound. At first, only a few wanted to work. But as the days passed and the monotony set in, more and more folks came forward looking for things to do. Some augmented security, some maintenance, some even with the household chores. We had a couple of teachers who started setting up classes for the kids, much to the children's enjoyment.

Richard rounded up a few others and helped design and build huge greenhouses on the back of the property to start working on fresh food. Turns out we had a few green thumbs who, after butting heads a few times, settled down to get crops going.

A few days after our fearless heroes left the compound for Houston, we received our first envoy from another vamp community. It was a smaller compound from down near Marble Falls. They had heard about the change in leadership from one of the three vamps who'd departed our compound and had sent someone to investigate.

All they wanted was to establish communication. Pagoda's previous courier, Reynold, reported to me to confirm all the information the Marble Falls courier had brought. We exchanged ideas on maintaining compounds best and keeping our "herds" in order before they returned to Marble Falls.

By this time, life had returned to the dullness I'd experienced before that fateful evening at Drakes. To combat the boredom I started working my way through the few, more competent vampires we had and started grooming one to become Mark's vampire second since he was adamant he wasn't interested in becoming a full vampire himself.

Some humans can be so dense. Why you wouldn't want all the benefits that come with this life is beyond me. But it was his call...and since I'd somehow ended up bloodbound to him, I didn't have much of a say in the matter.

I did find it terribly entertaining that he seemed to genuinely fear me. He had good reason, but I guess he didn't understand how deeply bloodbinding worked. I, of course, did nothing in the way of taking advantage of the situation in the slightest.

The vampire I eventually settled on was Adira. I wasn't sure how she'd work out with Mark, as she was just as headstrong, ruthless and cunning as I was. Not as hot, of course, but she seemed to get along with Becca, so I had a feeling it would be a good match. That, plus I went through her mind and didn't find any secondary agenda there.

While Adira didn't care one way or the other about Mark himself, she did care about the safety and well-being of the compound. I figured this would be enough to keep her honest, mostly. Besides, Mark was like a fungus. The more you were around him, the more he grew on you.

All this time, Trish was still following me around like a puppy. Well, not entirely like a puppy. She occasionally had something better to do than stalk me, but not very often. I swear I did nothing to lead the girl on, but she still tried. While I never accepted her advances, I never told her to go away either. I don't know if it was the ego trip of having someone want you or what. All I know is she kept at it, never becoming discouraged, just seeming to bide her time.

I knew I'd never have a normal relationship; that just wasn't me anymore. That little teenage fantasy I had of a white picket fence and a dog and all that was long gone and not just because I was a vampire. Nor was it because of the zombie apocalypse. It just seemed every time I tried to have a relationship, things...never worked out.

I mean, there was James, that was about as abnormal as you could get. I...liked the guy and loved having sex with him, especially in the more public areas he was so uncomfortable with. There was just something so delicious about watching him squirm as his anxiety and lust battled each other for control.

Yes, there were other people in the compound I could hook up with if I wanted to. With Pagoda's "hands off" decree gone, nothing held me back. There were plenty who were hot or they just tasted good, but I didn't trust any of them enough to let myself desire them. Not to mention they were all still terrified of me. Besides, regardless of how easy he was, I had fun with James.

And yes, I know I said I loved him last book, but that was then. Besides, there was still Shae. I couldn't wrap my head around the fact she didn't care that James and I were having fun. I didn't understand her and I had to admit it scared me a little bit. Most people were pretty simple to figure out, she was anything but simple.

[WAIT...*why the hell am I telling you all this? Is this that hack writer trying to get me to give you a rundown on my relationships or something? Oh God, it's a "feelings check" isn't it? He must have done another of those crappy writing courses. He still hasn't figured out that's where the real money is, not writing but hosting writing courses. FINE, I'll do it; as long as all you know this wasn't my idea.* --Rhi]

I'd gotten to know Shae a little better in the two weeks before they left for Houston. We'd even had a few civil conversations. The more I was around her, the more something told me that she and James wouldn't be around much longer; regardless of what Nat said.

Of course, Nat also said we're all bound together in some supernatural bondage shit that I don't understand. I still don't get what she was talking about. I mean, our minds blending together? What sort of moonbeams and sunshine, new age crap is that?

Luckily, I was saved from my boredom by a summons from Natalie. Yeah, a summons. Not a "hey, can you come over?" but a "get your ass over here." Apparently, the portal to Houston was repaired and our heroes needed backup.

So, I'd put together some of my old kit: a pair of old green cargo pants, a pair of tan combat boots made by Nike, a black tank top that didn't quite cover my abs, an old OD green military blouse that I rolled the sleeves up on but left open and untucked as it looked badass and finally an old black SWAT cap that I wore backward just because.

I made sure none of it was my Sunday best, as I was going to be around James. Somehow, my clothes tended to get ruined around that man, and not in a good way. Don't get me wrong; my clothes were still high-end, this is still me we're talking about, they just weren't from this season's apocalyptic line.

I tied my hair up in a tight braid to try and keep it out of the way. My gun belt hung crooked and low on my hips with a Kimber 1911 and a couple spare mags on it. I had a couple of pouches with basics I used to carry in the service and a long titanium blade. It wasn't quite long enough to be a machete, but it was curved and wicked-looking. I kept it strapped horizontally on the back of my belt. Finally, I had a boot knife and a small backpack filled with essentials.

So, I gathered up my gear and used the trap door to go to Drakes. That thing is the damnedest way to travel. First, you drop down into this trap door. The next thing you know, you're stepping forward into Drakes. There's no transition-one minute you're in free fall, the next you're taking a step. So weird!

Drake and Natalie were waiting for me at the bar when I emerged. From what I'd gathered, Houston was a bit hotter than they had expected and James and Shae needed Moi's help.

Drake showed me to a back room where another portal sat. This one wasn't a trap door but an actual door-door. Drake said they'd had to do some jury-rigging to get this portal to work again, so the trip might be slightly different than what I was used to. Since I'd only ever been through one of these things all of five minutes ago, I didn't know what "normal" was supposed to be.

I should have known something was up with what Natalie said just before I stepped through the door. She handed me my bag, which I hadn't realized I'd put down, and said, "Have fun and study hard."

But like an idiot, I was more worried about walking through this portal than what she was saying. It would be another six months before I realized they'd done this to me on purpose. I cursed them until...but I'm getting ahead of myself.

All in all, I was getting fucked again, and not in a good way.

OK, sorry, enough griping and foreshadowing. I'll get on with it.

The first time I'd stepped through a portal, it was instantaneous. Even though this was only the second one I'd been through, I instantly knew something was wrong. For one thing, it lasted WAY longer. Instantaneous seemed to go on for about an hour. And it was cold, teeth chattering cold, even for me.

When I finally emerged on the other side, my knees buckled, and I hit the ground. Right afterwards my lunch decided it had enough of sitting in my stomach and decided to go for a walk. Once my body stopped retching, I blinked away tears enough to look around.

Lifting my head slowly, I saw the floors, walls, and ceiling were stone, as was the rectangle bar that was always the centerpiece of Drakes. A set of stairs off in the corner indicated a second story, but the catwalks and balconies were gone. They were replaced with a stone ceiling.

There was no furniture, no bottles, no lights, nothing. It was as if Drakes hadn't moved in yet. Either that or it was Barney Rubble's house.

When my legs finally started working again, I stood up shakily and looked at the door I'd just fallen through. It opened at my touch but didn't reveal a portal back to Austin. Instead, it revealed the "outside."

"Outside" appeared to be a massive cave. The silent, dark shapes of more stone buildings surrounded me, but aside from my footsteps, there wasn't another sound.

Stepping back inside, I searched the place from top to bottom: no Drake and no magic portals.

"Drake!" I growled into the air, but nothing replied as I began to talk aloud. "OK, let's think this through. I'm obviously not in Houston, Dorothy. So that means something went wrong. This place doesn't look lived in, so maybe it's not done yet or it's abandoned. So, if that's the case, let's see if we can find whoever built or is building this place. Failing that, find ANYONE AT ALL!" I growled aloud in frustration.

I paused at my outburst. I normally wouldn't get this rattled, even at something this unusual. It was like something was prodding me but I couldn't figure out what. Well, I wasn't about to let it win. I took a breath, hitched up my big girl britches, and got to work.

The streets were chilly, but not as cold as you'd expect a proper cave to be. They were also deserted and dark. It wasn't pitch dark like it should be though. A light source from somewhere up above gave off a faint glow, but I couldn't make out exactly what was generating it. It gave the entire cavern the equivalent of a twilight feel.

And don't start with the FANFIC BS from that series, alright? Twilight was a time of day LONG before those movies, so zip it.

I spent a long time searching the surrounding stone buildings. I didn't go through each one top to bottom; it was more like ducking my head in and glancing about for anything out of the ordinary before moving to the next building. None of the buildings were more than four stories high.

My watch said I'd been searching for over 12 hours when I took a break. The entire time, I'd not seen or heard another soul, or a bug, or snake, or anything, which was weird for a cave. The lighting never changed either. It stayed that same dull glow. Luckily my enhanced vision allowed me to see as if it were daytime.

I climbed to the top of one of the taller buildings to have a look around. All I saw were rooftops disappearing into the distance in all directions. The cave's ceiling a good hundred meters above me. This cavern was insanely massive. I'd never heard of any cave being this large before, let alone having an entire city within it.

Desperation finally kicked in. *Nat? You there, Nat?* I waited a few moments. *Ha-ha, it's not funny anymore, Nat. Where the hell am I?* Still no answer.

James?

Shae?

Anyone?

I hear you. The voice in my head whispered to me.

Shut up, head. Even though I hadn't heard from the voice in my head in over two weeks, I wasn't in the mood.

Really? Nobody? Well, if you can hear me, I sure as hell ain't in Houston. I'm in some stone city inside the biggest damned cavern I've ever seen. I took a breath. *It sure would be nice if one of you could get me the hell out of here.* Silence remained my only answer.

My frustration eventually made me tired. I tried to get a few hours of sleep, but the silence of the place made me uneasy. Even my enhanced hearing couldn't hear anything. In the immortal last words of every schmuck about to die in a war movie, "It's too quiet."

Sure as shit, something happened.

It was during one of the many times I tried getting back to sleep. I rolled over, and a light caught my eye. It wasn't terribly bright by normal standards, maybe a regular flashlight, but to my eyes, it was like a flare going off. I was instantly on my feet and started moving towards the light. I stuck to the rooftops to ensure I didn't lose sight of it.

When I got close, I slowed down and started stalking. The light was cautiously leading a group down the street. I waited at the next intersection to see what the parade was all about.

I swear to God, if it's zombies, I'm gonna strangle someone, I thought.

Can you strangle a zombie? my head asked.

Shut up, head, I said automatically.

I'm just trying to help...and remind the readers I'm in this story too.

Shut it, I snapped.

Sourpuss.

Six figures appeared in the intersection below me and I had to blink to make sure I was seeing this right. They were all dressed as if they'd just come from a Renaissance Festival.

The first was a young boy, probably in his early teens. He had a mess of light brown hair and freckles on his cheeks. He wore brown leather pants with a loose-fitting blue shirt tucked into it. The shirt had a faded symbol on it that I couldn't make out and he wore a pair of well-worn leather boots. He carried a knife in his hand, and his eyes were darting everywhere at once.

The next figure carried the light source. She was dark-skinned also wearing brown leather pants, but her shirt was white and more form-fitting. She wore what looked like leather forearm bracers and leather boots that came up to her knees. She wore what I could only describe as a metal shield on her back with two swords tucked into it. In her hands, she carried what looked like some sort of amulet that was emitting the bright light.

The third was a man who looked Middle Eastern. He was wearing a ridiculous goatee and blue robes. Leather straps adorned his robe at the waist, knees, and elbows. A small pack was on his back and he stumbled every few meters. He didn't look like he was doing too well.

The fourth figure was also a man in robes, this time white. He was taller than the previous man, had short blonde hair, and was clean-shaven. His features were thin and long, almost like he'd been stretched out. He carried a staff that he didn't use for walking.

The fifth looked like a petite, leather mummy. But this mummy didn't shamble; it moved with a grace I'd only seen in my own kind. Instead of bandages, she (you could tell it was a she because of how tight the outfit was) wore a series of leather straps that covered every part of her. A deep red cloak helped to conceal her person. As she walked there was the glint of blades strapped to her thighs. She even had a leather mask with mesh eye slits. Whatever was underneath that getup, she didn't want anyone seeing it.

They saved the biggest for last. Bringing up the rear was a beast of a...woman? I wasn't sure. It stood a good head and a half taller than the tallest of their group and was pure muscle. I'd never seen anyone as tall or as big as she was. Maybe she was Andre the Giant's mom or something.

Her entire outfit appeared to be made from animal furs. As she walked...no, lumbered, not walked. As she lumbered, I could see leather beneath the fur, which appeared to be armor. She carried the most enormous axe I'd ever seen. This thing had blades on either side and looked to weigh 40 pounds easily. The ease with which she shifted it from hand to hand, you would have thought it weighed nothing.

The entire group was battered and bloody. They'd obviously been in a fight where they hadn't exactly won.

I watched them creep down the street quietly. From their manner, I didn't think they'd been here before. I shadowed them from the rooftops, listening as they spoke a strange language I'd never heard before. It was made up of sounds I'd never heard either. I couldn't even get the gist of what they were whispering, but something smelled wonderful! I didn't know what it was, but it practically made my mouth water. I wasn't particularly hungry, having lost my lunch when I arrived here, but I'd never smelt anything like this before.

I was so distracted by the smell I didn't sense the thing approaching me until it was too late. The rustle of what I'd later learn were wings alerted me a split second before the thing swooped down on me.

I rolled, barely managing to avoid the thing's talons as it screeched in fury. Sadly, the only place I could roll to was off the roof. I was in an unexpected freefall and said the only thing appropriate, "OH SHIIIIIIIIIIIIIIT!" I managed to hit the ground in a rough tumble that sent me sprawling.

It took a few moments for me to recover and get back to my feet. By then, the six had formed a rough semi-circle around me while the winged lizard perched on the roof across the street. Instinct told me to blast my way out of here fast and get to safety. The problem was, I didn't know where safety was anymore.

"Blah blah, blah blah blah blahblah!" The one who'd been holding the light bellowed at me, a rather impressive sword in each of her hands now. Of course, she wasn't really saying blah to me. I had no idea what she was saying, but her eyes said she was deadly serious.

"BLAH BLAH!" the big one yelled at me, her axe now in both hands in a threatening manner.

The boy was looking around now, trying to see where I came from and if there were more of me. The blue-robed man seemed to be swaying on his feet unsteadily while the other robed gentleman held his staff out towards me.

I didn't sense hostile intent from staff boy, more like curiosity. He gave me the old "elevator eyes" coming to rest not on my boobs, but rather my pistol. He looked away quickly as if not wanting to draw attention to what he'd been looking at.

The last was mummy girl. She had a dagger spinning around each index finger with inhuman ease. It was her that smelled so good! I had to drag my eyes from her as the light girl spoke again in her "blah blah" language.

I had to fight back a laugh as a line from a vampire movie popped into my head, "I don't say blah-blah-blah."

Again, I considered bolting, but what good would that do me? I still had no clue where I was or how to get home. At least these folks weren't actively trying to kill me, well sort of. That was a good sign. So, I slowly raised my hands above my shoulders and didn't move.

This seemed to give them pause. They weren't expecting me to surrender, apparently. They glanced at one another nervously, and a few words were exchanged before the big lady barked something at me along the lines of "blargety blargety."

I shrugged my shoulders helplessly and kept my hands up.

The big girl frowned as silence descended on all of us.

I glanced over at blue robes who was starting to teeter. They were all focusing on me and not paying attention to him. I watched as his eyes rolled up and he began to fall.

For some STUPID reason, I decided to play hero just then. I totally blame James. This was the type of bonehead maneuver he would pull. I should never have let that man put his dick in me...probably infected me with his "goody two-shoes" juice. Regardless, I bolted forward at my full speed and caught him before he crashed to the ground.

Of course, their roaring started as I gently laid him down and sprinted back to my original spot before they could close in on me. I was back in position with my arms back above my head before they'd taken two steps towards me.

The whole group froze, looking at me, except for staff boy. He squinted at me momentarily and then knelt to examine the man I'd caught.

Light girl...OK, that's not really cool since she was Black. *Calling her light girl, is that racist somehow? Do they have racism here? What the fuck am I doing? They're still pointing sharp, pointy things at me. Shut up and hold still,* said my inner monologue.

Anyway, light girl yelled something at Biggie Smalls and went to check on her fallen comrade.

Biggins...I couldn't believe her breasts were each the size of my head! Biggins took a step closer and seemed to take up a guard position, keeping an eye on me while they attended to their friend.

A high-pitched warbling sound came from the staff that too-tall-Jones was carrying. It sounded electronic; I'd never heard anything like that in nature. I wondered what that was all about.

Light girl and Jones exchanged words and then looked at me suspiciously.

"Hey, don't look at me. I just caught him as he was falling. I didn't do nothing!" I said defensively.

I saw three of them react: light girl, Jones and the boy. If they weren't already looking at me, they definitely were now.

"You speak the ancient?" Light girl's words were slow, almost like they were being carefully picked and weren't used often.

I looked at light girl now as she stood up and approached me.

"I speak English," I said slowly.

She nodded. "Who...you?"

"My name is Rhiannon," I supplied.

"Why here?" Light girl asked.

I felt like I was in one of those old westerns where the white man was trying to talk to the Native Americans. Of course, in those movies, it was always the Native American who was trying to speak English, not the invading white man.

"I'm lost," I said finally.

Light girl looked at the boy, and they shared a look. Then she blah blah blahed over her shoulder to the others, apparently telling them what I'd said.

"I Sh'teena," she said and was starting to point towards the boy when Jones snapped something at her, and she replied, pointing towards one of the buildings beside them. Jones picked up the collapsed man and carried him into the building while the others followed.

"Come?" Sh'teena motioned towards the building.

I nodded and looked at my hands and then back to her. She seemed to get it and nodded, so I lowered my hands slowly. Biggins seemed to tense a bit, but aside from that, we all went into the building.

Inside, the building was warmer than the street had been. While there were no signs of a fireplace or any sort of heating system, the chill in the air was definitely gone. When I placed my hand on the wall, it wasn't warm, but it wasn't the same cold roof I'd tried to sleep on earlier, either.

Jones laid his cloak out on the ground and lay the man on top of it before that high-pitched whistle came again.

"Is he OK?" I asked.

"No," was Sh'teena's reply. "He hurt greatly by magistrate."

"Magistrate?" Was I dealing with escaped criminals? Not that I minded, it would explain their current state. "Were you in prison?"

"No. Magistrate held us captive because we wouldn't break law to help his war. We escaped, but many wounds." The strain of speaking the "ancient" was taking a toll on Sh'teena.

I nodded, noting the various bruises and contusions among them. I leaned against a wall and slid down to the floor. My lack of sleep was starting to catch up to me. I felt strangely comfortable in their presence despite having only known this group of "criminals" for a few minutes. I chalked it up to the fact I had been alone in this strange land for nearly a day and just hungered for company.

Or, you recognize your own, my head chimed in.

Shut up head, I said.

Sh'teena seemed to read me like a book.

"Sleep. We rest," Sh'teena said.

I looked up at Biggins, who was still eyeing me warily.

"You will be safe. My word," Sh'teena assured me.

I pulled myself into a corner, wedging my pistol and knife against the wall and got as comfortable as possible. I took one last look around and was out.

Gang's All Here

<u>RHI</u>

I jerked awake a moment later. Glancing at my watch, two hours had passed. Several of the others had curled up on the semi-warm stone floor and were sleeping. Blue robes seemed to be looking better; his color had returned. The boy and the mummy girl appeared to be on watch.

"What did I miss?" I yawned.

The boy looked at me. "Not much. Not a lot happens in a dead city."

"Dead city?" I asked.

"Sure, seems like a dead city to me," he said.

"You speak...what did you call this language?" I asked.

"Ancient," he supplied.

"You speak ancient rather well," I said.

He glanced at Sh'teena sleeping in the corner. "Yes, language has always been easy for me. But it's not polite for a page to show up his knight."

"Knight?" I raised an eyebrow.

"Yes, my lady is a knight of the Rodor Kingdom," he said.

"What's your name?" I asked.

"I'm Gathers."

"And what's the name of the woman who smells so good?" I nodded at mummy girl, who was staring out a window.

"That's Tara," Gathers said.

"Tara?" The name felt...familiar somehow.

Tara was good. If you didn't know what to look for, you wouldn't have noticed her shifting slightly so she could peer at me through the sides of the mesh eye holes. She stiffened and turned away when I winked at her.

God, I wish I had fangs so I could sink them into her, the thought popping into my head unbidden.

You don't have any idea what she looks like, my head argued.

Who cares? Smelling like that, she must taste amazing! I had to swallow because my mouth had begun to water again.

You know I know everything you've ever done, right? So, when I tell you that was the creepiest thing you've ever said, take it for what it's worth, my head said.

I grimaced. *Yeah, that did sound bad, didn't it?*

Ya think? my head agreed.

I glared at the voice in my head.

I'd never had an attraction like this before. It wasn't anything remotely sexual, I don't think. I hate saying it, but the easiest way to describe it was a...hunger. The thought made me shudder cause, I didn't act like that. That wasn't me. I was always in control.

Yeah right, the voice in my head scoffed. *Hey, that reminds me. Why haven't you given me a name?*

Because either you're me, or you've never told me your name, I snapped back.

Oh. I hadn't thought of it that way, my head said and then was quiet.

The voice in my head had been with me from the moment I woke up in the VA hospital. Most of the conversations with myself I'd had were one or two sentences long and usually ended with me telling her to shut up. Most people will talk about voices in their head, but this was an actual voice, not my imagination. Course, that's what a crazy person would say, isn't it?

"What about your lizard friend outside?" I asked aloud.

"The Averian? He doesn't have a name that I know of,"

Gathers said.

I couldn't take my eyes off Tara. I eventually had to put my hand over my eyes to try and block her distracting figure from my mind. *What the hell, man?* I shook myself trying to snap out of whatever control she was having over me.

"Will he try to take my head off if I go for a walk?" I asked. Something was compelling me to keep looking around this place. There had to be more to the mystery of my being here. Besides, I couldn't stand sitting around listening to people snore.

"I shouldn't think so. You're not a prisoner. Aren't you tired though? I noticed you didn't sleep well," Gathers said.

"No, I don't sleep that much. Besides, I still haven't finished exploring this place," I said.

The boy shrugged, "As you wish."

I slowly stood up, making sure no one was going to jump me.

"Y'all will be here when I get back, right?" I couldn't keep the slight tremor out of my voice. They were the only people I'd encountered so far, and I didn't want to lose them. Being alone in this "dead city" wasn't exactly my idea of a good time, which made me wonder why I wanted to take a walk so badly.

"As long as you're not gone too long," Gathers said.

"Thanks kid," I said.

His grin soured a little at my calling him a kid.

"Don't worry," I stepped forward and patted him on the shoulder. "It's a term of endearment." I could tell he didn't understand the word and I wasn't about to explain it to him.

When I exited the building, I noticed the chill outside this time. I stretched, feeling like I'd been cooped up for days, not hours. I could sense my leathery friend up on the roof. I could feel his eyes on me, so I waved at him without looking before heading off.

First, I backtracked to Drakes. I couldn't lose this place, so I needed to embed its location firmly in my memory. Nothing had changed. On a whim, I pulled out my boot knife and started carving into the rock of the bar. It didn't take long; the natural stone easily gave way to my carbon steel blade. All I wrote was, "Drake – Find me. Rhi." I didn't think it would do any good, but I couldn't see how it would do any harm.

I headed back out into the city and continued to search. I decided to change tactics and followed one of the cavern walls to see how far it went. I ran this time, not worried about exploring the buildings as they all seemed to be the same. I kept my speed down to a light jog as there weren't many people, AKA food, around. I had to conserve my energy as much as possible until I could find a good food source.

My eyes had become accustomed to the pattern of one stone building after another. So, when I came across a spot where a building should have been, I stopped in my tracks. Glancing around, I saw more missing buildings and some partially constructed ones.

The buildings didn't appear to be pre-fabricated. They had been carved out of the cavern itself. Each building was part of the cavern floor. It looked like someone had removed the entire upper section of the cavern before cutting the remaining cavern into massive city blocks. It seemed the buildings had then been carved into each city block. I couldn't imagine the time it would take to do such a feat. The more I looked, the more I could see the details in the carving; it was amazing.

As I continued to walk, I came to where the sidewalk ended. Before me, stretching from one side of the cavern to the other, was a gaping chasm. I couldn't tell how far it was across, but think Grand Canyon size and you'd be getting there. I could faintly hear a river far below me.

I kicked a rock over the edge and never heard it hit the bottom, causing me to take a few extra steps back. I looked to either side and found some of the buildings had also fallen into the chasm.

"Sinkhole," I said to no one in particular.

Makes California look like a crack in the wall, doesn't it? my head said.

That makes no sense, I said.

You make no sense, my head retorted.

Shut up head, I frowned.

I decided to head back to the others as they should be waking up soon. The feeling of being watched had intensified after I left Drakes during this little walkabout. I figured my flying lizard was the culprit, but I didn't bother looking for him.

Would that make him a dragon? my head sounded excited.

Shut up head, I repeated.

So, when the smell hit me, I was so surprised it stopped me in my tracks.

"Tara?" I called, slowly turning around to find her standing in a nearby doorway.

Tara stood watching me for a few moments, then slowly approached. She stopped just out of arms reach.

I could almost make out her eyes behind the mask. The smell was intense now; it made me hunger for her all over again. I still had my full senses, I just really wanted to taste her. Like the smell when you drove by the Buttercrust Bakery in Austin before it closed. The smell of the freshly baked bread made your mouth water, but it didn't make you want to jump out and attack the bakers.

"What is it?" I asked as she stood silent.

She extended her hand out to me. It made a complex series of movements before stopping, still extended to me with her palm down.

I looked at it momentarily before slowly extending my own and taking hers. As soon as we touched, she clamped down hard and something bit into the side of my hand, causing me to gasp before the whole world exploded.

I couldn't move and spots filled my eyes like I'd been rubbing them hard.

Tara spun me around and dragged me back into the house she'd been standing in a moment before. Once inside, she stood behind me, one arm around my chest holding me up and I still couldn't move.

I heard the sound of cloth and leather scraping behind me. Her free hand grabbed my head and roughly pulled it to the side. The next moment she was biting into my neck.

She has fucking fangs! my head screamed at me in panic as I felt both fangs pierce my neck before Tara started to feed.

My body shuddered at the feeling of her lips on my neck. I couldn't feel her mind at all, but with her in such close proximity, unmasked, my hunger for her flared.

My hand broke free of my paralysis and reached up, grabbing the back of her head. Instead of pulling her away, my arm betrayed me and pulled her face harder into my neck. Every nerve ending in my body tingled from her touch.

The arm around my chest moved from restraining to caressing me as if on cue. A strange mix of pleasure and pain rippled through me at her pinching and teasing.

What the fuck is going on? I gasped, unable to comprehend the conflicting emotions pulsing through me.

Suddenly, she pulled away from my neck and spun me around in a bone-crushing embrace. I was a rag doll in her tiny, yet powerful hands as her bloody lips met mine. The spots were clearing, but my vision was going red with something I'd never experienced: bloodlust.

Her hand on the back of my head pulled me roughly away. As I watched, one of her knives flew up under its own power and delicately cut her neck before flying back to its sheath on her thigh. She pulled my mouth to the fresh wound.

I didn't think she could taste better than she smelled, but oh God, was I wrong. I sucked ravenously at the wound, hearing her moaning beneath me. I pushed her back up against a wall roughly, losing myself in the act.

I felt as if I were watching this all happen from outside my body. This bloodlust filling me acted of its own accord, but at the same time, I found I wanted the same thing it did. I was confused, to say the least. Luckily, my brain was smarter than I was. It pushed away my doubts and leaned into the creature before me.

My hands roamed across the soft leather she was encased in, wishing there was some way to get rid of it. And then it was gone. Soft, smooth, hot flesh was under my fingers, and I touched her everywhere. Running my nails down her back, I found she had a thin, soft but firm tail protruding from the base of her spine.

One of the times my eyes weren't rolling up into my head in pleasure, I managed to glance at her. She had straight, raven black hair cut short at her shoulders. Her skin was red...no, not red, crimson. The most striking...most beautiful crimson I'd ever seen.

"You think I'm beautiful?" she whispered, her voice husky. Then she was back, kissing my neck, nipping, biting.

"You have no idea," I managed honestly, my voice dry and hoarse, as she continued to touch and tease me. The fire between us seemed to be ebbing, but my determination blazed as I wasn't letting her off that easy. I swear I felt like Jim Kirk banging that green chick.

Where did that come from? my head asked. *You've never even watched Star Trek.*

I ignored my head as my tryst with Tara continued. I have no idea how long we were there. How long we ravished each other. It was sometime later before I came back to my senses. We were lying in each other's arms, exhausted, and covered in sweat and blood.

I still didn't understand what had happened. Sure, there was some sort of animal magnetism thing going on, but...I didn't bat for the other team. I hadn't even done the whole "experimented in college" thing. Yeah...while in Japan, I was taught certain things, but that didn't mean I pursued them. Nat doesn't count, nuff said about her.

Now, looking at this red-skinned goddess before me, I just knew I'd pursue her to the end of this world and the next. And I didn't even know her!

I looked into her eyes; they were the same color as her skin, with black irises and darker pupils.

"I can't get over how lovely you are," I kissed her again, running my tongue over one of her fangs. "Damn, that's sexy," I mumbled into her lips.

Somehow, all of my anxiety was gone. I started to wonder how she had done this to me. This was something straight out of a twisted romance novel, not reality.

"What have you done to me?" Tara whispered back.

"What have I done to YOU?" I shook my head. "You started this, remember? What did you do to me?" I ran my fingers slowly across her smooth body.

"I couldn't resist your scent," she sighed at my fingers.

"My scent? You're the one that smells like a walking buffet."

My head was starting to fog up with lust again.

"Wait," she said softly, and my fingers froze.

"Problem?" I asked.

"Questions," she said.

"Fire away," I resumed my playing with her. For some reason, I was completely at ease with this woman now. It was like a warm blanket had smothered all my reservations. I don't know how she did it, but this didn't feel wrong or that I should stop. Here I was in a strange land with a creature I'd never seen before, and I was fondling her like it was prom night.

"What are you?" Tara asked.

"Me?" I grinned. "I'm just your run-of-the-mill vampire."

"Vampire? What's that?" she asked.

That caused my fingers to freeze again in the act of pinching.

"Ow!" she squealed.

"Sorry!" I released her from between my fingers. "You don't have vampires here?" I asked.

"I don't know the word," she said.

"You've touched my mind; just take it from there," I offered this stranger my mind without a second thought. I had no idea what was going on with me, and my inner voice didn't seem to be any help. And...I didn't care. I knew I should, but I just didn't.

"Touched your mind?" she asked.

"Yes, when we shared blood," I said.

Tara cocked her head at me in confusion. "When we were in the house with the others, I tried to keep my distance, to guard myself. But then I heard your words and followed you when you left. Then, we were so far away from the others...and you were so close. You trusted me enough to take my hand. As soon as I pierced you, all of my apprehensions fell. I couldn't control myself anymore. It was almost like I was feeding off something," she said.

"I sometimes have a hard time controlling myself. But, you didn't touch my mind?" I asked.

"How would I do that?" Tara questioned.

"Yeah, it just felt like sometimes you were doing exactly what I was thinking," I said.

"Yes, yes, I felt the same way," Tara agreed.

"What are you?" I asked. I hadn't been able to touch her mind when I had the chance. It wasn't like she was resisting me; it was more like there was nothing there to touch.

"Macock calls me a Daemon," Tara said.

"Demon?"

"No, Daemon. Apparently, there's a difference," Tara said.

"Do Daemons drink blood?" I asked.

"I never have before," Tara said.

This caused me to blanch. "Never?" I wondered if my hunger had somehow passed to her when we touched. I looked at my hand where her clawed finger had first pierced me when we held hands. Had I just inadvertently, in a roundabout way, raped her? But she bit me first. Had she raped me?

I could feel the voice in my head shaking her head silently.

"Have you at least been with a woman before?" I said, trying to calm my spinning head.

"I've never laid with anyone before, man or woman," she said shyly.

"Oh crap," I groaned.

"What is it?" Tara asked.

"I think this may have all been my fault. I'm sorry," I genuinely felt bad for her now. *Poor kid. Somehow, she must have fed off of my own sick and twisted desires and unknowingly mirrored them?*

"I'm not a child. I'm 110 cycles old," she said.

"Wait, what? You heard that?" I asked, confused.

"Yes," she said.

"So you can touch my mind," I said.

"No," Tara shook her head.

"But I said that in my head," I said, frustrated.

This gave her pause as she considered it. "No, I'm pretty sure you said that aloud."

I frowned at her and decided to change the subject as I was getting confused and needed something else to latch onto.

"How'd you make that knife move?" I asked, remembering the knife that levitated as it opened Tara's throat.

"I've always been able to control metal with my thoughts,"

Tara said. "I must admit, I don't really understand what happened here."

"I think," I started carefully. "That when you came into contact with my blood, you sorta sucked up my thoughts and emotions. In this case, my slutty side. Then, as you acted on them, I gave in to them and sorta created a feedback loop."

Wait, that doesn't make sense, my head said. *You yourself said you don't like women "in that way." So why would you want her?*

I don't know. I mean, she's not human, so she doesn't technically count as a woman? I said lamely.

My head gave Tara the elevator eyes. *Oh, she's a woman, alright. You want to talk about what you've been repressing all this time?*

Shut up; this is hard enough as it is, and you're not helping! I yelled at myself.

"Well, I don't know about all that. I enjoyed myself...even the blood part. But I was speaking about the city," Tara said.

"Oh." I felt like an idiot.

"Is this an old city abandoned or a new city not finished?" Tara asked.

"I'm pretty sure it's new," I guessed.

"Then why's it not finished? I haven't heard any signs of construction," Tara said.

"Maybe the bottom fell out of the market. Or it may have something to do with the sinkhole over there. Looks like half the city fell into it...which means the bottom really did fall out," I grinned.

"Oh my," Tara said.

"How's your stomach?" I asked.

"Fine," Tara shrugged.

"And you said you've never had blood before?" I said.
She shook her head.

"Strange. You should be getting sick if your body can't handle it. Looks like you can ingest blood." I couldn't take it anymore. "OK, what's the deal with the tail?"

"What about it?" Tara looked apprehensive.

"I mean, what's up with it?" I said helpfully.

"It's my tail," she shrugged.

"What does it do?"

"What all tails do...tail things," she said as if talking to a small child.

"Can... I touch it again?" Something slid up my inner thigh to my stomach, giving me goosebumps. "Wow, you have that much control over it?"

"Sure," then Tara narrowed her eyes at me. "What did you have in mind?"

[The world froze as the fourth wall slid over the top of the scene blurring the images beneath it. "Uh, yeah. This is one of those Book -1 scenes I mentioned earlier. It's basically your typical drunken sorority make out session...there's nothing to see here, really. Just...move along. I mean it's all blurred out so you can't see anything, anyway."

<Snaps fingers, taps fist, and looks around uncomfortably>

"This may take a while so, why don't we just skip ahead." --Rhi]

A short time later, I was shuddering uncontrollably.

"Anything else?" Tara smiled seductively.

"This is just too damned surreal." I'd given up fighting whatever this was between Tara and I. For the time being, I shelved the part of myself that was still trying to figure it out. It was getting in the way.

"Wait..." I looked at her, my eyes a little out of focus. "How the hell are you talking to me? I didn't think you spoke this "ancient" language or whatever."

"Oh, I didn't. I learned it when I touched hands with you," Tara said.

"What else did you learn?" I asked suspiciously, my heart still trying to calm down.

"That you're not a threat." She looked away from me before continuing. "And that you can keep a secret."

I looked at her carefully. "Why keep all this wonderful covered up?" I couldn't help myself as I slid my hand down her again. I couldn't keep my hands off her.

"My smell, the one that makes your mouth water, it doesn't do that to anyone else. In them, it makes them so randy that they lose their minds."

"I can relate," I grinned.

"No," Tara said, suddenly serious. "As in violently losing their minds in rut," Tara said quietly.

That sobered me. "Oh, I can see where that could be a problem."

"Ever since I turned 14," she said quietly.

"You've been covering yourself since you were 14?" I asked.

"It was the only way to keep my village safe. They found me in the highlands when I was just a babe. They adopted me and nursed me back to health. They'd never seen anything like me before; no one had. Everything was fine until I "grew up." Then, bad things started happening. Once we figured out it was my smell, I've been covering it ever since."

"Wow, and I thought my puberty was rough," I sighed.

"How is it you don't have to cover up as well? I figured with how you smell, you would have to." Tara cocked her head at me.

"Me? Seriously?" I frowned.

"Oh yes. Something about you causes me to willingly abandon my nature. Still, being this close to you makes me want to start this whole thing over again. Right now, I'd do whatever you asked of me; it's very off-putting," she said, the color of her cheeks darkening slightly.

"So weird," I said. "I'm feeling the same way." I shook my head, trying to break whatever was starting to happen between us again.

Tara also seemed to try and resist, "But before that happens again, we should probably be getting back to the others." Tara looked at me again. "That is," she looked down at the floor, "if you were planning on coming with me."

I stood and offered my hand to her, "Yeah, I think we should stick together. But we'd better get going before...you know." I shook my head, wishing for a bucket of cold water right about now.

She took my hand and stood, looking me in the eye the entire time.

I forced myself to break her stare and looked down at the tangle of clothes around us. "Wish there was something to clean up with."

"Try the tap," she said.

"What?" I asked.

"The tap. Water was running in the other house," Tara said.

I stepped over, and sure enough, water came pouring out of a stone spigot when I turned the knob.

"It's warm!" I was amazed. Whoever built this place was amazing.

We cleaned up the best we could before getting dressed. Watching her levitate all the dark-colored straps and bands that covered her body was trippy. It was almost like she was being encased in hundreds of snakes.

"Ever considered working at Helga's House of Pain?" I joked, fighting the urge to kiss her before her mask was back in place.

"I'm sorry?" Tara said, a confused look slowly being hidden by leather straps.

"A joke, just a joke. Never mind." I was still flummoxed about what just happened, what she was and why I couldn't touch her mind when we were together. I thought about it as we walked back.

[Flummoxed? Really? I mean, it's a good word for 1837, but come on hack! --Rhi]

"You won't tell anyone, will you?" Tara broke the silence.

"About what?" I looked at her.

She motioned to herself.

"No, not if you don't want me to," I said.

"Thank you," she said.

"It is a shame to cover all that up, though. You're amazing," I couldn't help but gush over this woman. I didn't know where the new feelings came from, but they felt genuine.

"It's nice of my wife to say so," she nodded.

"Wife?" I glanced at her.

"Yes, of course, my wife," she said.

"Wait, what?" I said.

"We've shared blood and bed. We're bonded now," Tara said cheerily.

"Uh..." was all I could say. Was this just some local custom, or was she messing with me?

"It's OK; I understand if you don't want to tell anyone. I am...well..." She again motioned to herself. It was a sincere gesture; she was obviously ashamed of what she was.

"No, you silly thing, you're wonderful; don't say things like that," I found myself defending her automatically as if it were the most natural thing in the world.

What the hell is going on with me? I asked myself, but there was no response.

She latched onto my arm, wrapping herself around it. "I think you're pretty great too," she said as she put her head on my shoulder.

Oh crap, I thought as I could hear my inner voice rolling across the floor of my head, laughing herself silly.

Newlyweds

RHI

Tara separated herself from me as we got within sight of the house the others were in. I still hadn't figured out what I was going to do when we walked into the room. Everyone was up and seemed to be sharing some sort of green bark. It kinda looked like those hard, flat granola bars. I guessed it was edible as they appeared to be chewing it noisily. The blue-robed guy was still not looking so well.

"What's with him?" I asked Tara in a quiet aside.

"He was injured in our escape. That plus he's been pushing himself way too hard to keep us alive," Tara said.

"Pushing?" I said.

"Yes, he's a Soil Master. In our flight from captivity, he was forced to do some things that, in his words, 'weren't so smart.'"

"He doesn't look so good. Is he going to make it?" I asked grimly.

She shook her head and shrugged her shoulders. "I'm not very familiar with his kind, so I don't know."

I watched as Sh'teena seemed to be hovering over him, tending to him

"My wayward sister returns!" The large woman bellowed. Her eyes widened when she saw me. "AND MARRIED!" She was on her feet, the green granola bar forgotten, and embraced

Tara in a huge hug. She was surprisingly quick as I found one of her large arms sweeping me into a three-way hug.

Luckily, I didn't have to breathe, although I did hear some of my ribs creak.

"Married?" Sh'teena stood up quickly, the injured man forgotten.

"Yes, my young sister, can you not see the bands?" she said, releasing us from her grip.

Having escaped the crushing embrace, I noticed Tara was also drawing in a massive lungful of air.

"Or have your eyes failed as much as your taste for companions?" The large woman's grin was bigger than my head, which was terrifying. It led to thoughts of her being able to bite my head off literally. I shuddered, trying to think happy thoughts.

I felt a tugging at my sleeve and looked over to see Sh'teena pulling up the sleeve of my right arm. I started to jerk away when the sight of my skin caused me to freeze, my eyes bulging. I yanked my arm out of her hand and ripped off my overshirt.

Swirling bands of black tattoos covered my arms from the tips of my fingers all the way up to my shoulders. While they weren't "full sleeves," there was more ink than skin showing. The bands were identical on both arms; they swirled in and out of each other, forming strange symbols and patterns. They reminded me of the old Rorschach tests.

"Tara! How could you?" Sh'teena barked.

Tara seemed to take a step back at the woman's ferocity.

Without thinking I pushed Tara behind me, putting myself between her and Sh'teena.

The giantess bellowed laughter. "Yes, they are bonded, alright. See how she is already protective of her? Perhaps you should rethink your hasty words, little sister," she said with a touch of seriousness.

Sh'teena blushed. I'd never seen someone with skin as dark as hers blush before; it was intense. She seemed to take a moment to regain control of herself.

"I'm sorry, Tara, that was uncalled for," the knight said formally.

Tara bounded past me and embraced Sh'teena deeply. "I accept."

A moment later, Sh'teena looked at me. "And to you, I also apologize. That was terribly rude of me."

I was so lost on what was going on I stopped trying to understand it and just went along. "Don't sweat it. Um, when did you all start speaking English?" I asked cautiously.

"That would be your bond," Jones said.

"That's one way to break the language barrier," the giantess chuckled.

"I don't understand," I said in even more confusion.

"This is going to have to wait," Gathers called from the front door. "We've got company."

Everyone was on their feet, food and marriage forgotten. Even blue robes managed to get to his feet. When we reached the front of the building, nothing was there.

"Where is it, Gathers?" Sh'teena asked, scanning the street.

"Shadows moving, two from either side of the street, one up top, across the street."

"Shadows?" Blue robes asked.

"As you know, Mr. Gathers is intimately familiar with shadows," Jones said.

"But there's nothing here to steal," Blue robes replied.

"YOU ARE TOO EARLY," The voice seemed to come from all around us. It was deep and definitely had the "Big Giant Voice" thing going on. I looked around to see if there was a curtain somewhere hiding the sound system.

"What is it talking about?" Giantess said.

"This city must not be finished yet," Blue robes managed.

"There was a huge section in the back that looked like the floor gave way. There's a lot of damage and unfinished buildings there," I added.

"Unfinished cities are off limits," Blue robes groaned, as if it hurt to speak.

"Great, so what do we do?" I frowned.

Blue robes limped his way to the front of the building and stepped outside. "Builders," he began.

"Builders?" I asked.

"They are the ones who build the cities. They are not to be seen," Jones said.

"We have trespassed in error. We were not aware of this city and stumbled upon it by accident. If you will permit us, we will leave immediately," Blue robes said.

"WHO DISCOVERED THIS CITY?" The voice asked.

Silence fell over the group.

"You were here before us, weren't you?" Tara whispered to me.

"That depends," I said slowly.

"On what?" she whispered.

"On if I'm going to get my head cut off or not." Her look made me sigh. "Fine." I stepped outside to stand next to Blue, who was teetering again. "What is your name anyway? I keep calling you Blue, and you ain't my boy."

"I'm Tober," he said.

"Tony?" I asked.

"No, Tober."

"Well, with your sad little goatee, you look like a Tony, so you're Tony. Remind me to kick your ass if I get killed out here."

Turning to the empty street, I tentatively held my arms out and tried to put some sense of respect into my words. "I was first here." I glanced around, waiting for a big foot to come down from the sky and squish me or something. When it didn't I continued, "But if you could send me back to my world, I sure would appreciate it. I didn't exactly choose to come here either."

There was a long, long silence. A silence that got pregnant, had twins and got pregnant again; it was that long.

"YOUR NAME HAS BEEN RECORDED. ONE CYCLE DEFFERMENT," The voice said.

Tony's mouth fell open in stunned silence.

"The hell's that mean?" I said to Tony out of the corner of my mouth. "Am I on the naughty list or something?" I asked.

Before I could pry an answer out of him, the voice came again.

"YOU MAY LEAVE BY THE NORTHERN CHAMBER, NOW." Then the voice was silent.

"Wait," I started, my arms still held out like an idiot. "I can't leave, I have to figure out how to get back." Tony, of all people, was pulling on my arm.

"Being here is punishable by death," Tony said, pulling weakly on my arm. "It's unheard of that they're letting us go." He continued to tug futilely on my arm, his weakened strength not budging me.

"But..." I started.

"No buts," Sh'teena said from the doorway. "Move before you get us all killed."

"Please," Tara begged, peeking out a window.

Gawdamnitt! I growled in my head, much to the amusement of my inner voice. *You're enjoying this way too much.*

Yes, ma'am, I am. My head said.

Tara's voice broke through my resistance, and I moved in defeat. Tara smiled at me and handed me the overshirt I'd pulled off.

Tony led us out of the city; apparently, his Soil Master "powers" let him know which way we were supposed to go. It wasn't the way their group had come initially. The archway at the far wall was enormous. It was at least a hundred meters wide and a good fifty meters high. Outside the city entrance was a large chamber with three tunnels leading off it.

"Which way?" Sh'teena asked.

Tony looked around, then closed his eyes, a look of concentration crossing his face.

"Both of those tunnels lead nowhere; there's nothing in either direction," Tony said, pointing at the two tunnels with his eyes still closed. "The left one heads back towards Krodon, or at least in that general direction."

"Left it is," Sh'teena said and headed off that way. The group followed as we moved into the dark tunnel.

The tunnel narrowed to about forty meters wide and thirty meters high. The rock here was smooth and showed signs of fresh carving. As the light from the cavern faded, the others grew uneasy.

I could still see pretty well so when light suddenly burst forth from in front of the group, it blinded me. Blinking the spots out of my eyes I saw the silhouettes of the people in front of me. I realized it was Sh'teena and the medallion she wore that doubled as a flashlight.

A moment later, a light source appeared behind me. When I turned, Jones— "Wait, what the hell is your name?" I asked him.

"I am called Macock," he said.

"My cock?" I asked, biting my lip.

"No, Macock," he said.

"Right. Like I'm going to be able to say that with a straight face." Anyway, Macock's staff...Oh my Gawd, I just said that didn't I? And here I go again; the tip of Macock's staff was glowing brightly.

I couldn't help it; I laughed out loud. A few of the others looked at me strangely. I just shook my head. "Nope, can't do it, you're Matlock now."

Matlock frowned at me.

"Hey, where is..." As if in answer, lizard boy flew past us overhead and sailed off into the darkness. "I'm starting to think he's doing that on purpose," I huffed.

"What's that?" Tara asked. "Who's doing what?"

"The author. Being cute," *I scowled at the fourth wall.*

"I don't understand," Tara said, trying to see where I was looking.

"Don't worry, I'm just like this sometimes. Pay me no never mind," I waved her off.

We continued in silence. I noticed there were lights built into either wall, but none of them were on. This was a weird combination of technology and something out of a bad fantasy movie. When we stopped for the "night," all the questions I'd been holding in bubbled to the surface.

The group had broken out the weird green granola bars for dinner again.

"What is this stuff?" I looked at the small, misshapen piece of colored cardboard. It smelled faintly of seaweed, but I didn't want to taste it for fear of what my body might do with it.

"This is yutow," Tony said, leaning back against the wall,

his face pale.

"You tow?" I asked.

"No, yutow. It's a standard traveling food that will stay edible for quite a while."

I passed mine back.

"You must eat; we still have quite a way to go," Sh'teena said.

"Not really hungry, thanks," I offered.

"Strangely, neither am I," Tara said as she also returned her food to the "community pot."

"Tara—" The Giantess said.

"I'm sorry, what is your name?" I interrupted her.

"Rafly," The Giantess said.

"Rafly, got it, thanks," I didn't say a word about her name. Turning back to Tara, Rafly looked at her. "Why aren't you eating sister?"

"I don't know. I just don't feel very hungry," Tara shrugged.

"Is that normal?" I asked.

"No," Rafly said, looking slightly concerned. "She normally eats like a horse."

"Rafly!" Tara gasped.

"What, am I lying, sister?"

"I use my hands like a normal person. I do not put a bag on my head!" Tara said indignantly.

I wasn't sure how this whole bond thing worked, but I was afraid Tara's body may be trying to mimic my own. I wasn't sure how it worked, but I needed to keep an eye on it to make sure she didn't end up getting sick or starving.

"Why do you call her sister?" I asked Rafly.

"She is my sister. My great-grandmother was the one who found her all those cycles ago. She has lived with my family ever since. She is as much my blood as if she'd come from my mother's womb. She's been through the blood rites and has full status as my tribe sister."

"I heard you call Sh'teena your sister as well. Was she also from your village?" I asked.

"HA!" Rafly barked in laughter. "No, no. She is a battle-sister. One night, not too long ago, she appeared in my village chasing down a winged monster that had been terrorizing our countryside. It took many moons, but we did eventually take down the beast. Didn't we, little sister?"

Sh'teena held up her green granola bar in salute.

"She did our village and all the surrounding villages a great service that season and was blooded into the tribe. Now, she stands as my battle-sister, and we take care of each other. Don't we?" Rafly's huge hairy eyebrows waggled at Sh'teena in a strangely disconcerting way.

Sh'teena's wide grin and nod back was just as disconcerting.

"But now," Rafly said, turning to Tara. "Do tell us about this marriage of yours. Did you literally chase her down and wrestle her to the ground to get her to blood with you?"

I had a feeling Tara was blushing violently beneath her mask right now. She sat against the wall beside me, her shoulder touching mine. I felt strangely comfortable beside her.

Tara didn't speak.

"By Tor, you did, didn't you?" She laughed heartily. "Well, my sister, you've never shown an interest in the past. To be honest, I wasn't sure if you could. But when you finally found it, you didn't hold back, did you?"

"She smelled too good," Tara said in a tiny, embarrassed voice.

Rafly leaned forward and gave me a good sniff. The smell of her furry armor was powerful. I didn't know how she could smell anything at all over its musk.

Frowning, "It must be your nose, sister. But you follow it; you deserve some solace," Rafly's look sobered momentarily, "Is there anything we need to know?"

Tara shook her head. "No, she is a good woman, although she doesn't believe it herself. I'll convince her in time."

"I bet you will," Rafly broke out another of those head-eating grins.

"Her land is strange, her ways stranger still. She had a quest but was sent here...by accident?" Tara turned and looked at me.

I sat there looking at her, eyes wide. "I thought you said you couldn't read my mind."

"No, I can't. But you still share things with me; you do it all the time. You're worried about a man named James...and a woman called Shae. This you think about a lot. Are they family? Friends?"

"Something like that," I managed. Was my brain leaking? Was my inner voice sending her smoke signals or something? How was she pulling things from my head, but I didn't get a peep out of hers?

"You said your world?" Tony asked. "What did you mean?"

I looked at Tara for some reason just then. It was as if I was asking her if I could trust the others with the truth. She seemed to have already pulled part of my past out of my head. I don't know if she understood my look, but she nodded to me, and it compelled me to explain.

"I'm from another world, one that's nothing like this place. We don't live underground but, on the surface, beneath the sun, moon and stars. We have cities very similar to the one we left, but they are made of metal and glass, not stone. We have vehicles that move us across the surface and through the sky. We've made technology ease our way of life in so many ways. We got along, for the most part, as a people. We had music and plays and movies. We had fast food, beer, and drugs that kept us healthy because of all the bad things we did. It was good for the most part, that is, until our blight."

"Blight?" Tony asked.

"Yeah. For some reason, a disease appeared unlike anything we'd ever seen before. We don't understand how it happened as it didn't seem to start in one place and spread from there. It was more like the whole planet became infected overnight. Every person it infected went insane and soon died."

"That is a horrible plague," Sh'teena said.

"It would be if that was all it did. The ones that died didn't stay dead. Their bodies returned to 'life,' although the person inside was gone. All that was left was a corpse that wanted to consume every living thing it could get its teeth into. Now our lands are covered with these monstrosities, and we hide behind walled cities and compounds trying to keep what little civilization we have together."

The group was quiet then.

You sounded like a caveman there for a moment. My head interrupted the silence.

I did, didn't I? I said, realizing I was trying to simplify my world for people from one without technology.

"I've never heard of such a plague," Rafly said.

"Be glad. There's no cure. If you get bit or inflected, you're dead," I said somberly.

"How horrid," Sh'teena gasped.

"And you want to go back there?" Tony asked.

I nodded. "I have to. My friends...my family is in trouble."

"So, how'd you get here then? To an unfinished city of all places?" Gathers chimed in.

"We have a place called Drakes. It's a bar. Well, more than a bar really. Apparently, it can magically whisk you away to other places. I was supposed to go to another city near my own to help my family who was in trouble. Somehow, I ended up here, in a building that looked very much like the Drakes I had just come from...only stony," I finished lamely.

My, but aren't you Ms. Motor-mouth suddenly? My head said.

It was true. I wasn't usually one to blurt out my whole life story to people I didn't know.

[OK, so yeah, I did do that with y'all in Book 1, but that's different. You ain't people. These people are people, so...yeah. It's all the hack's fault anyway. --Rhi]

Regardless, I was being way too chatty with these folks, and it was weird.

"Isn't there a tavern in Krodon that goes by that name?" Tony turned to Matlock, who nodded at him. "Perhaps you might get some help there?"

"Best proposition I've had all day." Then I thought about it and turned to Tara. "Second best," I smiled at her.

She laid her hand on top of mine.

I still didn't understand where these emotions and feelings and...other things were coming from. I'd already done the whole "love at first sight" thing with James, and look how that turned out. This wasn't anything like that. James made me feel all 14 again and shit.

I barely knew Tara, but it was like she was a part of me that I'd forgotten about. And now that I remembered it, I couldn't understand how I'd ever gotten along without it. I wasn't sure if this was love or something else. It didn't feel like anything I'd felt before. Maybe because she was a girl? Perhaps because she was from another planet? Maybe because she was this crimson-skinned hotness? I dunno, I was still confused and—

Would you shut the fuck up with all the laughing!?! I bellowed at myself.

Oh, stop being a drama queen. My inner voice stopped laughing and chimed in. *As that moron Clatie Williams said, 'relax and enjoy it.' If you overthink this, you're gonna fuck it up.*

As if you care, I grumbled.

Of course I care, you twit. Yeah, I razz you every chance I get, but that doesn't mean I don't give a shit about you. We're still tied together, no matter how much you wish we weren't. She's cute and seems a bit naïve, but I'm interested in how this turns out. So don't fuck it up! Besides, she's much more entertaining than that James idiot. Tail beats dick any day, my head informed me.

"Where are y'all going anyway?" I managed, trying to wrestle myself from my internal conversation. "From what I was told, y'all were in prison and managed to escape?"

"Those are the most recent events," Sh'teena offered. "Right now, we're trying to get back to Krodon. We were investigating a tunnel collapse between the cities of Krodon and Sanbu. Well, Tober was..."

"Tony," I glanced at him, but he appeared to be asleep already. That was good; he looked like he needed the rest.

"Must you?" Sh'teena asked.

"Oh yes," I assured her. "Just wait; you'll get your turn. I just haven't figured out a good one for you yet."

"What about me?" Rafly said.

"Are you kidding? Rafly is totally badass in itself. You're good to go, girl!" I said with finality.

Her gargantuan smile reminded me again why I wasn't going to provoke her in the slightest. Anyone who could accidentally bite my head off if she sneezed too hard, I was leaving alone.

"HE," Sh'teena continued. "Was investigating the collapse; Gathers and I were just along for the ride."

"And he's some sort of dirt bender?" I asked.

"I don't know what that is, but he does have the ability to move the ground. It's a very rare ability and a respected position here," Sh'teena said.

"Sure, in an entirely cavernous society, I'm sure his dance card is full every night," I grinned.

This actually got a slight smile from Matlock.

"And what about you chuckles? What's your deal?" I asked.

"My deal?" Matlock said innocently.

"Yeah, what's your story?" I said.

"I am but a simple healer. I tend to the sick and injured," Matlock said humbly.

"Right, with your tricorder staff there, huh? Maybe I should call you Bones instead." My words didn't get a rise out of him, which irked me to no end.

Another Trek reference? Have you been sneaking late-night reruns without me or something? My head said.

No, I don't watch that trash. That's something...James would watch. It dawned on me. *Did I...absorb memories from him? Can I do that? Why would I want to do that?*

I felt my head watching me, and I tried to ignore it.

I turned to Sh'teena and Gathers, "I get the whole Camelot thing you two have going, but what's with lizard boy?" I nodded to the far side of the passage where he'd landed a while ago without anyone else noticing.

They turned as a group and looked.

Sh'teena was the one who answered. "I rescued him from slavers a while back and freed him. I thought he'd gone away, but later, he saved Gather's life. He's been traveling with us ever since. Well, with us is a bit of a loose term. He's just...around."

"Does he ever speak?" I glanced at him now. He was observing us. The light reflected off his jewel-like eyes, casting an eerie glow.

"None of us have ever spoken with him. I don't know if he can," Sh'teena explained. "Our story continues. We arrived in Krodon after a few misadventures." She looked at Gathers, who was pointedly staring anywhere but at her. "The head of the city had gathered his army, thinking that the cave-in was some sort of trick from Sanbu. Come to find out, both cities were overpopulated and trying to find ways to deal with multiple resource shortages. The tunnel that had collapsed was the only way in or out of Sanbu. Tober..."

"Tony." I interrupted.

"He's not even awake for you to pester. Why do you bother?" Sh'teena said testily.

"Gotta keep in practice," I noted the slight protective note in her voice and decided to dial it back a notch. "OK, fine."

"Thank you. Tober..." She waited to see if I was going to interrupt again. When I didn't, she continued. "Managed to make a safe passage for us to move around the blockage, and we made our way to Sanbu. That's when the trouble started. We were met by Sanbu's army, who had also been spun up. They took us to the magistrate, who told us of how Krodon had collapsed the tunnel in an attempt to kill them all through starvation. Once his subjects were dead, they would move in and take over the city without a fight.

"That's when the magistrate started trying to persuade Tober to help him overthrow Krodon and make them pay for the tunnel's collapse. Of course, Tober refused, but this didn't stop the magistrate. In the days that followed, he continued his attempts at persuasion through any means possible: treasures, land, women. But Tober was having none of it. By the third day, the magistrate had become tired of playing nice and had us all arrested, all but Gathers here, who has a talent for not being where he's supposed to be."

"You're welcome." Gathers bowed slightly.

"Just be glad the corrupt magistrate had turned off the city's theft protection," Sh'teena said.

"Yeah, kinda hard to be a crook if your own safeguards bust you. But I'll have you know I didn't steal a single thing."

Gathers said proudly.

"Of course not." Rafly chuckled. "I stopped you just before you tried."

"Gathers!" Sh'tenna scolded.

"Hey, there was no way I was going to be able to break you out without money." Gathers said defensively.

Rafly took over at this point. "On the surface, we'd received word that our little sister had gone into a hole in the ground and hadn't come out again. So, Tara and I packed up our gear and traveled to see this farmer who'd been building a well when he found a massive cavern. For a mission of such importance, the King had to send his very best knight to explore this new wonder."

Sh'teena snorted.

"He was just looking for another excuse to hide her away again," Gathers said in exasperation.

"Gathers!" Sh'teena scolded again. "That's our lord!"

"But he treats you like garbage. You're a knight! The first female knight in 300 cycles! And what does he do? He assigns you to garrison duty in some outlaying hold. Or he gives you border patrol duty on the outskirts—not the outskirts that have all the skirmishes where you are needed, but the outskirts of the wastes, where no one lives."

"Even still," she nodded. "It is our duty to obey our lord."

I didn't like this at all. I wondered if there was something I could do here. I never liked bullies. Then I realized this was how James thought and shook my head, trying to clear it.

"So, we picked up their trail and followed it all through this giant rat's maze until I found this little thief trying to relieve someone of their purse. I know how Sh'teena felt about it, so I stopped him." Rafly said.

"You picked me up off the ground! Scared the life out of me is what you did," Gathers said.

"Maybe you'll think twice next time." Rafly smiled. "So, Gathers here fills us in, and we form a rescue plan."

"Your 'plan,'" Gathers mimed air quotation marks. "Was to charge the prison and slaughter everything that moved."

"It was a good plan," Rafly defended herself.

Gathers rolled his eyes. "The plan we used actually worked and didn't cause a bloodbath. Tony...er"

I pointed at him, winked and made a clicking sound with my mouth.

"I mean Tober, used his powers to get us out of the city. He opened a passage but had to seal it behind us constantly. We walked to keep the army from coming through after us. Normally, shifting the walls and floors is a very delicate process that requires a lot of pre-planning as all of the soil moved has to go somewhere and that somewhere could be far away. What he had to do on the fly was very dangerous and somehow hurt him. That's why he is the way he is now. Normally, he's the flamboyant one," Gathers finished.

"I take it you two didn't get along?" I could tell there was more to this than he was telling.

"I wasn't a fan in the beginning. But seeing what he did to get us out of there changed my mind," Gathers said cautiously.

"That's very grown up of you, Gathers," Sh'teena added.

"Oh, don't start." Gathers shook his head.

"That's when you met us," Sh'teena continued for him. "Tober had accidentally brought us into that cavern as we were making our escape."

"Sounds like it would be an exciting book," I said.

[I turned and looked at the author. *There, happy douchebag? I did your stupid little plug for your other story. Now, can I go home?* And, of course, the fucktard didn't answer. --Rhi]

Things settled down—

[Wait, why the hell do you keep ending my asides with "--Rhi"? Who else would it be? I'm the only one that talks to/about you in these books. Knock it off already. --Rhi]

[Seriously?]

[Thank you.]

[--Rhi]

I sighed heavily while counting to ten.

Things settled down for the "night" after that. Gathers was pulling watch duty as everyone else bedded down.

I noticed Sh'teena and Rafly seemed to cozy up together, a bit more familiar with one another than simple friends.

With benefits perhaps? I considered.

Most definitely, my head confirmed.

But every so often, Sh'teena would glance over at Tony. Something was going on there, but this little love triangle was even more fucked up than what I was used to, so I left it alone.

"You didn't ask about me," Tara said when we were resting in that drowsy time just before sleep. "Don't you want to know about my story?"

"You have no idea. But I don't want to do it in front of all these people," I said sleepily.

I could almost feel her raise an eyebrow at me.

"Trust me, I want to drill you for every last detail," my words slurred together as my eyes were getting heavier.

"Good," Was the last word I heard before I drifted off.

Honeymoon Hot Tub

RHI

The next day was boring as shit. It consisted of walking, then some walking, and then some more walking. The entire time down a featureless dark tunnel with no end in sight.

The others played a travel game consisting of a cross between I spy and cloud watching. Apparently, the builders hide pictures and symbols throughout their construction. It was supposed to keep travelers alert and aware of their surroundings in case of trouble. It was weird, and had I understood some of their references, I might have enjoyed the hidden Mickey hunt.

I'd started keeping an eye on Tara's eating habits now. She did manage to eat a bit that morning and a bit more at lunch, but she still wasn't eating anywhere near what they said she should.

"When the fuck do we get to Mordor?" I complained after lunch.

"What?" Sh'teena asked.

"Never mind, just passing the time until we can get rid of this ring. Should have taken the eagles," I mumbled.

"What?" Tara asked.

I looked at Tara and shook my head. My companions hadn't learned to not listen to me yet when I rambled. Then a stray thought hit me.

"How is it one so small can snore so loud? Through a mask,

no less," I asked Tara.

Tara looked at me and held up a finger as if to say something, but a moment later dropped it and shook her head.

"Yo Tony, what was the deal with Bob the Builder back there?" I asked quickly, afraid Tara might decide to say whatever she was holding back. When I saw Tony's confused face, I continued. "The builders, in the city. What was all that about?"

"The builders have been around long before any others. It is rumored they were the first people to inhabit these caverns. Some say they were the first to migrate, others that they had been here all along. We don't have a history that goes that far back. That plus there's never been any confirmed encounters with them that brought back any evidence."

"If that's true, where'd you get those rules about the cities? Burning bush? Stone tablets?" I was surprised by his answer.

"Actually, yes. When our people discovered the first city, the centermost building had the rules engraved onto its walls. As the population grew and the city filled, another city was discovered, and again, the same writing on the centermost building. It continued that way, a new city being discovered just as the population reached maximum capacity for the current city." Tony said.

"What were the rules?" I asked.

"They were pretty simple:

> -No building was to be modified or destroyed. Everything was put in its place for a reason.
>
> -If a building breaks, do not attempt to repair it. The builders will take care of it.
>
> -A family will never own more than one home.
>
> -No digging of rock is allowed in a city or corridor.

-When a new city is found, the one who finds it gets the first choice of homes."

Tony turned and looked at me. "When they said your name had been recorded, that means you were registered as the discoverer. You get the first choice when it's done."

"How does that work?" I asked.

"There is a housing council that handles all building management and disputes. Once a new city is discovered, the name and location of the city, along with its discoverer, was sent to the council from the builders."

"What, does it just appear on the wall or something?" I asked.

"Actually, yes. The center building has a wall listing all the known cities in the region. No one has ever seen someone inscribe something in the stone, but it always appears," Tony said.

"Wait, you said a new city appears when the population warrants it. Didn't you say those two cities with the cave-in were overpopulated? Is 'my' city, the one we just left, anywhere near either of those cities?"

Sh'teena looked at Tony, who cocked his head in thought.

"Yes, I believe you're right." The more he thought about it, the more his face seemed to brighten. "Depending on how long ago the sinkhole you described happened, it might account for the delay in the city opening. The delay would cause the other two cities to overpopulate if it went on long enough. And those other two tunnels could be branching out towards the other two cities, just on an odd route." He looked at me. "That's an excellent observation." He was obviously impressed with my brainpower.

"Do you think that information would make a difference?" Sh'teena asked. "Would it stop the two cities from warring if they knew another was on the way?"

"Hmmm, I don't know. Sanbu would still need to be dug out, at least enough to allow trade. From the way the magistrate spoke, they wouldn't last a cycle. Plus, we'd need to prove this.

Hmmm..." Tony stroked his goatee in thought.

The following morning, I woke up to find Tara had curled up to me in the middle of the night and had thrown her cloak around us both. Waking up to her smell made my mouth water. She still had the leather straps, which I'd learned were infused with some sort of floral oil mix to try and mask her scent. But nothing could stop that wonderful aroma, at least not from my nose. I nuzzled her neck, pulling her tighter to me and felt her shudder.

It was then I realized how warm she felt. It wasn't a shudder; it was a shiver. My body temperature had dropped overnight. I sighed and slid away from her, wrapping the cloak about her tightly before taking stock of my body.

A quick rundown let me know I was running low on blood. It wasn't dangerous yet, not for another few days, but I would need a proper feed soon.

I looked around me and started thinking about my options. I automatically rejected the group. They were beat up and weary as it was. Tony already looked like he would need someone to carry him soon. Besides, I didn't know anything about their physiology. Sure, they mostly looked human, but I didn't know how they'd react or if I could even feed on them. Shae's story about what happened when she tried to feed on James made me gun-shy.

I knew I could feed from Tara, but she'd just started getting her appetite back. I didn't want to risk her losing that again. I kicked myself mentally. I needed to find somewhere to sit down and talk/experiment on this link we shared. I made a mental note to ask Rafly about it later.

With the party out, I turned to the only other option I knew. I hated wildlife feeding, but I didn't have to worry about that option since I'd yet to see any wildlife here. I hadn't even seen a bug down here. The lack of creepy crawlies was creepy.

So, unless we came across someone else, or a random herd of cattle, I was screwed.

You could always whammy one of them, My head chimed in helpfully.

*Not a good idea when they're all I got at the moment. And

again, I don't know if that might kill me!* I yelled at myself.

Wow, drama much? my head said.

You know what, where the hell have you been? I hadn't heard from you in a couple of weeks, and ever since I got here, you haven't shut up. What's the deal?

Ask Nat, Was the only response I got.

At lunch, I asked Rafly about the link I shared with Tara.

"Ah yes, your link. It is part of our way of life in the highlands. When two choose each other as life mates, they become bonded through blood and bed. Once they've shared both, their minds and bodies are entwined for life."

"For life?" My voice actually squeaked.

"That is generally what life mate refers to," she chuckled. "The bands on your arms are identical to one another. As time passes for you, they will change to document your story together." She had me pull off my overshirt. She held out one of her giant hands and waited for me to put my arm in it.

"This here," she indicated a section on my left hand. "This represents you." There was a small symbol that looked like a four-pointed star with small lines branching from it sitting between the knuckles of my index and middle fingers. She pointed at the space between the knuckles of my middle and ring fingers where a small line with sharp looped edges beneath it rested. "This is Tara."

She ran her finger to another symbol on the webbing between my thumb and index finger: "This is both of you at the moment of your marriage." Sure enough, there was a small symbol that appeared to combine the two symbols.

"Any children you have will appear on your knuckles themselves," Rafly grinned.

"Children?" I looked at her strangely. "But..."

"But what?" Rafly said.

"But we're both female."

"So?" Rafly said bluntly.

"We can't have children together," I said.

"Of course you can," Rafly said slowly as if explaining to a slow child.

Her statement startled me. Maybe their reproduction worked

way differently from mine.

You got pregnant from a tail! My head said, as helpful as ever.

Shut up, I mumbled to my head.

"Of course, Tara isn't physically of my tribe, so things may work a bit differently for her." Rafly smiled kindly at Tara.

"About that, how does your tribe's bond work for her if she's not originally of your tribe?"

"Oh, but she is. She was brought into the tribe long, long ago. The acceptance ceremony is permanent and knows no bounds." Rafly snorted. "Even little sister over there has been through it. If she ever completely loses her mind and chooses a mate such as Tony there, she will inherit the bands, just as he will.

"It's one of the perils of bonding with our tribe. You are marked for life. Even if your mate perishes, your bands will remain for all to see. That way, if you find another mate that is of the tribe, they will know your history."

"That is...one of the oddest marriage customs I've ever heard of," I said honestly. But the more I thought of it, the cooler it sounded. "But still nice." I smiled at Tara. "Wanna have some red-skinned vampire babies?" I meant it as a joke, but she acted as if I'd physically slapped her.

"Now?!?" she screeched.

"No, my dear, I was teasing," I said, smiling kindly. "I don't know of any of my kind who have ever had children. I honestly don't think it's possible." I watched as her shoulders slumped and suddenly regretted my words.

Tara may be over 100 cycles, or years, or whatever old, but she still acted as if she were a young girl. I leaned over and touched the side of her leather-clad face gently.

"But don't listen to me. I've seen more fantastic and incredible things in the past few days than I'd ever thought possible. Just as Mr. Bond said, never say never." I leaned over, kissed her leather lips, and rested my forehead against hers.

To anyone else, I'm sure I looked like a complete fool, but that didn't seem to stop Rafly. I heard a loud sniffle behind me and turned to see her studying her axe very intently, keeping her from looking in our direction.

"So, the bands will keep changing?" I asked.

"Oh yes. They can grow as well," Rafly said.

"Grow?" I asked.

"Spread." Rafly nodded.

"Spread? How far?" I asked warily.

"It depends on what all befalls the pair of you. I've known mates who only had the arms; of course, they were pretty tame and never left the village. Then others have nearly been head-to-foot in bands. They were ones who traveled afar and had incredible adventures."

"So, the more nutso you live your life, the more bands?" I asked.

"Eh." Rafly shook her hand from side to side.

I looked at Tara. "You and I are going to end up darker than Sh'tenna; just you wait." I grinned.

I could see Tara's shoulder shaking as she laughed, and Rafly joined in.

Later that night, I tried to get Tara to show me her hand so I could compare our bands side by side, but she refused, saying it was too dangerous. I considered dragging her off down the hall, but that didn't seem like a very nice thing to do to your wife.

The following day, Tony couldn't walk. We managed to get him to wake up, but he didn't seem to be able to move. His face was pale, almost gray. When Matlock examined him, I peeked at his chest and saw a nasty collection of dark bruising.

"There's nothing more I can do," Matlock said. "I've been able to ease his pain, but I would need the surgery in my home to do more. He's going to need serious medical treatment soon."

That was the most words I'd heard Matlock say since I'd met him.

"That's not the only thing," Sh'teena said. Lunch will consume the last of our food. We've stretched the meager supplies we could appropriate in our flight from Sanbu, but there's just not enough left. The same goes for water. If this tunnel doesn't lead us somewhere with food or water soon, we're going to be in trouble."

"Should we turn back?" I asked.

"No use," Matlock said. "Tony sealed the tunnel we used to

escape from Sanbu to keep us from being followed. He's in no shape to open it back up. Besides, they'd probably just kill us on sight."

"So, forward it is," I said grimly. They nodded in agreement.

Rafly volunteered to carry Tony. "It's no problem; he weighs less than my axe." She chuckled.

That night was a grim scene. Everyone was hungry, Tony seemed to be drifting in and out of consciousness, and I was starting to feel the effects of lack of blood. I had a tremor in my hands and the flu symptoms I'd been trying to ignore all day were getting worse.

In the morning, Tony wouldn't wake up. He was still breathing; we just couldn't get him to rouse. It took me an effort to overcome the lethargy I felt and get moving. While I'd tried to hide my rapidly worsening condition from Tara, she'd seen right through it. She was worried and hovering over me constantly.

By afternoon, we couldn't go any farther, literally. The tunnel had come to an end. There had been no branches up to this point and all that was in front of us was a smooth wall.

I collapsed on the floor beside where Rafly had left Tony. The others were arguing with each other now, trying to decide what to do. They didn't think they could make it back to one of the other tunnels in the off chance it might actually lead somewhere, and we couldn't just sit here.

I looked over at Tony's unconscious form. At least he didn't know what was going on, he wasn't suffering. If this was the end, he'd never know. I caught myself staring at the pulse in his neck.

Why not? My inner voice was tiny with the suggestion. She knew it was wrong. *If he's going to die anyway, you might as well stay alive a while longer. He could easily keep you going another week, possibly two.*

Shut up. I said weakly.

Just being practical, my head said.

I know; that's why you need to shut up.

You'd rather die? my head asked me.

*I've never killed someone while feeding, never. I'm not

about to start now,* I growled at her with a grim determination.

FINE! But when he keels over, I'm taking over and keeping us alive!

Good luck. I said defiantly but suddenly wondered if, in my weakened state, she might be able to take over. Or did I want that as an excuse to let me say it was her fault so I could do it?

STOP! I screamed in my head.

"Rhi?"

When I opened my eyes, Tara was kneeling next to me. I didn't feel good, and judging by the sound of her voice, I didn't look good either.

"I just need to rest," I managed, my words coming out slurred.

"You do know you can't lie to me, right?" The amount of concern in Tara's voice startled me.

"The bond again?" I asked.

She nodded. "You're ice cold, and you look as pale as Tony."

"I'll be fine..." I started, then thought better of it. "No I'm not. I'm not doing so good."

"Do you need to feed?" Tara asked.

I nodded weakly.

"Then take from me," Tara said.

"I can't," I said hoarsely.

"Of course you can," Tara said.

"No, I'm too low now. If I start, I may not be able to stop. Besides, you need your strength too." My eyes were feeling heavier by the minute.

"You are my strength," Tara said.

"You're a sweet kid, sappy but sweet." I wanted to reach up and touch her face, but I suddenly didn't have the strength.

"I am your elder, you know," Tara said, a bit put out.

"Then you should moisturize; your skin looks terrible. All leathery," I chuckled weakly. "Don't worry about me. Even if I shut all the way down, I won't die."

"What do you mean?" Tara asked.

"I'll look dead: no breath, no heartbeat, nothing. But if you found me enough blood, I would come back."

"How?" Tara asked.

"It's a mystery. It defies all logic and science we know. We stopped trying to figure it out and just accepted it. Most chalk it up to magic." I tried to shrug but failed.

"Magic?" Tara asked.

"When all else fails, fall back on magic or God—the two great catch-alls. I'm just glad I don't have a mirror. They say you begin to rapidly age when you run out of blood."

"Not at all, my sweet. You're still as lovely," Tara said.

"Now, who's the bad liar?" I said.

No one could decide what to do, so we chose to stay put for the night. The lack of food and water had soured everyone's spirits and drained what little energy we had left.

Tara tried to curl up with me, but I was so cold she couldn't stop shivering. I managed to get her to settle for just holding my hand.

Somewhere in the middle of the night, everything went to hell.

I was startled awake by the sound of Tony gasping for breath. Sh'teena and Matlock were over the top of him calling his name.

I couldn't feel my body anymore. I could still move a bit, but I couldn't feel anything anymore. I tried to open my mouth to speak but found nothing came out. Tara's visage suddenly filled my field of vision. She was making noise, but I could no longer make out what it was. I couldn't make out anything anymore.

God, I wish I could see her face. I know she must be terrified. I wish I could let her know I'd be OK. She needed to worry about herself, take care of her. I hoped they figured something out before...before—

I thought I was hallucinating when Tara's face became a silhouette as a blinding blue light appeared behind her. Then, hands were touching me—lots of hands. I was weightless. Then, I was underwater. The water was lukewarm, but I'd take that over the cold any day.

An infinity later...I must have swallowed some of the water because I could feel heat in my chest. Then someone was torturing me as fire ants crawled all over me. I could hear this loud gulping sound and soon realized I was swallowing down large mouthfuls of something. It didn't taste like blood to me, but it seemed to have the same effect.

I could feel my senses coming back. I could feel my body again. I was sitting, chin-deep, in a pool of steaming hot water. I could feel bubbles around me. Not the intense bubbles like a hot tub, just an occasional trickle tickling my legs and chest. The hot current flowed around me seductively, like a lover caressing me. My eyes were the last to clear. When I could see again, it wasn't the current but my Tara caressing me.

Tara was in the pool with me. The room was rough-hewn rock, not the smooth rock of the tunnels. Electric wall lamps lit the room with a soothing, gentle yellow light; not the typical harshness of fluorescents. There were lights in the pool as well, one on each of the four walls, illuminating the hot spring that poured up from the darkness below.

Tara's beautiful crimson was before me in all her glory. She'd shed her leather cocoon and sat beside me, her hand delicately running up and down my naked body. She wasn't trying to be arousing; she was just touching me.

When I tried to speak, my voice croaked.

"Shhhh," Tara commanded, putting her finger to my lips. "Drink." She handed me a semi-opaque plastic pouch with a tube coming out of it. She put the tube to my lips and nodded.

I drank. It was what I'd tasted before. Again, it wasn't blood, but it filled me, nourished me as if it were. My hand came up and took the pouch from her. I held it out and looked at it.

The liquid inside was slightly cloudy like water accidentally mixed with a bit of coffee creamer. I swallowed again. It wasn't as savory as blood, but it wasn't bad either. It sure as hell beat starving.

I was feeling quite good by the time I finished it. I set the pouch off to the side of the pool's rock ledge. There were several additional empty pouches already lying there. I started to speak, but Tara handed me another pouch.

"You eat, I'll talk," Tara said.

Who was I to argue with a beautiful naked woman in my bath who was feeding me...not-blood? I took the pouch gratefully and began to sip.

"First off, we're all safe, even Tony. The Sisters of the Order rescued us. Apparently, we'd camped out just outside the secret entrance to one of their temples.

"They'd been watching us the last two days as we approached the tunnel's end. They saw we were out of supplies, and when you and Tony were dying, they stepped in. Seems they are yet another of the mysterious factions down here that prefer to remain apart from the others. They do not like to involve themselves in the affairs of others but couldn't stand by and let us die when they could so easily help us.

"So, they took us in. They took Tony away, not even letting Matlock go with him. They fed us all and brought you here straight away. If I hadn't been as worried as I was, I would have laughed at how they tossed you into this hot pool. It seems they knew better than to try and keep you from me, though, and they let me accompany you.

"They brought me food and drink after they tried to offer me one of the pouches you had. I tried it, but it didn't agree with me. Instead, I fed it to you, and it brought you back. We've been here ever since. A few of the others have come to check on us, but I've sent them away when they came to the door."

"How long?" I managed, my throat dry despite everything I'd drank.

"A few days," Tara said. "I think."

"How are you...with no clothes?" I asked.

"The sisters do not seem affected by my scent—the others I don't allow in the room for fear of it. Rafly let me know Tony is up and about again. He's not 100%, but he's getting better. The others are also on the mend. While not very talkative, the sisters said we can remain here until we are all well enough to travel."

"You've been with me, in this pool, for a couple of days?" I asked.

Tara nodded.

"How are you not a prune?" I asked.

"A prune?" she asked.

"All wrinkly," I said.

She shrugged, making her look even younger than she acted.

If I had to guess, Tara looked like a human in her late twenties or so.

"What is this stuff?" I looked at the pouch again.

"They didn't say. They keep bringing it in when the tray is empty," Tara said.

I looked over, and several full pouches were on a small metal tray.

"This place would make a killing as a spa in my world," I said, sighing deeply as another wave of hot water spread across my body. "This water must be near boiling. Doesn't it bother you?"

"Oh, it's warm but comfortable. The hard part is staying awake with how soothing it is. I've nodded off once or twice." Tara smiled.

"Come here, you." I pulled her into my arms. "Sorry if I worried you. I'm sure seeing me like that wasn't any fun."

Tara nodded, and I thought I saw a bit of glistening in her eyes.

"Hey now, none of that. I'm fine. I told you I'd be OK. I'm a lot tougher than I look." I kissed her on the cheek. "You know," I started to say something, realized it was stupid, and stopped. "I like you," I said instead and kissed her on the lips briefly. "A lot." I touched her face again, running my fingers across her smooth crimson skin.

"Glad to hear it." Tara smiled at me.

"And since we finally have some time and are alone, we can... talk," I said.

"Talk?" Tara cocked her head at me.

"Oh yeah. You and I didn't have much of a courting period, so if we're going to be spending the rest of our lives together, maybe we should get to know each other a little bit?" I suggested.

"OK, what would you like to know?" Tara asked.

I stared at her for a moment, not knowing where to begin. "I haven't seen your arms yet."

She held them out next to mine.

"Amazing. They're absolutely identical," I marveled.

"Yep. I was always jealous of the others in the village with them. I didn't think I'd ever find someone who could stand to be around me without going insane," Tara said.

"Oh, trust me, I go a bit nutso around you," I leered gently.

"You know what I mean. It was one of the reasons I started traveling with Rafly, hoping I might find someone," Tara said.

"And how's that working out for you?" I asked.

"Beautifully," she said as she kissed me. It wasn't a deep kiss, but it wasn't a short one either.

"Woah, easy there, tiger." I cautioned.

She seemed to take a deep breath to try and get a hold of herself.

"It's just too easy between us, isn't it?" I said, something popping into my head and causing me to smile.

"Is that a bad thing?" Tara asked.

I started to answer, thought better of it and gave it a moment's thought. "I don't see how it can be," I laughed.

"What?" Tara asked.

"It's just...Shae..."

"Your friend-family from home?" Tara asked.

"Yes. She says the same thing about her and James. How easy it is for them to be around one another. I didn't understand that until now." I smiled again, liking the feeling Tara gave me.

Tara put her head on my shoulder.

"Now, let's get a bit serious now, shall we?" I said.

Her eyebrows shot up.

"Not like that," I said gently. "No lies, no coy games. Just some serious truth. Think you can handle that?" I asked.

"Sounds serious," Tara said.

"Let's just say I've been around a lot of people who had serious ulterior motives and could lie to me without me having the slightest clue," I said.

"That sounds horrible," Tara said.

"Only when they keep doing it." I looked at her then, pulling her chin off my shoulder. "How long have you been able to hear my thoughts?"

She searched my face for something.

I sighed. "I know you can do it; I know you have done it. I'm not mad. Where I'm from, we can do it anytime we touch someone's blood."

"It's not a good thing here," Tara said cautiously.

I took her hand. "Just be honest with me. There are a lot of things in this world I don't understand yet. You are one that I want to understand completely."

"Sometimes," Tara started, taking a deep breath. "Sometimes I get flashes, or words...feelings. Like the night we were brought into the temple. I felt you fading away from me, and I became a bit...distraught."

"I'm sorry I scared you," I said.

"Another time you said you wanted to eat me...or bite me...and another when you said I was pretty," Tara said, running through her memory.

"Surface thoughts." I nodded. "That's a rare gift. I've only met one other person that could do that."

"I wouldn't call it a gift," Tara said.

"You can do it with other people?" I asked.

"A little. It's really hard. With you, it seems to be getting easier every day. And your thoughts are never ugly, unlike others I've seen," Tara said.

"On the flip side, I get absolutely nothing from you. Even when in bloodtouch, I can't hear you or sense you. It's maddening," I said in frustration.

She grinned at me.

"What?" I looked at her sharply.

"I hide myself," she said quietly.

"You what?" I yelped.

"I hide myself, my thoughts, all the time," Tara said.

"You can do that?" I gasped.

"Once I learned I could sometimes hear other people's thoughts, I didn't know if others could hear mine. So, I practiced building a wall around my mind. From what you just said, it works. I've never known if anyone else had tried. It's good to know all those cycles of practice paid off." Tara nodded.

"So you can lower it then?" I asked.

"Uh, I don't know. I've never tried to let someone in on purpose before," Tara said cautiously.

"We can try sometime if you want. Merging your mind with

someone else is...an experience." I grinned.

She looked skeptical.

"I'll be gentle, I promise." She gasped as my fingers unexpectedly tweaked her.

"You are a vicious woman!" Tara said.

"You have no idea," I grinned evilly. "So, tell me your story."

Tara sighed. "It's a boring story."

"I'm not going anywhere. In fact, I might try to join this order if I can have this room," I sighed.

"Well, you know I was found as a small child somewhere up in the mountains by Rafly's family. I don't really remember anything before my life in the village. They were kind to me, but even so, children are unintentionally cruel by nature. Not only was I much smaller than anyone else, I was red and had a tail. There were old tales from the village wise woman that spoke of red-skinned devils that flew and used to raid livestock and carry off small children."

I grabbed her shoulders and spun her around to inspect her back. "Where do you hide them?"

"What?" Tara said suddenly.

"You're wings," I snapped.

"Oh, shut uuuuuup..." Her last word dragged out as I started to massage and knead her shoulders.

"You're as stiff as a board." And she was. Her shoulders were hard as rocks.

"I've been a little stressed," Tara offered.

"I'll work, you talk." I continued massaging her shoulders. While I wasn't a certified masseuse, I had been trained in pressure point work and sensual massage in Japan.

"So, I bore the brunt of that teasing for some time until I lost my temper and flattened a boy who had been teasing me far too long. Of course, I was scolded for losing my temper," Tara said.

"You get a spanking?" I asked.

"Yes," Tara murmured.

"You enjoy it?" I leered at her.

"What? Of course not!"

"They must not have done it right," I teased.

"Stop that! Did you want to hear this or not?" Tara asked

testily.

"I'm sorry. Please, continue."

"Then I came of age, and my body developed," Tara said.

"I'll say." I couldn't help it; the girl had an effect on me.

Tara sighed. "At first, no one knew it was me causing all the problems. They took all the increased sexual appetites from people due to the spring or some such. But after a while, they began to notice a pattern with me. Everywhere I went, people wanted to...you know. It started getting out of hand, so the village chief came to talk to our family.

"We tried several things to try and cover it, but the only thing that seemed to work was the leather. The infusion of the floral oil helped mask it and keep the leather from getting too smelly. I used to have to sneak off into the middle of nowhere to bathe."

"Used to?" I asked, curious.

Tara sighed again. "No, I still do. But it was during one of these trips I learned I could command metal. I was bathing in a stream and thought I heard someone. In my rush to get my clothes back on, I reached out, and my clothes flew to me. It took some time before I realized it was the metal rivets that I could control.

"After that, I experimented with every type of metal I could find. I was already somewhat good with knives, they being the only weapons the village made that were small enough for me to handle. Being my size in a village of giants caused so many unforeseen problems. But I became something scary when I started practicing my metal moving with my knife fighting."

"Oh really?" I said, my fingers roaming.

"Don't start...not yet... it's hard enough sitting here with you. If you start, I'll start, and then I'll never finish this," Tara pleaded.

"Yes mistress," I huffed.

"Bad, bad girl," Tara's voice was husky, nowhere near her normal tone.

My hands froze on her shoulders, holding her tight as my mouth moved to her ear.

"This whole shy girl thing is an act, isn't it?" I whispered.

Tara looked back at me over her shoulder, and I saw a different set of eyes looking back at me. These eyes were older, and I didn't recognize them.

"But why?" I asked.

"I'm older than people normally get here, Rhi. You know the one constant I've encountered? People are terrified of what they don't understand. But I sense this doesn't bother you, does it?"

"Being 'old?' No. Age is something you kinda let go of when you become a vampire. We can live a long, long time and I was taught to let go of such prejudices while living in Japan," I said.

"Well, that's not the way people think here. As such, I find it easier to act this way than to be chased out of town with a pitchfork." A sly grin flashed across Tara's mouth. With a blink, the old eyes were gone, replaced by the coy girl's eyes again. "It's one thing to come face to face with a smart, determined monster. It's a whole other situation if that monster acts scared, confused and timid. The first, they'll kill without thought; the second, they'll adopt as a pet."

"Now who's the bad girl?" I whispered, gently biting her earlobe, and then started rubbing her shoulders again. "Back to your story." I suddenly realized there was a lot more to this girl than I'd originally thought, and it sent a shiver of excitement through me.

"It took a long time for the village to become completely use to me, about 40 cycles to be exact. Once the next generation had grown up with me, I became a staple. I started traveling with the traders of the village to other nearby villages. We made a modest trade in furs, armor and some weapons.

"Occasionally, we'd receive a request from one of the neighbors whom wild animals or the occasional bandit were harassing. We'd usually make short work of them. Being the only giant village in the area, we surprised bandits as they were expecting normal farm folk.

"When the king annexed our lands, not a lot changed. Once a cycle or so, a man would come to collect the taxes. We'd pay in our normal wares, not having dealt with coin before. Only once did a king's patrol come through, trying to cause trouble. Anyone who comes to a giant's village thinking they can cause trouble quickly realizes their mistake. While we didn't kill any of them, they made a point to change their patrol route to avoid us in the future."

"You bunch of troublemakers," I said.

"That's why we lived out in the middle of nowhere, so that we could cause problems for our neighbors." Tara smiled. "By my 80th cycle, I'd learned all of the jobs in the village. I could fill in anytime someone got sick or needed a break. I'd become strong, too. I could almost beat them at arm wrestling."

"What about regular wrestling?" I grinned slyly then tried to knock it off. I couldn't help it with this girl; she was my new drug, and I couldn't get enough.

"No one tried," Tara smiled sadly. "My chief and every other chief said no one should try, if you get my meaning," Tara said.

"Oh yes, I know exactly what you mean. My last chief did the same thing to me. No one was allowed to touch me. It made things...lonely," I said.

Tara turned her head, reached back and pulled my lips to hers. "More for me then."

I smiled into her kiss. "I'm all yours."

"The First chance we get that we're not running for our lives, stumbling into empty cities, or being taken in by secret societies, I say we lock ourselves away for a week and discover what we missed," Tara said with a vehemence that surprised me.

"Sounds good to me. But I was only off-limits for a handful of years. I'd be afraid you'd break me in half," I offered.

"You'd be lucky if it was just in half." Tara's other eyes flashed for a moment before they were gone again.

"Sh'teena showed up in our village chasing her monster not long after that. We'd not realized it was the same one that had been terrorizing some of the surrounding villages. We'd thought it was just a pack of wild animals, not an actual monster. It was a pretty intense couple of weeks trying to track the thing down and kill it. Sh'teena delivered the final blow and is the one known for the kill. She received multiple honors and was taken in by my village," Tara said.

"I hope she warns her husband what he's getting into," I said.

"Husband?" Tara asked.

"What?" I asked.

"Why does it have to be a husband?" Tara asked.

"Sorry, from what I saw, she was digging on Tony there," I said.

"Now. It wasn't so long ago she and Rafly were battle buddies," Tara said.

"Sh'teena...and...Rafly? How does that even work?" I asked.

"It's very common in my village for those that go into battle together to form tight bonds regardless of sex. Sometimes, they can be away from their families for a long time. Battle buddies take care of each other in ALL things," Tara said.

"No, I meant physically...with the size difference, I figured she'd get lost up in there." I made a hand gesture.

Tara splashed water back at me chuckling, "Be nice."

I kissed the back of her head. "How nice?" I felt her hand on my thigh, and my pulse quickened.

"Not yet," Tara chided.

"Spoilsport," I complained. I didn't understand why my libido was so jacked while I was around this woman, but I was starting not to care anymore.

"Do women not get married in your world?" Tara was suddenly very still.

"It happens, more than people know, but it's kept quiet. There are still a lot of closed or narrow-minded people in my world. The human society there is way too uptight sometimes. But, usually, the pendulum swings the other way every 30-40 years or so. I expect things are going to loosen up here in about 20 years. Actually, with everything that's happening with the zombies, it might be more like next year."

"So, if I were to go to your world..." Tara started.

"You..." I was startled. With how hectic things had been, I'd honestly not had the time to consider her coming home with me. "You would want to come to my world?"

Tara turned around and looked me in the eye. "You do know what forever means, right? Where you go, I go. I don't care if you go into the Shadow Lands. As long as we're together, I'll go anywhere."

"Even Jersey?" I asked absently.

"Even Jersey...whatever that is." Then Tara kissed me, long, hard, and deep. It was a while before we came up for air. She patted my cheek and had me switch places with her so she could rub my shoulders.

"After that," Tara continued as if nothing had happened. "Sh'teena spent a few months patrolling our lands. When she left, Rafly and I tagged along. Actually, it was me who tagged along; Rafly came along to keep me out of trouble."

"That's what big sisters are for," I said.

"Yeah. We trooped around for a while until the King called Sh'teena back to the garrison. At that point, Rafly and I headed home. It was a good time later that we received a message from Sh'teena. Apparently, she'd been sent to investigate a cavern. She arranged that a message would be sent to us if she didn't return within a specific time.

"Rafly was packed within the hour and we were on our way. We found the cavern entrance easy enough. A farmer had discovered a large hole in one of his fields and had sent word to the king for help. The king had sent Sh'teena to investigate.

"Apparently, the king wasn't thrilled with having a female knight as they hadn't had one in over 300 cycles. Add to that, she was from a southern tribe that wasn't exactly 'knight material' to him. I'm so glad I never met the man," Tara said.

"Would you have set him straight?" I teased.

"No, I would have castrated the man. The most obvious case of testosterone poisoning I'd ever heard of." Tara smiled.

I looked down at her hand on my shoulder. "Give me that." I took her hand and pulled it over my shoulder to get a better look at it. In the process, I "unintentionally" made her press up against my back.

I turned her hand over in mine. It was as normal as you'd expect, save for her claws. Where I had fingernails, she had onyx claws. They weren't that long, maybe two centimeters. I'd seen fake fingernails that were longer.

"How do you keep from cutting yourself open with these?" I asked.

"How do you keep from biting your own tongue?" Tara countered.

"Well, I don't have fangs either," I volleyed.

"Carefully. I frequently scratched myself when I was younger, usually trying to get at an itch a little too fast. Since then, I've learned to take my time," Tara said.

I looked down and found her other hand quietly snaked around my side and cupped me. I could see the tips of her claws digging into my flesh but not cutting. I could feel their sharp pressure, but there was no tearing.

"That, and I learned how to trim my nails." Tara squeezed gently before slowly withdrawing her hand, dragging her claws across my skin.

I shuddered, watching as tiny red lines appeared on my skin before slowly fading.

"You and I are explosive, you know that, right?" I managed.

"I do like you so much better naked," Tara purred at me. "I can smell you so much better. It stirs things in me I didn't know I had."

"So, you're saying you're affected by me, how other people are affected by you?" I asked.

"In a way. The people I affect are never interested in me for whatever reason. Whereas, I only want you," Tara said.

"I'm still amazed we've lasted this long, being this close to one another," I said.

"And naked," Tara added.

"And naked," I acquiesced.

"What?" I asked when Tara was quiet for an unusually long time.

"Does this feel wrong to you?" Tara asked.

"Does what feel wrong?" I asked back.

"Us. How we feel about each other. It's been a whirlwind since we began and I haven't had time to stop and think about it till now," Tara said.

"Well, yeah. I mean, I've never met someone and had a bond like this form so quickly. I don't understand it, but at the same time, I don't want to end it," I said as I searched my feelings and found it to be true.

"So, we both understand this is wrong...well, not wrong but extremely unusual. Knowing this, we're still OK with our relationship but the fact we're OK with it feels wrong?" Tara seemed to get lost in her own thoughts while trying to figure out that sentence.

"Yeah, almost like some hack is doing it to us on purpose," *I glared at the fourth wall.*

"Hack?" Tara asked.

"Nothing, never mind," I said. "I'm happy. You're happy. Let's not jinx it and just enjoy being happy. Sound good?"

"I'm happy with that," Tara said and chuckled.

I continued to explore her hand. I slowly turned it over, examining each of her claws in turn. They were the blackest black I'd ever seen. The longer I stared at them, the deeper the black became. "These are amazing." I pulled one of her fingers to my mouth and ran it over my lips before opening my mouth and sucking it inside. My tongue gently explored every crease of her finger and claw.

"Quit it," Tara said, gently pulling her finger from my mouth.

"Back to my story. We spent a while getting to the bottom of the initial cavern. While it didn't have a city in it, it could easily have held one. We followed the trail Sh'teena had left until it disappeared. Things got easy once we found the hidden door they'd used to get into the first city. It wasn't hard for people to remember seeing Sh'teena. She's pretty distinctive down here."

"How so?" I asked.

"You'll see when we get to a city. By the time we caught up to them, they were already captured in Sanbu. Luckily, we stumbled across Gathers and pulled off a daring escape. You've pretty much heard the rest."

"Does that mean we can fuck now?" I asked a tingle in my stomach.

She slapped me in the back of the head. "Why are you so crude sometimes, then so gentle others?"

"Yeah...about that. I'm not entirely right in the head." I spent the next twenty minutes or so explaining my time in the Army and subsequent injuries.

"Maybe you should ask Matlock to see if he can do anything? Where your science failed, his magic may prevail?" Tara said.

"I'm pretty sure his 'magic' is more science than everyone thinks," I said.

"Oh?" Tara said.

"Just a hunch. Besides, don't you enjoy my quirky personality?"

This time, she wrapped her legs around my waist and pulled my shoulders back until I was reclining on her. Using her feet, she spread mine, allowing the hot water to make fresh contact with my more intimate areas.

I gasped at the contact.

"There are many things I enjoy about you, one of those being your mind," Tara said.

"Mmm, wait until you get inside it proper." I rolled my head back and turned to face her as she looked at me over my shoulder.

"You mean like this?" With that, she bloodied her lip before kissing mine and drawing blood. As our blood merged, I felt doors opening within her.

The cavern faded away as I drifted into her mind.

Hard Rock Drakes

RHI

"It lives," Rafly called as Tara and I entered the room.

After soaking so long in that blissful heat, we finally pulled ourselves from the hot tub room. Walking through "normal" temperature caverns was downright freezing. The sisters of the order had cleaned my clothes before returning them, for which I was eternally grateful. They were getting ripe.

"It does." I smiled at Rafly.

Rafly was sitting on a large bench against a back wall. Sh'teena, Tony and Matlock were seated at a large stone table while Gathers leaned against the wall next to another door.

"Glad to see you're feeling better, Tony," I said. I was so relaxed after my "interlude" with Tara that I almost felt comfortably numb to everything. I floated over to a chair at the table and settled into it.

"Uh, thank you," Tony managed, looking questionably at Sh'teena.

Tara sat down next to me, taking my hand. I didn't mind; we were both still so warm that even through her glove, it was like holding a small, soft coal.

"So, what's the haps?" I looked around the room.

"The sisters wanted to talk to us once we were all back on our feet," Sh'teena said.

"OK, what did I miss while I was out?" I asked.

"I'd like to be brought up to speed as well," Tony said.

"Oh," Sh'teena glanced at Matlock before continuing. "Not a lot. We've pretty much been stuck here. They've taken care of us, so I can't fault them for that."

"Nothing much?" Rafly barked out a laugh. "You're going to stick to that?"

"Rafly!" Sh'teena hissed.

"You should have at least made up a lie I could agree to be silent over." Rafly turned to the rest of us. "Seems our little group likes secrets."

"What do you mean?" Tony asked.

Rafly looked at her battle sister.

"Fine," Sh'teena growled. "I'm here because my king sent me to explore the caverns discovered beneath a farm. The caverns lead to the city I met you in." She was talking to Tony. "We were still...I was still in shock at our discovery and didn't dissuade you from thinking I was a member of this order. Later, I let you keep thinking it because I couldn't think of what else to do."

Tony looked at her a moment. "So, you're not a Golden Knight?"

"Oh yes, I'm definitely a Golden Knight. I was inducted when I was 12, before I went to be a page. But I'm a Golden Knight from my tribe on the surface."

"Not one from this order?" Tony asked.

"No," Sh'teena said quietly.

"Wait, the sisters here are called Golden Knights?" I asked, ignoring the little lovers' quarrel beginning in front of me. I knew all about keeping secrets and honestly didn't want to get involved in whatever this was.

"Yes. It's a secret organization that lives down here in the tunnels between cities. They want to keep to themselves and seem to value their secrecy more than anything else," Sh'teena said.

"So, you lied to me?" Tony was looking at Sh'teena.

"No. I am what I am; you just believed I was from a different order than I am. We share the same name," Sh'teena said cautiously.

"Don't mince words; you led me on," Tony demanded.

"Famous last words," I mumbled to Tara.

"Oh, she's not the only one here who's not been completely honest," Rafly chimed in.

"Fine," Matlock said flatly, turning away from Rafly's stare. "I'm also here to investigate the war between Krodon & Sanbu."

"Why?" Tony looked at him sharply.

"I believe there is another like myself who may be causing trouble amongst factions down here. I believe he's selling arms and may even be responsible for the cave-in," Matlock said.

"One like yourself?" Sh'teena asked.

"A...healer," Matlock managed.

"Oh please, Mr. Spock. If you're a magical healer, I'm the Queen of England!" I chimed in, just because I love stirring the pot.

"I never said magical," Matlock said.

"But again, that's what you're letting these people believe. You're using tech that is probably beyond that of my home. Is that forbidden down here or something?" I asked.

"What?" Tony asked.

Matlock sighed. "I'm not from these caverns either."

"You're from above ground?" Sh'teena asked.

"So to speak. I am from above ground...well above the ground." Matlock said slowly.

"The floating cities?" Gathers asked excitement in his voice.

"Higher," Matlock said.

"Enough with the labor pains; give us the baby!" I said, exasperated.

"I come from a place that floats above the world, even above the floating cities," Matlock said.

"You're talking about satellites, aren't you? Space stations?" I asked.

"Yes," he said slowly. "How do you know those words?"

"Oh, we have hundreds of satellites back home. Only one big manned space station, though. Last I heard they were planning on putting a colony on Mars, but that wasn't for another 20 years or so. There was a book—"

"Please, focus." Tara squeezed my hand.

"Since we're all being honest, there's something I should say. The cave-in was my fault," Tony said.

"What? Why?" Sh'teena asked.

"I saw the two cities about to go to war. I knew this would probably destroy both cities, so I blocked them before their armies could march." Tony sighed.

"That's why you could so easily make a course around the blockage," Matlock said.

"Yes." Tony turned to Matlock. "But I'm from right here, and I'm not working with anyone, so your man must be elsewhere."

Matlock cursed under his breath.

"Anyone else with any revelations they want to share?" Tara asked.

"Don't look at me; I've told y'all all the f-ed up stuff that's happened with me," I said. I had a slight clue about everything they were talking about, but I'd have to ask Tara to fill me in later.

"I ate the last of the yutow," Rafly mumbled. She said it so matter of fact that it momentarily caused the room to go silent. Then, a slow chuckle started rolling around the room, picking up momentum. After a while, it settled down, and we sobered.

"Now what?" I asked once everyone was done.

"Now," a voice called from the door. "Now you all leave." A woman entered in sand-colored robes, followed by two other women in robes. "We will provide you with rations, put you on the proper path, and you should be in Krodon in about three days."

Tony rose and approached the woman. "I can't thank you enough for what you did for me and my companions. If ever you need anything, ask for me and it's yours."

"I'm glad to hear you say that. Because none of you are allowed to breathe a word of our existence here. If our sanctum is discovered, it will end our lives as we know them. And I assure you, so will yours."

I could tell it wasn't an idle threat.

"Now, gather your things; Annabeth will show you to your

exit. Don't come back, don't try to find us. Don't mistake our charity for weakness. We still have the ability to defend ourselves as needed." Then her tone softened, and she turned to Sh'teena, holding out a small metal box to her.

"When you return to your tribe, and you will as it is written. Give this to your elders and tell them you are all welcome to return home. Banishment has ended."

Sh'teena took the small metal box and opened it. Within lay a small leather book with gold inlay on the cover. I couldn't read it, but it was about the size of a standard paperback book and just as thick.

"Is this a Rodeen?" Sh'teena touched the book reverently.

"This is THE Rodeen," The woman said. "So guard it well. I pray your elders understand what it means that I'm giving it to them."

"What does it mean?" Sh'teena asked, her voice that of a small child.

"It means all is forgiven. The children have grown and understand now what they lost then," The woman said.

Sh'teena closed the book and bowed, her hand making a strange gesture close to her chest. The woman returned the action and then smiled.

Annabeth stepped forward and motioned us out of the room. Once, we were down a corridor and around a corner, she spoke. "You must forgive The Mother. Things have been...shall we say, tense as of late."

"Why is that?" Sh'teena asked.

"We live in exciting times. This is the time of prophecy, and your coming has been foretold. The Mother knows what this means and has much to prepare."

"Prepare for what?" I asked.

"I'm not allowed. We are not allowed to know the entire prophecy to safeguard from attempts of tampering. But know that you all have a hand in it...a part to play." She seemed to scold herself for her words. "Already that is too much."

We came to a wall a minute later. "Once through this door, go to your right. Continue straight until you come to the main corridor. Then right again. You will arrive just as The Mother said." She handed each of us a small pack and gave Sh'teena an extra one. "This is for Fantill; please ensure he gets it."

"Who's Fantill?" Sh'teena asked.

A smile was all the answer she got. "Good luck, safe journey, and may Behemoth guide you."

The door opened, and she ushered us out into the narrow crevice. As we exited, the door closed and became part of the wall. It was seamless, and you'd never know a door had been there.

Just as she said, the main corridor was down to the right. Electric lights blazed on either wall, lighting our way. A few meters down the corridor, I turned back to find the crevice we emerged from had blended back into the corridor wall, just as the door had.

That night, our winged lizard showed up. It walked over to Sh'teena and took the extra pack without a word.

"You're Fantill?" Sh'teena asked.

It didn't answer; it just moved to the side of the small "pull-off" we were camping in and started going through the pack.

My pack was relatively barren. While the other's packs were filled with everyday foodstuffs, mine was stuffed with the small not-blood pouches. They reminded me of those old Capri-Sun packs my mom used to send with my school lunches.

Luckily, the straw was already attached to these, unlike the old Capri-Suns, where you had to pull the straw off and stab the pouch. I always made a mess. I could never get the straw to just pop in, like in the commercials. It would either punch through both sides or rip the package, spilling stuff everywhere.

These pouches were easy. All I had to do was suck. I guessed it had a one-way valve in there somewhere. The pouches themselves were made of a material I'd never seen before. It was tougher than an MRE package, so tough even my knife had trouble getting through one (as I found out later.) Whatever it was, it did not fit in with this fantasy setting at all. This was a high-tech material if I'd ever seen one.

Our spirits seemed to rise the closer to the city we got. I think it was more that nothing weird had happened; we hadn't been attacked, and we still had food. Before I knew it, I could hear the sounds of life. People noise: the noises ordinary people make on an ordinary day. It was music to my ears. When we rounded the corner and could see the opening to the city, it took everything I had not to break into a run.

The entrance was just as large as the one I'd seen in the dead city. The cavern beyond was not the dim twilight as the other, though. Bright yellow sunlight poured in from around a massive corner at the far end of the cavern. It cast beautiful rays across the city. Even though the source was around a corner, it still lit the place evenly somehow.

The city itself was alive and thrumming with life, overflowing as it were. People were everywhere: hanging out on the street, in doorways, sitting on top of buildings. Then I remembered this city was supposed to be overpopulated, one of the main reasons for the big war.

A troop of soldiers stopped us at the entrance, but Tony spoke with them and demanded to be brought before the council immediately as they had news of Sanbu. The soldier appeared to doubt his story until Tony showed him something that caused him to bark orders out to two of his subordinates. We were quickly escorted to the center building of the city.

"Keep an eye on your belongings," Gathers said. "I don't like the looks of these streets."

"I thought you couldn't steal here," I said.

"Oh, you can steal, but if you get caught by whatever magics protect these cities, you'll be stabbed to death by shadows," Gathers said quietly.

"Wow," I said.

"Yeah, I don't recommend it," Gathers said.

I ensured all my gear was tight on my body and kept one hand on my pistol, just in case.

We arrived at the large stone structure and were ushered inside. A man rose from behind a large desk as we entered. He had the words bureaucratic monkey practically written on his forehead.

"Elementalist Tober," the monkey began.

"Tony," I mumbled under my breath, causing Tara to elbow me in the ribs. "Sorry, reflex."

"We had feared the worst when we'd not heard back from you. Our scouts said you'd found a way around the blockage," The monkey said.

"I did. We need to speak with the council as soon as possible," Tony said.

"Of course, please wait here, and I'll let them know you're here." And with that, the flunky monkey disappeared down a hallway.

"So, what is this?" I asked.

"A council rules this city. They were the ones who provided us with information and help when we first arrived here," Sh'teena said. "They did not wish war with their neighbors and were willing to send us as their emissaries if we could get through."

"When they let us in, please remain silent. Actually, if you wish, you don't have to go into the council chambers at all." Tony turned and looked at us; well, me, really. "All we need are Sh'teena, Macock and myself."

"Matlock," I mumbled and Tara elbowed me again.

"The rest could return to the estate if you wished," Tony suggested.

"The estate?" I asked.

"Yes, one of the councilmen offered to share his residence with us while we were here. While it wasn't huge, it still had enough room for us," Tony said.

"Hmm...stuffy, boring council meeting...or R&R." I held my hands out, weighing my options. "Tara?"

I could feel her rolling her eyes as she turned away, heading back out the door.

"I guess we'll have to pass on the council meeting. Sorry, Tony, but my wife is just so demanding. Women, right?" I shrugged my shoulders in mock defeat and followed Tara outside, Rafly chucking as she fell in behind me.

"Gathers, go with them," I heard Sh'teena say behind us.

"But—" Gathers started to protest.

"Someone has to keep them out of trouble," Sh'teena said.

"When did I become the responsible one?" Was the last thing I heard before we were outside in the bustling streets.

A few minutes later, we entered a four-story building and were greeted by what I guessed were servants. Later, I'd find out they weren't servants in the traditional sense. They lived on the premises, and it was their home. The councilman, who lived there and paid for everything, was more like a tenant than a lord. He cleaned his own room, did his own clothes and even did chores around the house when needed. The others who lived there cared for the house and cooked meals for the entire building. They all ate together informally. It was a weird bed and breakfasty, European thing. Not Southern Plantation or Doughton Abbey at all.

A room was made for our group. They gave Rafly, Tara and myself a small room they'd been using for storage. We helped take the storage items up to the roof for the duration of our stay. Rafly told us once we finished that she would remain on the roof to allow Tara and I some privacy.

Tara had hugged her enthusiastically. Tara's gratitude seemed to embarrass the big woman, which was strange to see her normally boisterous persona humbled like that.

After so many nights sleeping on the ground, using my arm as a pillow, the bed in the room was heavenly. Of course, my favorite pillow was still beside me. Sadly, Tara couldn't remove her leathers due to the dense population, but that didn't stop us from enjoying each other's company. Just the opposite, really. It made our time together more precious.

We didn't catch up with the others until the next day. The council had kept them long into the night discussing matters. We all gathered at the midday meal to talk.

"So wait, the dead city is already on the wall?" Tara asked.

"Yes," Tony said between bites of some brownish meat that tasted vaguely of pork. "It actually appeared a week ago. The council has been trying to figure out what was going on. The location lists it as close, between the two cities, but their scouts didn't find any way into it."

"But," Sh'teena continued, "the interesting part is what's listed alongside the location."

"What's that?" I asked.

"You. Your name is listed as the founder, so it's official: you are the discoverer of the new city," Sh'teena said.

"Cool. Does that mean I get to name it? I think 'Bob's Town' had a nice ring to it. Or maybe 'Autobot City?' 'Megazone?' No? Nothing? I'm so wasted here." I grumbled as no one understood any of my references.

But wait, were they my references? That sounded more like something James would come up with. Shae told me about her conversation with Nat concerning our group "rapport." We were all supposed to be merging minds or some such nonsense. The idea was a psychologist's worst nightmare.

But I thought it was only while we were together. Was this whole "sharing minds" thing a permanent change? AKA, were James's geek ideas stuck inside my head forever? Did he have some of my ideas in his head? The thought of it all worried me. I had enough extra thoughts in my head as it was.

"No, the city already has a name. The builders name all of them," Tony said.

"What's it called?" Tara asked.

"Kison," Tony said.

"Huh," I grunted. "I still think Bob's Town sounds better. Or maybe name it after the Hero of Canton? We could build a big statue and wear stupid tuques; that would rule!" I looked around the room with absolutely no understanding from my comrades. I also didn't understand why I said the word "rule." "I need to get home," I mumbled.

What you need to do is stop using James's references. Do you even know where half that crap you just said comes from? Although you did make me laugh when you said, "That would rule!" my head said.

Oh, look who it is. Nice of you to show up, I grumbled inwardly.

Hey, your WIFE doesn't really like me, my head said.

What? I asked.

Yeah, we had a nice long conversation in the hot tub room. It seems she thinks I'm a terrible influence, my head said.

You ARE a terrible influence, I agreed.

True, but I'm just you remember? my head said.

You actually talked to her? What did you say? I asked

suspiciously.

Why? Worried I might have said something I shouldn't?

You're not an ex talking to my current girlf-, er wife, I said, stumbling.

You're right. I'm so much worse: I'm you, untethered. And don't even get me started about what she said to the autho—

Shut up, head, I'm trying to hear this, I said blocking her out.

"But, in yet another first, there's an opening date attached to this one. It's roughly a cycle from now. That's never happened before, so the council's a little worried. When we explained what we found, with the chasm in the back of the city, that seemed to clear it up for them," Tony said.

"What about Sanbu?" Rafly asked.

"Yeah...about that. They want to send a diplomatic party. If they can get the magistrate to calm down and listen to reason, then they should be able to avoid bloodshed," Sh'teena said.

"Reason isn't a word y'all used before when talking about that guy," I added.

"True," Tony said. "But the writing's on their wall just as it is here. He can't argue with that as no one but the builders can write on that wall."

"Of course, you're the only one who can get them through," Tara said.

"Also true, and he's not exactly happy with me," Tony said.

"He's unhappy with all of us right now," Sh'teena added. "I don't see how our presence could do anything other than more harm there. Considering how he imprisoned us the last time, I don't think he will honor the diplomatic truce."

"That's for the council to figure out. In the meantime, we have a few days to relax and recoup while they figure out what they want to do," Tony said.

"I should start looking for my target again," Matlock said quietly.

"You're leaving?" Sh'teena asked.

"No, not yet. But I need to start putting out feelers to see if anyone has any information. I think I'll tend to that now. Excuse me," Matlock said as he rose from the table and left.

"Anyone else think there's something off with him?" Sh'teena asked.

"Of course there is," I offered. "We yanked the rug out from underneath him when Tony revealed the truth about the—"

"Shhhh!" Sh'teena hissed, looking around. "With this many people around, there are literally ears all around us. No one needs to know anything about who's done what, especially this close."

"Well, he thought he was on the right track, and there's nothing worse than finding out you've been wasting what little time you have. I think he'll be alright after a while. I just hope he gets a lead soon," I said.

Matlock did get a lead the following evening, just not for what he was looking for.

"Come with me," Matlock said.

"No, Matlock, the line is 'come with me if you want to live.'" I corrected.

Looking at me strangely, he said, "Come with me if you want to live?" With absolutely no hint of an Austrian accent. I mean, come on, everybody can do an Arnold accent!

"Better. Lead on, wait. Where are we going?" I asked.

"Just follow me," he said as he turned and left the house.

I looked at Tara, who shrugged, and we hurried out the door after him. We were practically running to keep up with him in the crowded streets. The streets were always crowded, even in the middle of the night. I couldn't imagine living here for years at a time. I'd get claustrophobic.

"Here." Matlock stopped in front of a small, narrow, three-story building.

"Wow, how do they do that?" Tara asked, staring wide-eyed at the building.

"What?" I asked.

"Get the door to burn like that," Tara said.

I looked over at the building and found the door bursting with colors, ringed by fire. As I watched, the colors danced around and formed into letters, "Drakes."

I reached up, pulled Matlock to me and kissed him full on the lips. "You beautiful bastard, you found him! Thank you!" I left him standing there, wide-eyed and stunned before heading for the door.

"What is so special about this place?" Matlock asked Tara, who just shrugged and followed.

The door swung open easily at my touch. The first thing I saw were rough-hewn wooden tables and chairs. The walls and ceiling were stone, as was the rectangle bar that was always the centerpiece of Drakes. There were a few fluorescent lights in the ceiling, but there were also candles on the tables, half of which were lit. It was identical to the one I showed up in.

Several patrons were in the bar, all of whom looked like they'd just come from a Renaissance fair. They were all staring at me, as I stood in the door dumbfounded.

When my legs finally started working again, I stepped inside and spotted Drake behind the bar, also dressed for Scarborough Fair.

"Drake!" I growled and advanced on him.

"May I help you, mistress?" he asked.

"Oh, cut the crap with that. I want to know what I'm doing here and why the hell I'm not in Houston." Tara was by my side then.

Matlock stood just inside the door, staring at his surroundings as he noticed the internal dimensions did not match the external ones.

"Please." Drake motioned to the stools at the bar.

I sat down angrily and put both hands on the bar.

"What can I get you?" Drake's tone was his usual calm and charming voice, acting as if nothing was wrong.

"I don't care," I growled.

"Something cool and sweet, please," Tara said, all smiles and her coy girl self.

Drake set to work on drinks. "Anything for your friend?"

"Dunno, don't care." I was drumming my fingers on the stone top.

A moment later, Drake handed Tara a glass of what looked like white wine while he gave me a ceramic mug.

"Where are your...brothers?" I asked.

"Oh, they only come in when it gets busy," Drake said.

"I'm sure." I picked up the mug and sniffed it; it was the same non-blood stuff the sisters had given me.

Drake saw the look on my face and looked around at his other customers.

"We should be OK," Drake said.

"What?" I asked.

"First off, I have no idea what you're talking about," Drake said, nodding his head.

"Drake," I sighed, trying to bleed off my anger. Tara's hand touched mine, and the anger seemed to evaporate. I looked at her and smiled, "Thanks."

"Anytime." Tara smiled back.

"Drake, I don't pretend to understand how you work, and frankly, I don't want to know. Contrary to popular belief, I do enjoy a bit of mystery. But what I do know is that you're all connected. Somewhere in the back, you have a special door that can send us to any of the other Drakes out there. I want to use it to get home." As an afterthought, I added, "Please." I was starting to think Tara had control over my emotions as well.

He looked at me for a long moment and cocked his head. "That is a fantastical idea! If we had such a thing, think of the money we could make ferrying travelers from one city to the next. All the people and things that would traipse in and out of here."

Drake looked at me calmly, waiting for me to get it.

"Oh, I get it Drake; I just don't care. I'm obviously not supposed to be here," I half-growled.

"Aren't you?" He looked down at Tara and my joined hands.

"Wait, what's that supposed to mean? Are you saying you and Nat did this to me to so you could set me up on some sort of blind date?" I stared at him incredulously. "You know what, I don't care. Just send me home."

"Us," Tara said quietly, bringing me up short.

I turned to her quickly. "Sorry." I kissed her hand. I turned back to Drake, "I meant us."

"Understand something. For the sake of argument, let's say such a doorway existed. Theoretically," Drake started.

"Theoretically," I repeated in an exasperated tone.

"And it was connected to other Drakes. It would probably only be connected to the other Drakes here. Moving cities is one thing; moving worlds would be incredibly perilous, if not foolish. Again, theoretically," Drake said.

"So, for the sake of argument, the doorways wouldn't normally send someone to another world?" I asked.

"I'm just shooting in the dark here, but that sounds logical. Instantaneous Matter Transference, while theoretically possible, would be insanely difficult just to move a cup across the room. Then, step that up to a human, so to speak, and move them from one city to another and remarkably difficult becomes near impossible. Imagine trying to move worlds. Theoretically," Drake offered.

"So, the fact...er, if it were to happen, it would be a mistake?" I tried to connect the dots.

"An error," Drake said.

"Could the error be reversed?" I added, "Theoretically."

"Theoretically, anything's possible. But you'd need to recreate the conditions of the...error...as closely as possible. Same weather, temperature, time, location..." Drake said.

"Location?" I asked.

"Yes," Drake confirmed.

"I appeared in a Drakes that was part of the new unfinished city," I said.

He was looking at me, waiting patiently.

"What if, theoretically, one of these doorways was in a location that wasn't complete yet?" I asked.

"A doorway would need its normal power and such that comes with a completed facility," Drake said.

"You're saying I have to wait until the city is finished and that particular Drakes is properly open? Couldn't you just use magic or something to get it going long enough for us to jump through?"

"Theoretically..." Drake started.

"Seriously, can we drop that? I'm pretty sure no one in here even knows what that word means." I sighed as he continued, undeterred.

"Theoretically, each of these doorways would be unique in

every way. They would run off their own kind of power, material, etc. This way, each could be identified by the others, similar to your fingerprints," Drake said.

"So I don't have a choice, do I? I have to wait the year." I slumped on my stool and drained the cup in one long pull.

"Theoretically." His smile was a kind one.

"Drake?" I said.

"Mistress?" Drake said.

"Do you have a room available?"

"Of course," Drake said.

"Does it have amenities?" I asked.

"All you would desire."

"Will it hermetically seal?" I asked.

He smiled, "ALL, you desire," Drake said.

"Put it on my tab?" I asked.

"Of course."

"Matlock," I called, and he approached. "Have a drink here. You will never find its equal. Then let the others know Tara, and I will be here for the duration. If they need us, you know where to find us."

He nodded as I stood up and pulled Tara to her feet. "Come on you."

"Where are we going?" Tara asked in that coy voice I was starting to think was sexy as hell, even if it wasn't real.

"To get naked," I said.

Drake handed me an actual key, not a keycard, and I headed towards the stairs.

Matlock watched us go with a strange look on his face before sitting down at the bar and turning to Drake.

The room was everything I could have wanted, precisely as Drake had promised. As the door closed, it hissed shut.

"Do you know what that sound means?" I said as I turned to Tara.

"What?"

"That means we're sealed in here. Nothing gets in, nothing gets out." And with that, I started to undo her straps, starting at her feet and working my way up. At one point, she began to try and help, but I stopped her.

"No, not this time," I said. I took my time, strategically removing a strap here and another there. I pulled some tighter, just to feel her body react, before releasing her. By the time I got to her mask, she was visibly trembling.

"And what if I just left you like this?" I asked, grabbing her arms and holding them at her side. I pressed her against the wall, pinning both her hands above her head. My own body was a taunt string, practically thrumming on its own. I couldn't tease her much more as I was ready to break.

I pulled her towards the bathroom that I knew would be fit for a queen, but her restraint broke first, and we didn't make it that far.

DFA

RHI

A good time later, we were lounging on the bed.

"So, what was all that about?" Tara asked.

"I figured that was obvious." I grinned, and she slapped me lightly on the thigh. "Yes, please," I purred.

"I meant downstairs," she said.

"Looks like you're stuck with me here for at least another year," I said.

"You can't try to go home until that new Drakes opens?" Tara asked.

"Looks like it," I said.

She was quiet for a while. "Good," she said finally.

"Good?" I asked.

"Yes, if you're here for another cycle then I will take you home," she said with finality.

"What?" I sat up on one elbow.

"I will take you to my home. Introduce you to my family," Tara said with vigor.

"A little late to be meeting your folks after the wedding, isn't it?" I teased.

"Oh yes!" She flipped over and stared at me with huge, excited eyes. "We can have the wedding!"

"Uh, that's not what I meant." But she was off and running.

Apparently, the wedding ceremony in her village wasn't as complicated as the party afterward. She went on and on for at least an hour about things she wanted and how she would do them.

Me though, I was never a white dress and flowers kind of girl. I never daydreamed about the ultimate fairytale wedding or anything. Even as a kid, while I watched other girls practicing writing their married name, usually with a celebrity's name, I never had the inclination.

"I need to tell Rafly." Then she looked around. "Why don't we bring our group here instead of the manor? It definitely has enough room."

"I don't know about that," I warned. "Drakes is a bit...private. Only certain types of people are allowed in here. Hell, only certain types can even see the doorway."

"Well, I've seen it," Tara said.

I looked her up and down, "You're my type."

"Yes, I am." She kissed me, those older eyes flashing again. Then she pulled up short. "But Matlock saw it too, didn't he?"

"You said Matlock," I grinned, which caused her to roll her eyes and shake her head. "But, yes." I chewed my lip. "That one's had me thinking for a while now."

"About?" Tara asked.

"About what he is," I said.

"What he is?"

"Normal humans don't come here; they're not allowed," I said.

"Oh," Tara said.

I shook my head. "That's something for later; right now, I want a shower."

"A shower?" Tara asked, confused.

"It's like a bath, but standing up. Come on," I pulled her to her feet, noticing her toes had claws like her hands. "You're going to love this."

But as soon as I entered the bathroom, I froze; Tara practically running into me.

"Holy shit," I said in shock and then moved to the mirror.

"What?" Tara said in a worried tone. "Are you OK?"

"No," I said, blinking, trying to make sure my eyes weren't lying to me.

"What is it?" Tara asked, concern straining her voice.

"My eyes."

"What about your eyes? They're lovely," she said.

"They're fucking black!" I hollered.

"Actually, they're red and black if you want to be specific. What about it? They're the same as mine, only in reverse." Tara shrugged.

My entire eyeball had turned black while the iris was red and the pupil an even darker shade of red. "How long have they been this way?"

"Ever since our bonding. What's the matter?" she asked.

I hadn't seen a mirror since then.

"It's part of our bond," Tara said. "Sometimes, we take on traits of the other. You have my eyes albeit reversed. It's not completely unheard of for that sort of thing to happen. *Especially when he screws it up in Krita.* Do you...not like them?" Tara's voice trembled slightly.

"Do I not...like...them?" I managed, distracted as I moved my eyes all over the place, trying to get used to my new visage. I finally stepped back and took a deep breath before blowing it out. *This is going to take some getting used to.*

Hey, at least you don't have to worry about red eyes after your next hangover, my head chimed in.

Shut up, head.

"Rhi?" Now, Tara's voice sounded worried.

"I'm sorry," I said, grabbing her arms. "I just wasn't aware...I didn't know..." I looked back at the mirror over my shoulder. "Just wow." I had to admit it was striking as hell. I mean, they had literally stopped me in my tracks when I first saw them. I can't imagine what someone else would think. I turned my head this way and that, taking them in again. "They're actually kinda badass." I turned back to Tara.

What does she think of mine if she doesn't like hers?

Tara's thought sent a bolt through my heart. Not only had I heard her mind, she was afraid I didn't like her.

"Silly girl," I said, taking her in my arms and squeezing

tightly. Your eyes are amazing. Mine just shocked the hell out of me. I mean, you look at the same face for 30-plus years, and you get used to certain things. Having something like that sprung on you is a bit of a shock."

"I'm sorry, I thought you already knew. This doesn't happen in your world either?" Tara said.

"No." I smiled and pulled her chin up so I could kiss her lightly. "But, like I said, they look pretty badass. I like them."

She smiled.

"Just don't be surprised if I'm looking into the mirror a lot more in the near future."

"I'll cover them. Wouldn't want you falling into ponds and drowning," Tara teased.

"Shut up." I smacked her hard on the ass, and she jumped. "Shower, now."

"Yes, 'mistress.'" Tara said in a mocking imitation of Drake.

"Then you're going to tell me how you know about *him*," I *glared suspiciously at the fourth wall* and then got distracted by Tara's beautiful tail.

[Did you really just change that last sentence to try and distract me from the fact I'm starting to think my wife can talk to you? Originally, I just looked back at Tara, but now you've got me being distracted by her tail? Well, I mean her backside is amazing...and that tail just accentuates her...]

∞∞Ω∞∞

RHI

We spent a pleasant few days together until we were pulled back to reality...or at least some semblance of it. I spent most of the time learning more about my new wife in our room. Tara spent most of the time walking around naked, happy to be free from the leather prison she'd worn most of her life.

The more time I spent with her, the more I enjoyed her company. Having a wife wasn't so scary anymore. I mean, I have no idea what my mom would have said. She probably would have psycho-analyzed me into the ground, but as long as I figured out how to give her grandkids, she wouldn't have cared who I married.

My mom...yeah...I never did mention what happened to her after Z Day, did I? There's a reason for that.

Our group had gathered in the manor courtyard to discuss the "plan." The council had decided to send an emissary party under a flag of truce to discuss the new city. Since one of the council was going to be in the party, by law, the party wasn't to be harmed. Since our group had initially gone to the other city on their own and not under a flag of truce, they were not protected by the law. While Sh'teena and Tony had their doubts, they were willing to give it a try in the name of peace.

I thought it was a damned foolish idea. Let the council send their own peace party; just leave us out of it. But I was outvoted. By now, the rest of the party knew about my one-year prison sentence here in this world and Tara's idea to bring me to her home.

Rafly hadn't stopped grinning since Tara mentioned the wedding at home. It was...unsettling to say the least.

The current plan was to get this whole war thing straightened out between the two cities and then split up.

Tony would remain here in order to clear the tunnel.

Matlock was going to continue his search for his bad guy.

Sh'teena and Gathers were going to return home to report in.

The rest of us would travel with Sh'teena before returning to Tara and Rafly's home.

Nobody knew what Fantill would do as the flying lizard wasn't around much.

That was the plan, at least until our lunch was interrupted.

The food smelled good to me, but I wasn't about to try it just on the off chance it didn't agree with me. That and I didn't want to have to get rid of it later. The others were enjoying their meals, though. Everyone had recovered from our tunnel adventures and seemed in good spirits. Of course, the flowing wine and mead appeared to help the atmosphere as well. We were leaving for Sanbu in the morning.

Then, there came cacophony sound. It started with a loud piercing boom followed by a ripping sound like sheets being torn apart but painfully loud. It ended with another boom that sent a shockwave out, shattering glass for blocks around us.

Everyone was dazed, trying to figure out what just happened when there was a whoosh followed by the wall to the right of me exploding, showering us in stone shards.

I lunged sideways, pulling Tara down as my Army reflexes kicked in. I tucked her under my arm and leaped over the next wall, taking cover behind it as something whooshed over our heads and struck the building across the street, causing the wall to explode.

I could hear screaming now, and I had my pistol in hand.

"What the—" Tara started.

"Stay down!" I glanced over the wall and saw the deserted courtyard we'd just been in. Sh'teena was standing in the doorway of the building, both swords drawn, while Gathers was sitting on the ground beside her, holding a bloody rag to his head. Rafly was on the side of the building, axe in hand, scanning her surroundings. Tony was crouching beside a wall with Matlock standing beside him, his staff raised.

I only caught a glance of a shadow before I heard the whooshing sound again and ducked behind the cover of the wall. The wall where my head had been exploded. A shower of rock fragments cut into my cheek and arm as I pushed Tara away from the scene. I scrambled five meters and came up from behind cover firing.

My first shot was solely for covering fire, the sound barrier bursting as my pistol fired. I caught sight of my target and shifted fire, squeezing off another shot that went wide but caused my target to dodge to the left.

"Fucking Iron Man is shooting at us, stay down!" Was the best description I could give. Whoever was up there was hovering in some sort of powered armor. It was easily bigger than Rafly and covered in iridescent metal.

I rolled another five meters and popped up to find my target gone and a second flying armor swinging wide as if to flank me. I fired off two shots, leading it just a bit and was rewarded with the sound of one of the bullets striking home. My ammo wasn't anything special, just your standard ball round. Whatever I hit was allergic to lead as smoke billowed out from the back of the armor.

A moment later the armor shuttered before careening into a building. It smashed through the wall and buried itself into the building's depths. The entire upper floor collapsed on top of the armor in a huge cloud of dust.

My victory was short-lived as the wall exploded behind me, the concussion knocking me off my feet. I tried to roll with it but failed and ended up sprawled in the street.

"Rhi!" Tara screamed and broke from her cover to run to me.

I looked up just in time to see one of the white discs the flying armor had been shooting fly over my head and glance Tara's arm.

Tara went down screaming.

My vision went red; my limbs seemed to crackle with energy as I span up to my knees and began to fire toward the armor. My hands were already reaching for a spare magazine before the gun ran dry and locked open. Muscle memory had my spare magazine in the gun half a second after the spent magazine started to fall. I emptied the gun again before the first spent magazine hit the ground.

The ground exploded around me, but I didn't notice as I reached for my last magazine and slid it into the magazine well.

I knew I was hitting; I could see the holes appearing in the armor, but my luck had been spent on the first target, dropping it into that building. The roaring noise in my ears was deafening, and I didn't realize until later that it was my own screaming.

My leg erupted in fire, but I ignored it as my pistol locked open, my last round spent. I dropped it, bringing the knife up from my boot and throwing it with everything I had.

I wasn't very good with the knife, but the sheer power I put into it helped drive the point into a shoulder seam. It seemed I hadn't spent all my luck after all. I was pulling my blade from the sheath on the back of my belt and starting to rise when my burning leg refused to support my weight and I collapsed in a heap.

I looked up just as the armor was redirecting its fire at me. I saw the gun barrel start to blaze, and then a bolt of crackling energy enveloped the armor. All of its joints seemed to lock up as the entire armor spasmed.

Following the energy trail, I found it coming from Matlock's staff. His face was grim as he continued to pump more energy into the armor.

I looked back at the suit just as it started to smoke. I could see the energy being channeled through my knife, still embedded in the armor's shoulder seam.

Matlock didn't stop until I could smell roasting meat. A moment later the armor crashed to the ground, unmoving and smoking.

The threats eliminated, I span around and half crawled, half hopped over to Tara. She was twitching on the ground, a large black burn on her right arm. By the time I got to her, she'd stopped twitching and lie still. I listened but didn't hear breath or a heartbeat.

My injured knee screamed as I pulled myself up and knelt beside her. I shifted her head and gave her two breaths before starting CPR. It had been a long time since I'd had a class, but I still remembered the basics. I just hope it worked on her.

"MACOCK!!!" I bellowed at the top of my lungs. "I NEED YOU!!!" And I was breathing into her mouth again, watching her chest rise and fall with each of my breaths.

I heard a grunt of effort and metal slicing through metal coming from behind me, but I ignored it as I counted my compressions. Tara was my world right now; nothing else mattered.

The sound of sandals slapping on stone, and then Matlock was beside me.

"Whatever.those.things.were.hit.her.with.electricity.and.stopped.her.heart." I managed between compressions.

He dropped his smoldering staff beside him and felt various parts of Tara.

"What are you doing? Scan her with your stick already!" I gave Tara a breath.

"Burned it out," he said shortly as he examined the wound on her arm.

"I'm.having.to.be.really.careful.not.to.break.ribs.here." I grunted each word as I gave Tara chest compressions.

"Break them if necessary; it will make it easier," he said calmly.

I didn't have time to spare him a look.

He then started to pat his robes like someone checking his pockets for car keys. He reached into a pocket and pulled a small string out before tying it around Tara's head. He wet his fingers in his mouth and touched the tied-off ends before his eyes lost focus. He remained still, staring off into space. "Third-degree burn site, ventricular fibrillation, blah blah, blah, blah blah blah."

I stuttered in my count as I realized I couldn't understand him anymore.

"Matlock?" I said slowly and then shook my head and returned to my compressions.

Rafly came lumbering up and knelt next to us. "Blah blah blah, blah?"

"You're bond allows you to understand the languages each other knows." Matlock's words came back to me from last week. Ever since I'd been bonded with Tara, I'd been able to understand everyone in the party. The fact I couldn't understand them anymore only meant one thing.

"Oh, hell no!" I growled and redoubled my efforts. I heard a crack under my hands and winced but continued.

Matlock continued to babble incoherently in his trance-like stare and Rafly kept interjecting.

When I went to give Tara the next set of breaths, I found her face wet. It took a second for me to realize her face was wet from my tears.

[*OK fucker, I know you're drunk and just finished playing Catan with your family; I don't care. You made me care for this woman; now you're going to help me save her. I don't give a shit what sort of crazy bullshit you pull out of your drunken ass; just bring my girl back to me. You hear me? If you don't, fuck you. I ain't playing no more. And I*

know who you based me on; you know I can do it. Hell, I'll tell her, and she'll kick your ass...or just hold out on you until you fix this bullshit you're pulling. You just had to have a fight scene, didn't you? Add to the drama. Well, you're not George R.R. fucking Martin. Fix it fucker. You know I'll do whatever you want, just bring.her.back.
--Rhi]

I paused my CPR long enough to **grab the fourth wall.**

$$\infty\infty\Omega\infty\infty$$

{Have you ever been in a dark room of a silent house, busily hacking away at a story on your computer when a ghost-like arm seemed to come out of your monitor and take a swing at you? No? Me neither. It had to be my imagination. I'd had a bit too much to drink tonight, and I should really go to bed cause it's late. But first...you know, just in case.}

$$\infty\infty\Omega\infty\infty$$

RHI

The rubble from the collapsed building shifted, causing me to glance at where the other flying armor had crashed.

"Rafly, grab the gun!" I barked.

She recognized her name but nothing else.

I paused long enough to gesture at the other power armor and mime shooting the gun it still held. I wasn't sure if Rafly understood me or not, but she disappeared as I continued compressions.

Dust rose from the collapsed building and out of the corner of my eye I saw the power armor rising from the rubble. The armor scanned the area until it found us in the middle of the street. Dropping down to street level, the armor slowly hobbled towards us.

A thud marked the strange energy gun dropping beside me

from Rafly's hands. I slapped Matlock's hands away from his string and pushed him to take over for me as I picked up the gun.

A glance revealed there were no selector levers or safeties, so I pointed and pulled the trigger. A very satisfying white disc slid from the barrel and arched toward the approaching power armor.

The armor dodged my shot and slowed its approach.

"Is the Daemon dead?" A metallic voice called from the approaching armor. The voice sounded female and seemed to have a prissy British accent.

The armor was still surveying the scene as I yanked on the trigger again.

It easily sidestepped my shot.

"Good," the armor said, leaping into the air just in time to dodge Rafly's charge. Streaking skyward, the horrid sound from before ripped through the cavern once again, the armor disappearing in a flash of light.

I scanned the sky for a moment before realizing the armor was truly gone and dropped the gun.

Turning back to Matlock, he was still doing compressions but looked as if he was tiring. I pushed him out of the way and took over. I'd keep going no matter how long it took. I wasn't about to let my wife die.

Matlock returned to the string headband.

"Electrical impulse increasing," he said, and I understood him clear as day.

A second later, Tara moaned and took a painful, wheezing breath. I immediately stopped and felt for her heartbeat. It was slow but seemed steady. Her breath rasped through her lips, but it was strong. I sobbed in relief, collapsing next to her. "Matlock..." I managed as he took over, examining her.

[Thank you...but don't ever do that to me again. --Rhi]

Sobs rocked my body as I finished the prayer. It was the best I could offer to the closest thing I knew as a god.

"Let's get her inside," Matlock said. He and Sh'teena picked

Tara up and moved her into the building.

Rafly pulled me to my feet and held me up with one massive arm. Her eyes and the battleaxe in her other hand continued to watch for additional threats.

I paused long enough to scoop up the energy gun.

Rafly started to follow the others, helping me towards the house, but I redirected her to the fallen power armor.

The closer we got, the worse the smell became. It reminded me of fried pork, which was disturbing in itself.

The suit was blackened in multiple spots radiating out from where my knife was embedded. I glanced at the knife, but it was slag; there was no saving it.

The front of the armor was made of something similar to a lightweight polymer. Light and perfect for flying, but not for resisting bullets. I could see where several of my rounds had penetrated, but none seemed to have sunk far enough into the armor to make a difference.

"Rafly, pull this into the house where we can look at it later," I said.

"Right," she said and looked at me.

"Just leave me here, I'll be OK. We need to get this off the street now before others come looking," the urgency in my voice seemed to spur her into action. She easily lifted the strange armor before dragging it inside the manor.

Looking around the neighborhood at the havoc and destruction reaped in the last few minutes, I realized how lucky we'd gotten.

I managed to hop over and collect my pistol and magazines before Rafly returned. She helped me recover as many of the shell casings as we could find. I hoped I could find someone who could reload them for me. I'd used every round I had trying to protect Tara and even sacrificed my best knife.

Once I was satisfied the scene was as secure as it could be, I let Rafly help me into the manor to check on my wife.

It was obvious the attack had been meant for Tara. The final statement of the departing armor proved that beyond a shadow of a doubt. Now, I just needed to find out why.

Terran-Far

RHI

Tara was laid up in bed in one of the spare rooms the group had been sleeping in. She was still unconscious, but her heart and breathing had returned to normal. Matlock and I bandaged up her arm; it wasn't pretty, but there wasn't much we could do about it at the moment.

When I asked Matlock about healing, he said he needed to repair his staff if he could. He'd locked himself alone in a room ever since.

My leg was pretty bad. The energy bolt had caught me at the side of my left knee, but luckily, it was only a glancing blow. It had still given me third-degree burns, though. On one side, it didn't hurt; on the other, it was ugly. I'd left it unwrapped as I knew it should be healed up by morning, fingers crossed.

The constable's arrival was a surprise, but it shouldn't have been. I'd not seen any security or police force since I'd arrived aside from those at the city's entrance. I wasn't sure what I was expecting, but he showed up looking like a Spanish Conquistador, all shiny breastplate and helmet complete with plumes. His regular officers wore plain, plated leather tunics that appeared much more comfortable as well as practical.

The constable wasn't a very tall man but carried himself with the air of an aristocrat. I kept expecting him to have this high-pitched nasally voice, as it would match the image he portrayed. So, when his too-loud, grizzly voice demanded to know what had happened, I was surprised.

Tony took over talking to the constable, giving a toned-down version of what happened. When he was done, the constable sent his officers to go and assess the damages. He closed the door once they left, and you could see the man visibly sag. He pulled off his helmet and dropped it on the table. It rolled over, bending one of his plumes.

"Alright," he said in a casual, tired voice that I recognized from most of the combat veteran NCOs I'd served with. "Now, what really happened?"

Tony looked shocked, as if he couldn't believe the constable didn't believe his story. I spoke up when it was apparent Tony's charms had failed and he was at a loss.

"Alright chief. Two people piloting flying armor attacked our group. In the process, they did a lot of property damage before we could stop them. One was killed, and the other flew away. Two of us were hurt. That about sums it up," I said with a shrug.

The man's tired eyes evaluated me for a minute. I twisted my leg so he could see my burns. He didn't touch my leg but seemed to take a look from various angles.

"That is no ordinary burn," the constable said.

"You're telling me. I don't think you guys have lightning guns yet," I guessed.

"The only thing I've seen that looks similar is when a child had been burned while tampering with one of the wall torches." He looked up at me suspiciously.

"What? You think I tried to break into a wall torch with my knee?" I stared back. "Go take a look at the flying toaster downstairs if you have doubts."

"Oh, we will; I'll have it brought down to the hall for examination," the constable said.

"The hell you will," I growled, causing him to stare at me again. I wasn't about to let him take the only evidence that might help me figure out what the attack was all about. Besides, I seriously doubted they knew what to do with an Iron Man suit.

The constable bowed up a bit, "That thing attacked my city. I need to find out what it is so we can prepare defenses for any future attacks. It IS coming with me."

Surprisingly, Matlock stepped into the room and spoke up. "I believe what she is saying is that she is claiming Terran-Far." He glanced sideways at me, "Correct?"

I recovered quickly. "Yes, of course. Terra-Firma."

I could tell the constable was having none of it. But whatever this Terran-Far was seemed to tie his hands.

"Will you allow us to have a look at it at least?" he growled, clenching his teeth, "please." The word seemed to physically hurt him to say.

"Of course," Matlock answered before I could. "We will send word to you as soon as Ms. Rhiannon is back on her feet."

Then Matlock did something I'd never seen before, he smiled. It totally creeped me the fuck out.

It had the same effect on the constable, who picked up his helmet without another word and shoved it on his head. "I will await Ms. Rhiannon's word—" His voice cut off with my name. "Not the..."

"Yes, THAT Rhiannon," Matlock said.

The man looked at me and nodded once before turning. He slammed the door open and stormed out, the effect somewhat thwarted by his bent plumes.

"What's Terra-whatever?" I asked.

"It's one of our old laws, but still on the books." Tony gave Matlock a look of new-found respect before turning to me. "Basically, it comes down to 'winner takes all.' In the early days, there wasn't as much law as there is now. If you killed someone in defense, you could take all their belongings. As you can imagine, certain people tried to take advantage of the law, and eventually, measures were implemented. But they never removed the original law from the books."

"Why not?" I asked.

"That's a good question. It has come up several times, but the council has always kept it in place. Rumor has it there is some big power in the background that wants to keep the old tradition. Who knows?" Tony shrugged.

"Also, the name of a city founder has a bit of weight to it as well," Matlock added.

"How so?" I asked.

"Traditionally, they end up on the council of the city they discovered," Tony said.

The councilman we were staying with showed up about then.

"I hear you upset the constable," were the first words out of the councilman's mouth.

"The constable will get his way soon enough," Tony said.

"Oh, that's good. Is everyone OK?" The councilman asked.

So, we related the story again and showed him the damage to the compound. As before, we kept the fact they'd been after Tara to ourselves. A freak attack was one thing. But, if anyone found out the attack was targeted, we wouldn't be welcome anywhere for fear of collateral damage.

When satisfied, the councilman returned to work in order to discuss the new threat.

As soon as the councilman was gone, I turned to Matlock and anxiously asked, "Did you get it fixed?"

"As well as can be expected given the tools I have," Matlock said.

I groaned, "Can you heal or not?"

"Of course." Matlock stepped over to the bed and I cleared out of the way for him. As the others watched, he brought his staff down and waved it once over Tara's body.

"You did well; she only has one cracked rib," Matlock said.

"Yeah, yeah. What else?" I prompted nervously.

"No permanent damage to her heart or the muscles surrounding the site. She was very, very lucky. All she really needs is the dermal regeneration at the point of impact." Matlock paused and looked at me, "I'll need to remove the dead tissue first, of course."

"Will you be able to, considering her...'condition'?" I asked.

"I believe I can resist the temptation," Matlock affirmed.

When we'd brought Tara in, the only exposure of her skin had been where she'd been burned. Luckily, the burnt tissue didn't seem to emit her "scent" and we'd bandaged the entire site to help prevent infection. Matlock would have to remove her straps this time and risk exposure to her scent.

Rafly had already pulled replacement straps from Tara's pack and left them beside the bed. Apparently, Tara carried several "patch kits" in case her aging suit was damaged. She'd previously mentioned it was getting close to time to replace it entirely anyway.

"But, I believe the rest should vacate the area," Matlock said all deadpan-like. "I already have her under sedation. She'll be out for several more hours, it's for the best."

I stared at him for a minute, "Can I—"

"I work best alone," Matlock said gently.

"OK," I finally nodded.

"Would you like me to tend to your knee?" Matlock asked.

"No. A little vitamin M and I'll be right as rain by morning." Turning to the rest of the group, "Let's go check out our spoils of war," I said.

The power armor had been brought into an inner courtyard where Gathers sat watching it.

"It hasn't moved," Gathers reported.

"I should hope not," I snorted. "Rafly cut its friggin head off earlier." I pointed to where the head sat a meter or so from the body.

"I don't trust anything anymore," Gathers nodded, still watching the armor.

"That is a healthy attitude, Gathers." I patted him on the shoulder. "One that will help you live a long life...or give you an ulcer."

Gathers frowned at me. He'd grown accustomed to only understanding about half of what I said anymore and didn't bother to ask for clarification.

The armor sat in the middle of the courtyard. The helmet, complete with the head still inside, sat off to the side. Dark red blood had dried onto the floor in multiple places.

"That's gonna be a bitch to get out." I slowly circled the scene, taking it in from all angles before moving forward. I'd managed to find a makeshift cane to help me hobble around until my leg healed. No one else wanted anything to do with our dead guest, not that I could blame them.

I started with the helmet as it seemed the most straightforward. Getting the head out was a bit tricky as it was still strapped in. I found several buttons on the side of the helmet, but they appeared to have been damaged. I ended up with the grisly task of having to do a little cutting. I saw Gathers turn green before bolting for the door when the head finally popped out, mostly intact.

It appeared to be a woman. She had a very long, narrow face, sharp nose, and high cheekbones. If she had hair, it had been shaved off, leaving her bald. Her skin was dark pink, like actually pink, not Caucasian pink. Her eyes were downright troubling. They were black, except for the Iris and pupil, which were two shades of red. They were similar to my own, only slightly paler shades. I was starting to get a very uneasy feeling in my gut. Very carefully, I peeled her lips back and sure enough, there were fangs just like Tara's. I tentatively sniffed at the woman, trying to ignore the burning smell still in the air. Thankfully, she smelled nothing like Tara.

I put the head down and picked up the helmet. Inside were all sorts of pads that looked like they were sensor inputs, not cushions. The visor was opaque. There wasn't much gore in the helmet itself, although the smell of burned flesh remained. I searched around until my finger found a small metal stud. When I pressed it, the front half of the helmet swung up.

I thought about it momentarily, then stopped breathing and put on the helmet. I snapped the front half of the helmet closed, dropping myself into darkness.

There was a slight tingling in my scalp as the helmet's pads adjusted to cradle my head. Then the visor lit up in violent color. Everything was in extremely high definition, so sharp it actually hurt my eyes. Strange symbols scrolled across the visor.

As I looked around, small squares and circles tagged various objects and people around me. When I focused on them, more small symbols popped up that I didn't understand. There were several red flashing symbols at the bottom of the screen. I guessed they related to the helmet being disconnected.

The enormous energy gun was about four times the size of a

standard pistol; the hand grip seemed designed for the power armor's larger hands. While I could still wield the thing thanks to my strength, it was big, clunky and awkward. I also had no idea how it worked. There were no sights, no magazine, or any other moving parts aside from the trigger.

I reached down and picked up the energy gun. As soon as my hand wrapped around the grip, a bright green diamond appeared on the screen. It tracked the gun's muzzle as I moved it around the room.

"Now I know how to aim," I said.

"Woah," Gathers gasped, having returned from losing his lunch.

"What?" I asked.

"Your voice, it sounds strange," Gathers said, wiping his mouth with the back of his sleeve and desperately trying to ignore the strange head on the floor.

Approaching the main body of the armor, red indicators started flashing where the helmet had been severed and each of the bullet holes I'd given it. I found another release stud on the wrist. Touching it, the seam along the forearm split open, allowing me to gently pull the armor off from the elbow down.

The skin matched the same dark pinkish flesh from the face. It looked like a normal human arm and hand, save for the black claws on the tips of the fingers, just like Tara's.

This thing had to be a species related to Tara's in some way. They shared too many characteristics. I wondered if this "woman" had a tail, too.

I spent the next hour carefully removing the armor to reveal what would ordinarily be considered a human female, save for the eyes, skin, claws, and the fact she was nearly two and a half meters tall. It turned out she didn't have a tail or claws on her feet though.

She wore some sort of thin bodysuit that covered everything but her head. I tried to cut it off, but it wouldn't tear, no matter how hard I tried to shove my knife through it. It took a while, but I found a seam under the armpit. When I touched it, it split open like the top of a Ziploc bag. I pulled the garment off and stowed it away for later. There was no way I was letting something like this out of my sight. I just had to figure out a way to resize it for me.

I looked at the inside of the chest piece and found where my bullets had hit. They'd punched through the thin exterior but had been caught up in some sort of weird, sticky honeycomb liner on the inside of the armor. I wondered how it would fair against high-powered or armor-piercing rounds.

The knife wound seemed to have hit the shoulder seam perfectly and slipped through the joint. My one-in-a-million shot had allowed the electricity from Matlock's attack to channel past the armor and straight into the pilot. If I hadn't hit it just right, I'm pretty sure the suit would have ignored Matlock's attack.

We'd gotten lucky. The fact I'd dropped a building on one and it had flown away was a testament to how tough these things were. We'd gotten damned lucky to bring one down.

I looked at the gun again and wondered if it would have any effect on the suit. I wasn't about to try it in here, so I put it on the back burner. Instead, I pulled out my phone and started taking pictures of everything. My phone hadn't been much help here, so I'd had it turned off to save the battery. Now, I documented everything.

It was about this time that Matlock appeared again.

"I'm done. Tara's fine and should be up and about in an hour or so." Matlock stopped and stared at what all I'd done.

"Good. Does any of this look familiar to you?" I asked.

"The tech looks odd, nothing like we use in our suits. It's much too sleek." Matlock paused, tilting his head. "Do you see this?"

I looked at several segments of the armor he was pointing, "What?"

"Look at these spiderweb patterns. These cracks aren't from our fight, they're older. Much older," Matlock said, indicating several spots.

The more I looked, the more stress fractures I saw.

"These are old," I agreed.

"Most of these pieces don't show the same wear. It's like the armor is piecemeal together from various other armors,"

Matlock continued his analysis. "And it's not very well maintained," he frowned. "If these parts had been properly maintained, I'm betting your knife would not have penetrated." Matlock looked at me, "You're very fortunate."

"Yeah," I frowned, not really understanding what I was seeing.

"I don't recognize the race either, although..." Matlock said, shifting his attention to the pilot.

"Yeah, I see the similarities as well. Do you think they're from the same place? Some sort of genetic off-shoot?" I asked.

"Rumor has it Daemons live in the remote regions of the high mountains, mostly underground. They are extremely reclusive to the point we don't know of any colonies. We aren't aware of them being from somewhere other than our world, but anything is possible," Matlock concluded.

"Well, leave everything as is. Once Tara is up, I want her to take a look at this thing before we let the constable touch it. I wonder if it will ring any bells for Tara," I pondered.

"You should really take the helmet off before then; it's rather disconcerting," Matlock suggested.

"Oh, yeah." The armor's helmet was so comfortable I'd practically forgotten I was still wearing it. I touched the metal stud on the side and pulled the helmet off. I set it aside and took a breath of fresh air. The burnt-flesh smell still clung to my head and I wondered how long it would take to go away.

Open For Business

RHI

When Tara was finally up and around, she didn't recognize her attacker. Not the person, not the armor, not the smell, nothing. I let the council look at it, but they looked even more baffled than Tara. Eventually, I stored the whole thing, body and all, at Drakes. He said he had a "cool room" that would preserve everything until I could come get it.

Due to the fight and subsequent healing needed, we delayed the trip to Sanbu a few days. When we finally managed the trip, it was relatively uneventful. It seems in our absence, the city's aristocrats had found out what the magistrate had done. Imprisoning and torturing an Elementalist was one of the worst crimes you could commit. They had burnt the man alive and separated his ashes; it was that bad.

The peace talks went relatively well. Both cities agreed that a cycle was manageable as long as the tunnel blockage could be mitigated. Tony promised he could have the passage clear for minor foot traffic within the week, small caravans within the month and completely clear within six months.

Having your name on the wall as a discoverer of a new city apparently came with perks. Everyone was kissing my ass as they knew they couldn't move into the city until I did, and knowing what day I would do that had advantages. Needless to say, it was a pleasant week we spent in Sanbu. But soon enough, it was time to go.

With peace seemingly restored, or at least a calm cease-fire, it came time to part ways.

Tony and Sh'teena seemed to have gotten a bit closer in the last week or so, as their parting was a bit...mushy.

We hadn't seen Fantill for almost two weeks and wondered if he'd left the party.

The rest of us made our way back to the cavern Sh'teena had come through initially. Along the way, we passed another city perched on the edge of a massive waterfall that shamed Niagara.

Once we were topside, Matlock went looking for the farmer who'd originally reported the cave. Something the farmer said to Sh'teena made Matlock believe he was the man he'd been looking for. Of course, the farmer wasn't there anymore, but that didn't deter Matlock. He said his farewells and made his way off, away from the direction we were heading.

During all this, Sh'teena and Rafly noted my "horrendous" blade skills and took it upon themselves to teach me. It was compulsory. While intrigued by my titanium long knife, they said it wasn't a proper weapon for someone of my "skills."

So, they began to teach me swords, using Sh'teena's blades. They weren't crazy long, maybe one and a half times the size of the machetes we carried back home. But they were sharp along both edges and crazy heavy.

I tried to figure out what they were made from, but when I asked, all that came out was "Laftan." Whatever the word was, it didn't translate. Tara told me it was an ore found in the mountains above her home village. Sh'teena's swords had been a gift, a part of the adoption ceremony by Rafly's village.

I learned to fight with one sword rather quickly. Picking up two swords was a lot harder. With one, it was a relatively simple movement set, easy with my coordination. Adding the second one made me feel like I was fighting with myself more than I was with my sparring partner, which amused my partners to no end.

We made it to Sh'teena's home, or at least the castle of her "King." My eyes drew a lot of attention, and we ended up not staying very long. I met the pompous ass she called "King" and told her she needed a new line of work or to promote his heir quickly. She didn't like my suggestions, and we left shortly afterward.

It didn't take us long to get to Tara and Rafly's village and the event I'd been dreading arrived: my wedding. Just as Tara said, the ceremony was relatively short and straightforward, seeing as we'd already done the two main things that were required. That, at least, I was grateful for. Apparently, the consummation of a marriage here required the entire village's witnessing. Talk about performance anxiety.

The party, on the other hand, was legendary. It lasted a week. I don't remember half of it because I was completely and totally wrecked. Whatever the giants brewed up there as alcohol put me so far under the table that I thought I was back in Krodon.

Luckily, Tara took care of me. She could handle her drink much better than I could. Either that or she was purposely getting me sloshed just to mess with me. Either way, when I finally swam back to sobriety at the end of the week, we'd been given a small house on the outskirts of the village near Rafly's family home. The week-long celebration was meant to keep the newlyweds so shit-faced it gave the town time enough to build them a home.

As weird as it sounds, I was honestly touched. I'd never owned property before or had a place completely mine, or ours as it were. It felt weird and rather final.

I know you're wondering, "But Rhiannon, how did you not burn to a crisp without your UV treatment? Or did you return to the nightlife?"

Those are excellent questions, and it has a really kick-ass answer: I didn't need to. While underground, whatever light source they used didn't affect me at all. When I got topside, it was more of the same. I don't know if it was their sun or their atmosphere, but whatever it was, there was no burning. I swear, I'm going to make this place into some sort of vampire retreat if we ever get out of the zombie apocalypse. Between that and the fake blood, this place would be paradise.

And that's another thing, blood. Turns out the blood here is digestible, and giants have a shit-ton to spare. Once we explained my dietary needs, my new "family" didn't blink an eye at sharing with me. I later learned there wasn't anything you didn't do for your family. I guess Vin got that one right, as I have several not-so-nice memories attesting to it.

My sword training continued in the following months, and I steadily improved. I wasn't crazy super-ninja good, but I was getting there.

Tara and I set out on our own for a while. We went up into the mountains to see if we could find any trace of where she'd come from. We finally had to give up as we never found a trace of anything other than wild animals. If her family had been there, they made sure no one would ever find them again.

At our six-month anniversary, Tara gave me a set of swords similar to the ones Sh'teena carried. These swords were fitted to me and felt like natural extensions of my arms. They were insanely sharp and damn near indestructible. I eventually found out the metal was ore they'd crafted from what I took as a meteor from how they described it. I was hoping they weren't radioactive, but then again, superpowers would be cool.

The swords made me better. By the time a year had passed and it was time for us to start heading back, I was scary, crazy super-ninja good (it's a technical term.) We'd had some problems with bandits that gave me a chance to test my skills. I'd been able to dispatch twenty men in under a minute. It was something out of a superhero movie, well, not the murder part. I guess it would be a cool anime show instead? Curse James and his fucking geek memories.

I'd also come to truly, honestly love Tara. I don't know when it happened or how, but I knew it wasn't because of the link. Yes, the link bonded us in ways I couldn't describe, but I knew my feelings for her were my own, from my heart. It still surprised me. Never in my wildest dreams had I thought I'd fall in love this deeply with someone...lust, sure, but love, no. But here I was, happily married to someone I couldn't imagine living without.

Tara had shown more of her hidden side, but she was still teasing me, never being truly and completely honest about her true self. While it was sexy and intoxicating and all that, at the same time, it was aggravating. She continually told me I was far too impatient for someone as long lived as I was supposed to be.

Sometimes, when it was quiet and we were alone late at night, she would open her mind to me. I would experience things alien to me, and it would take a long time of us talking about it before I'd understand what I'd witnessed.

Something about these little jaunts into her mind scared me. It was as if she were trying to get me used to her other side or prepare me for something coming. When I would ask her about it, she'd give me that smile, complete with her "old" eyes. Damn, she could be annoying.

Meanwhile, she knew damned near everything about me. I didn't have any big, deep, dark secrets...well, not compared to her. She seemed to be able to walk into my mind at will now. When I asked her to teach me how to block like she did, she taught me. But I never knew if it worked or not since she was the only person I knew who could get into my head.

Saying goodbye to Rafly had been hard. She'd become the sister I'd never had during the past year. The thought I'd probably never see her again hurt. But it was worse for Tara. She'd watched Rafly grow up, so she was more a daughter than a sister to her. Watching them say goodbye was painful, and it almost made me change my mind about leaving until Tara gave me a look that steered me away from that decision.

We stopped by Sh'teena's "home," but the guards told us she'd been sent away on a mission for the king, so we continued on to the cavern. Nothing had changed from the last time we'd come through; the hole was still there in the middle of the farmer's field. Nothing down below seemed to have changed, either.

On the other hand, my clothes had changed. The rough and tumble life I'd been living in the mountains pretty much shredded my old clothes. The new ones were a compliment to Tara's. I wore dark red leather with similar buckles and straps, but I didn't wear a mask as she still did.

I did have a badass coat that Tara had made for me. It was red leather, of course, but it was sleeveless, buttoned across the chest, and flared back into a three-quarter trench that covered the back of my thighs to the knee but left the front open from the waist down. I looked good, and I could fight well in it.

I had seen firsthand what Tara's scent had done to one poor lad who'd tried to spy on us once. We'd gone far away from the village for a bath. They had to tie the poor kid up for several days until he finally calmed down. Tara had been upset for a long while, and no matter how much I told her it wasn't her fault, she wouldn't listen to me. Sometimes she could be so stubborn. I can say it, not you!

We reached Krodon and found out Tony had also disappeared. The tunnel had been cleared on time, just as he'd promised. But as soon as it was done, he'd gone back out into the world and no one knew where he was.

The housing authority said the city was ready now. Apparently, the morning I arrived the "coming soon" label on the wall faded away. They sent a representative with us to help guide us and make everything all official-like.

Sure enough, as we approached, a large, new hallway emerged from the darkness and led us to the city. It was one of the two side tunnels Tony had mentioned previously. It seems he was right yet again. The passageways were lit now: a bright, clean light that cast the tunnel into a much more cheerful scene than when we'd been lost in the dark.

The city was also lit up. The dull glow that had previously been above us was replaced with bright daylight. As we entered the city, the housing official led us to the center building, usually reserved for the housing authority.

The representative double-checked to ensure the wall here reflected the same information as the others. He then told us no one else would be allowed in until I'd made my choice of buildings. The tunnel we came through would remain hidden until then. I had as long as I needed to choose.

Curiosity, more than anything else, made me head to the rear of the cavern. Sure enough, the vast chasm had been repaired, and city block after city block of completed buildings sat where the huge hole had once been

I already knew which building I wanted, but having an entire city to ourselves was just too much to pass up. The two of us strolled through the streets like school girls, giggling and thinking up wonderfully wicked things we could do in a city all to ourselves. But once we were done playing, we made for the building where I'd entered this world.

It was still how I'd left it: an empty stone building, barren of life. I searched it top to bottom again just to be on the safe side, but no one was home. The message I'd carved into the bar was still there, untouched.

"Ready?" I asked Tara, who just smiled and nodded. We went outside and closed the door. Just as the official had told me, I placed my hand on the door and recited the words.

"I claim this space as my own." Then I waited. There wasn't a flash of light, a roaring sound, or even a tingling in my hand. Frowning, I reached down for the door handle, intent on opening and closing it to try the whole thing again.

As I touched the door handle, the door flashed to life with another of Drakes flashy door signs. As I opened the door, the inside was no longer empty. Warm light filled the room, accented by candles. There were tables, chairs and booths. There were barstools in neat rows next to the bar and bottles of various shapes, colors and designs behind the bar. And, as always, Drake was standing behind the bar polishing a glass.

"Ahh, the mistress of the house returns!" He bellowed out to the air.

I looked at Tara, who shrugged and followed me inside. "Drake," I said, closing the door.

"And what can we do for you today, mistress?" Drake beamed.

"You do realize, until about 10 seconds ago, none of this," I motioned around the room, "including you, existed?"

"Of course. We weren't open for business yet. Thank you, by the way," Drake said, nodding slightly.

"For what?" I asked.

"For choosing this place. It makes it special." Drake said with pride.

"How so?" Tara chimed in.

"This is your franchise," Drake said to me. "While it is

always Drakes, it is your Drakes."

"What does that mean?" I asked.

"Exactly what I said," Drake said, totally not clearing things up.

"What you said didn't make sense, Drake." Then I thought about it. "Nothing you ever say makes sense." I glanced down at where I'd carved my message to Drake and ran my hand across the now pristine surface; no sign I'd ever vandalized it.

He sighed and shrugged his shoulders, "It's the nature of the thing."

"Whatever Drake. Listen, can you...wait. Does that mean I get a cut of the profits or something?" I asked, dollar signs flashing in my eyes. Then I remembered money didn't mean anything back home anymore.

"Or something." He smiled wickedly.

"Am I your boss now? Cause I have to warn you, I don't have an MBA or anything. We could be the first Drakes to ever go bankrupt," I warned.

He chortled. "Oh, mistress. No, none of that you have to worry about."

"Well, good then," I said, pausing as a thought came to me. "If this really is my Drakes, then I should call it something else to make it my own."

"Like what?" Tara asked.

"I dunno, something catchy you can put on merchandise. But, I'm not that creative," I frowned.

Tara looked at me for a long moment before saying, "What's Hard Rock Café?"

"Get out of my head!" I slapped her lightly on the arm with a grin before shaking my head. "I'm not sure how Hard Rock Drakes would look on a coffee mug," I laughed, then thought about it. "It's not like they could sue me...this world doesn't have lawyers, thank God."

I chuckled once more before an awkward silence fell over us. I realized I was unsure how to proceed.

"Would you like to go home now?" Drake offered.

"What? No theoreticallies and shit?" I scowled.

"No shit mistress. This is your house." These words didn't

sink in until much later when it was too late.

"Yes, Drake, please take us home," I practically groaned.

"Of course, mistress, this way," Drake said.

"Shit. Drake, this is my wife Tara. Tara, Drake." I introduced them officially.

"I think we've met before," Tara said.

"Of course, mistress." He bowed slightly. "It's still a pleasure." He led us to the backroom where the portal had been in the Austin Drakes. He motioned to the door, "As requested, mistress."

"And this will take us home, to my world?" I asked.

"Of course, mistress, as long as that is what you desire," Drake said.

I paused. "What I desire?"

"Think of what you desire and then open the door. The portal will do the rest." Drake bowed slightly.

"Wait. Drake, the other Drake, said that this was worse than insanely impossible," I said cautiously.

"Normally, yes." He smiled. "But you are the mistress of this house; it obeys you now."

I wasn't sure if I liked the sound of that, but it was too late now. I was up to my ass in it, and there was no turning back. I turned to Tara, "Last chance to back out of this."

She gave me a look. "After all the work I've put into this marriage, you think I'm just going to give up on you now?" she grinned. "Besides, I've been looking forward to meeting your 'friend-family'."

I looked at her suspiciously. "Why do I suddenly have the feeling you're just using me to get to the big PX in the sky?"

"Love you long time GI," she somehow magically pulled from my mind.

"How the hell do you know that reference? Wait, never mind. I don't want to know how much rooting around you've been doing in my nugget again. You ready?" I asked one last time.

"For you? Always." Tara smiled.

I pulled her to me and kissed her deeply before turning back to the door.

"In the words of who I figure will end up narrating my life, 'hold onto your butts!'"

I opened the door.

Back Through the Rabbit's Hole

RHI

The trip took just as long as before, but it wasn't as cold as it had been. So, when I emerged on the other side, I didn't collapse like I'd done the previous time. Thank God for that because we walked right into a shit storm.

As I emerged, I stumbled into someone. It only took a moment for my senses to realize it wasn't someone I'd bumped into but something. The zombie fell back into the arms of the zombies surrounding it...surrounding us.

It was Drakes, a modern-day one that was trashed from the four hundred zombies crammed inside it. Drake told me to think of home before I grabbed the door handle and stepped through the portal. This wasn't what I pictured my home to be at all.

I glanced behind me at the still-open door and saw the monstrous, military truck James called the "Dilla" blocking the doorway. Tara appeared as I watched, just stepping out of thin air right through the open door.

"Down!" I yelled as I drew my swords and span, blades flashing out. The immediate row of zombies around us dropped as my blades sliced through flesh, muscle and bone as if they were nothing more than tissue paper. The dense blades made short work of the bodies around us.

"Back out the door into the truck!" I yelled as the room erupted with moans, the swarm turning towards us. I backed up until my back was against the truck.

I glanced behind me to see Tara in the truck.

"Are there any guns in there?" I began to drop zombies in ones and twos as they could no longer surround me thanks to the door acting as a choke point.

"Uh," was all Tara said, and I felt her rooting around in my mind.

What are you doing? Tara and I had never mastered the whole talking in our heads thing. It worked sporadically, mainly when stressed or something serious was up. We normally kept talking aloud.

Looking, she said. "Yes, there's an MP5 in this box and several magazines."

"Perfect, hand her over and feed me mags as I call for them."

"You got it," Tara said.

I felt the sub-machine gun brush my shoulder and sheathed my swords. I figured if James had parked this thing here, he was probably trapped in here somewhere. "Stick with me; here we go!" I thumbed the safety off and pressed the trigger.

Nothing happened.

"Well, that was anti-climactic," Tara muttered, her voice trying to conceal the anxiety she was feeling.

"Shut up," I said, pulling the cocking handle back and pressing the trigger again. The small gun barked and spat flame this time, dropping a zombie.

"Wow," Tara said as she watched me begin my headshot marathon. Tara had never seen me shoot a gun, seeing as I'd used all my bullets in the arrival of the flying power armor a year ago. I'd never found anyone who could reload bullets for me, so she'd tapped into my memories when I talked about gunplay. Now, she watched as I began to clean house.

"Mag!" I hollered and she put it in my outstretched hand as we slowly made our way back into Drakes. The old magazine fell away empty as I slapped a fresh one home and continued to shoot.

On my fourth magazine, I glanced up and could see James

and Shae fighting on the balcony. They were using machetes and had two gray, jumpsuit-clad people with them who were wearing MITCH helmets. They seemed to be hanging back and letting Shae and James do the fighting. One of them seemed to be supporting the other.

I returned my attention to my targets as my gun clicked dry, and I called for another magazine.

"Last mag!" Tara said as she handed it to me.

Nice of you to join the party, James's voice chimed in my head.

Better late than never, I sent back. I realized that having him in my head felt totally different than Tara. I dropped the gun as it ran dry and pulled my swords. The zombie to my right sprouted a knife in his eye socket as Tara covered my transition.

"Careful, watch your back; these guys are everywhere," I cautioned.

"Tell me about it," Tara said as she guided the metal of her throwing knives to find their targets.

I'd spent many a night explaining zombies to Tara to make sure she understood what was going on in my world. Luckily, all the memory sharing had prepared her for today. I didn't want to think about what would have happened if she'd been dropped into this situation cold.

How'd you get here? James asked.

Long story, fight now, talk later. I had to focus on the training exercises Rafly had taught me and relax my mind so my body would move more freely. It sped me up, and the area around us suddenly opened up as I dropped more and more shamblers.

Dang girl! Shae chimed in as she caught sight of my swordplay. *Where did you learn to do that?*

I am Japanese, you know. I said sarcastically.

You're mom's Japanese, you're from Marble Falls! James shot back.

Well, I visited. I grunted. I'd forgotten James had somehow pulled me into a talk about my family when we were rolling around naked at the Alamo. The man had the damndest talent for saying the wrong thing at the right moment.

I shook my head trying to bring my focus back to the here and now. *Y'all OK up there?*

*Better than you, they can only come at us from one direction." James said.

I reversed my swords, switching up my muscle groups and style. It was a trick I'd learned to keep from tiring myself out. These swords were heavy. A normal person would have been spent after only a minute or so of use. With the number of shamblers here, I needed to pace myself.

What the hell is this? I asked just as I misjudged a swing and my blade embedded itself in the skull of a zombie. *Shit!* I cursed, putting my foot on his chest and yanking my blade free. Costing me precious seconds, the error allowed another zombie to close inside the range of my blades. Luckily, Tara was there protecting me with another throwing knife to its eye.

Not sure, James answered. *We found these two holed up in here and then got trapped by the mob. I didn't think they could climb stairs; it seemed I was wrong," James stopped talking a moment to focus on his fight, then continued. "See that room on your right? The one far back on the right wall? That's where they're coming from.*

It's a friggin clown car! I said as I saw two more zombies shamble through the indicated door.

We think it's a portal to somewhere else...and somehow... it's stuck open, James grunted as he fought his own battle.

Great, I muttered as something raked my left side. I'd been paying too much attention to the conversation in my head. I kicked hard, knocking the zombie back and glanced at the damage. Its nails had left marks in my leathers but hadn't cut through. I mentally thanked my tailor and focused back on the fight.

No more chatter, I'm busy, I sent and silence followed.

Minutes followed of arm-aching combat. I kept trying to make my way towards the back door but had to keep stopping to take out the zombies that flanked us. Tara had to get in too close for my comfort using her knives, so I kept "helping out," which slowed our progress to a crawl as the crowd kept washing over us.

I was turning back from taking out the zombies on my left flank when I stumbled over a body and sprawled in a most embarrassing way. The front line of zombies closed on me.

"*Stay down!*" I heard Tara yell both aloud and in my head.

I felt the air around me suddenly vibrate and almost crackle with energy as I heard Tara growling over me. There was a sudden pressure in my head as she screamed and bodies fell around us. A lot of bodies.

"OK," Tara panted.

I was on my feet and glancing around. There wasn't a zombie standing within five meters of us. There had to be at least fifty zombies on the floor who had been standing only a moment before.

Instead of asking Tara what had happened, I took advantage of the break and made a beeline for the back door. A glance down revealed that each zombie Tara dropped had multiple holes in its head.

I made quick work of the few zombies between us and the back door before slipping inside. It was the same back room we'd taken a portal out of from my Drakes. However, the portal door was wide open, and I watched as a zombie stepped through it into the room with us. It didn't materialize as Tara had by the front door; it seemed to shuffle in from the darkness beyond the door frame.

I took its head off easily and kicked the door shut.

Door's shut! I managed. Then, just for kicks, I cracked it open again. There was no longer darkness in the doorframe, just the bare wall.

Portal's shut down, I sighed heavily. Glancing at Tara, "You OK?"

"Yeah, I think so," Tara said in a shaky voice.

"Ready to get back in there and finish this?" I asked.

Tara rubbed her head and slowly nodded.

"You OK?" I asked, concerned.

"Just a bit of a headache, I'll be OK," Tara said.

I'd learned Tara's body language pretty well over the last year. It's amazing how much the body can express when the face is covered. Right now she was showing some signs of fatigue, but nothing serious.

It took another ten minutes to clear out the remaining shamblers and then another ten to go through and make sure all of the decapitated heads were dispatched. No one wanted to step on a zombie head landmine.

We met up with the others at the foot of the stairs. Even though we were both covered in gore, James embraced me.

"Damn good to see you, girl," James said as he hugged me fiercely.

"You have no idea," I said, returning his hug with bone-crushing force. I'd forgotten how good he could smell, even if a bit worse for wear.

When he pulled back, "Holy crap, what happened to your eyes?!?"

"Long, long story. Hey, Shae," I said as she stepped forward and also hugged me, just not as rough as James had.

"Hey, yourself," she said, surprised by how freely I embraced her now.

"This is Beth and Rachel," James said, pointing over his shoulder at the two women sitting on the stairs. "We found them in here and came in to rescue them."

"Some rescue," Beth mumbled.

I laughed and turned to Tara. "This is Tara," I took a breath and blew it out, bracing myself, "my wife."

Shae had been starting to hold her hand out and froze. "Wife?"

"We leave you alone for a week, and you go and get hitched?" James was grinning ear to ear as he held out his hand to Tara.

"A week?" I managed, my throat suddenly tight.

Tara looked at James's hand momentarily before mirroring him but not shaking his hand.

I watched one of James's eyebrows raise. "She's not really one for touching." I provided.

"What a shame." James leered in that annoyingly playful way of his before withdrawing his hand.

"Good to see some things never change." I rolled my eyes and watched Shae nod at Tara. "So, this is Houston Drakes, and it's only been a week since y'all left Austin?"

Shae looked at me. I could tell by her expression she knew something was off even though I tried to keep my voice "normal."

"Yup, and when we get back, Trish is gonna be pissed!" James grinned. "Now let's see what we have to do now." James moved towards the back door while Shae continued to stare at me.

Later, I thought, and she nodded before turning to follow James. Thanks to my training, James was kinda badass, but Shae was the brains of the pair. She had a talent for noticing things others didn't; it made her scary dangerous on a whole other level.

While the others went to check on the portal door, I quickly swept the place with Tara to ensure we hadn't missed any stragglers. We hadn't.

"Your friends are...nice," Tara said while we were checking the upstairs.

"Yeah...?" I questioned cautiously.

"They didn't ask anything about how I was dressed and just a little comment about your eyes," Tara said.

"So?" I said.

"I'm used to a more...vocal reaction," Tara said.

"Give them time; they're just busy right now. The questions will come later, trust me," I said.

"Even still, it's a nice change not to be treated like a leper from the get-go," Tara said.

I watched her non-verbal; she was holding something back, "What?" I said.

"Nothing," Tara said.

"Right. Everyone on this planet knows when a woman says 'nothing,' it's always something. What?" I demanded.

"James." Tara grinned sheepishly.

"What about James?" I asked cautiously.

"He's...interesting..." Tara said.

"Oh, don't you start," I warned.

"What? I am linked with your mind...part of this is your fault," Tara said sincerely.

"I know, that's why I said don't start." I could feel her eyes on me. "What?" It was my turn to feel defensive.

"Should I be jealous?" Tara asked.

"Not if you're the one lusting after him," I said.

Tara laughed. "I never realized..."

"Realized what?" I said cautiously.

"How twisted you could be," Tara said.

I gave her my best look, "You've never complained before."

She chuckled and wrapped her arm around my waist. "And I never will." She squeezed and then let me go.

A warm feeling ran through my body that made me inadvertently grin sheepishly. "How do you do that?"

"Do what?" she said innocently.

"Make me feel this way," I said, feeling a blush brush my cheeks.

She grabbed me with both arms and pulled me to her suddenly, catching me off guard. Her face straps fell away, and she kissed me. It wasn't a peck, and it wasn't lusty; it was warm and soft and made goosebumps break out all over my body. When she finally let me come up for air, she said, "What way?" And then her mask was back in place, and she released me, walking across the room, leaving me with my mouth hanging open.

[SIDE NOTE: *Some of you may have noticed that I don't seem as nutso as I did when you first met me. I'd love to say I became a bit more sane or gained more control over myself, but 1) where is the fun in that? And 2) I can't take credit for it. Apparently, this little mind meld that Shae, James, and I were sharing was always on. Not only was it always on, but it was a two...er, three-way street. Meaning I somehow shared minds with both of them. As a result, my brand of crazy was spread amongst the three of us while all their good and bad things were shared with me. As a result, I got weird urges but didn't want to kill anyone over them...mostly. I guess it was a win.*

I didn't really notice the difference until I returned to the presence of what Nat called our little "gestalt." I suddenly felt this blanket of calm that seemed to rest on top of my brain. It was a weird kind of cool, but at the same time, now I had to try a bit harder to be nutso.]

"Who's Trish?" Tara asked in mock innocence.

"A girl back in Austin," I supplied.

"You do seem to get around, don't you? A ship in all ports?" Her voice had a grin, but I could sense a slight unease.

"She's not my girl. She only wishes she was," I said.

"You don't seem the type to play hard to get," Tara said.

"I used to, but not so much after living in your village for a year. Y'all were pretty upfront and honest with what you wanted," I said.

"That's why I bagged you. I knew I couldn't wait," Tara said.

"That's not how it seemed at the time," I said.

Tara shrugged. "So, when we get back to Austin..."

"Trish? You don't have to worry about her," I said honestly.

"Oh?" Tara said.

"No, it's Nat who'll try and get you into bed. She seems to have a knack for it. As a matter of fact, I wouldn't be surprised if she was from your village. She'll tell you exactly what she wants up front."

"You do surround yourself with interesting characters, don't you?" Tara said.

"I think I've got some sort of weirdness magnet in me somewhere," I said. I looked at the carnage around us. Bodies were covering the floor and gore splattered the walls. I stopped and looked back at Tara.

"You've been in my mind Tara. You've seen me, the real me," I said.

"Yes?" Tara stopped and faced me, sensing my unease.

"You know I'm addicted to violence. Both as a sport and," I motioned around us, "in real life. It...excites me."

"Yes," Tara said simply.

"That doesn't bother you?" I asked incredulously.

"Rhi, you've seen my world. It is a world of constant violence, much like the one you now live in. I've known strife my entire life. While I don't seek it out, it doesn't bother me as long as it's not senseless." Tara took my hand in hers. "I know your desires...even the dark ones. They're a part of you and I love ALL of you."

Tara started to continue but I placed my hand on where her

mouth would be to stop her.

"OK," was all I said and let it drop.

When we rejoined the group, they were sitting around the bar in a sea of corpses.

"What a lovely place you've found here," I said as Tara and I walked up. "The ambiance is so relaxing, I could just die." I really wanted to sashay up, but with so many bodies on the floor, they ruined the effect.

"What's a sashay?" Tara asked.

"I'll show you later." I smiled and proceeded to punt a decapitated zombie head out of my way.

"Hey!" James cried out.

"Hey what? You want me to take the zombie's feelings into consideration? Fuck them. They shouldn't have become a zombie, you know?" I climbed up on top of the bar, letting my legs dangle over the edge.

"So, what's the deal?" I said, watching Tara sit on a stool next to me.

James shook his head at me and said, "We're waiting on Drake. We made contact with Nat, and she's contacting Drake." James paused and looked at us, "How did y'all get here?"

"Front door," I said pointing my thumb over my shoulder.

"But the portal was supposed to be broken," Shae said.

"Hey, don't ask me; I only work here," I shrugged.

The two women in jumpsuits had taken off their helmets and appeared to be drinking warm beer.

"Holy shit, you're Jayne!" I hollered, completely started by the super-star, pop singer sitting a few stools down from me.

The woman chuckled and nodded. "Guilty. Or at least I was," Beth said.

"I friggin' love your music. 'Out-And-Out' makes me cry every time," I admitted, just the slightest fan-girl coming out in me.

James looked at me and made a face.

"Back up off me," I warned, and he held his hands up in surrender.

Beth made a face. "What song?"

"'Out-And-Out.' You know," I sang the opening line, but her

expression didn't change. "It's off your most recent album."

"*Fallout?*" Beth asked.

"*Fallout?*" No, *Truisms*," I corrected.

"I haven't done an album by that name. You must have me confused with someone else. The song sounds cool, though," Beth said.

"What?" I was at a total loss. *Fallout* came out like four years ago, with *Truisms* following the year before last.

"Uh," James interrupted. "This may sound really weird Beth, but...what year is it?"

The year Beth said caused James, Shae and I to exchange surprised looks.

"What?" Beth asked. "What the hell's that look for?"

"That was four years ago," James said.

Then, something clicked in my head. "You said you found them in here, right?" I asked.

"Yeah," James said slowly.

"Beth, how'd y'all get stuck in here?" I asked.

Beth shrugged. "Easy, we got separated from our team by a herd we weren't expecting. Rachel and I retreated in here, thinking we could barricade or get out the other side as the place was crawling with zombies. Turns out we couldn't secure the front door, and when we went out what we thought was the back door, it brought us right back into the same room. I thought we'd gotten turned around somehow in the rush, or it was some funhouse trick and tried to go back through the door, but it wouldn't let us. It acted like a black wall.

"When we checked the place out again, there weren't any zombies. We tried to go out the front door, but it wouldn't open. I wasn't sure if it was jammed or what, but we couldn't budge it, and we couldn't break it down.

"By then, we were wiped. We'd already been up for over twenty hours, so we climbed into one of the booths and racked out. The next thing we knew, we woke up and the place was crawling with zombies again. We climbed up on top of the canopies and started shooting. That's when Delta Force here stormed in." Beth jerked a thumb at James.

"Uh-huh," I added.

"What is it?" Shae asked.

"Sounds like you might have gone through the portal at the exact same time I did." I saw the blank looks and started to explain how I'd been called down to Drakes to come "save" them because Nat said they were in trouble. "When I stepped through the portal, I didn't end up here in Houston."

"Portal?" Rachel asked, looking up from the rifle she appeared to be cleaning. She had it broken down into several pieces on the bar and was taking her time making sure each one was immaculate.

"That 'black wall,' it's a portal that connects these places. It can transport you to another bar," I said.

"Talk about a pub crawl," Shae whispered, looking at me. "Where'd you end up?"

"Another planet," I managed.

"Another planet?" James said incredulously.

"Or another dimension, I don't know. All I know is that it wasn't here." I then took the next little while to give them a very condensed version of what happened to me. When I was done, no one said anything for a long time.

"A year?" Shae muttered. "You were there over a year?"

"Yup. Time must have run differently over there." I shrugged.

"And you think we did the same thing?" Beth asked, her voice incredulous.

"Maybe. Any differences you noticed aside from the year?" I asked.

"Parking lot's different," Rachel chimed in, not looking up from her rifle. "We went and looked a while ago. On our side, the lot wasn't full of zombies and there wasn't a row of buildings on the other side of the parking lot; it had been a field."

"There's also the fact you don't remember me." James looked at Beth.

I still think you're making that drunken make-out session up, Shae said through our heads.

You made out with Jayne? I gasped. *No shit?*

Shut up, you two. Focus. James chided, but I could almost

feel the blush in his voice.

"I also don't recognize some of the weapons you're using, and I've never heard of your unit," James added.

"The Roughriders were formed shortly after the second zombie war started. They—"

"Second zombie war?" I asked.

"It wasn't a second war," Rachel interrupted.

"It's all semantics," Beth said.

"No, it's not." Rachel put the rag she was using to clean her rifle down and looked over at Beth. "The zombie war broke out, and after about a year, it was under control enough that the government decided to declare "victory" as a propaganda stunt. So, everybody relaxed instead of finishing the fight. Then, six months later, it started all over again, and this time, we were on the losing side. It's all the same war." Rachel picked her oily rag back up and continued cleaning.

Beth sighed. "Anyway, the Roughriders were spun up and have been around ever since," Beth said.

Shae looked her in the eye. "Our outbreak is only four months old."

Beth and Rachel stared at us.

"Could they have traveled in time?" I asked.

"No." James shook his head. "That wouldn't explain her not knowing me and not having done her most recent album. I'd say you're not in Kansas anymore," James said to Beth.

"Great. How do we get back?" Beth asked, seeming to take this revelation much more calmly than I would.

"We'll ask Drake when he gets here. If anyone knows, it'll be him," Shae supplied.

"In the meantime." James grabbed one of the few unbroken bottles from behind the bar and poured himself a drink. He held the bottle up, but there were no takers. "I'm sorry, I've been trying to be polite, but what's with the full-body outfit?" James pointed at Tara with his drink.

Told you, I sent to Tara.

"I have a condition," Tara said. "I give off a scent that tends to drive people a little...insane."

"Insane?" James asked. "At least you're in the right

company." James nodded at me.

I silently gave him the finger before adding, "It will make people screw themselves to death." I grabbed a warm beer from a dead cooler. *Not that it wouldn't fit in with our group,* I admitted.

"OK, didn't see that coming. Important safety tip." He smiled.

I watched as Shae put a hand on his arm. I think he was going to try and make another joke, but she restrained him with a touch.

"In that case, what's with the eyes?" James was relentless.

"Wedding present." I smiled. "Seems when Tara and I bonded, we ended up sharing a few traits. One was the eyes," I started pulling off one of my arm gloves. "The other was matching tattoos," I revealed my arm and the dramatic tattoos on it.

"Oh wow," Shae sighed. "That's beautiful. May I?"

"Be my guest." I offered my arm up. I had already noticed the "bands" had started spreading. It had only been a year of being together, and they had already grown past my arms and into my shoulder blades.

"And Tara has a matching set?" Shae said, gently lifting my arm and turning it this way and that.

"Identical in every way, and they also change," I sounded like a schoolgirl with a new dress.

"Change?" James asked.

"Yeah. It will change to reflect our life together as we go on," I said, taking a sip of beer with my free arm.

"That is so cool," Beth said. "Beats the hell out of a tramp stamp."

"You have a tramp stamp?" I asked half-jokingly.

"No." She and James said in unison, causing Beth to look at him.

"Sorry," he apologized.

"When you said we knew each other, exactly how well did we know each other?" Beth asked.

"Just a drunken make-out session," James supplied.

"Or six." Shae grinned, causing James to give her the evil

eye.

"That well, huh?" Beth shook her head.

She's filing that one away for later, Tara said in my head.

I looked at her and nodded.

"Wait," James took a drink. "You said Tara's smell will drive you nuts. But you two...you've...well, you've seen her without her suit on." He seemed a bit embarrassed to talk about it. I hadn't seen him like that before.

"Yes, James, we've had sex, you perv. And while I find her scent intoxicating, it doesn't drive me to go around raping people." I turned and looked at her. "Well, maybe just one." I leered, and Tara just shook her head.

"What's with the swords?" Shae asked me.

I pulled one out and laid it on the bar. "They're made from a large meteorite that landed in the mountains near our village. It's a fantastic material. Heavy as hell, but I have yet to chip or nick the blades.

The dark gray material had sapphire blue streaks through it.

"They almost look like they glow." Shae touched the side of the blade and pulled her hand back quickly. "It's warm!"

"They're always warm, which comes in handy in the mountains in winter. And yes, the blue streaks do glow faintly in the dark."

"Is it radioactive?" James asked. "You did say it was from a meteorite."

"That would explain the glow and the warmth, but I don't know. The village has been mining the thing for years, and I didn't see any signs of radiation sickness." I looked down at the swords, "I hope they're safe; they're too pretty to give up."

"OK," James started, shaking his head. "So, you two are from an alternate world."

"Why is our world the alternate?" Rachel asked, chiming in for the first time in a while. "Why isn't this place the alternate?"

James frowned. "Fair enough," he conceded, turning to me. "And you visited, what, medieval world?"

"Actually, I think it was a post-apocalyptic world. They had satellites and technology and such, but it was all ancient," I said.

"I wonder how many of these worlds there are." James was lost in thought.

"Another question for Drake," I added. When's he supposed to get here anyway?"

"No idea," Shae added.

"Should we clear the parking lot?" I asked.

"No," James answered. "They can't get in unless they can..."

"Don't say it!" Shae hissed, cutting him off with a slap on the arm before he could make one of those statements that caused Murphy's Law to step in.

"They can't get in," he corrected quickly. "We'll just, wait on Drake," he said.

"Oh yeah!" I snapped my fingers suddenly and turned to Tara. "What did you do to drop all those shamblers?"

"Oh, that?" I saw Tara shift restlessly in her chair. "Well, when I was watching you 'gun' all those bodies—"

"Shot, dear. When I shot all those bodies," I said.

"Right. When you were 'shoting' all those bodies, I realized you were just throwing pieces of metal at their heads. So, I reached out and pulled back all of those shots—"

"Bullets," I corrected.

"Do you want to hear this or not?" Tara said testily.

"Honeymoon's over," James snickered.

"Hey, at least we're married." I gave him the evil eye, and he held his hands up in surrender.

"Anyway," Tara continued. "I grabbed all the bullets you had shot and shot them again. I just kept using them until there wasn't anything left to use. I would have gotten more if I'd had more bullets."

"You were amazing!" I squeezed her hand. "From now on, I'm not going to waste my time with shooting; I'll just hand you the bullets."

"I'd prefer you didn't." Tara seemed to pause. "That was really difficult and gave me a headache."

I smiled and patted her hand.

"Uh, what?" James asked.

"She's a metal bender." When it was apparent he didn't understand the reference, "She can control metal."

"Like Magneto?" James asked.

"No idea who that is," I said.

"Cool," James said.

"You can move metal with your mind?" Rachel asked incredulously.

In response, Tara reached out with her mind and picked up the rifle bolt Rachel was cleaning. Tara rotated it slowly and then gently returned it to its place on the bar.

Rachel picked the part up and examined it in detail as if she were worried it had been damaged in the demonstration.

"Amazing," Shae said.

"Bet you're amazing at pinball." Beth smiled.

"What is pinball?" Tara asked.

"Tell you later," I said.

"So, this world has proper monsters," Beth said. "Not...you," Beth said, indicating Tara. "Them." She pointed at James and Shae. "Vampires." She seemed to think about what she said. "That came out all kinds of wrong, didn't it?" She took another drink of her warm beer. "Tell me more."

James and Shae spent the next hour telling Beth and Rachel about our world and how vampires fit into it. Tara pretended not to listen, but I could tell she was glued to every word.

Shortly afterward, a series of pops and crackles came from various parts of the building, but nothing we could find or identify. We didn't smell or see smoke, so we hoped it was "normal," but nothing in Drakes was ever normal.

"Sorry for the wait," a new voice said from the back of the room. "It took a bit longer to get her up and running than I thought." Drake carefully stepped over the various bodies as he made his way to the bar. "Dear, oh dear, what a mess."

"Sorry 'bout that Drake, couldn't be helped," James apologized.

"Oh, think nothing of it." Drake waved a hand. "You've done me a great service, and I never forget my debts." Then he saw the rest of us. He looked at Rachel and Beth first and shook his head, "Oh dear." Then his eyes landed on Tara, and they actually looked startled. "Oh my!"

"What?" I asked.

"I'm so terribly sorry. It appears the damage here was much worse than I thought. I'll get to work on it straight away, not to fear," Drake said with uncharacteristic anxiety.

I stopped him as he started to turn away.

"Theoretically..." But his look stopped me.

"I do think we're well past that now, my dear. Just ask," Drake said.

"How long until you can send them back?" I threw a thumb at Rachel and Beth.

His mouth twisted. "I'm not sure, but it will take some time." His eyes then floated to Tara. "For her..."

"She stays with me," I said more forcefully than I intended. "Sorry," I tried again. "We're staying together, Drake."

He gave Tara another look and seemed to be debating whether to say anything. Finally, he sighed and said, "As you wish."

"Drake," I tried in my pleasant voice. "Can I visit my Drakes?"

"Of course, once the...door is fixed."

"My franchise, not Austin?" I asked.

"Obviously," Drake agreed.

"I don't exactly trust your 'doors' Drake. I did just what you said before arriving here. I thought of home and pulled the door open. Next thing I know I'm being mobbed by the dead. Not exactly the homecoming I was looking forward to," I said with a frown.

Drake cocked his head at me, "Home is where your family is."

I caught myself before I could snap at him. The more I thought about it, the more I came to agree.

What's a vampire health spa? Shae asked, having gotten flashes from my mind.

Ohhh no, you're not muscling me out of my million-dollar idea. I smiled.

"Your franchise?" James asked.

"Oh yeah, I own a Drakes back on the other side. But don't think that means you can freeload off me," I grinned.

"Wouldn't dream of it," he grinned back. "I'm sure we can

come to some sort of...arrangement," he teased, a bit of his old self emerging.

Shae smacked him upside the head.

"Knock it off before her wife kicks your tail," Shae said.

"I don't mind," Tara said quietly.

James and I both turned and looked at her.

"Besides, Rhi knows what will happen," Tara purred.

I could feel the grin that was hiding beneath her mask.

James looked from her to me. "What will happen?" He looked concerned now. It was good to see him on the defensive for once.

I patted him on the cheek. "Trust me, she'd wear you out." I winked at Shae, who hid a grin at the shocked expression on James's face.

Drake cleared his throat, interrupting our little scene. "I've managed to get a few rooms upstairs to reset if you'd like to rest and clean up," Drake offered as he pulled a brush and dustpan from under the bar and began cleaning up broken glass.

"Sounds good, Drake, thanks," James said.

Drake nodded as a second Drake appeared from the back room.

"This way, please." The new Drake said, indicating another door.

"What the?" Beth jumped. "Where'd that one come from?"

"It's a Long story," James said. "Come on, and I'll explain on the way."

Drake took us up to the rooms via an elevator that hadn't been there earlier when we'd searched the place. Each couple was given their own room and then Drake left us.

"I don't know about you guys, but I need a shower and about 30 hours of sleep," James said as he yawned.

"I don't know about 30 hours, but a shower sounds nice," Shae agreed.

"Is this place secure?" Rachel looked apprehensive.

"Yes," James said. "I don't know what happened before, but now that Drake is here, this will become one of the safest places on the planet. Plus, the Dilla is still parked out front, blocking the only entrance."

"I don't really get this place," Beth said, shaking her head.

Shae stepped up to her. "Easiest if you think of it as magic. It beats any other explanation I've come up with over the years." She smiled. "How about we meet back up in 12 hours? Does that sound good to everyone?"

I saw Beth glance at the watch on her wrist.

"Sounds good," Tara said.

"Night, y'all." I dragged Tara into the apartment and closed the door.

"You think I can eat the food here?" Tara asked me once we were inside.

I hadn't thought of that. I'd been worried about food when I visited her world. I probably should have thought of that before I brought her here. "Guess we'll find out, won't we."

"Sure, fine. But I want a bath first if it might be my last meal. Don't want to leave a dirty corpse. Coming?" she asked as she headed towards the bathroom.

"That a trick question?" I grinned.

Departures

[*COUGH-COUGH* My throat hurts from all that talking; I need a drink. Y'all listen to James for a while. I'll be at the bar. --Rhi]

JAMES

"What do you mean two weeks?" Beth said hotly.

"It will take at least that long to get everything repaired." Drake held his hands up defensively.

"But the local one is fine? You can send people to Austin?" I asked.

"Yes." Drake nodded.

"Are you sure?" Rhi asked with good reason.

"I assure you, that way is once again secured," Drake said.

"What are we supposed to do until then?" Beth threw her arms up.

"Hey, at least it's not a year," Rhi said before receiving an elbow from Tara.

The group gathered around the bar downstairs once again. All signs of damage and human remains had been taken care of, and the bar looked pristine once again. Strangely enough though, there were still no customers.

Shae tried to calm the situation. "Stay here, rest. We have to run down to Ellington Field anyway. We should be back in a day or so. That shouldn't be a problem, should it Drake?"

"Oh no, of course not. This is now one of the safest spots in the city," Drake said.

"Yeah, right," Rachel mumbled.

"No, it's true. Nothing can get through the door that Drake doesn't want to." Rhi pointed at the new front door.

"Yeah, tell that to the first door." Beth eyed the door speculatively, but then her ankle twinged. "Fine," she grunted. "It's not like there's anything for us to do anyway."

We planned on returning to Ellington Field to retrieve Pete and his mother. Even though NASA was just down the road from Ellington, the safety of Pete and his mom was paramount in my mind. That plus the compound back in Austin needed their computer guy back.

"You sure you want us along?" Rhi asked.

"As long as you don't mind the rumble seats," I replied.

"You expecting trouble?" Rhi asked.

"I honestly don't know. But I could use the extra guns...err blades, just in case." Rhi still had her blades but now wore her .45 as well. It was freshly reloaded with ammunition she'd acquired from Drake. Rhi had mentally kicked herself for not asking Drake for ammunition while on Tara's world.

Something Rhi did ask Drake about was this "not blood," as she called it, that she brought back from her other world. It was some sort of shelf-stable blood substitute served up in a pouch, complete with a straw. Drake had created something Rhi had described as "not quite as bad" as the original. So, now we had food we could keep with us instead of relying on acquiring fresh blood all the time.

Tara still only carried her daggers. When I inquired if she would like a gun, she declined, stating she didn't have the time to learn properly, so she'd stick with what she knew.

"Y'all ready to go?" I asked.

"Ready." Tara nodded.

"Actually," Rhi said. "There is one thing."

I didn't have to worry about the sun, but Shae and Rhi did. Drakes had a room set aside just for the sun protection process. It was a series of small pools, each with a slightly different sunscreen tint. This finally explained why Shae had such a varied skin tone back when we were first dating.

The process was simple. You picked your color, got in and let all the air out of your lungs so you'd sink. If you still had problems, there were weights you could use to help you stay submerged. Then, you had to wait for thirty minutes. At the end of the time, your skin would be stained with the protectant, and you would be good for about a week.

Watching them sit under the water like that still freaked me out. Of course, Rhi messed with me the entire time, making faces, lude gestures and such while Shae just seemed to take a nap.

For some reason, neither the tint nor the sun seemed to affect their eyes or mouths. I asked about it, and both of the women just shrugged. There appeared to be a lot about being a vampire that had to be taken with a grain of salt.

"Alright, let's mount up." I nodded.

The parking lot had also been tidied up during our sleep. I wasn't sure what happened to the shamblers and honestly didn't care. When it came to Drakes, I'd given up on trying to rationalize things. The parking lot was clear, and that was all that concerned me as we buttoned up the Dilla and pulled away.

Getting back onto Ellington Field was relatively easy. The guard recognized us and didn't even request we step out of the vehicle. This made me happy as I had no idea how I was going to explain Tara's condition or Rhi's eyes.

To cover for Tara, I thought up a story about her being horribly disfigured from a chemical fire or some such, but I didn't think it would fly. Rhi simply wore a pair of dark sunglasses she'd appropriated from Drakes.

Shae and I were with Pete and his mother when our good luck ran out. Pete's mom was finishing gathering her things when Rhi signaled us.

Trouble, Rhi called to us. *MPs are telling us to get out of the truck, and there's some officer looking all holier than thou.*

Secure the doors and stall. I sent, causing Shae to look at me. *We're on the way.*

"Stay here," I said to Pete and his Mom as Shae and I exited the main tent to discover COL Sureto with four Marines and four Security Forces members surrounding the Dilla. One of the

SF members was yelling at Rhi and Tara to get out of the vehicle.

"COL Sureto, what do you think you're doing?" I asked as we approached.

"Ahh, 'General' Sable, how nice of you to grace us with your presence," COL Sureto said my rank with distaste.

I recognized the tone; we were in trouble. "Tell your troops to stand down, Colonel."

"I think not. Tell your 'people' to get out of that military vehicle," he said, gesturing to two Marines who raised their weapons.

I felt Shae tense behind me.

"Colonel, as you can see, we in no way, shape, or form represent a threat requiring that escalation of force. What is all of this about?" I locked eyes with Rhi inside the vehicle. *Not yet.*

"Well, 'General,' turns out my command has no record of you in their system. So that tells me you're impersonating an officer, you've stolen military equipment, and I'm sure, several other things, all during a time of war," Col Sureto said smugly.

"Your command is misinformed," I said, keeping perfectly still.

"Be that as it may, I've been charged with doing everything and anything in my power to ensure the safety and continued operation of this installation." His smile was aggravating.

"And I'm sure you've exercised that power in ways your command knows nothing about," my statement caused two of the Marines to shift uneasily.

"When society is falling apart, we must do everything we can to keep and maintain good order and discipline," The Colonel countered.

"I'm sure that defense was used extensively at the Nuremberg trials. Look how far it got those folks," I volleyed.

"I tire of this. Take them to BDOC until we can move them to CC," Sureto said.

Now, I sent.

As the two marines moved forward, their rifles flew out of their hands, as did the weapons of the surrounding security detail. The surprised detail watched as their weapons moved to hover above the Dilla's turret.

"Colonel, where is your vice?" I asked calmly.

The Colonel reached for his sidearm, which flew into the air as soon as it cleared his holster.

"I ask again, where is your second in command?" I said.

The Colonel growled and ordered his troops to grab us, but none moved. Seems their battle rattle had a lot of metal in it.

"Colonel?" I repeated.

"Captain Ghrost is in his office," he growled finally.

"And would this be the same vice you had before all of this started?" I played out my hunch. Something had been eating away at me about COL Sureto since our last visit. I had several wild theories, but after having witnessed the roadblock on the way to Houston, only the darker ones seemed to come to mind.

"Of course," The Colonel said.

I noted one of the Marines fidget as the Colonel answered and turned to address him. "What's the truth of the matter, Marine?"

The Marine seemed to struggle with something internally before reluctantly answering. "Major Waldron is currently in CC, sir."

"Really? Let me guess, failure to follow? Desertion? Conduct unbecoming? Or did he jump straight to treason?" I asked.

"Failure to follow a lawful order," The Marine confirmed.

"Shut your mouth, that's an order!" The Colonel took a step towards the Marine and then also seemed to freeze.

"Colonel, please do shut up before you make an even bigger ass of yourself." Turning back to the Marine, I pulled a scrap of paper and drew a pen from one SF member's pocket. I scribbled something and then handed it to the Staff Sergeant SF member. "Does BDOC still have your secure uplink?" I glanced at the Dilla, and the SF member was released.

"Yes." The Sergeant looked down at himself in confusion.

"Then call this in. I'll wait," I said patiently.

The Sergeant looked around the scene again before reaching for his radio and taking the scrap of paper.

She OK? This could take a while, I asked.

Rhi answered, *She says she can handle it.*

I smiled.

It took several minutes for confirmation of my identity to come back through. It had been a breach of security to give open access to anyone not in the Phobos Project, but it was the only way I could think of to keep this from ending in bloodshed.

"It's confirmed, General." The Sergeant said, saluting.

"What? What's confirmed?" The Colonel bellowed.

"His identity, sir. Command confirmed it," The Sergeant said.

Looking around the group. "Does anyone need further proof of who I am?" When no one replied, "Good. I am placing Colonel Sureto under apprehension. Sergeant, please restrain the Colonel."

I waited as handcuffs were placed on the Colonel. "Does anyone else need to be detained, Sergeant?"

The SF looked around the group. "I don't believe so, General."

"Uh..." The marine whom I had spoken to cleared his throat. "I wouldn't let him go just yet, sir." His eyes indicated his fellow Marine.

The indicated Marine let loose with a string of profanity that also resulted in his being restrained.

The rest of the group was released, and their weapons returned. We moved to the confinement area as a group, and Major Waldron was produced. It seems the Major had disagreed with the Colonel's questionable methods of running the base and had been relieved of command and confined in the make-shift jail.

Now the Major was switching places with the Colonel at my order. There was no JAG on the base, so my orders were taken as absolute.

After a frank discussion with the Major, we were back on the road heading for Drakes. I had a feeling the conditions on that base would improve rather quickly.

The transfer of Pete and his mom back to Austin was painless. I was grateful something had finally been easy on this trip.

"How you feeling?" I asked Tara.

"I'm fine," Was all she said.

"Thank you, Tara. You kept a situation from getting way out of hand," I said.

"You didn't exactly help matters James," Rhi said.

"What do you mean?" I asked.

"You kinda escalated the whole thing at every turn," Rhi said.

"The Colonel was wrong. He needed to be replaced," I said in defense.

"I'm not arguing with you James. I'm just saying, you didn't exactly give the man room to back down now did you?" Rhi said flatly.

"I—"

"She's got a point there James," Shae added.

I just looked at her.

"Don't give me that hurt look. You're the one who's bragged about your 'verbal judo' training. I'm just saying you might want to remember what rank you really are."

I opened my mouth to say something, then closed it again. A moment later I turned back to Tara.

"As I was saying, thank you. I wasn't sure if trying to hold all that metal in place would put a strain on you or not."

"No, not to worry. I'm fine," Tara reiterated, not seeming comfortable with the praise.

"Yeah," Rhi chimed in, her flippant self returning. "I'm married to a tough old bird."

"Old?" Tara retorted, looking at Rhi sharply.

"Well, aren't you?" Rhi jibbed.

"Don't start," Tara countered.

"Love you too," Rhi said.

"Watching the two of you is just amazing," Shae said a moment later.

"How so?" Rhi looked at her suspiciously.

"I mean, to us, it's only been a week or so. I know it's been over a year for you. But you still both act as if you've been together much, much longer."

"Old souls," Tara said quietly.

"That, I know about," Shae said as Tara and she regarded one another for a long moment before nodding.

"Well, if you two grannies are done with your quilting bee," I said, causing Rhi to chuckle. "I need some rest. Thank you again for your help today, Tara; you were a lifesaver."

Nodding, she waved.

"What about tomorrow?" Rhi asked.

"What about it?" I replied.

"What are we doing tomorrow?" Rhi asked.

I frowned and looked at Shae before looking back at Rhi. "I honestly don't know right now." I pinched the bridge of my nose and shook my head, trying to shake off the headache I'd picked up.

Shae frowned at me for a minute, concern on her face.

"We'll figure it out in the morning," Shae said before she all but pulled me towards the elevator.

R2 Rescue

JAMES

"We want to come along," Beth said.

"What?" I looked up from the map I was studying. A couple of days had passed since Pete returned to Austin. We'd decided to take a day off before moving on to NASA, but then a massive storm moved through the area from the gulf. I wasn't sure if it had been a hurricane or not, but it had caused a lot of damage to the surrounding area. Drakes, of course, was untouched.

Ever since the storm, I had been studying a map of the JSC. I'd managed to pull up a little data from the uplink in the Dilla, but details on the complex were scarce except for the visitor center stuff. I wasn't sure where to begin.

"We want to go with you to NASA." Beth nodded. "We've been cooped up here for a while now and need to stretch our legs."

"What about your ankle?" I asked.

"It seems good to go." She stomped on the ground several times to show that it wasn't causing her pain.

"It won't be a comfortable ride," I said.

"It's not that long of a trip; we can handle it," Beth said.

I looked at Shae, who'd been silent the whole time.

"Two extra sets of eyes wouldn't hurt," Shae said, looking down at the map. "There looks to be a lot of open area. Either of you ever been there before?"

Rachel and Beth shook their heads.

"Well, grab yourself a t-shirt while we're there." Shae smiled. "What about you, Rhi?"

Rhi looked up from the corner where she was trying to get a stain out of her leather coat. "The space center? I went on a school field trip when I was a kid. All I remember was the freeze-dried ice cream they gave us. It tasted like strawberry cardboard."

"What is a space center?" Tara asked.

"Uh..." Shae started. Tara didn't have space flight where she came from. "It's where—"

"They make vehicles to get where Matlock was from." Rhi provided, not looking up.

"Oh, at orbit right?" Tara asked.

"Yes, above the flying cities, IN orbit." Rhi smiled, glancing up.

"Flying cities?" I asked.

"Yup." Rhi focused back on her jacket, ignoring me.

"You can't expand on that at all?" I pushed.

"Oh sure, just not going to." Rhi grinned evilly.

"Don't be a brat," Shae said, then paused and seemed to reconsider. "On second thought, we have been too easy on him as of late."

"True enough." Rhi agreed.

I looked from Shae to Rhi and asked, "What did I do?"

Rachel and Beth looked around, confused.

"What didn't you do, geesh." Rhi shook her head.

"He doesn't even remember!" Shae threw her hands up in exasperation.

"What?" I frantically thought about anything I possibly could have done to upset them both but couldn't think of anything. My face started turning red in frustration.

Tara suddenly burst out laughing, "You two are horrible."

"Tara!" Rhi gasped. "We need to work on your poker face, girl."

Everyone turned and looked at Tara's leather-clad face. A moment later, they all burst out laughing except for me, who was still confused.

Shae threw an arm around me and kissed my cheek. "You're surrounded by five women now; you need to stay on your toes."

"I hate you," I muttered, causing Shae to chuckle and kiss me on the cheek again. I shook my head, a little bit of my old self peeking through, making her smile.

∞∞Ω∞∞

<u>JAMES</u>

"How many people are in your world?" Tara stared wide-eyed out the window as the downtown Houston area flashed by.

"Huh?" Rhi shook her head, glancing down from the turret. There hadn't been enough seats, so she currently had her ass in a sling, literally. "Uh Shae, we're up to what, about 7 billion now, aren't we?"

"Sounds about right," Shae replied from the front seat of the Dilla.

"I don't know that number. What is a billion?" Tara was sitting in one of the rear passenger seats, Rachel in the other, and Beth in the space between them, leaning against the back wall.

As Rhi began her lecture on our numerical system, Shae looked over at me.

"You ever going to teach me how to drive this thing?" Shae asked.

"If you really want. Not a whole lot to it," I said.

"Oh, I seriously doubt that." She eyed me carefully. *How you doing?* She asked in my head.

My head still hurts, I said slowly, glancing around us as I dodged another snarl of cars.

JSC was only a few kilometers South of Ellington Field. I knew the route between Ellington and Drakes pretty well, considering how many times we'd traveled it now. If it hadn't been for the storm rearranging things, I could have practically driven it blindfolded.

Frowning, *Sorry. Wish there was something I could do,* Shae said.

Me too; I thought being a vampire let you avoid annoyances like headaches, I said.

Normally, yes. But never say never, Shae cautioned.

That's something we've learned a lot about lately, huh? I said.

There was a sound loud enough to be heard over the roaring Dilla.

"What is that?" Shae looked around outside the Dilla.

The sound grew louder and became a ripping sound that ended in a sound like a sonic boom.

"Was that?" Tara started, but Rhi cut her off.

"James!" Rhi yelled frantically. She'd recognized the sound. "That was the same sound as when—"

A blaring alarm filled the vehicle that I instantly reacted to by yanking the wheel hard even before the words "INCOMING! INCOMING! INCOMING!" came across our headsets.

A car in front of us erupted in fire as something smashed into it from above.

I jerked the wheel hard again while straining to see what was on us. "I can't see anything, Shae, Rhi?"

"Nothing here," Shae responded.

"Got 'em, two fast movers, seven o'clock high, moving West...maybe 150 meters?" Rhi answered, rotating the turret and pulling her pistol.

"Secure the turret!" I bellowed, reaching back with one arm and grabbing for her leg. Another alarm sounded, and I had to pull my arm back to swerve again, punching the accelerator just as asphalt exploded on our left.

Shae grabbed Rhi and pulled her down into the cab as Rhi slammed the turret cover shut and locked it.

"Grab the scope tablet!" I yelled over my shoulder at Rhi.

"There!" Shae pointed.

Rhi pulled the small tablet from the pocket beside the seat and thumbed it on, the screen instantly turning on. She'd never dealt with it before, but it seemed pretty self-explanatory. She touched the button that said scope, and instantly, a live image from the top of the Dilla appeared facing forward. She touched the tablet and the camera swiveled as she tried to find where our attackers had gone.

I flipped the cover off a button on the dash panel and smashed it, causing a small display panel on the dash to light up with the same image Rhi was seeing on the tablet.

We watched as the camera suddenly span wildly, and then we were looking at two familiar powered armors flying towards us. "What the—"

"INCOMING! INCOMING! INCOMING!" the computer voice blared again; this time, the Dilla rocked as the force of the energy projectile struck nearby, sending Rhi rolling. She grunted with the impact as she smashed into one of the seats. Instantly, Tara's strong arms grabbed her and held her in place.

"You see them?!?" I growled through gritted teeth.

"Yes, two of them, six o'clock high, 100 meters and closing."

"Double tap one of them," I ordered. Thankfully, Pete had talked our ear off during the trip to Houston. He's been going through the operating manuals for the various Dilla systems. This one had caught my interest due to its nature. I knew I could walk Rhi through the process.

Rhi did as I told her, illuminating one of the armors on the screen in red just as it released another salvo, "James!"

But I was already swerving, trying to find some place of cover, as we'd been caught out in the open on this part of the highway. I managed to dodge, and another car erupting, sending it slamming into us.

"Done!" Rhi called out.

"Tap engage, auto, engage!" I grunted, trying to keep the vehicle moving sporadically.

When she'd double-tapped the armor and colored it red, a new button had appeared on the display labeled "Engage?" She tapped it, and two extra buttons appeared below labeled "Auto" and "Manual." She tapped "Auto," and the "Engage?" button lit back up. When she tapped it, there was a loud whirring from the wall at the back of the vehicle, followed by a violent shaking.

To Shae, it sounded like the world's loudest chainsaw started up behind us. To Rhi and I, it was the symphony of a 20mm chain gun spinning up.

As Rhi watched the monitor, a stream of tracers arced skyward, tracking her target and punching through it like a hot knife through butter. A moment later, the armor exploded in a violent ball of blue and red flame.

The second armor immediately evaded and climbed hard.

"Got one!" Rhi hooted as she watched the gun screen begin to track the second one, but it seemed to be making a hasty retreat into the sky. She double-tapped it before she lost sight of it. The gun continued to track even though she couldn't see it anymore. "The other one looks like it's bugging out, but the gun is still tracking."

"Keep your eyes open. Save the ammo; engage only if it makes another run." I swerved off the road, down an embankment and pulled under a small overpass before throwing it into park. "Everybody OK?"

"Yeah, what was that?" Tara said.

I took the tablet from Rhi and scrolled through it. The computer had lost track of the target, but I left it actively searching now. I glanced at the video and froze it on the power armor just before the shot. "What the hell?" I showed the tablet to Shae.

"What sort of sci-fi is that?" Shae asked.

"That," Rhi said, pointing to the screen, "Is what attacked us in Krodon." Then, she spent the next few minutes retelling the story in more detail.

"And one of them got away?" I asked.

"Yeah," Rhi said.

"How'd they follow you here?" I asked.

"How the hell should I know, James? They're planet-hopping flying robots!" Rhi said defensively.

"Sorry," I said.

"I didn't hear that ripping sound a second time, did anyone else?" When we all shook our heads, she continued. "It must still be here somewhere."

"Probably wasn't expecting us to be able to fight back," I nodded.

"That's not what I was asking about. What was that sound?" Tara pointed to the back of the Dilla.

We piled out of the Dilla and gathered around the back. Part of the roof had rolled away, and what could only be described as R2-D2 with a Gatling gun stood on top of the truck.

"This is a mini-CRAM," I said.

"Or Big Ass Gun," Rhi supplied.

"It's a short-barreled 20mm cannon used to shoot down missiles, artillery, and such." I continued.

"And flying chicks in armor," Rhi helped.

"Well, we used up about a third of our ammo for this beast." I examined the damage to the side of the Dilla from where one of the shots had scored a glancing blow.

"A third? It fired for, like, a couple of seconds," Shae said.

"Yup, and at 75 rounds a second, it goes quick. This thing eats up about 3 tons of our weight." I slapped the side of the Dilla. "But you did good, didn't you?"

"Is he talking to the gun?" Tara asked.

"Yup." Rhi smiled.

"Does it talk back?" Tara continued.

"I hope not," Shae sighed. "We've got enough women issues in this group as it is." She turned and looked at Rhi, "Looks like someone else is in love." Shae smiled.

Rachel was right next to me, firing question after question as she couldn't keep her hands off the massive weapon.

"You got a hose I can borrow?" Beth asked as she watched her friend geeking out on guns again. "I have a feeling that's the only way I'm getting her back in the truck."

"Just offer her the tablet to play with," Rhi suggested. "But disable the fire controls, or we'll end up defenseless." She chuckled.

Bio-Habitat 00117 Observation Post 36211

CR'EON

The alert blared to life causing me to stop recording a new clip mid-fight. Silencing the alarm, I scanned the status board before my eyes went wide. My fingers flew through well-practiced movements, all thoughts of boredom forgotten.

ANGEL GUARD ALERT
BIO-HABITAT 00117

Observation Post 36211, Cr'eon reporting. Two Angel Guard Mark 72 craft entered Bio-Hab 00117 at the attached coordinates and time. The two AG units proceeded to engage a local ground vehicle. Same ground vehicle returned fire using local ordinance and destroyed one of the AG craft, designated AG1.

AG1 craft debris field is documented in attachment 12b.

The second AG craft, designated AG2,

disengaged and departed the area at a high rate of speed. Sensors quickly lost track of AG2, see attachment 13 for direction and speed vectors.

There is no indication AG2 has gated away and probability is high the craft remains in the area. The entire sector has been placed on highest priority for observation and I will continue to monitor.

The local ground vehicle has been tagged, is currently being tracked, and a backtrack has been initiated. See attachment 32 for currently known details of occupants.

It is unknown at this time if the gate-like activity spikes recorded over the past few days have any correlation. A request for CMCUS to analyze the relevant data has been initiated; see attachment 4.

I paused long enough to double-check my work, before flagging the report and sending it via DC OPSNET. I buried the anxiety I felt at sending my first alert and returned to my instruments.

Additional personnel will be here soon to verify and calibrate my equipment. Now that an AG incursion had been recorded in this Bio-Hab, it was considered an active battle space. DC patrols would begin round-the-clock overwatch and I would soon have many more personnel watching over my shoulder. Even though there were other observation posts, mine was the one that recorded it.

The days of keeping myself awake by recording battle clips were over.

Trespassing

JAMES

I left the CRAM active and on automatic now that it had a target profile. I didn't want to get caught by surprise again as we moved on.

The entrance to the space center was gated and closed. Unfortunately, no one was manning the gate. As far as we could see, the surrounding perimeter fence remained intact.

Beth and Rachel exited the Dilla' from the rear doors. Each took a knee and scanned their side of the vehicle like they'd been taught for any mounted patrol.

Rhi slid out of the turret and made a beeline for the gate. Hopping the fence, she entered the gate shack in search of the gate controls.

"No power!" Rhi yelled a moment later.

"Try the gate motor," I yelled back, then realized what I was doing. *The gate motor, check it.* I sent to her mind.

Gate motor? Rhi replied.

I killed the engine and climbed out. I hopped the gate and showed her the covered motor box. Peeling the cover off, it took me a minute to find the release lever. Once pulled, it was easy for the two of us to roll the gate open. I drove the Dilla inside, and Rhi secured the gate behind us.

Rhi hopped back into the turret as Rachel and Beth walked

alongside, scanning the buildings. We decided to half walk/half drive to give us better situational awareness. We weren't sure where we needed to go. I was heading towards the mission control building because it was one of the few I could identify. We scanned the surrounding buildings and trees for signs of life...or un-life.

"I remember playing over there when I was young." I nodded off to our left.

"Rocket Park?" Shae asked, reading the sign next to several static rocket displays.

"Yeah, but back then, the big rocket was outside. I ever tell you my uncle used to fly the escort fighters for shuttle landings?" I asked.

"Nope," Shae said.

"I never met him; my dad just told me about it and showed me pictures," I said.

A moment of silence later, Shae started to speak, but I cut her off.

I'm OK. I'm good. I said, sensing her concern as I stared straight ahead, not looking at her. I knew she had been worried about me since the roadblock. I couldn't blame her; that sort of thing would mess anybody up.

I had to admit I'd been a bit more testy than usual, but I was keeping it in check. Besides, I had a feeling she'd already talked Rhi into having another of our "therapeutic sessions" like the one we'd had back at the Alamo compound. That one had lasted over 12 hours. But Rhi was different now. A year of marriage seemed to have tempered her a bit. I wasn't sure if she'd still be interested in another session with me.

I almost felt Shae making a mental note to return to this later.

As we cleared the park containing all the rockets NASA had used in the past, Rhi slapped the top of the vehicle, and her voice came across the headset. "Contact, two o'clock, 100 meters. Two in the tree line."

The vehicle halted as Rachel took a knee, raising her rifle.

"Looks like...110 yards?" Rachel asked.

"Confirmed," Beth replied, raising her own rifle. "Plus a

straggler at 440 yards."

"Got em. Sending." The report of Rachel's rifle sounded twice, reverberating off the surrounding buildings. A moment later, a third shot rang out.

"Damn." Rhi whistled. Before I could ask, she continued. "There was a third about 300 meters past them that she popped."

With the amount of noise the Dilla made, we knew we would attract attention, so we had decided to take it slow and take out any "rotters," as Beth called them, that came close. I guess Rachel felt 400 meters was close enough. "I'm just glad Drake had been able to resupply her rifle," I said as Rachel and Beth stood up, and we continued forward.

Hatching

JSC PERSONNEL

"Hey, Jonesy."

Herman Jonesy stopped what he was doing and pulled the radio from his belt. "What's up, Johanssen?"

"Looks like the storm might have banged up Vent 2-3. I'm getting a red light on it. Check it out, will you?" Johanssen asked through the radio.

"Sure," Jonesy mumbled. "I'll add it to the list," he grumbled and returned the radio to his belt.

The hurricane that had blown through the JSC two days ago had gotten rid of the monotony, that was for sure. Instead of the routine maintenance Jonesy was used to, he'd been running from one maintenance tunnel to the next, trying to put out a never-ending string of brushfires. Normally, he was part of a much larger maintenance crew, but since only a handful of them had come back after Z Day, he had his work cut out for him.

The few buildings they'd managed to lock down didn't require much in the way of maintenance, honestly. Not since they had been overhauled after 9-11. But even the most secure building was susceptible to a hurricane. It may not take out a wall or something, but water still found some little seam that hadn't sealed properly, or a sub-contractor had "forgotten" to install, thinking no one would notice. But it was job security for Jonesy.

Finishing up his quick patch job, Jonesy wiped his forehead with a well-used rag and picked up his tool pack. That pack was now gold. Having been shut off from the rest of the world, he didn't think they'd get new tools anytime soon. As a result, he never let his tools out of his sight. He couldn't think of anyone who'd want to take them, but he wasn't taking any chances.

He'd found one of those airplane rollie bags and filled it with his tools so he could roll it through the maintenance tunnels between the buildings.

Jonesy seemed to have spent more time in these tunnels in the last three months than in his ten years at JSC. But when the surface was covered with those things, the tunnels were the only safe way to move from one building to the other.

When this had all started, JSC had managed to lock down and secure the gates. That had lasted all of a week before some idiot drove through the fence near gate four. Since then, those monsters had been slowly taking over the complex.

Luckily, Jonesy had been at work when Z Day hit. So many people had gone home and not come back. But Jonesy had stayed because he had a duty to the mission. It had nothing to do with the fact he had nothing waiting for him back at his apartment but a stack of bills he couldn't pay.

He ensured he was heading towards the right vent by double-checking his tunnel map. Each of the tunnels had these surface access blocks to ensure proper ventilation. The blocks were about a meter high and roughly three meters by three meters. A small vent portal on each side allowed the wind to swirl through, keeping a fresh supply moving through the tunnels. It also helped to vent any trapped gasses from machinery. Houston's summer heat was known for not being very forgiving on machinery.

Jonesy didn't see anything out of the ordinary when he arrived on the scene. He checked each vent, and they didn't appear damaged. When he tried to close them though, one of the four refused to move. Upon closer inspection, he found what looked like the piece of a tree had gotten wedged in the hinge. He would have to push the vent open more than usual to free the limb. When he tried, his hand slipped on what appeared to be the grease they used to lubricate the hinge system.

Jonesy hissed as he saw the blood well up from the cut on his palm. It wasn't deep; he wouldn't need stitches, thankfully, but he didn't have any Band-Aids on him at the moment. He wrapped his hand using the rag he'd used to wipe his brow earlier and tied it on until he could get to a first aid kit.

Turning back to the vent, with a curse Jonesy pushed the limb free. Now unhindered, the vent closed automatically. Had Jonesy not been so distracted by the cut on his hand, he may have noticed the limb was still wearing a shoe.

"Johanssen, try it now." Jonesy spoke into his radio. The vent opened and closed as he watched.

"Looks good, thanks, Jonesy," Johanssen said.

"I'll put it on your tab." Jonesy sighed and pulled out the rest of today's checklist. He shined his flashlight on it, made a small tick mark and moved on to the next job on the list.

Several hours later, Jonesy hung up his hard hat in the small maintenance locker room.

"You look like shit," A coworker said.

"Gee, thanks." Jonesy shook his head at the man. He hung up his tunnel scrubs and closed his locker door, looking at his hand. It hadn't bled long, and he'd been able to clean it up and get some proper band-aids before his next job. He swore he'd never leave his gloves in his locker again. Then he returned to his locker, opened it, and retrieved his gloves before shoving them into his tool bag.

"You on detail again tonight, Jonesy?" Kurt, one of the actual cooks at JSC, asked as Jonesy wheeled his tool bag into the kitchen.

"It's Tuesday, ain't it?" Jonesy growled.

"What's got you in a foul mood tonight?" Kurt asked.

Jonesy sighed, "Sorry, Kurt, just one of those days, I guess." Chuckling to himself, "More like one of those months."

"Yeah, but whatcha gonna do?"

"Right?" Setting his tool bag in the corner, Jonesy pulled an apron off the wall. "What can I help with tonight?" Jonesy wasn't a cook, never had been. The extent of his cooking ability had been not burning popcorn in the microwave.

Since only about 20% of the employees returned to JSC after Z Day, a lot of jobs needed extra help. So, the "survivors" had drawn up an additional duty list. Tuesdays was Jonesy's day in the kitchen for dinner.

"Could you start on those potatoes?"

"You found MORE potatoes?"

"What can I say? They're cheap," Kurt smiled. He was a nice guy; everyone liked Kurt, and not just because he could turn anything he found into a meal worth savoring. "Amazing thing, the potato. You can do anything with it," Kurt said.

"What are you doing with it tonight?" Jonesy asked.

"Good old mash." Kurt smiled.

Jonesy moved down to the end of the counter and started washing potatoes.

"Why are you here, Jonesy?" Kurt asked.

"Cause it's Tuesday?" Jonesy replied sarcastically.

"No, why are you here at JSC? Why'd you come back?"

"I told you, I never left."

"That's right, sorry," Kurt said.

"What about you?" Jonesy said.

"Me? Nowhere to go. The family was spread to the four winds before all this, Ex-wife as well. I went home long enough to grab JT and then high-tailed it back here. Figured I knew the food here; it was bound to be better than at one of those refugee camps."

"Where is JT?" Jonesy asked.

"Where else?" Kurt pointed up to the pass.

An orange tabby cat lounged lazily underneath the heat lamps. Before Z Day, an animal in the kitchen would have gotten the place shut down by the health department. Now, JT had become a part of the kitchen. Everyone coming for a meal would give him a scratch under the chin or behind the ear. He always responded with a loud purr.

"Hear anything new from the boys up top?" Kurt asked.

"Are you kidding? I work underground. You think those

guys are going to bother with me?" Jonesy snorted.

"You'd be surprised. Since our big family here got so much smaller, people are starting to rub elbows more with folks they'd never spoken to before," Kurt said.

"Well, I'd get one of their nice white shirts dirty if they rubbed elbows with me," Jonesy grumbled, sorting through the spuds.

"You should get out more," Kurt said.

"Ha!" Jonesy barked.

"You know what I mean, Herman. You spend all of your time down in those tunnels now; you need to come up for a breath of fresh air," Kurt said.

"That's why I'm here, for your sparkling personality," Jonesy waved a peeler at Kurt. "Besides, I don't have enough time to keep this place running as it is. This," he pointed at the pile of potatoes in front of him, "is the social highlight of my week."

Kurt chuckled. "OK, I surrender. I'll shut up." He reached over and turned up the MP3 player, filling the kitchen with some lively music.

The next morning, Jonesy's hand ached. He rolled off the couch in the small office he'd been sleeping in the last couple of weeks and headed down the hall to the bathroom. Peeling off the Band-Aids, he grimaced at the puffy red scrape. He'd need to stop by later and see if one of the medical guys was around. The last thing he needed was to get an infection from such a minor scrape.

Jonesy rewashed the wound and slapped on a new set of Band-Aids before setting off to work.

He skipped the cafeteria this morning on account of his stomach wasn't being nice to him. He probably shouldn't have had a second helping of dinner last night; it'd been too rich.

Arriving at the maintenance shack, Jonesy printed off the day's list of "chores" and set to it. There weren't as many today as usual. He crossed his fingers and hoped it would stay that way. As per the norm, it was a futile gesture.

Half the guys on the second shift didn't show up for work. Apparently, he wasn't the only one who'd had too many potatoes. Jonesy had already been to the bathroom three times and knew it was only a matter of time before there would be a fourth.

He only ate half the sandwich he picked up for lunch, wrapping the other half up and putting it in the fridge with his name on it. He managed to make it through the rest of his shift, but by the end, his head was spinning and he was having trouble with his eyes. Skipping dinner, he went straight to the couch in his room and died.

$$\infty\infty\,\Omega\,\infty\infty$$

JSC PERSONNEL

"How am I supposed to keep this place running? Huh?" George Carman threw his hands up. He was the acting superintendent. "We're already running with barely 20% of our original staff, and now you're telling me over half of them are sick?"

"George..." Kyle tried.

"Don't George me!" He spun around and shook his head.

"When was the last time you slept?" Kyle Atlas looked at the man forced into the hot seat after Z Day. Kyle'd been watching George literally aging into an old man the last three months. Kyle knew he was only in his mid-thirties, but right now, with the stress lines, dark circles and splotchy complexion, George looked as if he was well into his fifties.

"Sleep? What's that?" George half-joked.

"You can't keep people from getting sick. Honestly, I'm surprised it hasn't happened sooner. Everyone here has been working around the clock, yourself included, without proper rest," Kyle said.

"Rest? Who can rest with those things out there?" A vein in George's forehead throbbed.

"Yes, but we're safe in here. We've locked this place down tight, and the people we do have are keeping it that way. You need to get some rest before you give yourself a stroke," Kyle said.

"I've got three astronauts in orbit at the moment..."

"Yeah, and they're the safest people in our solar system right now. I guarantee they will still be there in eight hours after you've had some sleep," Kyle said.

They both turned as there was a knock on the door. "Come in Jimmy," George said.

The current head of security stepped into the office. His uniform was crisp and clean. No one knew how he did it. Most folks were happy just to have clean shorts. Jimmy had been promoted from deputy security chief when his boss hadn't returned after Z Day.

"Got the latest numbers," Jimmy handed the paper to George.

"That many are sick?" George looked up at Jimmy, eyes wide.

"They're thinking it was dinner last night. Kurt has thrown everything out and bleached the place from top to bottom twice. Whatever it was should be dead now," Jimmy said.

"Food poisoning." George shook his head.

"That's good!" Kyle said.

"Good?" George asked.

"Yes. People get over food poisoning in two to three days tops. It also means no one else should be getting sick; it's not contagious." Kyle breathed a sigh of relief.

"So we just have to stick it out a couple of days, and we should be back to 'normal,'" George sighed. "Thanks Jimmy, keep me posted. Anything else?"

"Nope, everything's still high and tight. All five buildings are still secure. We had some minor damage to one of the vent systems, but it was a quick fix." Jimmy nodded.

"What about the surrounding buildings? It wasn't that big of a hurricane, but still," George asked.

"Looks like some minor damage to a few buildings, but it appears superficial. Did you want me to send someone out to assess?" Jimmy sounded reluctant to send someone from security out. They had been hit worse than any other department after Z Day. Only three people from security had returned to JSC.

"No, as long as we're still good, let's keep it that way. Thanks, Jimmy," George said wearily.

Nodding, the security chief left the office.

"Hell of a way to start the day," George sighed.

∞∞Ω∞∞

JSC PERSONNEL

While what would have been called Hurricane Hilary (had the World Meteorological Organization still been around) wasn't a particularly strong storm, it was still strong enough to inflict damage. One such instance had been when a large piece of debris had been hurtled into a wall. Under normal circumstances, the wall would have been fine. But this section of wall hadn't set correctly due to a poor initial concrete mixture along with years of humid conditions and poor maintenance. As a result, a section of the brittle wall had collapsed upon impact.

Since the building wasn't one of high importance to the current Mission Control Center (MCC) priority list, it wasn't checked on frequently. Additionally, the breach had been on the opposite side from MCC, where it couldn't be easily seen.

Due to the fact the building wasn't kept under a watchful eye, it had become the favorite "go to" location for Rufus and Alexis when they were looking to share some alone time. Their frantic romance had sprung up two weeks after Z Day when Alexis had learned her fiancé had been killed in the panic. Rufus, who'd been after Alexis since she started at JSC, became that shoulder for her to cry on, which led to the torrid affair.

It is a well-documented fact that zombies have no manners. Unfortunately, neither of the two romantics had bothered to check the building this time when they snuck in from the tunnels. Had they bothered, instead of stripping the moment they were inside, they probably could have avoided the rude coitus-interruptions and would likely still be alive today. They likely would have remembered to close the maintenance tunnel door behind them as well.

∞∞Ω∞∞

JSC PERSONNEL

"So half of them are still sick?" George looked at the report the following day.

"Yes, sir," Jimmy said. "Half of them showed up for work this morning, they still look like crap, but at least they're on their feet."

"At least there's that. Let's make sure and have someone check on the others to make sure they're OK," George said.

"Already got someone on it."

"Thanks, Jimmy," George said, one less thing for him to worry about.

∞∞Ω∞∞

JSC PERSONNEL

"Yo, Roger?"

"Yep?" Roger said into his radio.

"This is the voice of God," Jesus said.

"And what is it you require, oh lord?" Roger said, playing along with the old joke.

"Looks like I've got an alarm light on door 472."

Roger glanced at his clipboard. "Uh, that's the machine shop, right?"

"Yeah, the maintenance tunnel access door. It's weird."

"How so?" Roger asked.

"The alarm just came on, but the door log shows it having been open for the past 16 hours," Jesus said.

"Gotta be a glitch."

"Gotta be," Jesus agreed.

"OK, I'll head over," Roger sighed, it seemed everything was a bother nowadays.

"Roger Roger."

"Don't start that crap again, please. I hate those movies," Roger said.

"How can you hate Star Wars and work for NASA?"

"That's NOT Star Wars. That is some stupid money-making scheme made up by Lucas. Star Wars started with episode 4 and ended with episode 6. End of story," Roger said with his usual finality.

"Touchy much?" Jesus offered.

"You try getting over food poisoning and then tell me how you're feeling," Roger said.

"I'm so sorry. Now suck it up and get back to work."

∞∞Ω∞∞

JSC PERSONNEL

Thompson looked down at her clipboard and then back at the number on the office door. It was the next room on the list.

She knew she was the lowest security member on the totem pole since there were only three of them. Add to this she'd only started two weeks before Z Day. Regardless, it still sucked that she'd been elected to go around and check on all the sick people. At least it wasn't contagious.

But still, so far every person she'd checked on had smelled like death warmed over and seemed to be expelling fluids out of both ends. If she'd wanted to deal with that, she'd have been a nurse. She didn't want to do that.

Thompson wanted to be the one calling the shots, busting people when they broke the rules. She didn't want the dangers that went along with being a street cop. Getting shot at every day wasn't her idea of job fulfillment. Busting pencil pushers whose britches got too big for them was more up her alley.

Glancing back down at the list, she knocked on the door, "Mr. Jonesy, this is JSC security. I'm just checking in on you to see how you're doing."

Most of the people she'd checked on today had taken quite a

while to come to the door. So, when the man hadn't come to the door after a minute or so, she wasn't ready to kick the door in just yet. When she didn't hear any movement from inside, she tried again.

"Can you please come to the door, Mr. Jonesy?"

There was a sound from inside and then a loud crash. Thompson fished her keys out of her pocket as she heard what sounded like a cry from inside.

"Mr. Jonesy, are you alright? I heard a crash; I'm coming in, sir."

The door swung open to a dark interior. The office wasn't very big, but someone had put something over the windows to block the sun. The clipboard indicated Mr. Jonesy usually worked nights, so he probably did it so he could sleep during the day. Still, the window job wasn't 100%. Some light still snuck through and caused the remains of a glass coffee table to glitter on the floor.

Her mistake was taking her eyes off the glass. Had she watched it, she would have seen the reflection of movement and probably would have had time to react. Instead, she looked to her left, groping for the light switch. By the time she finally found it, it was too late.

∞∞Ω∞∞

JSC PERSONNEL

"Sir? Can you come down to G4?" The voice on the phone asked.

"What is it?" George replied.

"We've got movement on JSC," the person on the phone said.

"If it's stumbling around, I don't care," George said.

"No, sir, it's not one of them," The voice said.

George made his way from his office to one of the control rooms, where he met up with Ryan, the controller he'd spoken to on the phone. Pointing at the screen, "What the hell is that

Ryan?"

"Some sort of military vehicle, sir," Ryan said.

"I figured that part out for myself. But what is it?" George asked.

"Got me, sir," Ryan said plainly. "Never seen anything like it."

They watched as the Dilla entered JSC and secured the gate behind them.

"That Gate 1?" George verified.

"Yes sir."

"What uniform is that?" George pointed at the two people flanking the vehicle.

"Never seen it before. Maybe a SWAT uniform or something?" Ryan guessed.

"No, look at that gun on top. That's military." George studied the vehicle a moment. "They look like they have an FM antenna. Can we contact them?" George asked.

"Not sure." The controller tapped his headset. "Barney, can you tap into local military FM frequencies? Yeah, check feed 121. George wants to try and contact them. OK." Turning back to George, "He says it'll take a few minutes, but he'll see what he can do."

"Good, make sure and—" George stopped talking when he saw the vehicle stop and the soldier on the left open fire. "Can you pan out?" George asked.

"No, but I can..." A moment later, a second image appeared from a reverse angle. Now, they could see what the military had been shooting at.

"Wow," Ryan said.

"What?"

"That was a good shot. Kneeling...had to be over 300 meters. Single shot to the head. Impressive." Ryan whistled.

"Really?" George had never touched a gun, let alone shot one.

"Yeah. My dad used to practice for hunting season. Sometimes, he'd drag me to the range with him. He'd let me shoot occasionally, but only off the bench, not kneeling. That is a difficult shot, especially with how quickly it went down," Ryan said.

George didn't care. He just wanted to know why the military had shown up on JSC after all this time. "What are they doing here?"

"George?" The panicked voice crackled in his earpiece. "George, are you there? We have a situation."

"What is it, Zweller?" George said.

"Uh...one of the security people is dead and—"

"What? What do you mean dead?" George hadn't meant to say it so loudly, but it had caught him off guard.

The few heads in the room turned from their consoles and looked at him, reminding George of meerkats on the Discovery Channel.

"What do you mean dead?" George turned away and whispered.

"The girl...I don't know her name, she..." The contact broke off in a screech of feedback. "Get away from it! Run!"

"Zweller? What's going on Zweller?" George tried to keep his voice level, but the last transmission was frantic.

"OK," Zeller said to someone else.

"Zweller?" George stressed.

"What? Oh, yeah, yeah, I'm here."

"What happened?" George demanded.

"Someone found the security girl in the dorm building. She was on the floor of the hallway, covered in blood. She looked like she had crawled out of one of the rooms. But it's OK now; we've locked off the dorm."

"What do you mean locked off? Why?" George barked.

"One of them was in there," Zweller said.

"One of who?" George asked. "You're not making sense."

"The zombies." Zweller's voice cracked. It took him a minute to get his voice back under control. "There was a zombie in there. It came out of the room she'd crawled from. We got the hell out and locked off the wing."

"We have other people in there, Zweller," George said.

"You want me to let the zombie into the main building?" Zweller offered.

"NO!" George said way too loudly. "Just stay there; I'll send Jimmy to you right now." Clicking over to the security frequency, "Jimmy, you there? Get over to the entrance of the dorm. Zweller is there and says he's locked a—" George covered his mouth and the mic with his hand so no one else could hear him. "He says there's a zombie inside the dorm. He also says one of yours is in there as well, and they're...down."

"What? What do you mean down?" Jimmy demanded.

"Just get there!" George was trying to maintain his calm, but he could feel his blood pressure rising in his ears now.

"Sir?" Ryan said.

Turning back to the controller, "Yes?"

"We think we can scan the frequencies, but we don't know if they'll hear us," Ryan said.

"Give it a try," George said.

Quarter and Search by Twos

SHAE

"Got fast movers on the right," Rachel called out.

Rhi looked that way but didn't see anything. "Where?"

"Building, second floor," Rachel said.

"Coming up on an open area on the left," Beth added.

Why do they do that? I asked as I looked first one way and then the other as the others called out.

Part of training. You see something, no matter how trivial, you call it out. You see an open area where we'll lose cover or something suspicious, you call it out, James said.

Doesn't that get tiring? I asked.

Yup, but you get used to it. Trains you to keep your head on a swivel, James said, scanning the area around us yet again.

No wonder you get headaches. I smiled and glanced at James, but he was paying more attention to our surroundings. I frowned as I could sense his anxiety coming through our link.

It seemed I was always worried about him lately. I knew it was starting to annoy him, but what could I do? I was his creator, and he was my fiancé. Worrying came with both jobs.

The radio crackled in our headsets.

"Attention, military vehicle, this is the Johnson MCC. Please identify yourself."

"James..." I started.

"I heard it. You got it?" James asked, not taking his eyes off the road.

I nodded, "This is..." and then I had no idea what to say; I'd never spoken on a military radio before. I glanced at James for help.

Have fun with it. He grinned.

Have fun with it he says, I rolled my eyes. *Fat load of help you are.*

"This is Special Agent Shae. We..." I took a breath and settled, falling back into my old court etiquette routine. "We're attempting to make contact with an employee here." I paused as a gunshot rang out. "Looks as if your security has been breached."

The voice on the other end replied hesitantly. "Yes, that's been a problem for a while now. Who are you looking for?" The voice asked.

Trent Miller, James told me as I mentally questioned him for his friend's name.

"We're looking for a Trent Miller. Is he still here?" I asked over the radio. I think I remembered Trent. He was one of James's high school friends who played Boffgaurd back then.

It took a minute for the reply. "Yes, he's still on the complex."

"Good to hear. Things out here seem to be a bit hostile," I said as another shot rang out. "Can you give me a secure location where we can contact you?"

This time, the delay was longer.

It's like they don't trust us or something, I mused.

Well, we are toting a BFG, James replied.

BFG? I asked.

Big Fuc—

"OK agent. Here's what you need to do," The voice cut off James's explanation.

We followed the directions and made our way between several buildings. Eventually, we parked against a large multi-storied complex of buildings that looked to all be connected. There were no windows on the ground floor of the buildings.

The only entryway seemed to be a large glass walkway

between two of the larger buildings. The directions had said to park in the parking lot, but James ignored that part and backed right next to the glass doors. We could see three people inside, watching us.

Once the parking lot had been cleared, we dismounted and secured the Dilla. As Rhi was locking down the turret, she grabbed the control tablet and jumped out.

Inside the glass walkway, secured doors led to the buildings on the left and right of us. Large red lights above each door indicated that they still had power.

A tired-looking man with dark, gray-streaked hair stepped forward and held out his hand to me.

"Agent, I'm Director George Carman." He shook hands with me before continuing. "This is my head of security, Jimmy Geist, and my personnel supervisor, Kyle Atlas."

"I would say it was a pleasure, but under the circumstances." I shook his hand with a diplomatic smile as he nodded in understanding.

"I don't mean to be rude, but do you have identification? We are still attempting to maintain some semblance of security here," George asked politely.

"Of course." I fished my military ID out and handed it over. I held my hand out to James, and he handed over his ID without a word. "Unfortunately, we're the only two still with ID cards; the rest have been..."

"Volunteered," Rhi said, smiling from behind her dark sunglasses. Figuring her eyes would add even more questions about our motley group, Rhi decided to hide behind her shades even while inside.

"Good a word as any nowadays." I threw a glance at Rhi.

I heard that look, Rhi sent.

"Needless to say," I continued, "we'll take whatever help we can get."

"That," Carman took James's ID, "is something I completely understand."

"This," I indicated James, "Is General Sable. That is Formerly Retired Captain Kachou and her aid Tara; please don't ask about her protection uniform." I flashed my most disarming smile. "Our precision engagement team—"

"Corporal Sinclair," Beth said with a nod.

"Specialist Ross." Rachel waved over her shoulder as she was eyeballing the parking lot. "S'cuse me." Rachel stepped outside the door with Beth pulling it shut behind her. While still standing, Rachel's rifle barked three times.

From inside, the sound was surprisingly dampened. None of us could see what she was shooting at though.

Beth looked over her shoulder. "Sorry about this. She's been unable to do any distance shooting in a while and gets kinda twitchy." Beth smiled and held the door open as Rachel came back inside. "Better?"

"Yes, thank you," Rachel said in a small voice.

"Well," Carman returned the ID cards, not taking his eyes off Rachel. "Mr. Miller is down in one of the control labs but should be here in a few minutes."

I noticed Carman glancing nervously over my shoulder at the doors behind us.

"If you would like to come this way, we can get out of sight of any of those...things," George offered.

"We call them rotters," Beth supplied. "Easier to remember." She nodded.

"Right. This way, please." George didn't smile and was obviously nervous but I wasn't quite sure of what.

We passed through a set of doors into the main building. Several doors lead off in various directions. I noticed the security chief made sure to double-check the doors we passed through to verify they were closed and locked. Once that was done, he checked the doors we hadn't used as well. He looked through a small window back into the area we'd just departed.

Something's off, I sent to James and Rhi.

What's up? James came back, looking around casually.

They're worried about the doors to the other building back there. At least one of them has been constantly watching them since we came inside, I said.

I did hear some thumping while we were standing there, Rhi added. *I thought it was just machinery or something.*

Rhi, pass it along to the others to keep an eye out, I said.

"James!" a new voice called out from up the hall. A man came bounding down towards us.

"Hey, Trent," James said as they embraced. "Glad to see you in one piece."

"The same. I haven't heard anything out of Austin," Trent said.

"I take it you know the General?" Carman asked.

"General?" Trent stepped back, giving James an appraising look.

"Field promotion," James grinned.

"Some promotion," Trent said, turning to Carman. "Oh yeah. James and I go way back..." Trent's eyes bulged as he saw me. "Is that who I think it is?"

"Yeah," James smiled. "Long story."

I smiled and nodded.

Beth snapped her fingers twice before the sound of Rachel's rifle bolt snapping grabbed everyone's attention.

"I hate to break up the reunion, but do you know you have rotters in the building, Mr. Carman?" Beth was staring out one of the door's small windows back the way we'd come.

Rhi was next to Beth instantly. *Yup, that's my thumper.*

By the way Trent is looking at Carman; they haven't told anyone, I said, putting it all together.

"Looks like we came just in time," I said to Carman. "Not to step on your security chief's toes, but do you need some assistance?"

Atlas spoke up when Carman didn't. "Yes, please. Our security detail has been drastically reduced—"

"Kyle!" Carman interrupted.

"What? We've lost that building, and we still have people inside. We can't do anything about it, and they're offering to help," Atlas said.

"The dorm is infected?" Trent gasped. "When did that happen?"

"It doesn't matter—" Carman started.

"Gentlemen," I said smoothly, stepping in and cutting through the growing chaos. "Give us a map and a personnel count. We'll happily rescue who we can for you." My voice was a practiced calm I'd often used when directing people without telling them what to do. I'd found that particular tone usually left little room for argument.

Geist pulled a small tablet from the carrier bag he wore. He thumbed it on, tapped a few keys and handed it over.

"This is the current layout of each floor," Geist began. "We've sealed off all the other access points from this building."

I looked at the tablet, "This thing is a maze!" The insane mish-mosh of connecting corridors and maintenance floors was an architect's nightmare.

"Add-ons," Trent said in way of explanation. "When it takes Congressional approval to build a new building, you don't call it a new building; you call it an annex."

"Jimmy," Carman said. "Send Victor to guide them through. If they're going in, they can't miss anything." Turning to me, Carman continued. "No offense, but it's still a secure area; you'll need an escort."

"Victor's missing," Jimmy said before I could respond.

"What?" Carman said.

"He hasn't reported in yet; he was one of the sick ones," Jimmy said.

"What about Roberta?" Carman tried.

"Unconfirmed reports are that she's...dead," Jimmy said reluctantly.

Carman didn't comment on the report; he looked like he'd already heard it. "In that case, you'll need to—"

"I'll go," Trent volunteered.

"Out of the question. Jimmy here will—" Carman started.

"What?" Jimmy cut him off incredulously.

"Mr. Carman, if I can be honest a minute," James cut in. "We really don't need the help. Yes, it will take longer, but bringing your personnel with us will endanger them and us."

"You're not going in there alone; it's out of the question," Carman demanded.

"Well, sending your security chief may not be the best bet." James turned to Jimmy, "Mr. Geist, do you still have power in that building? Comms? Video? Any monitoring ability?" James asked.

"All of that. We're all tied into the same power grid," Jimmy said.

"What about portable radios?" I asked, sensing where James was heading. "If Mr. Geist could provide us with radios, he could guide us through the building using the CCTV and keep an eye on our backs simultaneously," I offered.

"That's fine, but you're still not going in alone," Carman said.

I could tell the man wasn't going to budge. He'd been through an impossible situation, and he was hanging onto whatever procedures he could out of a false sense of security.

"Mr. Miller, if you still wish to, you may escort them," Carman relented.

Trent nodded reluctantly, just now realizing what he'd gotten himself into.

While we waited for Geist to get the radios, I turned to Trent's worried face. "Don't worry, we'll keep you safe. Just stick by James, and we'll take care of the rest." I gave him my most reassuring smile. "Our team has been doing this a while now."

"Yeah," Trent half-heartedly cheered.

∞∞Ω∞∞

<u>JAMES</u>

We spent the remaining time reviewing the floor plans and Trent explaining sections in more detail as we all asked questions.

When Geist returned, he had radios for each of us with earpieces. Everyone got a quick rundown on the radios before we discussed the easiest way to blanket search the building. When we were done, Geist handed Trent a security card that gave him full access and returned to the security monitoring station.

We waited until Geist did radio checks with us and then turned towards the doors.

"Ready?" I glanced around the room to see that everyone was good to go.

"Let's do this," Trent said.

I chuckled to myself. "Remember, keep quiet, keep within arm's reach of me at all times. Anything happens to us, you hightail it out of there." I paused and considered. "Do you want a gun?"

"James," Trent said, looking around. "If it gets to that point, plenty of guns will be lying around.

Nodding, "OK, let's go," I said.

Our group stepped into the lobby entryway and took up positions outside the door where "Thumpy" was still banging away. Rhi unsheathed her blades as Tara moved to the door. Trent slid the card across a panel, and Tara pulled the door. It was over as it began, and Rhi kicked the remains back into the building. We filed in wordlessly.

It was surprisingly dim inside the building. A reception desk was directly ahead of us, and a hallway led off in either direction. There was no movement in sight.

"Why is it so dark in here?" Shae asked Trent.

"They converted this building from administration to living quarters, for the most part. They keep the lights dim for those trying to sleep," he whispered.

Of course, to our core group, the lowlight wasn't noticeable with our night sight. Beth and Rachel both had flashlights but hadn't turned them on yet. Tara apparently could see rather well in the dark.

"Happy you came along now?" I whispered to Beth.

"Just thrilled, thanks," she chided back. "We're set." Beth and Rachel had set up a firing line on the left hall while Shae and I had taken the right, armed with the backup MP5s from the Dilla. Rhi and Tara stood in the middle, blades ready in case they were needed.

I still couldn't believe I'd forgotten about the submachine guns in the Dilla when Shae and I first entered Drakes. That's what I get for getting excited and rushing in.

"Whenever you're ready," I said quietly.

The relative silence of the building was shattered as Beth

began to bellow.

"THIS IS THE US ARMY. IN ACCORDANCE WITH THE INSURRECTION ACT, THIS BUILDING IS QUARANTINED. IF YOU ARE CURRENTLY SAFE, STAY THERE. WE WILL FIND YOU. AGAIN, IF YOU ARE SAFE, STAY—" was as far as Beth got.

"Fast mover," Rachel called out a moment before her rifle spat flame. The figure sprinting full out at them landed face-first on the carpet and slid to a stop.

"Uh, got two...slow ones," Shae hesitantly called out, not used to the jargon.

Don't worry about it. Call out what you see in simple terms. As long as we can understand, you're good. I watched the two shamblers appear from the middle of the hallway. We waited for them to get closer before dropping them.

"Another shambler, far right," Shae called more confidently this time.

*See, easier with practice." I glanced back at Trent, who flinched with each shot. "Might as well plug your ears; we'll be at this for a while."

We had taken a page from Beth and Rachel's playbook. Their team's tactic when entering an infested building was to set up a defensive position at the entrance and make enough noise to bring the zombies to them. They would methodically take down each one with well-timed precision. If things got too bad, they'd back out of the building and try from a different entrance or wait and try again later.

Trent nodded and put his fingers in his ears as the gunfire rang out again.

We continued for a good 20 minutes. The zombies came in ones and twos, allowing for easy pickings. Geist would give us a heads-up when he saw movement on the cameras heading towards us.

Rhi stepped over to give Beth a hand with a fast mover who'd gotten a little too close. Beth had only winged the zombie instead of putting it down. Rhi was in the process of dispatching it with her swords to save a bullet when—

"Look out!" Trent hollered, but it was too late.

The crawler was pretty much just a head and partial torso with one good arm. Pulling itself around from behind the reception desk took nearly twenty minutes. As a result, it had worn its fingertips down to the bone.

The leather around Tara's lower leg had become brittle with age. She'd been meaning to replace it but one thing after another had kept her from the maintenance.

Tara was completely unaware of the zombie when its hand grabbed her leg. Its bone-tipped fingers dug deeply into the leather and pulled.

At the same time the zombie pulled, Tara reacted and violently jerked her leg in the opposite direction. The zombie came away with a large chunk of Tara's armor, but not her skin. Because the armor ripped away so easily, Tara never noticed its loss.

Rhi brought her sword down reflexively, spearing the creature's skull.

"Fast movers!" Rachel and Shae called out simultaneously as the zombies rounded the far corners of both halls at full tilt.

"Who opened the floodgates?" I wondered aloud as all four guns opened up and more zombies rounded the corners.

"No, seriously, what the shit is this?" Rhi bellowed as she went on guard at the approaching horde.

"You OK?" Trent asked over the gunfire as he got Tara's attention.

"Yes, he didn't get me," Tara said.

"Are you sure? It looks like you're—" But Trent didn't get a chance to finish as I called for Tara to back us up. The wave of zombies was thickening.

Tara moved to stand between us, knives at the ready.

"If this keeps up, we might need your metal storm," I yelled over the gunfire.

"I'm ready," Tara replied, her body tensing for the fight developing in front of her.

Then, as quickly as it began, the flood stopped.

"Geist, what the hell was that? Where'd they come from?" I asked.

"Still trying to figure it out. Give me a minute," came Geist's voice over the radio.

"Rhi, how y'all doing?" I called over my shoulder.

Rhi looked at her two counterparts, who nodded, "Sittin' pretty. You?"

I glanced at Shae and Tara and then over my shoulder at Trent. "Good to go, but we're not out of the woods yet; stay frosty."

"Ice cold," Rhi muttered back.

I felt Shae watching Rhi and me. Her thoughts were inside my head, but she wasn't talking. It was like I could read her inner monolog.

Shae'd been smiling at how Rhi and I had fallen back into soldier mode so easily. About how much the two of us had in common with one another. Part of her was jealous she'd never have the same sort of relationship as Rhi and I had. She'd never understood the whole "brotherhood of arms" deal. But watching the two of us slip back into our soldier roles gave her a brief insight.

I wanted to say something, reassure her, but now wasn't the time.

We waited another few minutes, but nothing else shambled around the corner.

"By my guesstimate, we've got more bodies here than are on our personnel list. Where are they coming from?" Shae asked quietly.

"No clue," I said, glancing around. "OK, we're moving forward." I signaled the four of us (Tara, Trent and Shae) to advance down our hallway.

As we approached a door, Shae would cover the hall while I banged on the door and waited. If nothing moved, I'd open the door and go in with Tara right behind, leaving Trent with Shae to watch the hall. After we'd clear a room, we'd move to the next.

We worked our way to the end of the hall before following it around the corner. It was a slow process, and we occasionally heard a gunshot from the others as they worked down their hall.

"OK Beth, we should be about parallel now. Go ahead and start moving forward." I waited for her reply before continuing with our search and clear. By the time we had finished the ground floor, we had confirmed we'd put down more bodies than were on our list of missing personnel.

"Something's not right here, Geist," Shae said as we sat resting at the end of the hall. We'd all met back up in a corner near the stairs. We'd managed to secure each stairwell and were now sitting outside the last unsecured one on this level. "We've got way too many bodies. And some of these are old dead."

"I was afraid of that," came Geist's reply. "I think one of the maintenance tunnels might be open. If that's the case, they could be feeding in from another building.

"Maintenance tunnel?" Rhi chimed in. "Are you shitting me?"

"Rhi, relax," I said.

"No, I've already seen this movie. It doesn't end well," Rhi countered.

"Chill Rhi, you're scaring the women-folk," I said.

She flipped me the bird in reply.

"Are they always like this?" Trent asked Shae.

"What this? No, this is the tame brother-and-sister ribbing they've got going," Shae said.

Trent shook his head, not understanding the dynamic going on.

I had the NASA tablet Geist gave me out and flipped through it with Shae and Rhi. "What do you think? Secure the tunnel or the building?" So far, we hadn't come across a single living person.

"Just like Drakes," Shae suggested.

"Yeah, take out the monster generator first, then clear the building," Rhi added.

"Basement it is." I closed the tablet. "Geist, how's the basement look?"

"Dark," Geist said.

"What?" I said.

"There aren't any lights on down there. They're all manual; someone must not have left them on," Geist said.

Rhi just shook her head, "Great."

"OK, stairwell first, then down. Shae and I will take point

with the SMGs. Trent, you're behind me. Then Beth and Rachel. Rhi and Tara, you watch our asses," I said.

"With pleasure," came a reply, but I couldn't tell if it had come from Rhi or Tara.

"OK folks, let's move," I said.

The stairwell was well-lit and, thankfully, empty as we made our way to the basement.

Glancing one last time at the map, I signaled Shae to open the door, and we went in.

The darkness consumed our group until three flashlights clicked on. Beth, Rachel and Trent's flashlights cast eerie shadows on the walls as they cast them around. The silence on the floor was unnerving as each of our steps sounded like a bomb going off.

Trent reached for the light switch but found it was a secured switch, meaning you had to have a special key to turn it on.

"Lights are a no-go," Trent whispered.

"Sorry guys, I didn't think about that," Geist's voice crackled in our ears.

Shae's gun barked as we rounded a corner and a shambler was standing there. It crumpled to the ground. The sound was like someone ringing the dinner bell as the rotters started coming out of the woodwork.

"Careful of the machinery in there," Geist chimed in.

"Yeah, tell that to them!" Rhi barked as the muzzle flashes were messing with our night vision.

"There it is!" Trent pointed at a metal door across the room.

"Rhi, Tara!" I yelled and tapped Shae on the shoulder. *Shift fire left!* We set up a lead wall on the side of the door, shooting anything that crossed the line.

Rhi and Tara's blades moved forward as they quickly carved a path to the door and slammed it shut just as another shambler came up from the tunnels. They threw the bolt and turned to face the remaining zombies.

Door's secure, Rhi said.

"Companies picking up back here," Beth called out.

I looked as Beth and Rachel were cracking off shots back down the hall from where we'd come. Rachel had slung her rifle and was using her pistol while Beth was still using her carbine.

Rachel was missing shot after shot. When she did hit, they were body shots. With how well she could shoot her rifle, I couldn't understand why she did so poorly with a pistol. Shooting basics are essentially the same regardless of the gun. When the firefight ended, I approached Rachel and asked her about it.

"I've never been good with anything other than my rifle," she said honestly.

"Let me see your pistol." When she handed it over, I flipped it over in my hand. Using a multi-tool from my gear, I removed the small electronic site from my MP5 and attached it to her pistol. "We're at such close range; it shouldn't need adjusting," I said, returning the gun.

Rachel hefted the pistol and looked down the site. A crisp red circle and dot hovered just about the top of her gun.

"Put the red dot on the head and press the trigger," I said.

Rachel nodded and holstered the weapon.

We braced the tunnel door with some cabinets as pounding on it had already started.

"They'll settle down once we leave and stop making noise," I told Trent.

"I take it y'all have been doing this a while?" Trent asked.

"More than I'd like," I nodded.

We finished clearing out the basement and returned to the ground floor to rest.

"Not looking forward to those tunnels," Rhi murmured.

"We might not have to worry about that," I said and stopped when Rhi gave me a look. "What?"

"Yeah, right, Boy Scout," Rhi said.

"Hey, I was never a Boy Scout," I said defensively. "I never made it past Cub Scouts," I added.

I had originally planned on using the personnel roster to mark people off as we encountered them. With the hordes coming up from the tunnels, that plan had been shot all to hell. Add to the fact that most of them weren't wearing nametags anyway, and my plan had been doomed from the start.

"Just upstairs left, right?" I asked.

"Yup," Trent agreed.

"Gimmie a L.A.C.E.," I said automatically.

"Seriously James?" Rhi rolled her eyes.

"We're running low on ammo," Beth replied.

"So am I," Shae added. "What's LACE?"

"See James, knock off the military jargon, K.I.S.S.," Rhi said.

"Fine, fine. L.A.C.E. stands for Liquid, Ammunition, Casualties, Equipment. It's basically a quick after-combat report to see how everyone's doing," I said to Shae.

"And kiss?" Shae asked.

"Keep It Simple, Stupid," Rhi chimed in, sticking her tongue out at me.

"Should we go back to the Dilla?" Shae asked.

"No. We've secured these two floors; let's keep that and finish up. I'm just hoping there's someone left alive in here. It's been disappointing so far," I said.

We setup on the second floor as we had on the ground floor, complete with Beth's Army bellow.

The first room we came to was a conference room. I knocked and was about to open the door when I heard movement inside, lots of movement.

"Ah crap," I said, bracing myself.

"Hello?" A soft voice whispered from the other side.

Shae spoke up as I looked like I was about to have a heart attack.

"We're here to rescue you. How many are you, and is anyone hurt?" Shae whispered back.

"We've got about 12 people, and we're all OK," the voice whispered.

"OK, hang on. Beth, you and Rachel take this group back to the lobby and then high tail it back here," Shae said.

Beth gave her a thumbs up.

"Geist?" Shae called.

"Yeah?" he said.

"We're about to send a group to the lobby. It would be best to have some folks there to take care of them. They say no one's hurt, but you have to make sure. Do you understand? No bites, no scratches," Shae said, taking charge.

"We've got a couple of medics; I'll send them down," Geist said.

Good thinking, I complimented Shae.

"OK. Quietly, crack the door, and I'll let you know what to do," Shae said.

The door clicked open, revealing the pale face of a disheveled woman.

"Hi. OK, you're going to follow that woman there," Shae indicated Beth, who waved. "You'll go silently and single file, understand?"

The woman nodded.

"No one talks until you get to the lobby. Tell everyone now." Shae waited until the woman passed the word and turned back to her. "OK, quietly, go."

The door swung open, and the people filed out silently. Rachel followed the last of them as Beth led them downstairs.

Go or stay? Shae asked.

Rhi, you and Tara stay and secure the hall until they come back. Then catch up and we'll continue just like downstairs. Shae and I will keep moving.

You sure? Rhi asked. *I'm good, you can take Tara.*

Battle buddies, I chided.

Spoilsport, Rhi mumbled.

Hey, it's your wife; you trying to get rid of her already? I countered.

Rhi's look shut me up then and there. Apparently, the wife was a "no-no" subject.

That's not it, Rhi sent, reading my mind.

Then what? You get all prickly when I mention your wife, I said.

It's hard to explain, Rhi said.

Um, hello? Shae cut in. *We're in the middle of a zombie-infested hallway. Can we have our Oprah moment later, please?*

Yes, mom, Rhi and I said in unison.

Shae, Trent, and I continued forward. Being a body short now, we took extra time in our checks. We methodically checked each room for survivors with no luck. We were on our eighth door when Rhi came silently bounding up.

Where's Tara? I asked.

We switched. Everyone's safe in the lobby. Beth, Rachel and Tara are standing by to move down the other hallway on your signal, Rhi said.

I glanced around; we'd moved slower than I thought. We still had several more rooms before we'd be parallel with the others and they could move forward.

OK, next room, stack up, I said automatically.

Rhi pulled her blades and lined up behind me as I pulled on the door.

I stepped into the room silently, scanning with my shouldered MP5. It wasn't until I cleared the door I realized I'd been in such a hurry I hadn't knocked.

A sharp, burning pain lanced across my right forearm. The shock of the pain surprised me so badly that I froze while looking down at the rotter currently gnawing on my arm. As soon as my brain caught up to what it was seeing, it shut down.

Once More

SHAE

I felt James shut down and immediately knew what had happened. I'd been with him the last time it happened.

RHI! My frantic mental call sent a cold shiver down Rhi's back. Rhi had felt James "go away" just as I had.

"OH, YOU STUPID GODDAMNED SON OF A BITCH!" Rhi had hold of the back of James's neck and threw him behind her hard enough he smashed into the wall on the other side of the hall. Her action had dislodged the zombie, causing it to fall, a chunk of James's arm still in its mouth.

For a split second, I wondered what had happened to the zombie. It was a young male that looked like someone had tried to smash his head in and only partially succeeded.

Then Rhi's blades sliced the creature's head into three parts, finishing the job. A growl from the corner caused Rhi to spin to face it. There were at least five more in the room. Five wouldn't be enough to quench the fear-fueled fury that threatened to overpower her.

RHI! I called, having felt Rhi's rage threatening to overtake her. Somehow, my mindtouch calmed Rhi, and she cooly cleared the room of hostiles in moments.

I knelt beside James, who was comatose.

Trent glanced from James to the hallway on either side of us and back to James.

Rhi unholstered her pistol and handed it to Trent.

"I've never fired one of these," he protested.

"Oh, man the fuck up," Rhi dismissed him and knelt next to James. *What is it?* She asked me.

I think it's a PTSD trigger. I got a flash of the zombie before he went down. It felt similar to the last time, I said.

*Last time?" Rhi asked.

Long story, I said.

Rhi nodded. *What about his arm?* Rhi asked.

I examined the ghastly wound on his forearm.

That doesn't look good, Rhi shook her head.

No, it doesn't. And we still don't know if we can be infected, I said.

I thought they wouldn't attack us, Rhi said.

We topped off at Drakes right before coming here. They normally ignore us unless we're 'full,' I said.

Should I take his arm? Rhi asked, gripping her blade tightly.

What? I looked at her.

Worked in the movies, Rhi shrugged.

I looked up at Rhi for a long moment. *I have no idea if it would help.*

Rhi nodded, *Then, what should we do with him?*

Last time, I had to go inside his mind to pull him out of it, and even then, it took hours for him to come around, I said.

We don't have hours, Rhi said.

Agreed. I tapped my earpiece mic. "Beth? Pull back to the stairwell; we've got a problem."

Before I'd finished, Rhi tossed James over her shoulder as if he weighed nothing, and bolted back down the hall at top speed.

When Trent and I caught up with her, Rhi was kneeling next to James inside the stairwell. Beth, Rachel and Tara were at the door. I pulled them all into the stairwell and secured the door.

When I turned back to the group, Rhi was already reaching down for James.

Wait, I said.

What? Rhi said.

I should be the one doing that, I said.

Why? Rhi asked.

Because I've done it before, I stated.

You don't know what you're dealing with, Rhi shook her head.

Yes, I do; like I said, I've been there before, I said.

Rhi looked at me slowly.

As I watched, Rhi's face changed, and I suddenly felt an entirely new emotion from her.

No, Rhi said gently. *You haven't been there; I have.* And with that, Rhi bent down and kissed James, HARD.

∞∞Ω∞∞

RHI

The room was hot, damned hot and smelled of filth and blood, lots of blood.

"Help me, dammit!" James called out to me from where he knelt, beside a bed in the corner of the room.

I turned from the desert sun pouring in the open door to face the bed. On it was a young man, a boy really, in an Army uniform; part of his head was missing. James was talking to the boy calmly, trying to keep his voice level, and the boy was talking back.

"Keep pressure here," James told me as I approached. James had stripped off his Air Force desert uniform top and pressed it to the side of the boy's head.

I gingerly took over, keeping pressure on the head wound while James checked the rest of the boy's body. A quick glance at the boy's face and I couldn't miss the star-shaped burn around the bullet entry wound. The gun's muzzle had been right up against his skull when it went off.

"So, tell me more about your dorm room. How many anime posters you got again? What's your favorite?" James asked the boy.

My brain was fuzzy, the scene was surreal, and I had

difficulty focusing. James had briefly told me about this horror when he'd come to me the first time, back in Austin.

"I..." the boy started, his voice weak. "I have six—" the boy's voice cut off suddenly with a gurgling, choking sound.

"Shit!" James leaned over, "Hold his head!" James rolled the boy onto his side as the boy vomited blood and small chunks of gray matter.

I had seen some things in my life and even more in my afterlife. But the site of this boy coughing up his own brains was almost too much.

An eternity later, the boy stopped coughing. James rolled him back over. James felt for a pulse and then began doing CPR.

I watched as James did chest compressions and then the breaths. He didn't flinch as he made contact with the boy's gore-covered lips. I felt he didn't even notice I was there as he continued until the boy's eyes fluttered open weakly.

James sat back on his heels, his hands still on the boy, bracing himself as they both took a shaky breath.

"I don't want pancakes mom," the boy mumbled out of nowhere.

"It's OK, you don't have to eat them. What do you want instead?" James glanced at the door and the Air Force cop outside. "Where are the medics?"

"They're on the way," the cop said.

"Tell them to hurry up; this kid is still breathing!"

I watched the cop relay the information with his radio. I didn't know how much time had passed when I finally turned back to James, but it already felt like forever.

"Come on, kid, stay with me, just a little longer," James mumbled, focusing on the pulse in the boy's neck, ensuring his chest kept rising and falling. Another minute passed, and the boy's chest stopped. "Fuck, no pulse," he growled and began CPR again.

At one point, I watched as he had to reach into the boy's mouth and remove something from his windpipe. I didn't want to think about what it was. Amazingly, the boy came around again.

"I'm going to be late for practice, Dad!" the boy said as he tried to get up with more strength than I thought possible.

"Easy there, practice is canceled; you just rest up, OK?" James said.

I could see the trembling in James's hands as he spoke to the boy.

"Where the fuck are the medics?" James growled over his shoulder.

I could hear the cop telling his people over the radio to do whatever it took to get the medics out of the clinic. I didn't hear the reply from the other side, but the cop's follow-up comment made it pretty clear, "You've got guns, don't you?"

The boy's choking brought me back into the room as, again, James had to purge the boy's windpipe. I had no idea how he was still alive, let alone talking to us. The human body was an amazing and mysterious machine that no science seemed to be able to entirely explain.

Then, the boy seemed normal. "What's going on Sarge?"

"Lie still; you're hurt, but the medics are coming," James managed through gritted teeth.

"Why is it so dark? I can't see anything," the boy asked.

"You hurt your head, just don't move, alright? I've got you," James said.

The surge of emotion I felt from James when he said those last three words nearly choked me up as my eyes started to water.

"Does my lieutenant know? I don't want to be late for chow," the boy said.

"You're LT knows what's going on, don't worry, you're OK," James said.

"Good. My mom hates it when I'm late for dinner. I can't make her angry; she'll ground me again, and I got a date with Deidra on Friday," the boy said.

"No worries, you're not going to be late." The self-control in James's voice slipped before he pulled himself back together and continued. "Where are you taking Deidra on Friday?"

"Oh, dad's gonna let me take the car to the—" There wasn't any choking this time; the boy just stopped.

Another round of CPR followed, longer this time. James told

me it took the medics over 20 minutes to cross the 400 meters between the clinic and the room the boy lay dying in. This didn't feel like 20 minutes; this felt like 20 hours. But James kept going, bringing the boy back to life over and over again. Each time, he talked to the boy whether he was in his right mind or not.

How James had kept so calm about it, knowing there was no way the boy would make it, was beyond me. Watching this now was hard enough. Knowing it wasn't really happening to me did little to soothe my soul.

When the medics finally showed up, they helped get the boy on the stretcher and then to the ambulance. As we watched the ambulance head back to the clinic, I followed James back to the room. He stood in the doorway, looking at the nightmare within.

I caught his hand just as he started to step back into the room.

"It's over, James," I said softly.

"I need to get my blouse, LT," James said, having no idea who I was.

"Look at me, James," I said firmly.

He slowly turned to face me, his eyes hollow and distant. No one was home.

"I'm not the lieutenant. You know who I am," I said soothingly.

A momentary look of confusion crossed his face before he tried to turn back to the room.

"James, it's over. You're safe now," I said more firmly.

"I...I need to get my blouse..." he hesitated in more confusion.

"James, this happened a long time ago; it's in the past. It can't hurt you now; you're safe. Safe with me," I said, turning his face to look at me.

"But LT..." James insisted.

"Look at me, James." I was using everything I'd learned both clinically and personally now. "You know me, don't you?" I said softly.

"I..." James started.

"Look into my eyes, James; what's my name?" I said gently

but firmly.

He tried to turn away again, trying to be drawn back into the nightmare.

"What's my name, James?" I caught his shoulder and pulled him back down the stairs, away from the room. "Look at me now James. What.is.my.name?" I insisted.

"Rhi," Recognition flashed briefly in his eyes, "you're Rhi."

"That's right. And I wasn't there, in that room with that boy, was I?" I asked.

"No," The confusion in his voice grew. "You weren't."

"That's right. I wasn't there, and you're not there right now either. You're safe with me in Houston," I said, holding his eyes.

"I'm...safe?" James questioned, looking around.

"Yes," I said, bringing his face back to mine. "This is just a memory. You're safe with me at NASA, remember?" I pushed.

"NASA?" His brows scrunched in concentration. "The zombie!"

"Yes! The zombie." I watched his body tense all over again. "But you're safe now. I took care of it. You're safe now, here, with me at NASA...in Houston," I said.

"With you?" he asked.

"Yes. WE are safe," I guaranteed.

He took a deep breath and blew it out.

Safe, we said simultaneously as both our eyes slowly opened. I held his gaze as I gently pulled my lips back from his.

Still with me? I stared into his eyes. I sent a quiet aside to Shae *Give it a minute.*

Yeah, he said, looking up into my tear-stained face. *What happened? Why are you crying?*

Take him, I sent to Shae, practically pushing him at her. I was barely in control of myself. It felt as if the tiniest thing would push me over the edge right now. I turned away from them and retreated down the stairs, Tara following me silently.

∞∞Ω∞∞

JAMES

Heya you, Shae started in my head gently. She moved to kneel in front of me. *You back with us?*

Yeah. I was confused. *What...what happened?* But then I moved my right arm and hissed. There was a bandage on my arm and it burned like fire. *Did I get bit?* I asked, staring at the bandage in confusion.

Shae nodded. *Rhi rescued you when you had your...incident.*

Incident...I blacked out again, didn't I? I asked.

Yes, Rhi went in and brought you back. Shae tapped my temple.

I saw through Shae's eyes as she glanced over her shoulder and saw Rhi sobbing uncontrollably in Tara's embrace. Whatever Rhi had seen, it had to be worse than what Shae had experienced the first time I blacked out. I'd never seen Rhi like this, and I could sense Shae was desperate to go and check on her but restraining herself.

You don't remember anything? Shae asked me.

No, I said truthfully.

Maybe that's better for the moment, Shae said.

"How you doing?" Trent moved over to check on me.

"Whew, close call, I guess. Don't really know what happened." I made a show of rubbing the back of my head. "Must have hit my head pretty hard."

"I'll say, you looked like a ragdoll when you came flying out of the room like that. Scared the shit out of me," Trent said.

"It'll take more than a bump on the noggin to keep me down. I'm feeling better, thanks," I said.

"You sure? You were bleeding pretty good there for a while." Trent indicated my arm.

"We think James caught it on the door frame," Shae supplied. "Beth patched you up." She nodded at Beth, who'd only been half listening as she focused on the door to the second floor.

"Thanks, Beth," I said and got a thumbs up in reply as she didn't take her eyes off the door. Turning back to Shae, "What's our status?"

"We pulled back to the stairwell when you went down. We only cleared about a quarter of the floor," Shae said.

"Which means we'll have to start over," I groaned. "I'm sorry, it's my fault. I broke my own rules by rushing. I forgot to bang on the door before going in. Had I done that, none of this would have happened."

"You should have also waited for the rest of the team before starting out," Rhi added, rejoining the group. She looked rough but had pulled herself together. "That's two of your rules you broke: no rushing and never split the party." There was actual venom behind her words.

Leave it, Shae cut me off before I could reply. *Not now.*

I looked from Rhi to Shae and back. "I'm sorry," I said honestly. It didn't take puffy eyes and smeared makeup to see Rhi was still hurting.

"Right. You think you can finish this?" Rhi spat.

I flexed my hand. "Yeah, I'm good," I said, embarrassed I'd screwed up so badly.

Good, cause I'm gonna kick your ass as soon as we're through here. Rhi's voice was furious as she turned away from me.

What? I was more confused than ever.

Later...focus, Shae pressed me.

Trent looked around the group, confused by all the strange looks and behavior going around.

"OK, kiddies, let's try this again," Rhi started. "Tara, you take Trent, Shae and dumbass there and start over. We'll stay put until you give us the signal to move up. We're on the clock, people, let's move."

We found a few more pockets of survivors that we sent to safety and a handful of shamblers we dispatched without further injury. Having secured the building, we were heading back downstairs when Rhi hung back at the entrance to the stairwell.

Give me a minute, Rhi sent to the three of us. *We'll catch up.* She touched my hand and I slowed, letting the others pass. As soon as the door to the stairwell closed, Rhi slammed my back against the wall with enough force for me to actually see stars.

Of all the stupid, goddamned, idiotic, jackass things to do, you went and got yourself bit, you fucking moron! She started, her "mind voice" filled with fury like I'd never felt before.

Before I could reply, she slapped me hard enough to fill my vision with stars.

Like an idiot, I tried to reply but she cut me off and crushed her body to mine. She grabbed me by the back of the head and kissed me so hard she split my lip. Just as the kiss started softening, she pulled away and slapped me again.

Konoyaro bakayaro! she screamed at me before slamming the stairwell door open and catching up to the others.

I was still rubbing my cheek when I caught up to Shae. *What did I do exactly?*

James, Shae sighed, shaking her head. *You scared her...badly.*

I didn't mean to, I said lamely.

I don't know what she saw in your head, but it was enough to really shake her up, James. That was on top of getting yourself bit, which I will kick your tail for later, Shae said seriously.

But why would she— I continued my idiocy by speaking without thinking.

Shae looked at me. *I know you're not that stupid; stop acting like it. You know how she feels.*

But she's married now, I said, actually feeling the foot as it went into my mouth.

Oh for...James, stop thinking like a human, will you? Shae rolled her eyes and chuckled to herself. She grabbed my face and held it still, looking at something in my left eye.

For how old you act, I keep forgetting you're still a newborn in my world. Shae moved my head to the side. *She burst a blood vessel in your eye. Your cheekbone doesn't look too good, either. But you should be OK by tomorrow. Keep your distance for a while, or she might do something more permanent,* Shae said seriously.

Her thoughts sobered me.

We were approaching the entrance doors, avoiding bodies,

when Trent picked something up off the floor and handed it to Tara.

"Don't forget this," Trent said.

Tara turned and froze when she saw what was in his hand.

"Remember, it came off when that thing attacked you up here near the front," Trent said.

Tara took it from Trent and stared at it. "It's been off all this time?" she asked.

"Yeah, since we came in," Trent said.

Everyone's eyes followed Tara's gaze as she slowly looked down, twisting her leg to examine the large hole in her armor. The red skin of her exposed calf was there for all to see. Tara looked at Rhi.

"I was afraid the zombie had gotten you when I saw all that red. I thought it was blood." Trent said.

"No," Tara started. "Not blood. That's just...what my skin looks like." She looked at Trent and cocked her head.

"How are you feeling, Trent?" Rhi asked cautiously, stepping up to him and taking a close look at his eyes.

"Honestly? Tired. I don't want to go through that again." Trent tried to smile.

"Tired? That's it?" Rhi said.

"Uh, yeah. And maybe a little hungry," Trent looked around at the corpses. "Although I don't know how I have any appetite after all that."

"Beth, Rachel?" Rhi called.

"Yeah?" Beth said.

"Y'all feel OK?" Rhi turned to them, and they shrugged.

"Well, as can be expected," Beth said.

"Yeah, what she said," Rachel said.

What's going on? Shae asked openly.

What about you two? Any weird cravings? Sex, blood, food, anything? Rhi asked.

No, why? I asked.

You're freaking me out, Shae added.

Later. Rhi turned to Tara, who was jury-rigging the torn leather back into place using additional straps from the small pack she always carried. "You OK?"

"Yeah, just...concerned?" Tara said hesitantly.

"We'll figure it out later, in private," Rhi said.

"OK," came Tara's guarded reply.

We made our way back through the atrium and into the other set of secured doors. Carman and Geist met us just as the medics were packing up their kits from the impromptu field examinations they'd given the survivors.

"Any problems with the survivors?" Shae asked Geist.

"Aside from a few bumps and bruises, everyone was OK." He smiled. "Thank you for thinking of that, by the way. I would have hated to have this whole thing start again because we missed someone."

"Yes," Carman started, "thank you for your help." He seemed to wrestle with himself for a moment. "I apologize if I came across a bit...callous earlier. We're not what you'd call soldiers, and things here haven't been easy."

"Don't worry about it." Shae smiled. "These are hard times all around. We've seen people with half the responsibility you have not holding up half as well as you are."

"You're too kind," The man actually blushed. "Please, come this way. I've made room for you here in the main building. I'm sure you'd like to clean up. After you've had time for some rest, I'll give you the grand tour."

He's sucking up to us cause he wants us to clear those tunnels, I guarantee it, Rhi added.

"Thank you, Mr. Carman, we'd be grateful." *Time and place Rhi,* Shae sent.

Emerging Out of the Walls

SHAE

Carman showed us to a couple of offices that had been converted into sleeping quarters. From the way Carman talked, the previous occupants may be lying on the floor of the building we'd just cleared. When Carman and Trent left us alone, Beth and Rachel racked out while the rest of us gathered in another office.

"OK, what's going on?" I asked quietly.

Rhi went over and ensured the blinds were drawn so no one could look into the office. "You remember me saying why Tara has to wear the suit, right?"

"Yeah, her scent drives people crazy," I nodded.

"To me, it's just really, REALLY appetizing...in a whole Bram Stoker way, if you know what I mean. If Tara had her leg exposed all that time and no one reacted, something's different."

"Maybe it just takes longer?" James asked. "You know, cause it was just a small area?"

Rhi continued as if she hadn't heard him. "When I was on Tara's world, I noticed some things worked differently, like sunlight didn't burn. That sort of thing. Maybe her scent doesn't work the same here?"

"Worth a shot. It already looks like that's the case. All we have to do is test it." I turned to Tara. "Are you willing to trust us?"

"With removing my armor? I don't know..." Tara hesitated.

"It's OK." Rhi wrapped a protective arm around Tara. "It's going to be OK."

After a moment Tara nodded and slowly removed one of her gauntlets. When her red skin and black claws came into view, James gasped slightly and stared.

"Sorry, I'm OK," James said hesitantly, "It's just...pretty," his words were almost a whisper.

"Pretty?" Tara cocked her head at James, and he nodded in reply.

Rhi took Tara's hand and held it to her nose, breathing deeply.

"The hunger is still there, but it's more subdued. I don't know if I've just gotten used to it, or it was muffled somehow," Rhi said.

"May I?" I asked, holding my hand out. When Tara gave me her hand, it was my turn to gasp. "You're so warm!"

"You have no idea," Rhi leered, a bit of her old self emerging.

"Your ink is beautiful, by the way." I glanced at the exposed forearm, watching as the tattoos seemed to move beneath my eyes.

"Thank you," Tara said sheepishly.

Leaning down, I took a deep breath, putting my nose right up to Tara's wrist. "It smells like...some exotic spice I can't place. But aside from the pleasantness of it, I don't feel any different." I smiled up at Tara, "Thank you."

Tara smiled back and held her hand out to James.

James hesitated, inadvertently glancing at Rhi before taking Tara's hand delicately.

"Oh wow," James sighed. "You do smell wonderful." He froze after saying it and closed his eyes, embarrassed. "Sorry, that sounded...just wrong." Opening his eyes, he looked up at Tara. "But you do smell good. It reminds me of something I've smelled before." He let go of her hand and tapped his lips with a finger. "But for the life of me, I can't place it."

"Something from downrange, right?" Rhi said to him.

"Yes!" James said, obviously surprised Rhi had spoken

directly to him.

"I've been thinking the same thing but can't place it either," Rhi said. "Guess that confirms it. You're safe here, at least with us." Rhi hesitated, "Do you want to get comfortable?"

When Tara didn't answer, "You don't have to if you're not comfortable," I added.

"Are you kidding?" Tara's excited voice was practically giddy. As we watched, the buckles on Tara's outfit undid themselves and fell away—all of them.

James and I stood in stunned silence as we watched the leather armor fall away, revealing Tara in all her glory. Her red skin and raven-black hair were striking, but her eyes and fangs were mesmerizing. When Tara stretched up onto her tiptoes and stretched her shoulders, I managed to recover.

"James?" I cleared my throat and gently closed his open mouth.

"Wow," he whispered.

I could feel James's waves of pure lust through our link. But it wasn't due to some pheromone. No, what he was feeling was what any red-blooded person would feel when staring at a lovely naked woman. I had to admit, I was similarly affected, but I was more couth about it.

"I've said it before," I continued. "Girls don't like it when you stare."

"Wha...what?" James somehow shook himself free from the trance Tara's body had put him in.

"I don't mind," A new voice came out of Tara's throat, dripping with innuendo.

I didn't know if it was because Tara was no longer speaking through a mask or if she was doing it on purpose. What I did know was that I needed to get James out of here, maybe find him a cold shower somewhere before he drooled on the carpet.

I glanced over and saw Rhi eyeing James, not fazed by Tara's nudity at all. Rhi seemed to be waiting for something.

James...LATER. I sent to James hard, a borderline command.

My thought seemed to allow James to regain some semblance of control over himself.

"Rhi's right," James's voice was strained and it looked like he'd broken out in a sweat. "They're probably gonna ask us to clear those tunnels soon. We should probably get some rest," he managed to finish, but I could tell he was having a hard time of it.

"Awww," Tara pouted. "Do you have to?" She purred.

Rhi? I sent an unspoken warning.

If she wants him... Rhi mentally shrugged.

You said the two of you are linked, right? Meaning you share a mind? I asked.

That snapped Rhi out of her thoughts, causing her to pause. *Yeah. Even still...* she started, but I cut her off.

Do you think, after everything the two of you have been through today, now is the right time? I asked. Rhi knew I had no qualms about who James slept with as long as he didn't get hurt.

Rhi visibly flinched and grimaced. *You're right. I'm sorry. I don't know what I was thinking...I just...* Rhi's voice sounded confused in my head, as if she were having a hard time with her own thoughts at the moment.

I walked over and wrapped my arms around Rhi, surprising her. Rhi was stiff in the embrace, but that didn't stop me from holding her.

Later, OK? Then you can have your naked fun time, I grinned at her kindly.

Naked fun time? Rhi actually chuckled aloud and then wrapped her arms around me. *How...* Rhi started, not letting me go.

How what? I said into her shoulder.

How do you know the right thing to say all the time? Rhi finally said. When she pulled back, I felt the return of that tenuous hold on her emotions she'd had in the stairwell earlier.

I smiled and kissed Rhi on the cheek. *You may know how to take care of our screwed-up military boy here, but taking care of my family is my superpower, dear.*

Rhi looked away and made as if there were something in her eye.

You OK? I sent to Rhi.

I'll be alright, Rhi said, clearing her throat slightly.

I risked looking at Tara, who held her arms out to me. I chucked and let go of Rhi before embracing Tara as well. "You look lovely, my dear," I said before kissing Tara on the cheek.

"Thank you," Tara purred, not taking her eyes off mine.

As I looked into Tara's eyes, her gaze was intense and hungry. They weren't the eyes I was expecting to find behind those leather wrappings. I couldn't tell what was going on behind them, but they didn't seem to match the woman I'd gotten to know these past few days.

"But I think you overwhelmed James, in a good way." I grinned.

"Do you mind if I..." Tara suddenly seemed pensive, her eyes softening, but the hunger lingered.

I chuckled and turned to face James, "Would you go hug her so we can get out of here? I'm tired."

James awkwardly moved forward and embraced Tara, who immediately grabbed his ass and grinned up at him.

When James glanced over at Rhi, I heard Tara whisper into his ear, "Your time is coming; rest while you can."

Rhi rolled her eyes and made a "shooing" gesture at James as he made his reluctant escape.

She's already got him wrapped around her finger, I sent to Rhi.

She's not the only one, Rhi sent back.

When we were out of the room, James turned to me, "Are you sure there's nothing hypnotic about her scent or something?"

I shook my head. "Yes. Everything in there came straight from your pants, not her scent." I studied him momentarily as we entered our room and closed the door. He looked lost in thought...and guilty.

James, I shook my head before pinching the bridge of my nose and sighing.

Yeah? He looked up at me.

You do know it's alright to want her, I grinned at the conflicted man.

But, she's married to Rhi and... James started.

242

James, we're all married to Rhi. We may not have had a ceremony or signed a paper, but we're all family now. It's OK to have feelings; you're SUPPOSED to have feelings. The alternative is too horrible to think about. I sighed.

Up until four months ago, I was single and alone, James started. *Now, I have a family with multiple women who want to jump into bed with me. It's just...new,* James said.

It's supposed to be new. If it weren't new, watching you crucify yourself over your natural feelings wouldn't be half this fun. Anytime an attractive woman, married or not, takes her clothes off in front of you and throws herself at you, you're supposed to have feelings about that. I took his face in my hands and kissed him gently.

But right now, I'm the woman you're going to jump into bed with, I said.

He smiled into my mouth.

∞∞Ω∞∞

SHAE

A short time later, we lie curled up together, enjoying one another.

"You want to talk about what happened in that stairwell?" I asked, pressing back against him.

"Not really," James said honestly.

"You OK?" I asked.

"As well as can be expected," he said flatly.

"Doesn't exactly fill me with confidence. You do know Rhi is a psychiatrist, right? That's how she pulled you back. Maybe you should talk with her," I said.

"I don't know if that's a good idea," James said.

"She got scared, James. We lash out when we get scared. She'll get over it soon enough," Shae said.

"If you say so," James muttered.

"I swear, you look older, but sometimes it's like I'm still talking to that teenager from way back then." I sighed. "If she isn't already over it, she will be before you realize it. Trust me, the next time you sleep with her, you might want to talk to her afterward about what's going on with you. She says you're more...open about things then."

"I..." But James shut his mouth, staring at yet another alien ceiling. "Wait, you two...talk about me?" His voice almost squeaked before he cleared it. "About me when I'm...with each of you?"

I chuckled, "Of course. What do you think we talk about when you're not around? Purses? Makeup?"

"But—"

"James, whether you understand it or not, we're all family now. We look out for one another however we can. If that means comparing bedroom notes, then that's what we do. Besides, it's not like we can't look into each other's minds and see what went on."

"You can do that?" James asked.

I sighed. "We all can James. Now, it would ease my mind if you'd talk to Rhi. I think she might be able to help you get some of your past trauma under control." Before he could interrupt, I continued. "Just think about it, OK? For me?"

"Seems that sleeping with Rhi is becoming a common favor for you," he joked. "She's not giving you kickbacks or anything, is she?"

"No." I frowned. "She's too scared of me."

"She's the big, tough assassin," James said. "She doesn't seem afraid of anything; why is she scared of you?"

"You gotta learn to keep your eyes open, dear." Before he could cut in, I continued. "For more than just weapons. Start looking at people's faces and study their eyes. The eyes are usually the hardest thing to control. Well, that and the hips."

"Gateways to the soul?" James asked.

"The hips?" I grinned.

"No, the eyes silly," James said.

"Exactly. Now get some sleep," I said.

"Yes, Mom," he teased, knowing how much I didn't like being called Mom.

I slapped him on the thigh.

A quiet few moments passed before, "You two really talk about my bedroom habits?" James couldn't seem to wrap his head around it.

"Are you serious?" I asked. "Of course we do. Didn't you ever talk about girls with other guys?"

"Not the serious ones," he said.

"The serious ones?" I glanced back at him.

"Guys don't talk about their feelings with each other. We just...don't. Not really," James said.

"Guys are weird," I frowned. "And dumb sometimes."

"I'm not going to argue with your Shae," James chuckled. A moment passed before, "But you said Rhi was scared of you?" James said.

"James," I sighed heavily, shaking my head. "We're women; we talk about everything, especially boys. It doesn't matter how we feel—" I intentionally stopped talking.

"What?" James sat up, looking at me.

"Oh, nothing. I can't give away too many secrets now. Loose lips and all that," I said as I rolled over and closed my eyes. I could feel him still looking at me as I drifted off to sleep, a grin on my face. Sometimes it was fun playing with that boy he still had inside him.

$$\infty\infty\Omega\infty\infty$$

JAMES

The tunnels were something out of a bad nightmare. They were cramped, had all manner of pipes and conduits lining the ceiling and walls, and were musty and damp. They were only missing the blue mood lighting and slime-dripping aliens. Instead, they had gore-dripping, moldy zombies...almost as bad.

It didn't take long to determine where the breach occurred and seal it. We took it slow and methodically, clearing out the rest of the tunnels. I'd learned my lesson and every time I even started to get a little overzealous, Rhi reigned me back in. Shae had been right, Rhi was over it now. But she wasn't about to let me make the same mistake twice. She was making it her job to keep me on a short leash.

Beth and Rachel had overseen the removal of the dead zombies from the building while the rest of us had gone down into the tunnels. They made sure each body was actually and properly dead before some of the JSC personnel would drag them off. We didn't bother to ask where they were taking them.

By the end of the following day, we were just as filthy as we had been the day prior. It took a total of three days to clean up and dispose of all the bodies both in the building and the tunnels.

At the end of the third day, the MCC had restored its security over the five buildings it was linked to. The door to the building with the collapsed wall that had started it all had been welded shut. The black slime some zombie had smeared on a random intake air vent was also discovered and cleaned up.

All of this and not one additional case of zombiehood.

"You know what's been bugging me?" I said as I looked through the glass of the visitor gallery over the central control room.

"What's that?" Shae asked.

"What the hell happened to that Iron Man suit that flew off?" I asked.

"Good riddance," Rhi said from behind us. She was sprawled across two chairs with Tara rubbing her feet. Beth and Rachel were in the back of the room cleaning guns.

"I wish it were that simple," I sighed. "You said that the last time they showed up, you killed one, and the other went back to wherever it came from."

"Yup," Rhi said.

"But this time, the second one just flew away. It didn't go back to wherever it came from," I said.

"So what? As long as it's gone," Rhi said.

"I wish we knew why they wanted Tara so bad," Shae said.

"You and me both," Tara nodded.

"Have we had anything more out of the radar on the Dilla?" Shae asked.

Rhi pulled the tablet from her hip pocket and thumbed it on.

"Not a peep," Rhi said.

I frowned.

"Hey..." Rhi sat up suddenly.

I was about to ask her what was happening when Trent entered the room. Before Trent could offer a greeting, Rhi jumped out of her seat and approached him.

Wrapping her arms around one of his, "Trent! Just the man I wanted to see," Rhi purred.

Trent looked started but recovered quickly. Now he only looked slightly apprehensive to have the beautiful woman on his arm.

"Yeeees?" he drew out.

"Do y'all track radar in the local area?" Rhi smiled at him.

"We're tied into the local airports; why?" Trent asked.

"Would you be able to tap into them to pull up the telemetry for the last four days or so?" Rhi's voice was melted butter.

"Uh," Trent seemed to stumble. "Probably, it depends on if the airport was still online. Why?"

"Can I see? Pretty please?" Rhi purred, batting her eyelashes at him as she turned the charm up to 11.

"OK, let's go check." Everyone except Beth and Tara followed Trent down to one of the control room floors. We stood back as Trent approached one of the controllers and had a brief discussion with her.

"I thought the airports would have shut down," Shae said.

"Most airport systems are automated now," Trent said over his shoulder. "They'd stay up and operational until someone shut them down."

"What about power?" Shea asked.

"Auxiliary generators would kick in after the power grid failed," Trent said.

"How long would that run? Don't generators normally run on gas or something?" Shea said.

This time, Trent shrugged; he didn't have an answer for her and turned back to the controller.

"Ellington," I mumbled.

"What about it?" Shae asked.

"Ellington Field. They had their own airport, and we know

they're still operational," I said.

"And we were pretty close to them when it happened, weren't we?" Shae nodded.

Rhi interrupted Trent and relayed the information before giving me a thumbs up.

A few minutes later, we were gathered around a screen as the controller pulled up Ellington Field's radar footage.

"OK," The controller said as she started the playback. "I'm not an air traffic controller; I flunked out of that school."

"And now you're at NASA?" Rhi smiled.

"MUCH better job," she smiled back. "Ellington doesn't get a lot of traffic, so anything we see would probably be your bogey."

We watched as the time bar scrolled forward, and a blip appeared on the edge of the screen out of the West. The controller slowed the footage down to real-time, and we watched as a label popped up on it, calling it "EF117".

"What's the distance on this radar?" Rhi asked.

The tech squinted at the screen. "Looks like it's set at 100 kilometers right now."

EF117 made a slow, straight approach to Ellington and disappeared.

"Ellington marks their drones with "EF" so that's one of theirs," the controller said. The controller pushed the footage forward until another blip appeared. This time, the blip appeared in the middle of the screen. "They zoomed into 50 kilometers for this one."

As we watched, the single blip split into two and began moving erratically and extremely fast. A moment later, a label came up labeling them "Angel078" and "Angel079".

"That's gotta be them." The tech tapped the screen. "Angel is a designation for unknown targets."

We watched as the blips danced around before one suddenly vanished. A moment later, the other one shot away to the West. The screen flickered several times but remained blank.

"Wow." The controller leaned forward.

"What?" Rhi asked.

"The bogey took off, and the operator tried to zoom out, but it was off the scope by the time they zoomed out to 100 kilometers."

"It moved that fast?" Shae asked.

"Or it dropped off the scope...aka crashed," the controller said.

"If we were only so lucky." Rhi sighed.

"Anything else matching that signature show up since?" I asked.

The controller made a face. "That...will take some time." She turned back to the screen. Nearly an hour later, no blips labeled "Angel" had appeared.

"Well, that was disappointing." Rhi sighed.

It was about time for us to take our leave.

Trent and I sat down and had the catch-up conversation I'd been meaning to have since our arrival. We talked about his family and the online girlfriend he'd had, all of which he had zero contact with since Z Day. Sadly, my military survivor database hadn't been any help on either front, one way or the other

We talked about the possibility of Trent coming to Austin, but he declined. He wanted to stay at MCC and I could understand his reasons. Instead, I showed him how to tap into the nets to get a message to our Alamo compound if anything came up.

For now, the government networks were still working, and satellites were still flying. As long as at least one of them was still working we could link up if needed.

We said our goodbyes shortly after.

Zombie Movies & Malls

<u>JAMES</u>

"Argh." Rhi emitted a disgusted groan.

"What's wrong, Rhi?" Shae asked as the Dilla rumbled through dead traffic.

"I just dread saying this," Rhi said.

"What?" Shea asked.

"I told you to go before we left," I chided.

Then a huge smile spread across her face, "Hey mom? Like, can we go to the mall?" Rhi asked in her best valley girl voice.

Shae's face twisted in confusion. "What?"

"I want to get Tara some clothes," Rhi said.

"Why not just get them at Drakes?" I asked.

I could practically hear Rhi's eyes rolling at me.

"Oh.my.gawd. Could you be any.more.male?" Rhi continued her impression before finally dropping it. "You have to know what you want at Drakes, and I want to browse." Rhi looked over at Tara. "This fine specimen deserves only the best."

Tara had continued to wear her full leathers while at JSC, mainly not to scare the normals. As soon as we've left, she'd gone to wearing an odd mismatch of pieces that protected her modestly more than her body. She'd completely ditched the helmet. Under different circumstances, I'd say it was provocative. As it was now, it looked more like a five-year-old dressing themselves for the first time.

The sight of a nude Tara had tied my mind in knots back at JSC. There was plenty of lust there, but I'd realized I was looking at someone completely alien to my world. There was all sorts of fiction that mentioned creatures similar to Tara, but seeing her in the flesh so to speak, was something else entirely. It still blew my mind when I looked at her. I desperately wanted to sit her down and ask so many questions about her world but had yet to find the time.

That always seemed to be our group's problem. Since the moment we'd come together, we'd been on this non-stop whirlwind adventure. While exciting, it was exhausting at the same time. I don't know if I was getting older or what, but I needed a vacation. I was tired.

There was silence in the Dilla.

"The Galleria isn't too far from Drakes," Shae said.

Shaking my head, "Have any of you actually SEEN a zombie movie? Going to the mall is the absolute worst thing you can do. Hell, even Night of the Comet had a mall scene that went bad."

"Night of the Comet wasn't a zombie movie," Rhi countered.

"Go back and watch it again luv; they were bad make-up zombies, sure, but still zombies," I said.

"Wasn't that guy from Voyager in that movie?" Rachel chimed in from the back.

"Yeah," I answered.

"You know, we could use some new clothes as well. These uniforms are getting a bit ripe," Beth added. "We don't have a lot of civilian stuff on our side, you know?"

Then there was Beth and Rachel. They were so normal to me that I continuously forgot they were from a similar but different world. There were too many mixed-up emotions in my head over Beth for me to get too close. I felt I should ask her more about her world but was terrified for fear it might be a preview of what mine was heading towards. The fact I knew Shae had talked with Beth quite a bit already was a relief.

I sighed, shook my head and gave up.

Remember sweetie, you're traveling with five women, Shea said.

Yes, I know. My testosterone is suffering, I smiled.

The Galleria was a massive four-story complex that sprawled over several blocks of downtown. It had large parking structures, a hotel, an office tower, and over a dozen entrances. It was the perfect nightmare for security and might just be enough to give me a nervous breakdown.

"I still can't believe all of this is still here," Beth said.

"Yeah, downtown is pretty much burned-out ruins back home," Rachel said.

Being so close to downtown, the congestion was bad. I couldn't get us too close to the mall due to cars and debris choking the streets. So, we left the Dilla and hiked the last block or so on foot.

This time around, we opted for a quiet entrance. Figuring there was no way we could secure a spot in the mall, we didn't want to get swarmed or trapped. So, instead of shooting every rotter that got close, we crept from cover to cover until we were up against one of the entrances. The glass doors were still intact and luckily, unlocked. We slipped inside silently.

Power had failed some time ago. The crudded-over skylights provided the only illumination inside the complex. This made the hallways dimly lit and full of shadows, just like in the movies.

There was a stale, musty odor within, but thankfully, not an undead one. As we stopped and listened, we could hear shambling in the distance, but the tiled walls made the sound act funny, so we couldn't pinpoint where it was coming from.

As we knelt against the wall, Rhi suddenly stood up, startling me, and casually walked to a mall directory map in the middle of the corridor. I was about to say something when Shae touched my arm.

Is it really making a difference kneeling here? Shae asked.

I considered it and then slowly stood up. I had trained so long to fight against people I was still having a hard time adjusting to fighting undead.

Rhi tapped her lip for a minute as she seemed to make up her mind.

OK, let's hit this place first. Rhi tapped the map.

First? I started, but Shae's touch once again enhanced my calm.

I had always hated shopping. Anytime I'd been dragged to the mall when I was younger, I would usually escape to an arcade or bookstore. Sitting and watching my mother or sister trying on clothes had been torture.

We'll see what we can do about that, Shae promised.

The central part of the mall was a giant open area with stores clinging to the walls. The skylights running the length of the ceiling allowed light to penetrate down to the below-ground level where an ice rink once was. Glass half-walls marked the boundary to keep people from falling over the edges.

We could see several of the glass walls were already smashed and there was movement on every level. Mostly just ones and twos, but occasionally, there would be clumps of shadowy figures lumbering about. Luckily, the first store Rhi wanted to visit was just down on the left.

One of the larger commercial stores, it had multiple levels and covered everything from clothes to mattresses. We moved into the store quietly and headed to the back, where women's clothing was. The women's section was the entire back half of the store. We stalked, pistols out for Beth and Rachel and melee weapons for the rest of us.

I came across a "rotter," as Beth called them, standing near a jewelry counter. I knifed it through the back of the skull without a sound and lowered the body to the ground. The body reeked as it looked like it had been dead for a while now. Its skin sluffed off as I laid it on the tile floor causing my bile to rise.

Rhi beheaded one, just managing to catch the body as Tara caught the head, dispatching both as they put them down. It seemed they had become quite the pair.

As we entered the clothing section, Shae suddenly became a blur as she dispatched a zombie lying on the floor in the middle of a clothing display. It reminded me of how, as a kid, I used to hide inside the displays when my sister and I would play hide and seek while waiting for mom to try on clothes. Only I didn't try and bite my sister when she found me.

We kept Beth and Rachel behind us with their flashlights off.

We had told them only to turn them on if they absolutely had to. We tried our best to keep a low profile and knew light in the near pitch-black store would attract unwanted attention.

I insisted we make two sweeps of the area and the surrounding sections before I was comfortable enough for us to stop. While it had made Rhi grumble, she stopped grumbling when we found a rotter we'd missed hiding in one of the dressing rooms.

With the section so large and cluttered with display racks, finding a good overwatch point took a while. Most everything in here was still intact and seemingly untouched. In the first month of the pandemic, people cared more about food and weapons than about clothes. A sporting goods store further down in the mall had been ransacked from the looks of it. Anything that could be swung at a shambler's head had been in high demand.

I'd scaled up a display attached to the wall and perched on a small ledge. It gave me a good vantage point for most of the store. While my eyes could see into the darker places, I would occasionally use my rifle's starlight scope to scan the darker spots just in case.

The women went through just about every rack of clothes on display over the next two hours and were in and out of the dressing rooms trying everything on. They even expanded out to the nearby shoe section briefly.

Eventually, Rhi approached me.

Hey, Batman, it's time to go, Rhi said.

Standing and stretching, I silently dropped down to the floor beside her.

Batman? Would that make you Catwoman? I asked.

Are you nuts? Could you see me in a catsuit? Rhi replied.

Well, yeah. I grinned.

No, she grinned back. *I'm so Harley it's scary.*

The more I thought about it, the more the profile fit. Nodding, I suddenly had a thought.

Wait, how do you know all this comic book stuff? I thought you said you didn't like that type of stuff. I said.

She put her hand on my chest, stopping me.

James, what rating on the GAF is the most dangerous?

10, I said automatically, shrugging my shoulders, *why?*

Rhi stared at me, waiting.

What the fuck is a GAF? I asked, not having a clue myself. But the more I thought about it, the more I understood what it was and what it was used for.

Yeah, you can thank Nat for that one. Have you picked up any of my other little "quirks" from this personality blender we seem to be sharing?

When I didn't answer right away, Rhi smiled and patted my cheek roughly. *Don't worry,* Rhi said, returning to the previous conversation. *Harley wanted to fuck Bats too.*

It was my turn to roll my eyes as we headed to the next store. Whatever animosity Rhi had against me had faded, just as Shae had predicted. I should have known better than to question Shae. I just chalked it up to yet another thing I'd never understand about women.

What I was still trying to wrap my head around was the whole personality blending thing Rhi mentioned. Shae had explained to me what Nat had told her, but I still didn't understand it. Now I seemed to be unconsciously pulling information from Rhi's brain as if it were my own. What else was coming from this little group brain we were forming? I shook my head to derail that train of thought and bring me back to the here and now.

We passed a part of the mall where a small playground sat, abandoned. There were several mechanical animals around the perimeter, the kind you could put a quarter in, and they would rock back and forth or make noise. I remembered watching children on those things, their faces beaming with ear-to-ear grins. *Such simple joys.* I thought darkly as I noticed the dark stains that splattered a once pristine white pony.

∞∞Ω∞∞

SHAE

Shae? Rhi sent privately.

I felt it, I replied and glanced at James, whose eyes, which had been downcast a minute ago, were back to scanning this way and that, sharp as ever.

Rhi and I had agreed to keep a close eye on James since his incident at JSC. Anytime either of us felt or suspected anything out of the ordinary with him, we'd let the other know. With all the worrying we did over the man I was starting to think James had some issues we couldn't handle on our own. I hoped the quasi-normality of shopping might help to ground him a bit.

I'd had a long talk with Rhi at JSC after the incident. I was still worried about her even though she'd assured me she was doing fine. She refused to talk about what she'd seen, saying she needed to let it settle, let it get a little less raw before getting into it. I'd made her promise to talk to me when that happened and didn't plan to let it go. Whatever it was had caused James to block it out and nearly sent Rhi into a nervous breakdown. We couldn't have that festering.

Our next stop was upstairs at a designer clothing store that shared an open wall with another boutique next door. We'd had to dispatch three zombies on the stairs up, but the store itself was clear.

I mused to myself that shamblers didn't need new clothes, so why were they in here? Actually, zombies did need new clothes, but all they could do was window shop for the rest of eternity. There was a morale or something in there somewhere. I chuckled at the dark thought and wondered where it had come from.

The backroom doors were closed, reminding me of that convenience store so long ago. I'd shied away from them as James took up his post in the store's entryway. His head was, as he would say, on a swivel. He flinched every time a clothes hanger scraped on a rack.

Several times I heard James's silenced...I mean suppressed rifle "persuade" a shambler to go away in the form of a 5.56mm bullet to the face. The first time I'd said silencer in relation to a gun, James had given me an earful about how there was no such thing as a silenced rifle. I didn't care; he knew what I was talking about. I didn't understand his need to correct people when it came to guns so I just nodded and smiled.

At least James's guard duty was keeping him busy and distracted from our quiet giggling behind him.

I heard James say, *They're actually giggling.* Before he sighed and shook his head.

I don't think James understood what was really going on here. When Rhi first suggested this detour, I was annoyed. But the more I thought about it, the more I realized this little side-trip was a little slice of "normal" none of us had had in a very long time. We desperately needed some normal right now to keep our sanity. Even James having to wait for women to try on clothes in a store was "normal" to him; at least that's what I pulled from a memory of his.

I could hear him both mentally and physically in his agitation. I was starting to think James needed a very long vacation. To him, everything that wasn't about survival agitated him. He wouldn't let go and relax. I was worried the stress was going to make him crack in a whole new way.

Shae, Rhi whispered to my mind.

Yes, Rhi? I said, realizing I'd completely zoned out worrying about the man.

What's wrong with James? Rhi asked, concern lacing her thoughts.

You are such a girl, I grinned and felt Rhi's frown. *Guys hate shopping.*

No, that's not it. He's been acting weird for a while now. I figured he would have talked with you by now, Rhi said. *Or you would have pried it out of him.*

I sighed.

You know you do that a lot? Rhi told me for the second time since I'd met her.

What? I asked.

Sigh. You sigh A LOT, Rhi said.

It helps, and it's better than cursing all the time. I teased, then sobered. *I know James has gotten worse since the flashback.*

True, but I noticed something before that. Did something happen? When I hesitated, Rhi continued. *Wow.*

What? I said.

I've never felt you hesitate before. You've always been pretty forward with everything. If you're hesitating, it must be pretty bad, Rhi said cautiously.

Yeah, it is. So I spent the next little while telling Rhi about the rescue at the roadblock. While I managed to keep up the appearance of looking at clothes, Rhi stood still, listening and reliving the incident in my mind.

Christ, Rhi finally managed when I was finished. *How did...uh...I...* Rhi was having a hard time wrapping her head around it. *I mean, I know I've done some pretty bad things, but it was never on that scale. How...many?*

Around 40, I said solemnly.

And they were mostly asleep? Rhi asked.

Yes. I absently nodded. *James said he'd done similar things in the service, but I seriously doubt it was anything like that. You know how he is; he doesn't want to talk about the service unless we pry it out of him.*

Shae, it takes a lot to kill someone in their sleep, no matter how evil they may be. There are psychological issues that come into play, no matter how much the bastards deserved it. Rhi stopped. *But you knew that already, didn't you?* Rhi sensed I was holding something back but didn't press the issue.

Yeah, it's come up before, was all I volunteered.

This time, it was Rhi's turn to sigh.

Comforting, isn't it? I teased.

Rhi frowned, still worried. *Shae, this is serious.*

Coming from you, that would be funny. But I know what you're feeling, and you're right. What can we do? I had an idea, but I wanted a professional opinion.

Rhi was quiet for a long moment. *Shae,* she said with all seriousness. *This is pretty much beyond me.*

It's beyond all of us, but you're his best bet right now, I said.

What do you expect me to do? Rhi asked.

Just talk with him, I said.

You can do that, Rhi said.

I can be his friend; I can't evaluate his mind, I countered.

I don't think you give yourself enough credit, Rhi said.

Rhi, you're also a fellow soldier. As you like to remind me, you can relate. There are things a soldier will tell a fellow soldier but never their family, I said exasperated.

You're actually going to sit there and tell me you were never a soldier? Rhi probed.

Not in the sense the two of you are. I paused. *Please, Rhi, I'll beg you if that's what it takes.*

Rhi managed to bite her tongue to keep from firing off a comeback. Sighing, *I'll do what I can Shae, honest.*

It's all I can ask," I said, then nudged the subject. "You ever thought of opening up a business as a vampire shrink? I don't think I've ever seen one of those.

Huh. We do have our own unique set of problems, don't we? Rhi said.

Maybe you could offer it over at the resort you keep thinking about, I said.

Hey! Stay off my Kool-Aid; that's still my retirement plan! Rhi snapped.

Alright, alright. Now, let's get back to why we're here, shall we? I said.

Uh, Shae? Rhi said, apprehension tinging her thoughts. *You do know you can talk to me about things too, right?*

I stopped looking at clothes and turned to face her. *I do, Rhi, and thank you.*

Sure, Rhi said cautiously.

Rhi said it a little too cautiously for my peace of mind, so I continued with all seriousness. *But would I have to sleep with you first?*

Uh...I...uh.

It was rare to see Rhi speechless. I could feel how flustered she was at the thought, and I could practically see her blush even in the dark.

We already had an extensive collection of make-shift bags when we reached the final store Rhi wanted to visit. Of course, it was on the top floor, but as we came up the stairs, we had to climb over some debris in the stairwell. We would have been there sooner, but Rhi kept ducking into stores where she just needed to "grab one thing real quick."

The top floor was surprisingly void of undead as we made our way to the store. When we arrived, we started sifting through the racks while James once again stood guard.

His unease at the lack of shamblers was unnerving to me. Every time I felt him start to relax and settle down, a sound from downstairs or something we did would set him on edge again. The feedback I kept getting through our link was exhausting.

"What the...don't move!" A startled voice said from behind me. I'd been so distracted I hadn't sensed the arrival.

The man, correction, boy as he couldn't have been more than 16 years old had emerged from a set of doors at the back of the store. When he'd seen us he'd yelled and pulled a revolver that was now pointed at the side of my head.

James had already targeted the boy when I felt him make the choice to squeeze the trigger.

JAMES NO! I commanded, but I was too late. The bullet had already left the barrel and hurtled straight for the boy's left eye socket.

James told me the Air Force wasn't allowed to have "snipers." So, they sent them to the same training and called them "counter-snipers" instead. During this training, James had been taught striking anywhere in the "T," a line between the eyes and down the bridge of the nose, would normally shut a person down instantly. This wouldn't allow a hostage taker time to pull the trigger or even have a "death flinch" on their hostage.

James's aim was true and had the bullet struck, the boy would have dropped like the Goddess cancelling his subscription to life.

Instead, the bullet stopped about a foot from the boy's face and spun in midair.

It took a moment for the boy to realize what had happened. When he did, the boy jumped back, letting go of his pistol as it refused to move from its spot in space. The boy looked from the still-spinning bullet to his floating pistol and smartly chose to high-tail it back the way he came.

James let out a breath loud enough for us to hear over our now-ringing ears. "Everyone all right?"

"Thanks to Tara," I said, glancing over at her.

Tara was holding her head. As I watched, the gun and bullet slowly lowered to the ground. Rhi was beside her a moment later.

"Time to go," James said with finality.

"Wait, shouldn't we check on the boy?" Beth asked.

"He's long gone," Rhi tapped her ear. "There must be hallways behind all the stores. He could be anywhere by now."

"As we should be." James glanced around again and walked over to where Tara had put the pistol on the ground. Picking it up, he looked at it momentarily and then laid it on the counter. Without another word, he walked out of the shop and down the main corridor.

I looked at Rhi, who shrugged. We gathered our things and met up with him at the stairwell.

James? I sent, but he didn't reply. He just climbed over the barricade and continued downward.

He's not home, Shae, Rhi said as she bounded past me and caught up to James. *Gun up, Sarge, we're still on the clock.* This seemed to bring him back as he shouldered his rifle and began scanning again.

The gunshot was like an alarm clock to the once docile zombies in the building. Luckily the acoustics muddled the origin of the shot. The zombies didn't know which way to go.

Rhi stuck with James the entire way back, as she could tell he was just going through the motions. Muscle memory was running his body right now. He refused to say anything all the way back to the Dilla.

The ride back to Drakes was thankfully quick. No one knew what to say, so silence continued to reign.

I followed James up to our room, waving to the others as I closed the door behind us.

I found him standing in front of a mirror, just staring through himself. I jumped when he dropped his rifle but didn't otherwise move.

James? I sent gently.

I shot a kid, he said in a daze.

No. You didn't. I countered.

I saw him pointing a gun at your head. I knew he couldn't hurt you if I shot him just right. I pulled the trigger without even thinking about it, James said flatly.

You were trying to protect me, I stated.

The kid's gun was fucking empty, he hissed.

How could you have known that? I asked.

I shot a kid, James repeated.

No, Tara stopped the bullet, remember? The boy is still alive; he's OK, I tried.

James stripped off his gear and clothes without another word and climbed into the steaming hot shower.

I held off on following, instead opting to wait by the door and give him some time. I listened to him to ensure he wouldn't try anything stupid. I seriously doubted he would, but he'd been through the wringer lately—the roadblock, the bite, the flashback and now this.

At least the bite had healed without any signs of infection. Strange enough, the bite had scarred. Not even the injury he got in San Antonio had scarred him.

Usually, when a vampire healed, they returned to the state before the wound. I'd never seen an injury that caused scarring before. But better a scar than a zombie vampire. I hoped this meant we were immune. If this were true and I'd known it before, I wouldn't have had to suck on James's leg back in San Antonio.

Rhi checked in with me several times during the hour James was in the shower. I peeked in on him a few times, but he continued to lean against the wall under the spray. At one point, I wished we hadn't been at Drakes so James would have run out of hot water. Of course, knowing him, James would have stood under the cold water just to be prickly.

When he finally emerged, he was some semblance of his former self.

"Sorry bout that. Just needed a little time, I guess," he said, embarrassed.

I nodded and took him into my arms without a word. After a long while, we broke apart.

"The others are going downstairs in a while. They want to get gussied up and have a nice night," I said.

"Gussied up?" James asked.

"Not. A. Word." I cautioned.

"I don't know if I'm up to being social," James started.

"Bull," I said.

He looked at me.

"Pete found his mom, you found your friend alive and well, we saved NASA, and everyone has new clothes they want to show off so they can feel "normal" for a little while. You will clean yourself up, get dressed, and take me downstairs to have a nice, decent, civilized evening with our family," I informed him.

"Yes, mom," he mumbled, receiving a not-so-gentle slap from me for it. "I've got nothing to wear," he whined after a moment, that teenager surfacing again.

I rolled my eyes. "You've got stuff in the closet, you twit. Now go shave while I rinse off."

The After Party

TARA

Father: it's been several days since I last wrote you, for that I apologize. But things here have been very eventful and I've been kept so busy. Hopefully you can forgive me.

I've come to Rhi's world and to say it is different is much too simple. I fought the "zombies" I'd mentioned before. Rhi's description of them didn't do them justice. I've tried and failed to get the rotten smell of them out of my nose since our arrival.

Rafly would be proud of Rhi as all the training they did paid off from the moment we set foot here. Rhi is a beauty to behold when she gives herself over to the fight.

Speaking of fighting, I learned to control the "bullets" Rhi uses and can strike down a great many zombies using only my mind. It makes my head hurt, but a little pain is worth the victory.

You don't have to worry for my safety though. We have taken refuge in a place called Drakes. Apparently, it is a magical place that remains safe from the outside world and can produce the most amazing things. So, try not to worry.

I met Shae and James, Rhi's family friends. Shae is a formattable warrior with a mind like a razor. She has a kindly spirit and took me in as one of her own without question. She's also quite lovely. She is always watching out for our group. Even when two strangers travelled with us briefly, she protected them the same as any of us. I have a feeling, had the two of you met, you would have liked her.

James is more of a conundrum. He acts a warrior, but one that has been too long a soldier. He seems to suffer from battle sickness, such as Talon had during that difficult winter a few cycles ago. But Shae tends to him as his mate and Rhi as his battle sister. Together they seem to keep him on the path. It doesn't hurt that he's also quite attractive, but that may be Rhi's desires branching through our link again. I don't mind either way.

The world here is strange. Everything is so large. Roads, buildings, even villages are immense. There were so many people here before the zombies. But they're mostly gone now, leaving behind an empty shell of a world.

"You working on your journal again?" Rhi's voice interrupted my train of thought.

"Yes. I haven't spoken to my father is some time now and figured I'd take a moment to catch him up," I said, not looking up from the small book I was currently writing in.

I had several of these "journals" as Rhi called them. I'd brought them with me when we'd left our village heading for Drakes. I'd been documenting my life for many cycles now by writing to a father I never knew. I knew it was a pointless exercise, but it still brought me some comfort.

"OK, well I should be ready in a few minutes, so try to keep it short. You can write to pops later and let him know how it went," Rhi said as she affixed something to her ear and walked back into the bathroom.

"If you didn't take so long to get ready, I wouldn't have time to write him at all!" I said.

Rhi's head poked out of the bathroom and she stuck her tongue out at me before disappearing once again.

> *Alright father, I must end this shortly. Seems Rhi is just about ready to go downstairs. I will catch you up when I have more time. Until then, I love you and miss you. --Tara*

∞∞Ω∞∞

<u>JAMES</u>

After Shae got in the shower, I looked in the closet, and sure enough, a couple of new outfits were hanging in there. I wondered if she had picked these up for me at the mall or if she'd ordered them from Drakes. Regardless, I needed to scrape the whiskers off my face. It seemed I would be forced to be social regardless of whether I felt like it or not.

Sometime later, I was fastening my shirt sleeves and looking in the mirror. I was wearing a simple black suit with a white button-down and cowboy boots, of all things. When I asked her about the boots, she said she knew she couldn't get me out of boots, so she'd swapped my combat boots for simple black Ropers. I liked cowboy boots, but if I wore them too long, my feet began to hurt, so I didn't wear them that often. Her other reason was, "We're in Texas, stupid," which was good enough for me.

Where my outfit was simple, hers was elegant. It was a spaghetti-strapped midnight blue dress that hugged her body and sparkled as she moved. The color seemed to shift from blue to black to blue again with each step she took. She'd complained that she hadn't been able to find matching shoes, but Drake had come through for her with matching heels. She wore a black gauzy wrap around her shoulders and had slicked her hair back again, reminding me of our military dining out all those years ago.

When I could speak again, I tried to convey how good she looked, but no matter what I said, it fell short of how I felt. She kissed me lightly and took my arm, causing the tightness in my chest to loosen just a bit. Anytime she was on my arm, it made me feel better.

"You should have worn the tie," Shae pouted.

"Never again," was all I said as I escorted her downstairs.

Drake had magically produced a large, round, high-backed booth for the group in an out-of-the-way location.

"Where is everyone?" I asked.

"We're the first ones, silly. They wanted to make an entrance. So, we came down first to watch and applaud. There's no reason to get all dolled up without an audience. Rhi has been sharing her impressive vocabulary of swear words with me because we were taking so long," Shae said.

Drakes had started up business again. When we came downstairs, at least a dozen other customers were sprinkled across the bar. We didn't have to wait long for the fashion show to start.

Beth and Rachel were first down. Beth was wearing a blue, off-the-shoulder dress that fell about her body like water shimmering down a waterfall. It was simple, yet screamed runway model.

Rachel's dress was much more basic, being a typical "little black dress." It had a crisscrossed front that wrapped around her neck and was sleeveless. It went down to her knees, and she didn't seem very comfortable wearing it. If I had to guess, she hadn't worn a dress in a long time.

Shae and I laid on the compliments while, at the same time, the girls gushed over Shae's dress. I found it hard not to grin as I listened to them being "normal." It had been so long since I'd heard "normal" that I'd almost forgotten what it sounded like.

Rhi appeared next. She wore a cranberry cocktail dress that fit her like a glove and was slit up the thigh almost to her waist.

Her arms and shoulders were also exposed, which seemed to be the style of the night. Her tattoos were practically glowing in all their glory. Their beauty continuously drew my eye's attention and refused to let it go.

I couldn't help but smile as Rhi looked down on her admiring audience before turning to hold her hand out to Tara.

Where the girls had gone for lovely cover-ups, Tara had gone 180 degrees in the opposite direction. I guessed it could still be classified as a dress, but there was barely any material to it. The black v-front came low, almost to her waist, while the top wrapped around her neck in an open X-back where the material just managed to cover her rear, exposing nearly all of her long legs. It also exposed her tail, which swished to and fro as she walked. She'd opted for no shoes in an effort to expose as much skin as possible. She'd been covered up for too long and was done with it.

I felt Shae's fingertip touch my jaw and close it before drool could escape. We openly applauded as the final two made their way to the table. More giggling ensued, and I couldn't help myself; I chuckled along as they complimented each other on their outfits.

"What, no tie, James?" Rhi teased me when there was a break in the conversation.

"Cop rule number 1," I said, making Rhi laugh.

"What? What's rule 1?" Beth asked.

"Never give the bad guy an edge," Rhi grinned.

"If you're wearing a tie in a fight, it's one more thing the bad guy can grab and use against you. So we're taught as soon as we become cops, no ties. Ever," I explained.

"What about uniforms?" Shae asked.

"If we ever have to, clip-ons only," I said. "And those suck of their own accord."

Drake arrived with drinks then. There was wine for Beth, Rachel and Tara and blood for the rest. Rhi commented that this blood tasted nothing like the not-blood she'd had in Tara's world.

After the third round, I began to notice I was getting a buzz.

I thought we couldn't get drunk, I said.

Not on blood, not in the traditional sense, Shae answered. *And no, I don't count Natalie's blood as traditional.*

Then how am I getting a buzz? I asked.

Maybe Drake added something? Shae said.

I asked the next time Drake came by, delivering food for those who wanted to eat.

"Oh, it's a special vintage, sir. Only reserved for special occasions," Drake said.

"What, is it harvested from winos or something?" I joked.

"Oh no. There are no additional organic compounds; it is pure blood." Drake winked conspiratorially. "House secret, sir."

I shook my head. I shouldn't be surprised by anything in Drakes anymore. Seemed the "man" could do just about anything.

As the evening wore on, there was more food, drink and even dancing. Shae had asked Drake to turn on the music and made her selection. Everyone pretty much danced with everyone else, but the couples still favored their partners. I had reluctantly danced but had to be enticed to return to the floor every time. I just wasn't comfortable with it, no matter how much "encouragement" my partner gave me.

Shae and I sat at the booth when Rhi and Tara returned from the dance floor. Tara slid in beside me with Rhi next to her. I tried to avert my eyes as Tara's "dress" slid even higher than it had been.

"Aren't they cute?" Rhi slurred, her chin on her arm as she stared over the back of the booth at the dance floor.

It was a slow song, and Beth and Rachel were the only ones on the floor. They embraced one another and slowly swayed back and forth in time with the music.

"I wonder how long it's been for them?" Shae nodded.

"What do you mean?" Rhi asked.

"Beth said they'd been at war for nearly three years, and most everything was rubble. I wonder how long it's been since they were able to have a 'normal' night?"

"I wish things could be normal again. I miss things like..." Rhi faded a moment before continuing, "like shopping!"

"We went shopping dear," Shae said.

"That doesn't count and you know it," Rhi narrowed her eyes at Shae.

My eyes started to glaze over as I tried to remember normal. Tara's hand on my thigh snapped me back to the present.

"Where did you go?" Tara asked.

"What?" I said.

"Just then, you started to go somewhere." She took her hand off my thigh and tapped my temple with a delicate black claw, "in there." She then returned her hand to my thigh.

I didn't see Shae and Rhi's exchange of smiles.

"Nowhere, really. Just...trying to remember what normal was." My mind started to wander again, and then her hand squeezed my thigh and brought me back.

"No," Tara said.

"No?" I questioned.

"No," Tara said simply.

"No, what?" As usual, I was confused.

"No wandering into the past tonight." She smiled, her fangs showing. "Tonight is for celebrating the here and now." She picked up her glass and held it high as the others followed suit and drank.

"And on that note," Beth said as she and Rachel appeared at the table. "We, are going upstairs."

My intoxicated mind wondered if it was an invitation.

It's not an invitation, Shae clarified, shaking her head slightly at my male mind.

"Night all," Beth said and then the off-world couple were gone.

"Well now," Rhi said, signaling Drake for another round. "Now that the children have gone to bed, it's time to get down to some serious drinking." She grinned.

I imagined Rhi as one of those Japanese anime characters who tied sake bottles to their head and danced around in their underwear. I heard Shae chuckle, but it was lost as Tara's hand slid further up my thigh.

As another round passed, Tara turned and faced Shae and me both. "I don't have the mind link the three of you have." She took another drink. "I rely on my mate here," she reached back and touched Rhi's face gently. "But as you know, her judgment can sometimes be impaired."

"I'm not drunk yet," Rhi slurred, spilling some of her drink as she attempted to put her cup down and misjudged the distance.

"Prejudice?" Tara tried again.

"Prejudice?" Rhi straightened herself up, putting on an air of mock dignity. "I'll have you know I hate everyone equally!"

"Jaded then? Is jaded all right with you, my love?" Tara asked sweetly.

"Jade is a pretty green," Rhi continued to slur as she sank back down until her head rested on the table.

"And that will be enough for her." Tara slid Rhi's cup further away from her. "As I was saying, since I can't read your minds or feelings, you have to actually use your words to tell me how you're feeling."

A pounding began in my head as her hand squeezed something other than my thigh this time. The room suddenly felt very hot and actually span just a bit. I glanced at Shae carefully as the room took a moment to catch up.

Shae smiled at me and nodded with a slight grin crossing her face. She seemed to enjoy my panic.

When I turned back, Tara was nose to nose with me.

"You have to tell me what you want," her voice was husky and smooth.

I'd never heard this voice from her before, nor the eyes of which she now stared at me with hunger.

"Or show me," Tara said.

In response, I leaned forward and kissed her gently at first, which made her smile into my mouth. But then it became more and wasn't so gentle.

[Don't you dare screw this up.]

I don't know who Tara was talking to but what followed was something that should not have been done in public. It would have gotten the both of us arrested back home. I still had no idea how she kept from scraping me with her fangs. The image of her looking up at me from my lap was forever burned into my memory as one of the sexiest things I'd ever seen.

Afterward, the room was spinning from more than just the alcohol.

Tara sat back up, looking very pleased with herself and grinned at Shae.

"Well," Shae said, standing up. "I'll carry Ms. Jaded upstairs; you two coming? Or are you going to stay here and practice for your Amsterdam show?"

We all managed to make it upstairs a few minutes later, Shae having carried Rhi and Tara half supporting me as my head was still a bit loopy.

"How come you're not tipsy like the rest of us?" I asked Tara.

"Oh, I am, trust me. My whole life, I've had to fight for control of myself. Even drunk, I can't seem to let go of old habits." She paused as Shae fumbled with the door. Tara's normal, shy voice returned, "Was that OK, earlier?"

"That was amazing." I chuckled.

"Good. I was worried since it was the first time I'd tried giving one of those."

"Your first...never?" I asked, shocked.

"Not with a man." Tara grinned. "There are many things Rhi and I can share, but several we can't. Remember, she was the first person I'd met who didn't go crazy at the smell of me."

The door popped open, and Shae dragged Rhi inside.

"Well, I like the smell of you," I said, kissing her again before we stumbled inside and closed the door.

∞∞Ω∞∞

SHAE

I poured the sleeping Rhi into an oversized chair and sat on its arm as Tara and James stood at the foot of the bed, necking. I continued to watch over them as they got to know each other better.

"Mmmmm?" Rhi slurred.

I turned to find Rhi coming around and held my fingers to her lips.

"Good timing. I was afraid you'd miss the show," I whispered.

"What?" Rhi's voice was groggy, but her eyes cleared when she saw the bed. "That hussy! She said she'd wait so I could watch. What I miss?"

I filled her in on what had transpired downstairs.

"Damn, in public?" Rhi said, surprised. "I wanted to see how she did on him, her first time out and all."

"You really think you won't get another chance?" I rolled my eyes.

Then, all eyes were on Tara and James on the bed as they became one. They stayed that way for a while, locked together, unmoving.

"What's he waiting for?" Rhi asked restlessly.

"You're impatient, you know that? It's her first time, remember? He's probably making sure she's OK." I thought of something just then. "They are different species, after all."

"Oooh, I forgot about that," Rhi said.

"You forgot your wife isn't human?" I asked.

"Shh, they're starting," Rhi said, biting her lip in anticipation.

I stifled a chuckle at Rhi's excitement, then watched her face change. Rhi's eyes closed, and she seemed to relax.

"I didn't think you could link into Tara," I said suspiciously.

A smile crossing Rhi's face was her only reply.

Waves of emotion seeped through my link with James unbidden. I was not only surprised but also swept up in it.

"You are incorrigible, you know that?" I teased Rhi as waves of lust filled my head from her as well.

Rhi's eyes popped open, and she reached for me, "You can spank me later. For now, come here." Rhi caught me by surprise, pulling me into her arms and kissing me deeply.

As my lips touched Rhi's, her link with Tara poured into me causing me to shudder.

Rhi sensed James's feelings flowing into me. "You

hypocrite," Rhi teased. "You were tapping into James this whole time."

I chuckled, "Well, he is my tap boy." I pulled myself back from the events of the room enough to form a rational thought. *I thought you were afraid of me?* I sent to Rhi.

Rhi looked me in the eye, *Make me not,* she whispered.

Then, the mutual lust of four people mentally linked washed all rational thought from our collective mind.

I didn't understand how any of our mind links worked. Nat had thrown everything I understood out the window when she linked us. All I knew was I could touch the minds of James or Rhi pretty much anytime now. I knew James could sometimes eavesdrop on private links Rhi and I shared, and I didn't know how he could do that either. I wondered, as time passed, how much our three minds really would merge into one.

∞∞Ω∞∞

JAMES

By the time our group took a collective break, whatever intoxicant we'd ingested was long gone. We were sipping from the cups that had appeared on the table, but it was "normal" beverages, not the "special vintage" we'd had earlier.

"So?" Rhi asked, propped up on an elbow, lying beside Tara on the bed. "How was it?"

"You were there, you know already," Tara smirked.

"True, but I wanted to hear it from your lips." Rhi gently moved up and kissed those lips before returning to her elbow rest.

Tara glanced at me, who was resting beside her. Shae was sitting up, leaning against the headboard behind me.

"It was lovely." Tara smiled.

Rhi groaned. "You're so sappy."

Turning back to Rhi, "What do you want to hear? The fact I don't know if I can walk right now?" Tara said in exasperation.

Rhi raised her eyebrows and tilted her head, considering it.

"It's a start anyway."

This caused Tara to roll her eyes and Shae to chuckle.

I saw Shae and Rhi share a look I couldn't identify.

"OK, go shower. You smell of man funk," Rhi teased Tara.

"Bite your tongue," Tara said. "I think he smells amazing."

Rhi stuck her tongue out and pulled it back in before Tara could grab it.

"I need one too," Shae announced, standing up from the bed.

"In that case..." Tara said, scooching to the end of the bed and taking Shae's offered hand. "I haven't had a chance to catch your scent yet."

Shae shot me an apprehensive look as Tara closed the bathroom door behind them. It was my turn to chuckle as Shae's sudden panic.

Finally! Rhi said, turning to me as the bathroom door clicked shut. She crawled over and snuggled up next to me before tasting my lips.

I don't know what you're expecting, I said when we finally came up for air. *You were right; she wore me out.*

I said she'd break you. Rhi took hold of me, and I instantly reacted to her touch. *And I appear to have been wrong. It doesn't seem broken at all.*

I couldn't believe I was responding to her attention. With everything that had happened, I figured my body was spent for the night.

Rhi looked at me with a mischievous grin as she held her tongue between her teeth.

How are you doing that? I asked incredulously.

Oh, just something Nat taught me after the two of you left for Houston.

Do I want to know? I asked, trying to think straight as she was riling me up.

Well, it seems this little link of ours is more than just mental. It seems we can have some physical control over each other if done right, Rhi purred.

Uh... was all I could manage at the moment.

Let's just say...you'll never need a little blue pill...and...I can edge you as long as I want. Rhi's look was predatory.

I wasn't sure if she was telling the truth and part of me was more than a little afraid she was. After all, Nat had locked Shae and me away in her bed for two days. If anyone knew how to do what Rhi was describing, it was Nat.

I pushed all that to the "think about it later" part of my brain and tried to focus on the here and now.

My hand touched the back of Rhi's head, taking a large handful of hair and pulling it taunt. I knew what she enjoyed; she didn't hide it. Rhi was not a girl who wanted to be handled gently...most of the time.

I love you, I was surprised at how natural it felt to say as I kissed her again.

I'm glad, she said, running her hand across my cheek. *If you really love me, you'll talk to me.*

What do you want, foul language? I chuckled.

Maybe later...no, definitely later. Right now, I want you to talk to me, Rhi said.

Then it clicked and I tensed.

Easy...easy... Rhi said soothingly.

I'm not a horse, I complained.

That may be the case, She teased, gently squeezing me. *But you sure as hell spook like one.*

Shae asked you to talk to me, didn't she? I asked suspiciously.

What do you think? Rhi looked at me.

A moment passed before I spoke. *Seems you and Shae mended whatever fence y'all had.*

Sure, she found a way to push all my buttons in the right way. That, plus she likes that I take care of you, or at least that's what she tells me. The two of you have turned out to be the most fun I've had in years, but don't change the subject. I want you to talk to me, Rhi chided.

About what? I said.

About what's been bothering you lately. You seemed fine back in Austin, Rhi said

Yeah, that was before— I stopped myself.

Before the roadblock? When I looked at her, she nodded. *Yeah, mom told me about that. Now I want you to tell me,*

Rhi said.

What's the point? It was seriously fucked up, but it's in the past now. Besides, I've had to get my hands dirty before. It's nothing new, I'm handling it. I shrugged. When she didn't say anything I looked over at her. Rhi was staring at me.

James, you've passed out, what...twice now in combat? No team lead would have you in that state, you're a liability. Either Shae or I have to watch you like a hawk in case you have another episode. You're not combat effective anymore, yet you keep saying you've got it under control and you don't need help. You need to get your shit together and take the help we keep offering before someone else gets hurt covering for your ass.

I stared at her, trying to think of something to say but she wasn't finished.

James, Rhi said with all seriousness, *you were in the Air Force. Sure, some super-soldier program, but it was still the Air Force. Nothing you did could have been that bad.*

That was all it took. I knew I was stressed, we all were. But I hadn't realized how tight I was wound until that moment. The string of profanity that came out of my mouth was enough to make a Marine DI blush. I don't know if she did something in my mind, but it was like a damn broke in me. I started telling her the absolute worst things I'd done and the situations I'd been in. If it hadn't happened to me, it would have sounded like some bad TV show about the military. Horrible thing after horrible thing spilled out of my lips, and by the time I wound down, my cheeks were wet.

The shock on her face was obvious, as I'd never seen her eyes so wide.

You never told your shrinks any of that, did you? Rhi said accusingly.

No. I still needed my gun to work, and they would have permanently decertified me if they'd heard half of that. I tried to nonchalantly wipe my eyes.

No wonder they had you on so many drugs; they didn't have the info to give you the right one, Rhi said.

I stared at her, and she held up her hands defensively.

I'm just saying, she said, then kissed my chest. She made a face as my chest hair tickled her nose.

We felt the mental moan from the bathroom before the audible one reached us.

Seems our girls are getting along, I said.

Yes, it does, doesn't it? Rhi sighed.

I felt it as Rhi allowed herself just a moment to tap into her link with Tara before she pulled herself back.

Or did you mean these girls? Rhi sat up, allowing her breasts to brush against my chest. When I reached for them, she grinned evilly and laid back down.

Now, the rest of the story, she demanded.

So not fair, I complained.

Hey, I let you fuck my wife, Rhi said.

Yeah, and you did mine; so we're even, I countered.

Rhi looked at me, cocking her head to the side. *Are you? Married, that is.*

In everything but the law, I said. I was pretty sure it was the first time I'd referred to Shae as my wife in Rhi's presence. *Now, you don't change the subject,* I said.

She suddenly leaned over and took me completely into her mouth, but only for a few moments before releasing me and returning to my side. *Sorry, been wanting to do that for, like, the past hour.*

Really, I don't mind, I said, trying to recover from the shock of the touch.

Do you know how hard it is to give a blowjob and try to listen to someone? Rhi asked.

Actually— I started.

Why am I not surprised? She shook her head. *Get back to the story, mister.*

So, I explained the roadblock, the kidnap/rape gang, and how Shae and I murdered most of them in their sleep.

Rhi listened attentively. I could tell she was trying to put together pieces of the puzzle that was me.

I'm sick of killing, I mumbled out of the blue. *I'm sick of people making us have to kill them. Why can't people just be decent to one another?* I whined. *We used to have alternatives, jail, prison, and community service, but not anymore. People think just because there's no law anymore that, there aren't consequences. Without the law, we're back to the rule of the gun. And I slid into it so easily that I shot a kid yesterday without a second thought.*

But that's just it, Rhi interrupted. *You did have second thoughts, and you're assigning yourself guilt even though the boy is still alive. You care a lot. Enough to torture yourself over what you consider a mistake.*

It was a mistake, I argued.

Under the law you care so much about, was it a mistake? She threw that one at me, and it caused me to pause. *Would that have been a legal shoot under the UCMJ and your use of force model?* Rhi asked me. When I didn't answer, she went on. *You bet your ass it was a legal shoot.*

But what about the roadblock? I said.

Fleeing felon, Rhi said.

Bulllllllshit, I drew out the bull part.

Had you been enforcing the law back in the day, do you think you could have apprehended all those people, or do you think some of them would have gotten away to continue to rape and pillage? Rhi asked.

That's thin, I said.

You're right, it's practically fucking transparent. You said the two of you went through each person's mind before you put them down. So, how many people do you think each one of those monsters would have raped, tortured and killed if given the chance? Well, multiply that by 40, and that's the number of people you saved that night, Rhi sighed heavily.

I frowned just as heavy.

Is it the fact you killed a bunch of people or the fact you had to be judge, jury, and executioner because nobody else was going to do it? Rhi asked.

I hate the fact it was so easy for me to do, I said.

Again, it's not that easy if you're still torturing yourself over it, Rhi said. *James, you're the reluctant sheriff.*

The reluctant what? I asked.

The reluctant sheriff. When no one else is going to do something, you step in to do what you think is right. It's all about situational ethics and—

I know what situation ethics are, I interrupted. *I've read enough Heinlein to understand it. You can talk about culling monsters from our society all you want but when it's you holding the knife...*

Rhi touched my hand gently, *No justification will help you sleep better at night over this," Rhi continued. *The only thing that's going to help you is—*

Rough sex? I interrupted, desperate to change the subject and stop talking about this.

Is— Rhi continued.

Lots of booze? I interrupted again.

She put her hand over my mouth to stop my attempts to avoid the subject.

The only thing that is going to help you is you. When this comes back, I want you to tell yourself you made the best choice you could at the time.

But— I started.

Was there another way at the time? You've had three weeks to dwell in it. Was there a better way? Rhi stared me dead in the eye.

When I finally shook my head, Rhi said, *Say it.*

There wasn't a better choice to make, I droned.

You tell yourself that. Then you tell yourself there's nothing you can do to change that choice, Rhi said.

I can't change it now if I wanted to, I continued to drone.

And soldier the fuck on, Rhi said finally.

I looked at her, and she waved her hand in a "get on with it" gesture.

Soldier, the fuck on? I said, the barest hint of a grin on my face.

Good, that's your new mantra. Every time, and I mean EVERY time that pops up, you recite those three things before you do anything else. You keep saying them until they sink into that thick head of yours. You got me?

I've got you, I said quietly, flinching at the words.

What's with... Rhi started, but I felt the recognition of the memory. The boy in the desert with half a head and me comforting him with "I've got you."

I felt her mentally and physically shuddered at the memory.

James, that boy...that was fucked up. Rhi seemed to be collecting herself.

That's what you saw? I said incredulously. "Rhi, I'm sorry,* I said quietly, looking down. *You shouldn't have seen that.*

No one should have to see that, including you, Rhi said, pulling my chin up so she could look into my eyes. *But the same rules apply, say them.*

I—

Say them, James, Rhi held my chin sternly.

Is this part of your domineering side? I automatically went to humor to try and avoid this, even if it was bad humor.

James, Rhi said patiently. She surprised me because she wasn't getting angry or frustrated with me.

Fine, I sighed. *I made the best choice I could. I can't change it. Soldier, the fuck on.* I blinked at her. *Happy?*

Ecstatic, Rhi said, releasing my chin.

So, are we done with the psychoanalyzing? I asked.

That depends; you gonna stop being a mopey bitch? Rhi countered.

I laughed, an honest laugh that caused Rhi to smile.

Sure, I grinned.

Then we're good, for now. Rhi shook her head slightly.

What do I owe you, doc? I said, a bit of my true self emerging.

Rhi moved up and straddled me. Without a word, she reached up and wiped the tears from my face. I hadn't realized they'd returned.

Now, Rhi began, *there was mention of a hard fuck? But first, my girls really need some attention,* Rhi wiggled in front of me.

Yes ma'am, I obliged.

Goodbye, Desert Jayne

BETH

I took a deep breath and knocked on the door. While we hadn't known these people very long, we had fought alongside them, making them comrades, if nothing else. Their strange world seemed to read like something out of a bad novel.

[HA! She called your book crap! Wait, you wrote it, so does that mean you think your book is crap? My head hurts. --Rhi]

The door opened partway, and the woman named Rhi poked her head around it, looking at us. It was obvious she had been doing something strenuous as she was flushed and sweaty. I had a good idea what it was, but wasn't sure who with as this was supposed to be Shae and James's room.

"Sorry to bother you, but we're looking for James and Shae," I said.

"They're inside," Rhi shot a thumb back into the room.

"Oh," I said guardedly, unsure what to say.

"Would you like to come in?" Rhi's voice was laced with innuendo.

I've done some things in my life and not a lot flusters me. But this goddess of a woman offering me what I think she was offering caused my face to turn red. Then, a tiny squeak from behind me caused me to turn and see Rachel standing there with wide eyes.

"No, probably shouldn't," I said with a reluctance that surprised me. With all the oddities of this world, I was curious about what else might be different. "Um, they just told us that our door is fixed. We can go home anytime."

"Really?" Rhi let the door swing open and hugged me, oblivious to her lack of attire. "That's wonderful!" Rhi said.

I heard Rachel squeak again and spin around to look the other way.

"Yeah, we kinda wanted to talk about it," I said.

"Sure! Let me grab the others, and we'll meet you downstairs if you want." Rhi looked at my face, "What?" Then Rhi saw me glance downward.

At this point, I could feel my blush moving into my ears. Not to mention, it was suddenly sweltering in this hallway.

"Oh...sorry bout that," Rhi whispered. "Down in a few?" When I nodded, Rhi winked at me and closed the door.

I picked my jaw up off the floor long enough to mouth the word "WOW!"

We all met downstairs, thankfully fully clothed, about 15 minutes later. The place was deserted except for the Drake guy. We all sat around the center bar as we had on the first day we'd been here together.

"Yes," Drake answered James's question. "They can return home anytime they wish."

James looked at Rachel and me. "Y'all don't look that excited to go back."

Rachel and I glanced at one another. "It's not that we don't want to, so much as...well, things are still decent here." I sighed. "Neither one of our families is still alive there. The only real family we have left is our team."

"You're more than welcome to stay here. The compound in Austin could use Z-trained soldiers, especially those with the amount of experience the two of you have," James said.

"You two are the most experienced zombie fighters on this planet," Rhi added.

Rachel and I shared another look, one that lasted for a long moment.

"The two of you don't have to make up your mind right now," Shae offered. "Drake did say you can go anytime."

"It's just," I started. "It feels like we're abandoning our team. Enjoying this vacation when we were trapped here was one thing."

"Vacation?" Rhi cocked her head.

"Like Beth said, it's decent here. Not so much back home." Rachel looked around the room. "But now that we can go back, I worry that our guys might be in trouble. And if something did happen to them, I couldn't forgive myself."

I'd tried hiding my flinch when Rachel mentioned "our guys," but I was sure Shae saw it. Nothing got past that woman.

"I can understand that," James nodded.

"Really?" Rhi asked.

"Yeah," James said. "In World War 2, there were cases of guys who'd been injured and sent back behind lines to get patched up going AWOL to return to their unit. When the wounded soldiers found out they were being shipped home or to a different, closer unit, some went AWOL and made their way back to the front to rejoin their buddies. Some didn't bother to wait until they were fully healed to head back. It was that battle-buddy comradery. It gets into your head if you stick with someone long enough."

Rachel nodded before starting in on some of the stories from our world.

Shae motioned for me to join her away from the others.

"What was that about?" Shae asked after she pulled me off to the side.

"What was what?" I asked.

Shae nodded at Rachel.

"Oh, that. Rachel has a mad crush on our squad leader. He is literally old enough to be her father, which I think has something to do with it," I said.

"I take it you two..." Shae started.

I sighed heavily. "'We' started out with me being the big sis Rachel never had. You know, taking care of her, watching her back, keeping the assholes off her. Things just developed in the field. But I know I'm more serious about it than she is."

"What are you going to do?" Shae asked.

Smiling, "What I always do, look after the runt. If she wants to go after Grandpa, fine. If things work out, great! If they don't, I'll take care of her as long as she wants me to," I said.

"You can fight for her, you know," Shae said.

"Yeah...but like I said, I don't think she's long-term serious. Of course, nothing is long-term where we come from," I said.

"Then stay," Shae implored, taking my hands in hers.

Shaking my head, "It wouldn't work." I glanced at Rachel, who was still talking with James and Tara. "A little piece of her would always be back there with the Sarge wondering 'what if.' I can't do that to her; the guilt would eat me alive. Not to mention, she'd end up resenting me for it, even if she didn't want to."

"You could let her go back, and you stay," Shae offered.

"Then it would be me always wondering 'what if.' That, and knowing her, she'd get herself lost before she could find the team," I sighed again.

Shae squeezed my hands tightly.

"You are a wonderful woman, you know that?" Shae said.

"Yeah, yeah." I rolled my eyes.

I watched as Shae bit her lip, debating something.

"What?" I asked.

"You said things were bad back where you're from. What if I could offer you...a possible advantage?" Shae said cautiously.

"Such as?" I asked.

"I could try and turn you," Shae said hesitantly.

It took me a minute to catch on. "Into a vampire?" I said incredulously.

Shae nodded. "It's not a guaranteed thing; there's a big risk it could go wrong. But if it worked, you'd be more than able to handle your own against the rotters. You've seen how we fight."

I was quiet for a long minute, going over the idea in my head. "I can't," I said finally.

"It's OK; I wasn't sure if I should offer or not." Shae seemed to sigh in relief.

"Oh, trust me, if I were here...it would be much more

tempting. But we do all of our movements during the day AND...there's not a lot of 'food' left, if you know what I mean," I said.

"Ah, I can see where that would be a problem. Like I said, just a thought," Shae said.

I smiled, "Thank you, really."

"How soon are y'all leaving?" Shae asked.

"Pretty quick," I said. "It's been two weeks here. If what Rhi said is true, then only Behemoth knows how long it's been in our world. For all I know, it's twenty years later."

"Let's hope not." Shae paused and turned back towards the bar. "Drake?"

"Yes, ma'am?" Drake said.

"Once they go back through, can they come back?" Shae asked.

"I'm afraid not. Once back through, they'll be 'removed' from the establishment and not allowed back in, you know the rules." Drake said.

"Yeah, I thought as much," Shae muttered.

"Behemoth?" James chimed in suddenly. When I looked over they were all listening in on our "private" conversation. But before I could answer James, Shae was talking again.

"Wait, does that mean the Drakes on their side is working again?" Shae said.

"It had been damaged previously, which is how they managed to enter in the first place," Drake said.

"How long do you need? Did you want to rest up first?" Shae asked, turning back to me.

"Honestly, we only need about twenty minutes. We slept the night and have been up a while now. Some of us know moderation," I grinned, my ears getting warm again.

"Moderation is for monks," James said from the cheap seats of the peanut gallery.

Shae cocked her head and motioned me in for a private conversation.

A few minutes later I approached Rachel. "Hey, why don't you head up and start getting the gear together?" I said.

"Sure thing," Rachel said and bounded back upstairs, a

newfound spring in her step.

I waited for Rachel to depart.

"Too bad you can't stay. You could start up your own Roughriders here," James mused.

I watched until Rachel was out of sight and turned to him. "James?" I moved closer to him and lowered my voice.

James suddenly looked nervous as I put one arm around his neck and then the other.

"Yes?" he said cautiously.

"I want you to kiss me HARD and make me remember," I said, just as Shae had instructed.

"You want..." He glanced at Shae. "You want my memories of you...uh her...my Beth?"

"Yes," I whispered, pressing my body to his, trying to motivate him. I was nervous, but it was now or never. I locked eyes with him. I could feel his body practically vibrating beneath me. It was weird but kinda hot at the same time. It had been a while since I'd had this kind of effect on something. Shae hadn't said anything about this though.

"Christ, did you feel that?" Rhi asked Shae, who nodded slightly but didn't take her eyes off what she had set in motion.

"Are you sure?" James asked.

No, I wasn't sure. But...I didn't want to miss this chance; FOMO was spurring me on. Besides, I really wanted to know what the me in this world had been like.

Before I could chicken out, I swallowed the lump in my throat and nodded.

Something flashed in his eyes, and he seemed to hesitate before finally leaning in and kissing me.

∞∞Ω∞∞

<u>JAMES</u>

"You're having me escort who?" I asked, not believing my ears. I'd been on personal security details before, but usually for generals, politicians or corporate bigwigs the military used in the desert. So, when my handler told me I'd be guarding one of the prominent female pop stars out there, I had to hear it again.

"Jayne. You'll be guarding Ms. Beth Sinclair; she goes by Jayne professionally." Bob, my handler, said.

"I know who she is; what the hell is she doing in this hellhole of a country? Doesn't she know there's a war on?" I frowned.

Bob nodded patiently, used to me speaking my mind.

I had been a poster child for soldiering. I'd taken to the training well, responded to the treatments, followed my treatment schedule like clockwork and had a flawless performance record. But I did like to mouth off when I felt it was safe to do so.

"Of course she does. That's why the USO is bringing her here, for the troops," Bob said.

"If she wants to do a concert, leave her in Kuwait or Qatar where it's safe."

"She wanted to come here," Bob said flatly.

"What in God's name for?" I asked.

"That," Bob stood up, "is above my pay grade and yours." He handed me the chart. "This has everything you need to know. Her current head of security is a gentleman named Pedro Rios, a medically retired Marine, but don't hold that against him. Got himself blown up a couple of years back."

"Seems to be a lot of that going around," I mumbled, glancing at the sheet.

"Now," Bob started, ignoring me as usual, "he does private security for the stars. Spin him up on the detail, but make no mistake, it's your show from when she sets foot on this COB until she gets back on her plane."

"Got it." I frowned at the paperwork. This was going to be a twelve-hour pain in his ass.

"And James, keep it professional," Bob said.

"Of course, Bob. I'm the epidemy of professionalism." I grinned.

"Right..." Bob frowned.

Four hours later, I was standing at the foot of a C-130 cargo ramp, shaking hands with a beast of a man named Pedro.

"Welcome to COB shi— er...welcome to the COB, Mr. Rios.

My name's Sergeant Noble," I yelled over the still powering down aircraft engines. I'd caught myself before I lost my professionalism and called this place what it was, a shithole. "How much time do I have to brief you?"

Pedro looked at me momentarily and then back up into the plane.

"Maybe two minutes. She's up glad-handing the pilots," Pedro said.

"Good, here's the current itinerary. I just finished checking each locale, and security has been in place for the last three hours."

"Who's pulling the detail?" Pedro asked.

"Army PMO here is currently being run by an Air Force in lieu of team. I've been working with them for the past three months. You've got their A-team on tonight."

"For what that's worth," Pedro smirked.

"It's what we got. How many people did she bring with her?" I asked.

"Eight, plus three more security."

"Easy-peasy. The COB Commander is in the short bus over there," I pointed at the white bus that looked like a state-side airport shuttle. "He wanted to wait and do the meet and greet there. I think he's afraid of the heat."

"What, this?" Pedro motioned around at the 120-degree tarmac. "Just a warm summer day," he smiled.

I nodded and smiled back, taking a shine to the Marine.

"Pedro?" The voice came from inside the plane. The engines were almost down to a manageable level now, and the woman of the hour was approaching us. Beth Sinclair wore loose blue jeans rolled up over desert boots, an oversized brown Henley and a headscarf with dark glasses.

Beth looked tired, and from what I'd read, she had the right to be. The paperwork Bob gave me said she'd been on one airplane or another for the last 36 hours.

"Over here," Pedro called out as she approached us. He took one last look around the outside of the plane and turned to her.

"How we looking?" she asked.

"Good. This is Sergeant Noble; he'll be our security liaison while we're here," Pedro said.

"Ms. Sinclair," I nodded.

All I got was a nod in return.

"Where we heading?" she said in an exhausted voice.

"The boss man is over in the white bus waiting for us," Pedro indicated the waiting bus.

"Christ, it's hot. I thought the last place was bad. What did they do, piss off God?" she asked.

"Pretty much," I said, winning a glance from her.

I heard her sigh when she stepped onto the air-conditioned mini-bus. When I got inside, I saw her tired face was gone. She was all smiles and pleasantries with the commander. As the bus began to move, she kept up the banter all the way to the billeting room set aside for her.

It was impossible to keep a secret on a base with 20,000 people on it. Especially if they had nothing better to do. So, when we arrived, there was a small crowd out front. The cops held them back at a safe distance as we exited the bus.

Beth smiled and waved to the crowd while I kept telling myself to keep my eyes on the surrounding buildings and rooftops.

We had zero intel that she was a target for anyone. Her visit was impromptu, so it hadn't given any of the bad guys time to set something up, even if they'd wanted to. I couldn't help my anxiety though. Anytime one of my "packages" was out in an exposed area like this, I got nervous.

Pedro double-checked the billeting room before letting her inside. Once inside and the door closed, the pleasant façade dropped, and she flopped into an overstuffed chair.

"God I'm tired," was all she got out before the snoring began.

"Wow," I commented.

"Yeah, she drops off like that when she gets run down. Trust me, she'll be chugging energy drinks by the night's end." Pedro looked around and pulled a blanket off the couch before draping it over her. "Be right back." He walked over to the door, stuck his head out, looking for the rest of his team. He glanced back at Beth and me before stepping outside. He pulled the door most of the way, his hand keeping the door from completely closing.

This practically left me alone with the sleeping pop star.

I looked around the room but kept being drawn back to her face. I wasn't what you'd call an Uber fan. I had a couple of her albums and I enjoyed her music for the most part. I'd play them sometimes when it was quiet, and I needed to stay awake. Aside from her having an on-again, off-again boyfriend, I didn't know much about her.

Beth startled awake and caught me staring at her from across the room where I was leaning against the wall.

"What the hell are you staring at? Ain't never seen a girl sleeping before?" she said grumpily.

"You're cranky when you're tired," I grinned.

"Who isn't?" she growled.

"You've got about four hours. Why don't you try the bed? It's more comfortable than that chair." I thumbed over my shoulder at the other room.

"Where's Pedro?" she asked.

"Outside, briefing his team," I said, motioning to the hand holding the door mostly closed.

Beth frowned and stood up. Grabbing her blanket, she made her way to the other room, purposely avoiding eye contact and slamming the door behind her.

I was still chuckling when Pedro came back inside.

"What's up?" Pedro asked.

"Sleeping beauty woke up and went to go rack out." I pointed at the bedroom. "You staying in here?"

"Yeah, slept on the plane," Pedro said.

"Best time for it. OK, I'll be outside if you or grouchy in there needs me," I said.

Pedro laughed, "Wait, stay. I'm not sleeping anytime soon and promised myself I'd never watch another AFN TV commercial if I could help it."

"What? Who doesn't enjoy a good state quiz or infomercial from 1979?" I sat on the couch, and we talked for the next couple of hours.

Pedro joined the Marines straight out of high school and made it nearly 12 years before an IED medically forced him out of the service. He'd linked up with a security firm out of LA that guarded high-profile cases and been assigned to Beth's detail straight out the gate. Two years later, he oversaw the detail at her personal request.

We were swapping insulting Air Force versus Marine stories when Beth emerged from her room, causing us to stand up.

"At ease, boys, just need some water." Beth retrieved a water bottle from the mini fridge and plopped down in the other chair. She'd changed into pajama pants and a tank top. She'd removed all the makeup, and her hair was a spiky rat nest from all the gel in it.

"What?" Beth asked when she caught me staring again.

"Nothing at all, ma'am," I said, remembering Bob's words. Shooting the shit with a Marine who I was now on a first-name basis with was one thing. When it came to the client though, Bob's "be professional" kept repeating itself in my head.

"Bullshit," she said, taking a long drink of water.

"He's probably wondering why you stuck your finger in a light socket," Pedro chuckled.

She gave Pedro the finger as she took another long pull from the water bottle.

"Seriously, why is it so fucking hot?" She pulled on her shirt, trying to get a little relief.

To me, it was downright frosty in the room. Most of the barracks on base either didn't have AC or, if they did, it was constantly breaking down. Box fans were a golden commodity around here.

"Actually, this is probably the coldest room on the COB," I said, shrugging.

She frowned at me, "COB?"

"Contingency Operating Base," I said.

"Means they're only here till the war is over," Pedro supplied, and I nodded.

I looked at my watch. "You've still got a good hour if you want to hit the rack, Ms. Sinclair."

"Can't sleep with you chatterboxes going at it like two old ladies at a quilting bee," she said.

"Sounded like you were snoring away to me," I replied before my brain could stop me.

She gave me a flat stare and then turned to Pedro, "Can you believe this guy? Who'd they assign me, Gordon Ramsey's ugly brother?" She continued to drink her water.

"Be professional," Bob's words came back again, making me cringe.

"Yeeeeah," I drew out as I stood up, "sorry bout that. I'll wait outside so you can get some rest." I should have left it at that, but I couldn't help myself. "Maybe you can get that hedgehog off your head while you're at it."

Pedro howled with laughter.

"Oh no you don't," her voice caught me as I reached the door. "Sit your ass down."

When I turned around, she was wide awake and pointing at the couch. I held up my hands in defeat and sat back down.

"Pedro, see if you can teach this ape some manners while I tame my 'hedgehog.'" Beth frowned at me as she stood up and went back into the bedroom, closing the door.

"Hedgehog," Pedro chuckled.

"Too much?" I cringed.

"Hell no. Too many people tiptoe around her while she's on the road. It can go to her head. She needs a few more 'normal' people to keep her grounded."

"I don't know about 'normal,'" I started.

"Trust me, you're good." Pedro nodded. "Hedgehog. That one's going on the net tonight."

"What? She's got the weird short/long hair thing going on, and it was all spiky...and..." I started, but Pedro just waved me off.

A while later, Beth stuck her head out of the bedroom. I could hear the shower running in the background. I was pretty sure she didn't have the same three-minute shower limitation the rest of the base had.

"You married James?" she asked.

I held up my left hand so she could see there was no ring on my finger.

"Why doesn't that surprise me?" she said before disappearing back into the bedroom.

Pedro started laughing again.

"What the hell?" I looked at the bedroom door.

"Oh, my friend," Pedro started, "it's on like Donkey Kong."

"What? What's on?" I said, slightly nervous. Talking with Pedro had lowered my guard earlier. When that happened, I tended not to watch what I said and Beth had caught me off guard. I'd tried to recover, but her banter had caused me to drop my guard completely. I usually got in trouble when that happened, which I was worried about now.

"You'll see. Just be ready to return fire the next time she comes out," Pedro said.

"Where we going first, Pedro?" Beth called from the other room.

"Food at the chow hall with the big wigs, maybe some pictures. Then, autographs over at the rec center. The show ain't till tonight," Pedro said.

"Food?" She asked.

"Yeah, you know, the stuff you eat," Pedro said to the ceiling.

"Smartass. What are they having?" she asked.

I looked at my clipboard. "The peasants are having beef stew, but I'm sure they'll have something special for your delicate palate." I couldn't help it; I'd gone completely off the reservation. Bob was gonna kill me...again.

There was a long pause during which Pedro covered his mouth, trying not to make noise while he laughed.

"Pedro?" she said calmly.

"Yeah?" he managed.

"Why is he still here?" she asked.

"You told him to stay," Pedro said.

"Like a good dog," she said in the same calm tone.

Pedro's face was one long, silent "Ohhhh."

"Is she normally like this?" I asked.

"At home. But she's been on the road for a while now, plus she'd been up for like two days now. She's usually only like this with me and her handlers." Pedro chuckled and said, "But then again, no one's ever called her a hedgehog before."

"So, I'm OK?" I asked cautiously, still worried she might say something to Bob.

"Yeah, I think you're good. Just don't do it out there." He nodded towards the door.

"Of course not. I'm the poster boy of professionalism." I tried to look offended.

At the chow hall, the only thing that kept her from being mobbed was the ring of officers surrounding her. Had the fear of officer reprimand not been present, there would have been a riot. I hadn't been so much worried about the chow hall; it was the autograph session that worried me.

Pedro and I both were on edge as the fans were allowed to come up, get autographs, pose for pictures, etc. They limited it to one at a time, but there was only so much time, and I was worried about those at the end who might not get their chance.

Surprisingly, there were only a few groans and some cursing when it came time to shut down. Then Beth did something that surprised me. She had the rest of the people in line all bunch up and she took a selfie with the group. She told them she'd post it to her page tonight so they could get it. Then we were out the door and back in the van.

She caught me looking at her again, "What now?" She frowned.

"No, nothing. Just...surprised," I said.

"By what? That back there? Haven't you ever been a fan of someone? Gone to a concert or convention or something in hopes of meeting someone?" she asked.

"Sure," I said.

"Sucked when it didn't work out, didn't it?" she asked.

"Well, yeah," I admitted.

"I can't do everything, but I do what I can. If that one photo makes those 50 people happy, who am I not to do it?" Beth asked.

I cocked my head at her, "Huh."

"What does that mean?" she asked.

"I've been doing this a while now," I indicated our little group inside the vehicle. "Most of the people I guard wouldn't care, not many at least. But you..." I tried to find the right words to express what I wanted to say. "You try to do right by your fans."

"Why wouldn't I?" she asked defensively.

"It's refreshing, that's all. And nice to see someone who cares enough to try." I shrugged.

"Well, I'm glad I could exceed your expectations," she mocked.

"Oh, I wouldn't go that far," I said, giving her my mischievous grin. Someone had once labeled it my "come fuck me" look, but that's not what I intended. Just the mischievous part.

"And what the fuck is that look for? You need to use the bathroom or something?" She frowned again.

Pedro just continued to chuckle. "You two are free entertainment; you know that?"

"What, do I amuse you? Am I here for your amusement?" She did a pretty decent Joe Pesci impression.

"Well, actually..." Pedro started.

"Shut it, Pedro." She grinned. "What next?"

"Sound check at the venue," I supplied.

She nodded and sat back to look out the window.

No one spoke again until we reached the venue.

Pedro was out the door ahead of me. As I started to exit the vehicle, a hand on my arm stopped me. Turning back, I found Beth looking at me.

"You need to get better clientele." Her sunglasses hid her expression as she released me.

Before I could reply, Pedro opened her door and Beth slid out.

The venue was nothing more than a large hangar with the doors open. A stage had been erected against the back wall with some lights suspended above it. It wasn't much, but its lack of amenities wouldn't keep everyone on base from trying to show up tonight.

The sound check went quickly and Beth did a few run-throughs to see what she could get away with in the confined space. She was used to having stadiums with million-dollar lights and sound systems. Wire rigs that would allow her to fly around the room. But tonight, she would be getting back to the basics. She said she was looking forward to the more bare-bones approach.

Beth left the crew to finish preparations and returned to her room.

Once out of the spotlight and back behind closed doors, I had to ask. "So why here?"

"What do you mean?" she asked, running her hand through her sweat-soaked hair.

"I mean, why did you come HERE? Bigger, nicer, safer venues in Kuwait and Qatar are set up for this sort of thing. Why'd you come all the way up to this..." I tried to hold back, but I was pretty sure we were past the point of niceties, "shithole?" I finished, indicating our surroundings.

"Don't hold back; tell me how you really feel, " Beth mused. "I am hitting those other places too. But those are support bases, away from the fighting. I'm not belittling what they do; it's important. But the people here, they're closer to the action. They're always in harm's way and can't get to those other nice places. So, I come here and hope to make it a little easier for them. At least for a little while."

She looked at me, watching her. "Oh, don't give me that look. My dad was in the military. He used to tell me about how USO tours were the highlight of some of the worst places he'd ever been."

I didn't say anything; I just nodded.

"What?" she said.

"I didn't say anything." I held my hands up in defense.

She squinted at me and stood up. "Gonna get some rest, Pedro, don't let this one out of your sight."

"Yes, ma'am," Pedro replied as Beth went to her room, eyeballing me the whole time.

Later that night, I timed it. It took over an hour for them to get her makeup, hair and outfit just right before she was ready to go on stage.

We were backstage. The band was already playing the intro to Beth's opening number and she paused at the stairs leading to the stage.

"Hedgehog, huh?" Beth said.

I looked at her now combed, teased and styled hair; it was striking.

"A nice hedgehog?" I offered.

Beth rolled her eyes at me as she chugged the last of her umpteenth energy drink of the day.

The woman seemed to drink more energy drinks than a cop working a midnight shift. I figured she'd have an ulcer or a stroke before she got back to the States if she kept this up.

When I asked Pedro about it, he said she normally didn't do this. She was usually a bit of a health nut, even on tour. It was just the weird hours she'd been pulling on this trip. Besides, in Pedro's words, "Hey, it's healthier than doing crack."

She shook her head at me and pushed the now-empty can into my hands before taking the stage.

While I didn't get to watch the show properly, I got a few glances in when I wasn't scanning everywhere else. Beth was amazing. The energy, playfulness and joy she pressed onto the crowd was contagious. Halfway through, I found myself grinning and humming along...then I heard it.

The music was deafening, and the lights lit the place up like the 4th of July. It could be seen and heard from kilometers around, making it the perfect target.

I never would have heard it over the show if my ears hadn't been enhanced. Because I could, I was the first to act. I yelled at Pedro before leaping on stage. I pulled Beth away from the microphone just as the first round hit.

It was a wide miss, hitting out towards the runway. The bad guys who routinely rocketed and mortared the base weren't known for their accuracy. They seemed to enjoy blanketing the COB with high explosives and then running away before we could find them.

We were behind the hangar now. Pedro was trying to keep up with me as I sprinted for safety, carrying Beth in a most undignified manner.

The sound of the COB's CIWS reached my ears over the explosions as the 20mm guns attempted to shoot down more incoming rockets. The siren and continuous "INCOMING, INCOMING, INCOMING" from the COB's giant voice system filled the air.

Emergency bunkers were all over the COB. Most of them,

like the one I was sprinting towards now, were merely large concrete horseshoes turned upside down and surrounded by sandbags. They weren't big, and they weren't pretty, but they did protect from flying shrapnel.

I entered the bunker and put Jayne down as far in as I could. She was rubbing her neck when I heard the whoosh of the rocket overhead. I turned just as the rocket struck the corner of the hangar and exploded. Next thing I knew, I was picking myself up from where I'd thrown myself across Beth.

"You OK?" I shouted, my ears ringing.

Beth nodded, "Where's Pedro?"

Pedro was lying on the ground about halfway back to the hangar.

"Pedro!" Beth yelled and tried to go to him but my hands stopped her.

"Stay here, stay down, don't move!" I commanded and then sprinted out for Pedro. I knew it was a stupid thing; it was the wrong thing. You never leave your "package," ever. So, when I reached Pedro, I didn't check him, just threw him over my shoulder and hauled ass back to the bunker.

Once inside, I laid him down and popped on my surefire light.

Beth gasped at the blood spurting from Pedro's neck. Apparently, a piece of shrapnel had sliced him deeply.

Without hesitation, Beth jabbed her fingers into Pedro's neck, and the spurting stopped.

"Medic!" I yelled, looking around.

By this time, more people had started arriving to take cover. Luckily, one was a standby medic who had been at the concert. As missiles continued to explode, the three of us attempted to keep Pedro alive.

Finally, the 20mms cut out, meaning they weren't tracking any more incoming. At least, for the moment.

We didn't wait for the all-clear but made a dash for an ambulance parked nearby that had miraculously survived the barrage. We passed other medics tending to additional wounded, but none were as severe as Pedro.

We got Pedro to the base clinic and they took him straight

into the back. A nurse took over holding Pedro's neck from Beth, who'd been keeping him from bleeding out this whole time.

A nurse gave us the once over, but we were fine, more or less, and they had others to attend to.

A little while after arriving at the clinic, Bob showed up and tried to convince Beth to return to her quarters, but she wasn't having it. I waved Bob off and said I'd take care of it. He'd reluctantly agreed and left.

When Beth refused to leave, they'd let us wait in one of the doctor's offices as there wasn't a waiting room. Beth had taken one look at the rickety desk chair and promptly got comfortable on the floor. I kept an eye on her for shock and several times ran her through a few exercises to keep her grounded.

Eventually, Beth fell asleep leaning against me as we sat on the floor. Several hours later, Beth finally agreed to go back to her quarters after the medical staff said Pedro was in a guarded condition. He wasn't at Death's door anymore, but he was in the driveway.

I didn't quite carry Beth to her bed, but it was one hell of a lean. As soon as she hit the bed, she was out. I ensured she was OK and retreated to the living room so she could rest.

I pulled out the small tablet I carried and started working on my report.

Maybe 20 minutes later, Beth surprised me by emerging from the bedroom and sitting down next to me on the couch.

"Don't you ever sleep?" she asked groggily.

"Not that often." I continued to tap on the tablet, "Can't sleep I take it?"

Beth shook her head. "No, too much drama," she said through a yawn. "What are you doing?"

"The worst part of my job: paperwork," I grunted.

She chuckled and pulled her blanket tighter about her. "Do you mind if I just hang out here for a while?"

"It's your room; you can hang out wherever you'd like." I tried to smile, but her face made me hesitate. "You OK?" I finally put the tablet down.

"Stupid question," she mumbled.

"True, but I still gotta ask," I said. "By the way, that was pretty impressive what you did back there."

"What's that?" She asked.

"How you jumped in and held Pedro's neck. I know combat vets who would have at least hesitated at the sight. You dove right in," I said.

"What was I supposed to do, let him bleed out?"

"Oh course not. I'm just saying that took a lot of guts to do. You saved his life," I said with a healthy dose of admiration.

"You think Pedro will be OK?" she asked.

"Yeah, he's a tough one, he'll pull through. Might not be able to sing any duets with you, though." I nudged her with my elbow.

"Don't," she groaned.

"What?" I wondered if maybe she was hurt after all and just too stubborn to admit it.

"Don't try to make me laugh; I'm not in the mood," she said flatly.

"Then what are you in the mood for?" I asked.

"To get wasted," she said.

"Sorry, dry country here," I said.

She pulled a small bottle from under her blanket and twisted off the top. The smell of tequila wafted into the room.

"Where did you get that?" I asked.

"Being a celebrity has its advantages." Beth smiled and took a long pull off the bottle before offering it to me.

"No thanks," I said.

"Not a drinker?" she asked.

"Oh, I'm a drinker, alright. But I'm still on babysitting duty." I smiled.

"More for me then," she started and then stopped drinking. "Hey! I'm not a baby." Then she finished the swallow she'd started. "Is it always like this?" she asked a minute later.

"Like what?" I asked.

"The bombs and guns and stuff?" Beth asked.

"Not that often. Usually, the bad guy's aim sucks; they just got lucky tonight." I sighed.

"Huh." She took another longer drink.

"Take it easy there. You got work in the morning," I said.

"Hey, you didn't want any." Her voice was already going from groggy to slurred. She had to be dehydrated as hell from all those energy drinks. No wonder the alcohol was already hitting her.

The next time the bottle touched her lips I noticed it was already halfway gone.

"You know, I'll take some of that after all," I said. When she handed me the bottle, I pretended to drink it when she wasn't looking and set it down behind the couch.

"All gone," I said, smacking my lips loudly.

"Awww," she complained, swaying on the couch until she was leaning against me.

She was snoring before I could look down at her.

I tried not to move as I chuckled and pulled my tablet back out before returning to my report.

An hour later, a message came through that Pedro had been medevacked out of the country. Shortly after, another message informed me Beth's flight had been postponed until they could get the runway repaired from the missile attack.

Meanwhile, I held still and let Beth sleep on my shoulder. She woke up on her own sometime later.

"Better?" I asked.

"Mmm hmm." She yawned and stretched, looking around and then at her watch. "You still haven't slept?"

"I'm good," I said. That was true; I didn't need to sleep as long as I had enough medication.

Beth frowned at me and shrugged before heading to bed proper.

I let Beth sleep until she woke up on her own. She had nothing on her schedule as she was originally supposed to leave after the show. Later that day, after a lot of hydration, she asked me to escort her to the gym. She said she had a workout schedule she had to stick to.

Since it was impromptu, the gym wasn't crowded. She took the time to actually talk with some of the other soldiers who were working out. It was surreal to watch and not what I'd come to expect from "big shots."

We were eating when Bob showed up. "Good news, your plane just landed and is taxiing as we speak. They should be good to go in about 45 minutes."

"Any word on Pedro?" Beth asked.

"He's in a military hospital in Germany. They say things look promising." Then, Bob did something I'd never seen before, he knelt down beside where Beth was sitting.

"They tell me if you hadn't done what you did, he wouldn't be alive right now," Bob said gently. When Beth didn't reply, he continued, "When he's safe to transport, they'll send him back to the States for recovery," Bob said, standing back up.

"Ugh, bed rest. He's going to lose his mind," Beth groaned.

"Well, that's good." I eyed Bob, wondering why he'd come here as a messenger boy instead of sending me a message. Maybe he was a fan?

"Hear that princess? Your flying chariot awaits. In an hour, you'll be heading back to civilization, leaving us here to muddle through in our squalor," I said, hamming it up.

Beth just looked up at me over her spoon.

"Yeah, about that..." Bob said cautiously.

"Bob, if you say I have to come in on Saturday, I'm going to punch you," I said, quoting an old movie.

"Nope, I'm not going to say that. In fact, you won't have to come in for the next six weeks," Bob said.

Beth spooned a bite through now-smiling lips. As I watched, her smile grew.

"Hedgehog, huh?" she mumbled through a mouth full of food.

The next six weeks were relatively tame...as far as security went. Bob had loaned me out to her security team as a full-time liaison. Beth had several more concerts scheduled at the more "safe" bases in the area. There were no more rockets or mortar attacks, just me following her around, ensuring no one pawed her.

The extra security gave me more "downtime." As a result, Beth and I spent more and more time together. She taught me how to play pool. I'd only played a few times when I was younger, and she was some sort of pool-savant.

I taught her about guns, every type I could get my hands on. To this day, photos of the two of us shooting guns in the desert are posted up on a small range office wall somewhere in the sandbox.

Somehow, she always had alcohol around. I never learned how she did it, but she'd make a bottle magically appear late at night. We'd have a little drink followed by a bit of companionship, but it never rounded all the bases and made it home. Something would usually interrupt us, whether it was a knock on the door or a phone call from her boyfriend. Afterward, the mood would be broken, and we'd leave it at that. After a while, we stopped trying and just fooled around a bit before turning in.

Six weeks later, she returned to the States and, not long after, married her boyfriend. She sent me an invitation, but it reached me well after the date, not that I could have gotten away.

For a while, we talked by phone once a month or so. She asked about military life, and I asked about married life. But over time, the calls became more infrequent. They were always friendly like we'd just seen each other the previous day, but they dwindled, as they tended to do.

Pedro recovered and went back to working celebrity security. Sadly, his injuries prevented him from being in the field anymore. The few times I spoke with him, he seemed to be going nuts working behind a desk, but he was alive and grateful.

I received a package from Beth a year or so later. Her next album was due to be released in a few weeks, and she'd sent me an advance copy. A post-it note on the cover said, "Track six, thanks you."

When I listened to it, the song was about going above and beyond for the people you cared about. It didn't matter if you succeeded or failed as long as you kept at it. It was a good song, a little slow for me, but the more I listened to it, the more I came to like it.

Much later, Beth called me up from London, where she was doing a show. Once she found out I was in England on R&R, she invited me over to see her. I managed to catch up with her, and met her husband and her young daughter. Before the night was over, she pulled me off to the side and showed me the tattoo of a hedgehog she'd gotten on her hip. I laughed and tussled her hair.

In the few years between the London concert and Z Day, we'd spoken on the phone a few times, but never met in person. I had no clue where she'd ended up during the whole Z Day mess and no way of contacting her now.

$$\infty\infty\Omega\infty\infty$$

<u>BETH</u>

The kiss broke, bringing James and I back to the present.

"Wow," was all I could manage as I stepped back out of his arms. I made a face as I could still taste his blood in my mouth. I don't know why everything had to involve blood when it came to vampires. My tongue ran over the spot on my lip where he'd bit me, but it had already closed and healed like it had never been there.

"You OK?" James asked.

"Sure," I said, forgetting the taste in my mouth as my mind raced with what I'd just seen. I couldn't describe the experience. Seeing an alternate version of my life through his eyes...I thought I wanted to know. But, after seeing it...after...living it, I didn't know what to do with it. That woman acted like me in every regard back before Z Day. But I'd never done any of that.

"I swear I thought you'd made the whole thing up," Rhi said.

"Y'all were watching?" James turned to them.

"Duh," Rhi said.

"Do you mind if I keep that?" I said, drawing James's attention.

"What do you mean? You asked for the memories; I gave them to you. They're yours." James looked confused.

"Thank you. Those memories, they're confusing but...I think I'm glad I have them," I said. "Sorry, it's just so...overwhelming." I took a breath and got myself under control. "I can imagine writing that song after all that. I just wish I had the lyrics," I said.

"Here you go," Rhi stepped forward and handed me a CD. It was Jayne's most recent album, the one I hadn't written on my world.

"The liner notes have all the lyrics," Rhi said.

Rachel chose that moment to reappear with our gear.

Rhi turned to Rachel and handed her a small white box. "And this is for you."

"Ohhh, presents!" Rachel opened the box and found a strange-looking iPod already in a protective case.

"It was the latest model I could find," Rhi said.

"How?" I asked.

"All the little side trips at the mall," Shae said.

"Yup. And a little help from Drake. He helped me get most of the songs that came out over the last two years on there for you."

"Thank you!" Rachel said as she hugged Rhi ecstatically.

Rachel had managed to keep one thing from before her Z Day: an iPod her father had given her for her birthday. I'd watched her use a small solar charger to keep it running, but I knew she had no way to put different songs on it. She'd listened to the same music over and over again to the point I could practically quote her playlist.

Rachel was almost as fascinated by music as she was with guns. To her, ammo aside, new music was the best present there was.

"OK, I think we should go before this gets mushy," I said as we made our goodbyes to everyone.

"Thanks again for the rescue," I said, looking around at the group before me, knowing I'd never see them again. Swallowing a sudden bout of nerves, I said, "Good luck!" before turning and following Drake into the back.

∞∞Ω∞∞

JAMES

A few minutes later, Drake returned and nodded, "They're gone."

No one said anything for a few moments.

"Gonna miss those two," I said. "Seems like kinda a waste."

"What does?" Shae asked.

"Those two going back to what's probably a lost cause," I said.

"Would you leave your buddies behind in a fight if you knew they were in trouble?" Rhi asked.

"Fair point," I conceded.

"On a completely different note, I have a question," I said looking around. "Why are all our bloodtouches in the form of a kiss? I mean, Shae did it with my finger back in Austin. Why don't we do that normally?"

"We can do either," Shae said.

"Yeah, but kissing's more fun," Rhi interrupted. "What, are you saying you didn't want to make out with Jayne one last time?"

"That wasn't making out, shut up!" I said, blushing furiously.

Later that night, when Shae and I were alone, we were comparing notes on recent events.

"We definitely live in interesting times," Shae said, cuddling up to me. When she touched my chest, I flinched. "You OK?"

"Yeah, just a little sore," I said.

"Oh?" She looked at me sharply.

"Yeah..." I trailed off.

"What?" She narrowed her eyes.

"Tara...well...kinda...bit me." I pointed at my chest, where there was still a tiny bruise.

"Only once?" Shae smiled at me.

"Isn't once enough?" I didn't mind the occasional nibble, but I did not enjoy actual pain during sex.

"Oh, you big baby, you'll get over it. Her fangs don't hurt that much," Shae grinned. "Next time, just say no," she chuckled.

"Have you ever known me to say no?" I grunted.

"Not so far, but there's always a first time." She smiled at me.

Gotta Love Family

JAMES

"So, anything we need to know about this family of yours?" I asked as we were avoiding traffic snarls.

"I know, I know." Shae sighed. "I've been avoiding talking about it; I'm sorry."

"I figured you'd get around to it eventually...like when we showed up on their doorstep." I smiled.

"What's the deal, Shae, black sheep? Cousin It? What?" Rhi chimed in from the back.

"No, nothing like that. The place we're going is an actual ranch. It is where my master was based before she moved back to Louisiana. When she moved locations, she left behind a group to manage the property and keep it up in case she ever returned. The group that stayed behind kind of became my home away from home."

"Is this where the magical storage closet is?" I teased.

"ANYWAY," Shae continued, "the group was pretty much left up to their own devices for quite a while. They developed certain...eccentricities."

"Such as?" Rhi asked.

"They stopped feeding on humans," Shae said.

"Why?" Rhi said.

"Most of the tap boys went with my master when she left.

They had herds of horses and cattle, so instead of bringing in new tap boys, they used what they had," Shae said.

"Ick." Rhi made a face.

"It's not that bad," Shae tried and then gave up. "OK, I don't like it either, but it's what they do."

"Why is that such a bad thing?" I asked, confused.

"James, you've only fed on humans." Shae stopped me before I started. "That cow at the beginning doesn't count; you had no idea at the time. People who feed only on animals are looked upon like..."

"Like people who eat dogs and cats...and horses," Rhi supplied.

"I've had horse; it wasn't that bad," I said.

"Yes, but you understand the connotation?" Shae asked. "It's not wrong, just...not right in the eyes of our world."

"Wait, people eat dogs here? Why?" Tara asked.

"Is there any difference, physically?" My curiosity drowned out Tara.

"Aside from taste, no. Blood is blood. Doesn't matter where it comes from," Shae said.

"Anything else? Pentagrams, sacrificial virgins, anything?" Rhi grinned.

Shae scowled at her as we continued on.

"Wait," I started. "They were bound to your master, right? That would mean they ended up bound to Pagoda. How does that play in?"

"That's one of the things I want to check on," Shae said nervously. "It's been a while since I've looked in on them, thanks to Pagoda's little lockdown in Austin."

Suddenly Shae's expression twisted. "James?" Her voice was coy.

I glanced at her and saw she was looking at me with mischief in her eyes.

"Yeah?" I said cautiously.

"I've been meaning to ask since we're in Houston...did you want to check in on your kissing coach and make sure she's OK?"

I didn't have to look to know Rhi was suddenly leaning

forward with newfound interest.

"Oh?" Rhi said.

"Don't you think our relationship dynamic is confusing enough as it is?" I said.

"Oh?" Rhi said again, this time with more urgency.

"James had a girlfriend here in Houston who taught him all of his oral skills," Shae grinned.

I frowned at her.

"Oh really?" Rhi just had to chime in. "And where is this woman?" I could hear the evil grin on her face.

"We were just kids fooling around, it's wasn't a big deal," I said defensively.

"I dunno. Shae, don't you think we should thank this woman?" Rhi asked.

"I do," Tara chimed in.

When they didn't say anything after a moment, I glanced over and they were all staring at me patiently.

"Fine," I sighed in defeat. "She's in an evacuation camp in Ohio, her family all moved there a few years ago," I grumbled.

"I knew it," Shae grinned triumphantly.

"What? I...once I had access to the database, I looked up everyone I knew," I said defensively as Rhi laughed from the backseat.

"Not a big deal huh?" Shae grinned at me.

"Shut up," I grumbled.

"And that's why I love you," Shae said, leaning over and squeezing my arm gently.

Then Rhi broke the moment, as usual.

"Damn James, anyone you haven't hooked up with around here?" Rhi said.

The ranch was in an industrial area on the city's outskirts. A small private airport sat cattycorner from it. It looked as if the ranch had been there a while. The city appeared to have encroached on it as the years passed until the city eventually surrounded the ranch.

A sizeable two-story house sat well back from the road with low brush hiding part of it. A split rail fence surrounded the property, butting it up against two industrial parks with three-meter chain link fences.

"Well, I can see why she might want to move," Rhi said wryly.

"It used to be very quiet out here. But that was a long time ago," Shae said.

"Doesn't look like there's a lot of security." I frowned, not seeing anything.

"Doesn't need it anymore. They try to keep a low profile," Shae said.

The gate was closed, and a speaker box was attached to a pole. I pulled up and killed the engine as Shae got out and came around to the box before pushing the button. After a moment, the box crackled to life.

"If all you can do is moan, go away. If you can speak, speak," A voice said.

"It's Shae; please let me in," Shae said apprehensively.

"Mom?!?" The speaker bellowed.

I saw Shae cringe at the word, and I glanced back at Rhi, who mouthed the word "Mom?" I shrugged and turned back.

"Come on around back; we'll put you in the garage," and with that, the fence started opening.

"They still have power," Rhi commented as Shae returned to the Dilla.

"Solar grid as well as a tap into the hydro farms out East," Shae provided.

We rolled forward and skirted the house. The house hadn't appeared that big from the road, but as we approached, we realized the house went quite a way back. At the rear of the house was an oversized two-story garage that could easily hold five cars side by side. The doors opened as we approached, and I pulled inside next to three other vehicles. One was a large Lincoln SUV, which I could tell was armored. Another was a rather plain-looking mid-sized sedan, which didn't appear to be anything special, and the last was a—

"It's the Phantom!" Shae's reverence was almost holy. She was out of the Dilla before it could roll to a stop, running her hand along the car. "They still have her car."

When I finally got out and rounded the Dilla, I could see

Shae's eyes were misty. It was a 1927 Rolls Royce convertible that appeared to be in pristine condition.

"You don't think we'd get rid of the old girl, do you?" The voice came from the doorway into the house. A shorter man who was built like a steam engine, stood in the doorway wearing dirty coveralls and what appeared to be grease stains on his hands and face.

"Billy!" Shae squealed and ran to hug the man. She kissed him deeply and then pulled back, "Look how you've grown!"

Billy looked embarrassed, "Hey, be careful, I'm filthy."

"You've been turned," Shae's tone wasn't as happy as it had been a moment ago. Now, it was much quieter.

"Yeah," he rubbed the back of his head and shrugged. "Who are your friends?"

Shae put her arm through his and drug him over to the group. "This is James. James, this is Billy."

We shook hands, and his calloused hands had a grip like a vice. I also noticed Shae's arm was still in his.

"This is Rhiannon," Shae said as Rhi stepped out from the Dilla.

"Yo." Rhi gave a three-finger salute.

"And her wife, Tara."

"Woah!" Billy exclaimed as Tara stepped from the Dilla.

Tara had decided to rebel. Now that she knew she could expose her skin, she was determined to show off as much of it as possible. As a result, she was wearing cut-off jeans, designer "combat boots," and a short tank top.

I had to admit she did look good, even if she appeared to have just stepped out of a bad anime. I'm sure it was a bit overwhelming to someone who'd never seen her before.

"I really hope that's not a sunburn," Billy gaped.

"Guys, this is Billy. Close your mouth, son, you're drooling," Shae said.

"With reason!" He stopped and looked at Shae. "Do I want to know?"

"Just enjoy the show. Who all is home?" Shae asked.

Billy sobered. "Uh, Sean's here, Thomas, Randy is out and about (as always), David, Ron and Craig."

James noted Billy seemed OK until he reached the last name. From Billy's tone there was no love lost between him and Craig.

"What about Terrance?" Shae asked.

Billy's expression told me the news wouldn't be good. "He...didn't make it past Z Day."

"Oh no," Shae said gently. "I'm so sorry."

"It's OK, we push on." Billy nodded.

Shae ruffled his hair a moment later like she was trying to shake the memory from his head.

"How long you guys here for?" Billy asked.

"Oh, just a visit, we're making the rounds," Shae said.

"Really? For who?" Billy asked.

"Is that mom?!?" A new voice came from the doorway. A tall, painfully thin man emerged into the garage and wrapped his rope-like arms around Shae and Billy.

I figured I could literally break the guy in half over my knee.

"Ron, how are you?" Shae was grinning ear to ear.

A moment later, another man appeared and joined the group hug.

"Oh, Tom, it's good to see you." Shae kissed him deeply as well.

I began to wonder just what sort of family this was and then tried to rein in my sudden surge of jealousy. I could feel Rhi's eyes on me without looking at her. I couldn't get used to how this strange link worked. She knew I wore my emotions on my sleeve regarding Shae.

Glancing back at Rhi, I saw her glance at Shae and then back to me. I had a feeling her doctor shrink mind was picking me apart. Then I saw Shae glance at Rhi, then back to me. Now, I had no idea what was going on.

When Shae's little circle finally came up for air, she made the introductions again. All three men had dark hair and fair completions, except for Tom, who was about as Italian as they came.

We were ushered inside to a large room filled with comfortable chairs and couches. Before we could get comfortable, two more men came downstairs together. They were both rather tall, one with close-cut black hair, the other redheaded. They were both wearing simple shorts and t-shirts.

The redhead turned out to be Sean, while the other was David. They also flocked to Shae, both receiving hugs and kisses while they tried not to stare at Tara, who seemed to be basking in the attention. The two men sat together on a couch and joined in the conversation.

I noted none of the windows were boarded up or covered. Looking around the room, I noticed the front door wasn't barred. I couldn't see any precautions.

"Worried about security?" Ron said when he noticed where I was looking. "Relax, you're looking at one of the most secure buildings in the state. The windows, they're storm and bulletproof privacy glass infused with UV block. They're bolted into the walls and can withstand a hurricane without batting an eye. The walls are steel plate reinforced. After the fire in '83, we replaced everything with steel. Your suburban assault vehicle might make a dent, but that would be all it made. The front door is the same, with six-bar reinforcement. We could even make the place airtight if we wanted in the event of a chemical attack. There's no way those knuckle draggers are getting in here."

"That's impressive," I said honestly.

"Better be for the amount of work it took for us to get it all in place." Thomas chuckled.

"You'll did this yourselves?" I asked.

"Ron designed it; the rest of us provided the construction manpower." Thomas hesitated. "Course, there were a few more of us around back then."

"But that was pre-rat pack days," Sean chimed in. "Things got so much more interesting once they left." He leered at David, who shook his head. Sean slapped him on the shoulder. "Don't you roll your eyes at me."

"Somebody stop them," Ron groaned. "Otherwise, they'll be making out on the couch in a minute. I swear, it's like they've been in heat for thirty years."

"I don't mind," Rhi grinned, causing Tara to shake her head.

Shae just laughed, "Some things never change."

"Too true, mother, too true." A man in a three-piece suit, complete with a cane, stood in a nearby doorway. His presence seemed to suck the frivolity out of the air. He had wavy, dark brown hair, was clean-shaven and had dark eyes. He was European, and from the air about him, upper class at that.

He approached Shae and held out his arms, but the embrace was half-hearted as if he was worried Shae might wrinkle his suit.

"Hello Craig; please tell me you have more than one of these suits. I swear it's the same one I saw you in the last time I was here," Shae teased.

"Oh, I have three," he assured her. "What brings you here after so long an absence? Last we heard, you were chained up in Austin."

Shae leaned back, looking at Craig with a curious expression. She seemed to hesitate and then gave a brief synopsis of how she'd been assigned to Pagoda's court and put on lockdown. Then, after Pagoda's demise, we'd come to Houston looking for refugee families.

I noted she was very vague in her storytelling. I was sure it hadn't gone unnoticed from the looks around me. No one else had spoken a word since Craig had appeared, and all horseplay had stopped as well. Everyone was very attentive to Craig but not so much to Shae.

"And who are your friends?" Craig asked finally.

Shae made the introductions, and when it came to Tara, Craig approached her as if inspecting an animal at a stock show. When he attempted to walk around her to see her from all angles, Rhi stepped between the two, a well-practiced smile on her lips.

Craig took one look at Rhi's expression and promptly lost interest in Tara. Apparently, Rhi's reputation had made it here as well.

"Well, you are all more than welcome to stay as long as you like. Your room is still upstairs, as you left it, and there are a few other rooms to choose from for the rest. If you'll excuse me, I have a few things to attend to." With a nod, Craig turned and left the room, heading upstairs.

Once out of sight, the room seemed to let out a collective sigh.

"Swimming!" Sean said, breaking the silence. "David and I were heading to the pool. Would you like to join us?"

"That would be lovely!" Shae beamed. "I can't remember the last time I had a swim. James?"

I felt like she'd just remembered I was there, but it had to be my imagination. I shrugged and stood with the rest.

"We'll follow in a bit," Rhi said. "First, I'd like to get a look at this house; it's immense!"

"I can give you the ten-cent tour," Billy offered. "I need to clean up before I can get in the pool anyway."

Sean and David took Shae between them and led the rest of us down the hall to the far end of the building. Ron fell in beside me and started telling me of the other interesting architectural points he designed into the house as we went. I tried to listen, but I kept coming back to Shae.

The pool was Olympic-sized, of course. It seemed everything in a vampire house had to be grandiose. The room was one of the biggest solariums I'd ever seen. I couldn't imagine how much UV block the glass needed. The room was easily two stories high but all the glass made it seem even larger. I could see a walkout patio on the far end of the pool. The absence of the overpowering chlorine smell and Ron's continued narrative told me it was a saltwater pool.

Sean and David dropped their shirts on a pair of the many deck chairs beside the pool, followed by their shorts as they dove into the pool naked.

As I watched, the rest also began to strip, including Shae. I hesitated only a moment before joining them. I wasn't really comfortable with nudity in front of strangers. I'd been naked with other people before, usually the shower trailers downrange or the gym. But there was no social interaction, and my...girlfriend...fiancée...wife? Hadn't been present either. I really needed to clarify that soon.

A splash brought me back to the present and I quickly finished undressing. As I was jumping into the pool, I caught someone saying, "God, did you see those scars?" But then the warm, heated water enveloped me, muffling all sound.

I did have several scars on my body, a few from operations

but others from combat. Nothing had been terribly serious, bullet wounds excluded, but the scars always looked nastier than the wound had been. I'd hoped my rebirth would have done something about them, but apparently not. Shae had asked me about them in passing a while back but had never dug deeper.

When I surfaced, I wiped the water from my eyes and looked around. Shae was off to one side, talking with Ron and Tom while Sean and David splashed on the pool's other side.

Not wanting to intrude, I decided to try some laps. Aside from the cave diving I'd done to infiltrate Pagoda's compound; I'd not been in the water since becoming a vampire. Since most of that was short distance, I hadn't had a chance to try out my "new" muscles.

I started slowly to get a feel for moving in the water. I'd never been a great swimmer. I'd grown up being dropped off at the public pool with friends for a few hours, but we just played around. The kiddie swim lessons didn't count. And most military bases didn't have pools; or if they did, I never had the time to get to one. So, it took a while to get back in the grove. Soon enough, though, I was stretching out and moving faster than I'd imagined possible. It reminded me of using aqua-jets, little hand-held submersibles that pulled you through the water. They made you feel like you were flying underwater.

Suddenly, there was someone beside me, keeping pace. It was David. He moved like a sealion through the water and easily pulled ahead of me so fast I couldn't believe it. I was amazed as I watched David shoot back past me, heading the opposite way.

I didn't notice the wall coming up until it was too late. I threw my arms up as I crashed into the wall. I grabbed for the lip of the pool, pulling myself up and resting on the wall while my bottom half was still in the water.

I sat there trying to catch my breath and waiting for the room to stop spinning. Luckily, I'd been on the pool's far end, so no one had seen what I'd done, or so I thought.

"That looked like it hurt, you OK?" Sean asked, swimming up to me.

"Uh, yeah. Just got distracted, is all," I said, wiping water off my face.

"Let me guess. Not a lot of practice in the water?" He swam closer.

"Not since the change," I admitted.

"You OK?" David reappeared.

"Yeah, just...watching how you swim...that's amazing," I said.

David actually blushed. "I practice."

"Don't let him fool you." Sean wrapped his arms around David. "He was an Olympic hopeful back in his breathing days."

"Really? It shows." I nodded.

"Swimming's a lot easier when you don't have to worry about breathing anymore," David said.

I paused mid-breath, "Oh yeah." I'd completely forgotten I didn't need to breathe anymore. But my living habits seemed to still be with me.

"You must be pretty fresh," Sean said.

"Sean, don't embarrass the man," David chided.

"I don't mean anything by it," Sean pouted.

"It's alright. Yes, I'm only a couple of months old," I said.

"Since the outbreak, then?" Sean asked. Well, that explains it. You've been a bit distracted with other things, like staying alive. There's not a lot of time for swimming when you're out there."

"How bad is it?" David suddenly cut in.

"Y'all haven't been out there since this started?" I asked.

They both shook their heads. "No, we didn't get out a lot to begin with. We mostly hung around the house and took care of the animals. That sort of thing," Sean said.

"It's not good. There are a few refugee camps we've come across and a few towns that are struggling to keep it together. But those shamblers are everywhere. Cities are ghost towns now, and we're starting to see the first of the Mad Max gangs showing up."

"What about the military? Government? Anything?" David asked.

"The only military we've seen were the refugee camps. Last we heard, the government was hiding in Colorado, but we haven't heard anything from them," I said.

Sean and David looked at one another. "That's not good."

We talked a while longer, me filling them in on what we'd seen so far out in the "real world."

Rhi and Tara showed up a bit later and wasted no time stripping and leaping into the pool.

I shook my head at Rhi's lack of shame.

It's not shame if you're flaunting what you got, shugah. Rhi's voice was laced with a heavy southern accent and reminded me my thoughts weren't always mine alone.

"Why do y'all call her Mom?" I asked suddenly.

"Oh, that's easy," Sean said.

"Sean, be nice," David chided.

"Well, she is older than all of us," Sean said defensively.

"Sean," David scolded. Turning to me he said, "She was the one who always looked out for us. SOME of us were a bit more hot-tempered, or lacked restraint, or..."

"Or just liked getting in trouble," Sean finished, smiling. "You see, we're sorta...orphans. All of us were turned and then dumped for one reason or another."

"We weren't all dumped," David argued.

"Alright, honey, some were left behind." Sean patted him on the head. "We're basically the lost boys of the vampire world."

"That movie was so cool," David said.

Sean rolled his eyes. "Anyway, Doreen took us in and gave us a home in exchange for tending to the place. She had a soft spot for hard luck cases."

"All of you at the same time?" I asked.

"Oh no. We were spread out quite a bit. Seems our master took one of us in every decade or so. Anyway, Shae was around long before any of us showed up. So, when we started coming around, she kept an eye on us. It wasn't her job; it was more like we were a pet project on the side."

"I always thought it was part of Doreen's personality that had rubbed off on Shae during all their mindtouches," David said.

"Regardless," Sean continued. "The others in the household shunned us for the most part. Treated us more like hired help.

Shae didn't; she treated us like family. Whenever there was a problem or an issue we couldn't handle amongst ourselves, we'd take it to her, and she'd help us. The "mom" thing just stuck after a while."

Something slithered up my thigh and yanked me into the water without warning. I came up sputtering and cursing.

Rhi leaned against the side of the pool, her breasts bobbing in the water, with the most innocent expression. Her hair was slicked back, and water beads slid down her skin.

"Rhi!" I bellowed. The pool seemed to be getting warmer the longer I stared at her naked and wet form. I shook my head trying to calm myself down. Especially since I was naked and around strangers.

"Yes?" she said, packing more innocence into her voice. She touched her hand to her chest, "What? It wasn't me." Her eyes glanced down.

I had just enough time to see what looked like a red snake wrap around my ankle and pull me under again. This time, when I surfaced, the other three were chuckling.

"Not funny," I coughed as Tara surfaced beside Rhi, an evil grin on her face. "And you, I'll deal with later." I glared at Tara.

"Promise?" Tara teased.

"Randy!" Shae's squeal carried all the way to our end of the pool.

"Oh, Randy's back," Sean said.

When I looked, a tall man in motorcycle riding leathers was walking in. He had longer black hair and a thin chin-line beard. He had the rough "bad boy" look most high school girls swooned over.

Shae was out of the water and leaping at him. She wrapped her arms around his neck and kissed him longer and harder than any of the others. He returned the favor and picked her up off her feet, making her giggle like a little girl. He walked to the pool's edge and unceremoniously dumped her back into the water, laughing the whole time.

She came up sputtering and commenced to splash him until he finally jumped into the water, clothes and all and began to wrestle with her.

"Yep, that's Randy," David said.

I couldn't take my eyes off the two of them frolicking in the water.

"Race ya!" Tara said and was off like a shot through the water. David's grin was huge as he accepted the challenge and took off after her. Sean followed.

James, Rhi's voice had never, ever been as gentle in my mind as it was now. I probably would have missed it if it hadn't been so unusual. I blinked and looked over at her.

You know what you're feeling right? Rhi asked.

I nodded and looked back across the pool.

She pulled my face back to her. *You remember the words she told you when it came to me, right?*

Yeah, I said.

What were they? Rhi asked.

That if we... I started.

No, not that. The simple ones, Rhi said, holding my eyes with hers.

It took me a moment to bring my mind into focus with her and not on the splashing at the other end.

We keep faith, I finally said.

Rhi nodded. *Trust me when I tell you that you'll never lose that,* She nodded toward the other end of the pool. *As long as you keep faith in her.*

I watched Shae and Randy for a moment before returning to Rhi. *She called them family, like she calls us family.*

Oh, James, Rhi sighed. *I'd steal you away in a heartbeat if I didn't love you so much.*

What does that mean? I asked. Why do women have to be so confusing?

It means you need to relax, quit hiding out down here and go be social, Rhi snapped.

Never been good at that, I said.

Why do you think she sent me down here? Rhi asked.

She sent you? I said slowly.

Rhi kissed my forehead. *Talk with Mom later; I'll kick your butt if you don't. For right now, see if you can keep up.* Rhi leaped off the wall with the force of a torpedo launching.

It only took a moment for me to push everything else to the back of my mind and try to catch up.

They're Just the Best

JAMES

Randy turned out to be the most personable one of the bunch, which irked me to no end. He welcomed me and gave me a hug, wet leather and all. We all talked about the most mundane things; you wouldn't think a zombie apocalypse was going on. After a while, Sean and David excused themselves to tend to the animals while Billy arrived and joined the antics.

By evening, we'd been given a complete tour of the grounds and had way more information than we could absorb. A large barn had been built adjacent to the house to house their entire herd. It wasn't a slapped-together project either. It appeared to be just as sturdy as the house. Ron had chalked it up to needing to be prepared for hurricanes.

We'd spent three hours in the pool, and now I was feeling it.

"You shouldn't let Rhi goad you into racing like that," Shae said as she massaged my shoulders. We were in her old room, and she had me face down on the bed. Everyone else had gone their separate ways for a bit with the promise of a card game later.

"I don't know if it was that or your insistence on chicken-fighting over and over again, but—OW!"

"That didn't hurt, you big baby." Shae grinned as she put pressure on the knot in my shoulder again.

"Gonna start calling you the dragon lady—OW!" I grunted as she moved to a new spot on my shoulder.

Shae grinned and waited, continuing to rub my back. Finally, she sighed, "So, are you gonna talk about it or not?"

"Talk about what?" I asked.

Shae's hand left a red outline on my ass from where she slapped me.

"OK, ok...geesh. Never knew this would turn into an abusive relationship," I flinched.

"Oh, you call THAT abuse?" Shae threatened.

"OK, ok, uncle." I gave in before she could show me anymore. I was quiet long enough that I felt Shae tense up for another slap. "I don't have the right to be upset."

This caused her to stop what she was doing, too shocked by the statement. Instead of calling me an eejit as I expected, she said, "Oh?" and started rubbing again.

"I mean, there was Nat, then Rhi and now Tara. What right do I have in getting upset when you've let me be with them?" I said miserably.

She didn't stop this time but shook her head.

"If you recall, I practically threw Rhi at you more than once," Shae said.

"That's just it, you do, and you don't get upset. It's unfair of me to be upset when you're not," I said sullenly.

"This is my fault; I relax around you so much I keep forgetting how young you are. I wanted to ease you into my world, not throw you in the deep end. Normally, you wouldn't run into people like Nat or Rhi, definitely not Tara. You've just been one of the luckiest men I know. And I wasn't about to get in the way of that." Shae chewed her lip a moment in thought.

"Let me try it this way...and I may be making this worse, so just let me finish, OK? Rhi could do this better with all her mind shrinkage, but I feel you need this from me," Shae said.

I held my tongue.

"Do I get jealous?" Shae started. "Yes, of course I get jealous. Jealousy is one of the major human emotions. The fear of losing something precious to you is the primary trigger. I acknowledge that I fear someone may take you from me—"

"I would never—" I interrupted, starting to rise.

"I said let me finish." She pushed me back down on the bed forcefully. "Could someone take you from me? Yes. Is it probable? No."

"Hell no," I said fervently.

She slapped me. "I've been in contact with your mind long enough to know how you truly feel about me, which is a comfort. Knowing the people you've been with actually care about you is also a comfort. I would get upset if you were ever with someone who didn't care about you.

"But regardless, there will always be a little flame smoldering in the back of my mind. So, I acknowledge that little flame and tell it to relax, knowing that no matter what, you'll keep faith and return to me after you've had your fun," Shae said.

"But you shouldn't HAVE to feel that way," I protested.

"Really? So all that "you can love more than one person" rhetoric you fed me was a lie?" Shae asked firmly.

I took a minute to think about it before answering, "No, I know you can love more than one person," I admitted.

Shae gave me a knowing smile. "Ahhh, which brings us back to that jealousy monster being a constant."

"But it's not fair for you to have to feel that way," I practically whined. "I shouldn't do things that make you feel that way."

"The concept of "fairness" in the universe is moronic and childish. The only way to not feel that jealousy is—"

"To not be with other people," I interrupted again.

"Weren't you ever taught interrupting someone while they're talking is rude?" She smirked at me as I tried to look at her. "Do you honestly believe you could resist Rhi...or Nat, for that matter? No, you twit, there will always be something to threaten you and make you jealous. It might be a look someone else gives you, or an innocent conversation you're having that I don't think is so innocent. Heck, I could get jealous because you got a bigger portion of dinner."

"That's envy," I corrected.

"The POINT," she continued, "is that it's there. Trying to change your natural reactions, your nature as it were, won't work. For example, let's say that I and—"

"Randy," I mumbled.

"Randy? Really? That's who you're worried about?" Shae shrugged. "OK, fine. Let's say that I actually wanted to sleep with Randy. How would that make you feel?"

"Jealous, of course," I said.

"Of course, again, a natural response. You're afraid I might like him enough to leave and not come back to you. Now, what if you knew he loved both of us and respected us too much to want to try?"

"Well—" I started.

"And what if you knew there was absolutely no way I would ever leave you? Would you still be jealous then?" Shae asked.

"Uh—" I said intelligently.

"Of course you would. This isn't hard, silly; I'm not trying to play stump the chump. All I'm doing is describing things that are already going on here. So, if you keep banging that bimbo...DO NOT tell Rhi I called her a bimbo. Know I'll be a little jealous, but also know I love watching the two of you. And you don't know it, but you glow...mentally and physically afterward."

"I..." I didn't know what to say to that one. I had to admit that even knowing how much Shae loved me, I would still be jealous if she was with another man. I didn't think acknowledging my own jealousy would change how I felt.

"And what's that about?" Shae asked. "You would be jealous if I was with a man but not a woman? Why?"

I hadn't realized the thought had run through my head until she mentioned it. This link thing was nuts.

"I honestly don't know. Never sat down and thought about it." By this time, I'd managed to roll onto my side.

"You saying that the love between two women isn't as serious as that between a man and a woman?" Shae asked with a touch of heat.

I was at a loss for words. Did I think that?

"I could always call Sean and David in here; they've been married over thirty years now. Or how about I tell this to Rhi and Tara?" The heat in her voice had turned to teasing now.

"Oh God, no!" I said hastily. "I don't know..." I jumped on a train of thought I'd never expected. I didn't care who loved whom; hell, I wasn't exactly straight myself. Could I love a man as seriously as a woman? I didn't see why not, but I'd never met someone I'd been more into than just for casual fun.

Luckily, Shae took pity on me and let me off the hook with a smile.

"So now, if I want to go sleep with," she shuddered, "Randy, how—"

"OK, what's wrong with Randy? You sure didn't seem to shudder with revulsion when he came in today," I said testily.

"Ooooh, that's what's been sticking in your craw?" She thought about it. "OK, I was a bit overzealous."

"And naked," I said.

Shae laughed, "and naked. Don't tell any of the others, but Randy is my favorite. He is the oldest here and taught me how to ride a bike. But he's a brother to me; they're all brothers to me. Not like how some people treat their siblings; yes, I heard about your and Rhi's little role-playing weirdness. If I slept with anyone here, it would be Billy. But sadly, I'm not his type. Although I hear you are."

"Stop it," I said.

"Seriously, what is it that keeps having people fall into your lap...or onto it, as the case may be?" Shae asked.

I rolled over to lie on my back with her still atop me. "You tell me."

She pretended to think about it, "I mean, you're cute and all. Somehow, you've kept that kind soul thing going...but aside from that...nope, I got nothing," she grinned.

I tried to sit up and kiss her, but she put a hand on my chest. "Uh uh. You're not getting away that easy, mister, my turn," she said as she pushed me off the bed and lay down so I could rub her back.

"Oh, and next time," she glanced over her shoulder at me. "Just tell me what's bothering you; don't make me drag it out of you. I mean, I could do it Rhi's way, but I don't want to steal her thunder. It's so much easier if you'd just tell me what's wrong."

"Yes dear," I said, working on her shoulder blades.

"Oh yeah, I forgot to mention. Ron said if we're around on Thursday, we're welcome to his D&D game," Shae said.

"D&D?" I asked.

"Yeah, Ron is the DM for the guys. They're the ones who taught me about the game way back when. They play on Thursday nights and not even the zombie apocalypse can stop their game," Shae laughed.

∞∞Ω∞∞

JAMES

Everyone but Craig met up a little while later to play cards. It was the dealer's choice, but Texas Hold 'em seemed the most popular. Of course, Tara had to be taught the rules, which became entertaining the first time she laid down her hand, declaring she'd won because she had "three pairs."

What surprised me was the fact the guys had snacks out and were eating them. I'd started shying away from real food once I'd gone to a liquid diet. I loved the fact I didn't have to use the bathroom for anything more than showering anymore. But all of the guys were sitting around eating chips, pretzels and various other junk foods while drinking beer. Finally, I couldn't take it anymore.

"OK, I have to ask, what's with the food?" I asked.

"What?" Randy asked, mid-sip. "Who doesn't like beer?"

Shae stifled a chuckle and pointed at me.

"Seriously? How could you not enjoy this tasty golden beverage? It has everything you could ask for. You must not have had the right beer yet," Randy said.

"Nope, and I'm not starting now," I grinned.

"If the plumbing ever stops working, then we might stop," Ron said.

"Maybe," Randy replied.

"Alright, let's not start a holy war; let's just play cards," Rhi interrupted, putting down her cards and winning the $17,000,000 pot. Since money had become pretty much useless, the blinds were $500,000. The massive pile of cash on the table looked impressive, but it was as valuable as Monopoly money now.

"Give me that!" Shae said as she yanked a cigar from Thomas's hand. Only a moment before he'd pulled it from a case in his pocket and nipped the end when she spied it and grabbed it. "These things are bad for you!"

"Hey, that's a Louixs!" Thomas cried.

She looked at the ring on it and sniffed it gently.

"In that case, give me a lite," Shae said.

Thomas conceded and lit her up.

I watched as Shae took a small pull. Seeming to enjoy what she tasted, she took a bit of a longer puff and held it in her mouth with her eyes closed before letting the smoke roll from her mouth in the creepiest display I'd ever seen.

"Wow, that is good. What is that, cocoa and..."

"Spice. Yeah." Thomas nodded, hoping she would pass the cigar back. When it was apparent she wasn't going to, he pulled another from his pocket and coveted it.

The smell of the cigar was intoxicating. I had always liked cigar smoke, not so much cigarette smoke. But I'd never smoked myself.

Shae offered it to me, but I shook my head, "Gotta keep my poster-boy image, remember?"

"You're loss." Shae took another puff with practiced ease.

I was curious, but I'd seen how first-time smokers normally reacted and didn't want to lose any "cool points" in front of this crowd. "I've never seen you smoke."

"I don't do it very often. Up until not that long ago, it wasn't exactly a lady-like habit," Shae said.

Rhi snorted.

"Shut it." Shae pointed the cigar at Rhi, who quickly plucked it from her hand and took a puff.

"That's not half bad." Rhi nodded and started to pass it back when Tara nabbed it from her.

"I didn't know I was surrounded by smokers," I said.

"No shugah, cigarette people are smokers. To enjoy a cigar, you must be a connoisseur." Rhi's southern accent was back as she watched Tara fumbling with the cigar. Rhi cringed as Tara took a long pull.

Tara immediately began a coughing fit, not used to the strong tobacco.

"You take little puffs," Rhi coached, starting to take the cigar back, but Tara recovered and tried again, this time without the explosive coughing. "Better?"

Tara nodded and passed it back.

"Of course, I prefer a pipe." Rhi handed the cigar back to Shae.

"I think I have one upstairs," Thomas offered, but she waved him off.

"Come here; I want to try something," I said, pulling Shae to me and kissing her deeply. It wasn't like kissing a cigarette smoker, which was disgusting. The flavor of the cigar mixed with her mouth enticed me. "Yep, definitely don't need to smoke it to enjoy it," I smiled.

"Come on, Starbuck, it's your deal," Randy called out to Shae.

Shae rolled her eyes at both of us and turned back to the cards. "Where's Craig, by the way?" she asked as she began dealing out the next hand.

The room was silent for a moment before Randy looked around and spoke up. "He...sort of does his own thing now."

"What's up with that? He didn't used to be so standoffish. It used to be he'd be down here in the mix. Maybe sitting on a high stool, but he'd still be at the table," Shae said.

This brought smiles and nods around the table.

"What's up with him anyway?" I asked. "He seems a bit too...stuffy to fit in with this crowd."

"You saying we're lowbrow?" Sean put on his best hurt look, causing me to pause.

"Quit it," Shae wagged a finger at Sean.

Just playing mom." Sean frowned.

"That's twice now you've defended him, Mom. Is this another of our lost boys come home to roost?" David teased.

Shae rolled her eyes.

"He's no lost boy," Randy said, leaning forward and eyeing

Shae with a serious look.

Shae seemed to squirm under his gaze, and the slightest touch of color crept into her cheeks.

"Holy shit, she's blushing!" Billy chimed in. "I didn't know mom could do that."

They all focused on Shae, and I could sense her sudden unease.

"Hey guys, could we get back to the game?" I tried to steer them away from Shae, but when that failed, I racked my brain before throwing my cards down on the table.

"Fine!" I sighed loudly, drawing everyone's attention away from Shae. "If you must know, the council sent me down here to evaluate remaining strongholds as possible evacuation sites. Shae was assigned as my guard and escort as she had been through the circuit here in Texas more than anyone else."

"Evacuation sites?" Ron questioned; Shae momentarily forgotten.

Nodding, "The current sites are too near population centers and have drawn too much unwanted attention. The council is currently considering splitting up to ensure something survives in a worst-case scenario. The problem is they're having issues establishing a stable communication base with spreading out so much." I was pulling bullshit from deep out of my ass now.

"We still have an operational communications suite," Ron added. "We just haven't had a reason to use it."

"That's good; I didn't know that," I said.

"We still have the tunnel to the airport as well," Thomas chimed in. "I've maintained the tunnel; it's still dry and secure."

"The one across the street?" I asked.

Thomas nodded.

"I'll add it to the report," I said.

Sean grinned, "Could you imagine the look on Craig's face if a councilman moved in here?" The rest of them smiled at the inside joke, except for Randy.

Randy looked from me, then to Shae and back. He shook his head.

"You're so full of shit," Randy said flatly.

I looked him in the eye and locked my face down using all

my military bearing. I was starting to understand why Shae liked Randy so much; he had a good head on his shoulders. I was about to add something stoic when Shae's hand covered mine. When I turned to look at her, she kissed me warmly.

"I love you," Shae whispered. Turning to the rest of the group, she said, "James is my fiancée." She held up her hand where the tiny gold ring I'd bought her all those years ago rested.

Two heartbeats of silence passed before pandemonium broke out. The next ten minutes were hugs and congratulations, followed by Shae sitting down and telling them about how we met and some of the courting. She again skipped some parts they didn't need to hear and was creative in other parts to cover the strange and long engagement.

Much later, Rhi chuckled, "Well, I'm glad that worked out. I thought I would have to pop a boob out or something to break the tension."

"You still can if you want," Billy chimed in.

"I thought you batted for the other team, kid," Rhi said.

Billy shrugged, "Doesn't mean I can't appreciate beauty."

Rhi grinned, "I like this kid. I'm calling dibs!" She patted him on the cheek rather forcefully.

Tara gave Billy the once over and added, "Eh, why not?"

Rhi snorted a laugh and just shook her head.

Billy, for once, looked embarrassed.

The game eventually resumed, but several had lost interest and retired by then. Eventually, it came down to just the Austin team and Randy talking, the cards almost completely forgotten.

"To answer your question," Randy continued as if the conversation hadn't been interrupted several hours ago. "Craig is from a well-to-do New England family that sorta got themselves blacklisted."

"Blacklisted?" I asked.

"If you violate some of the golden rules or threaten our way of life, you can get yourself blacklisted," Shae started. "Once blacklisted, your entire family pretty much becomes outcasts."

"I thought you said there wasn't some big mafia family ruling over vampires," I said.

"There isn't," Shae answered.

"The council is nothing like what you're suggesting, James," Rhi said. "They don't rule, and they don't govern. They're more like an advisory body. If something is brought to their attention, they inform whatever governing body is in the affected area. Rarely does someone do something that causes them to issue something, like a blacklist statement. Even when they do, all they are doing is spreading what they have done to all governing bodies, not just the one in the immediate affected area."

"But don't let all that fancy talk fool you, James," Randy cut in. "If they want something done, it gets done. They just get to claim their hands are clean."

Shae frowned at him.

"Am I wrong?" Randy said.

Sighing, "you oversimplify things," Shae said.

"I call 'em like I see 'em." Randy shrugged.

"So, you two don't always see eye to eye on everything after all." I nodded.

"Not on politics." Randy shook his head. "She's always been too close to it."

"And you could never see the big picture," Shae fired back.

"Guys?" Rhi interrupted. "While I'd love to watch y'all get into a knife fight over stupid shit, we're tired and going to bed." Rhi said, standing up.

"I'm not THAT tired," Tara said, retrieving two of her hidden knives and laying them on the table.

"Knock that off!" Rhi said, grabbing the knives and pulling on Tara.

Tara grinned and allowed herself to be guided to her feet.

Rhi touched Shae's shoulder as she passed, "Night."

Shae reached up and touched Rhi's hand. "Night you."

When Rhi passed me, she flicked my ear, "Don't let her stay up too late." Then she and Tara were gone.

I watched them go, wondering about the little exchange between Rhi and Shae. They'd butted heads ever since that first night back at the Hacienda. It shocked me when they'd been intimate at Drakes, but I thought that was a heat-of-the-moment thing. What I just watched felt more like two sisters saying goodnight.

Shae returned to glaring at Randy, who glared right back across the table. I sensed this wasn't heading in a good direction and interrupted.

"Craig." The one word broke the spell, and Randy looked at me.

"What about him?" Randy asked.

"What's really going on?" I asked.

"What do you mean?" Randy said.

"You all tip-toe around him, which, from how Shae talks, isn't how it normally is around here. Y'all will also not really talk about him," I said.

Randy was silent.

"Why was Billy turned?" Shae interjected when Randy didn't say anything. "He was a tap boy with absolutely no interest in ever being turned. What changed?" When Randy didn't say anything, she continued. "He wouldn't talk to me about it either. What's going on here, Randy?"

"Wouldn't or couldn't?" I thought aloud.

"Wait, what?" Shae looked at me, then it clicked. "Craig turned him, didn't he?"

Randy continued his silence.

Shae stood up and walked across the room to stand before Randy, her eyes blazing. She took his head in her hands and leaned down to his face. He offered no resistance as she kissed him, HARD.

I had never ridden along on a mind link like this before. As she established the bloodtouch with him, he didn't offer any resistance, but he didn't offer any help either. I couldn't keep up with the images as she flipped through them in his mind, but I did hear when she spoke.

You're all bloodbound to him! He FORCED you all?!?

Her mental gasp rolled through me, along with a wave of disgust. Apparently, when their master had been killed, Pagoda had visited the ranch, and shortly afterward, Craig had enslaved them all. He'd forbidden them all to speak of it and been ruling over them ever since.

*That's why you stay away as much as you can. You can't

stand him anymore,* Shae said.

He changed after Pagoda's visit, Randy finally spoke. *I don't know what Pagoda did to him or if he did anything. I know he wasn't the same man afterward. Honestly, though, he hasn't done anything with his power. He runs the house, but there's really nothing in that.*

That you know of. Shae was fuming. *He could do anything he wanted and make you forget about it. Trust me, I know!* She hissed.

I could feel the waves of fury rolling off her.

Shae, I said quietly, trying to use the same tone she used on me.

My voice cut through the rushing sound that had filled her ears a moment ago, and she instantly calmed. Taking a deep breath, she let it out, *Thanks.*

You do it for me all the time, I sent.

Shae turned back to Randy, *I'm going to have to talk to him.*

Only talk? Randy said.

Of course. She was surprised that Randy would think she'd do otherwise. Then she remembered only a moment ago, she was practically seeing red. *I need to know what happened. I need to know what's going on with my boys.*

I sensed a strange pause as Randy finally spoke.

You never really had an interest in me, did you? Randy said.

You never showed any interest. Shae looked at him.

I was too intimidated by you, Randy said.

By me? I was just starting to pull myself together when we first met, Shae said.

I remember. You were so adorable but so fragile. It took you a long time to...accept who you were, Randy said.

You were the big brother I never had, Shae said.

Randy pulled Shae into his arms and held her gently. *By the time you were strong enough...you'd become my sister.* He sighed, *We never had a chance, did we?*

Her smile was kind, *I love you silly. But not like that. It would be too...weird.*

Randy broke their kiss, and with it, the mental contact the three of us shared. He kissed her forehead, "I love you too, kiddo."

Shae looked up at Randy and kissed his lips, gentle at first, then with more urgency, but it was forced and didn't feel right. After an awkward minute or so, they finally broke.

"Yeah," he sighed, "weird."

"Definitely weird," she agreed. "But I did try."

"Oh, that you did," he agreed, smiling.

"Who knows," I said, breaking the weird little scene and startling the both of them. They'd forgotten I was in the room. "Maybe you'll both eventually develop a sibling fetish."

"What kind of sicko are you marrying?" Randy grinned at Shae.

"You have no idea. The whole sister thing is just the tip of the iceberg. Don't get me started on his furry fetish." Shae grinned.

"Oh, come on!" I protested.

"And then there's the whole cosplay thing," Shae added.

This time, it was my turn to blush.

"Oh yeah, we still have all that stuff in storage in the attic," Randy offered.

Shae's eyes just about popped out of her skull as she smacked Randy. "Why'd you tell him that?"

"What?" Randy watched the smile curl across my face and winked at me. "You look good in some of those outfits," he said.

"Some?" She put more hurt in her voice than there should have been.

"Which one are you going to wear on your wedding night? Rogue? Catwoman? Or are you going all out with the whole slave-Leia bit?" Randy's grin was absolutely evil by this point.

Shae pushed herself off Randy's lap and walked away, grabbing my hand as she headed for the door.

"I guess that's goodnight," I waved.

"Night," Randy chuckled.

The next morning, a pair of large Rubbermaid containers was outside Shae's room. When I pulled them inside and opened one, I pulled out a thin, green spandex outfit and held it up as

Shae stepped out of the bathroom.

"I ever mention Rogue was my favorite X-Men?" I asked.

Shae's face turned bright red. She didn't say a word; she just turned around and went back into the bathroom, closing the door behind her.

I reminded myself to thank Randy the next time I saw him.

∞∞Ω∞∞

JAMES

I'd never lived in an all-vampire household before. I was still used to human rituals like meal times and such. But when you didn't have to eat every day, let alone every few hours, there really wasn't any breakfast, lunch or dinner routine. People just sort of did their own thing, maybe passing in the halls occasionally. I found it rather spooky.

The only ritual they seemed to have was chores. While half tended to the animals, Billy managed the vehicles and anything mechanical in the place, including the solar cells, while the rest kept up cleaning and such.

The barn the animals were kept in wasn't like any barn I had ever seen. It wasn't a wood frame with tin walls. This was an actual building with insulation, climate control, the works. These cows had it better than some people back at the Austin compound.

I was just about to ask Sean how they handled blood exchange when I was interrupted.

James! Rhi called.

Rhi? I said.

Get upstairs now!

The urgency in her voice had me already moving. *What's going on?*

Shae and Craig are getting into it. Rhi's voice was tense.

While I had never visited Craig's office, it was easy enough to find. All I had to do was follow the shouting. Rhi, Tara and Billy stood outside the office's closed doors as I approached. I

339 THE GESTALT COMPLETE

stopped when Rhi held up a hand, her finger to her lips.

"What do you mean it was the right thing to do at the time?" Shae shouted.

"You weren't here; you don't know what occurred after Doreen was killed." Craig paused, "A day after, Pagoda showed up here backed by actual US military troops! He was polite enough about what had happened, but as soon as he got me alone, he bloodbound me on the spot. Afterward, he ordered me to do the same to the rest. His men rounded them all up and watched as I did it individually."

I closed my eyes and focused on her voice. A moment later, I saw Craig staring at me from across his desk. The image was blurry and not very clear, but I was seeing what Shae saw. I didn't know how I was doing this, but it seemed to be working.

"What about Billy?" Shae demanded.

Craig sighed. "After figuring out what was happening around Z Day, I understood what was coming. There wouldn't be any room left for norms, at least not around here. We would need every strong hand we could get to protect this place, so I brought Billy into the fold."

"Against his will," It was a statement, not a question.

"He didn't understand what was at stake. If he could have seen the big picture..." Craig said patiently, as if he were explaining it to a five-year-old.

I glanced at Billy, whose face had gone white. As I watched, Billy was studying the carpet as if his life depended on it.

"The big picture! Nowhere in that big picture was there enough room for one man to keep his humanity?" Shae asked.

"You're being naïve," Craig said.

"No, I'm being human. What gives you the right to think you can go around and play God with all these boy's lives?" Shae asked.

"I'm the master of this house!" Craig bellowed.

"Says who?" Shae asked.

"Says..." he couldn't seem to find a good answer to her question.

"Yeah, that's right. I might add that a madman, a now-dead madman, put you in charge. Before that, who ran the place, huh?

All of you. You worked together to take care of this place. You didn't have someone in charge because you didn't need it. Each of you knew what needed to get done, and you took care of it," Shae said.

"Things are better now," Craig said.

"Better for who? For the slaves you have working downstairs or for the little rich kid who just had to be in charge so he can impress mommy and daddy?" Shae regretted the words the second they were out of her mouth. The look on his face reinforced her regret. Yes, she'd crossed the line, but he couldn't see what his dictatorship was doing.

"Get out." His voice was low, almost a growl.

"I'm sorry," Shae said as calmly as she could. "That was wrong of me. But you don't see what you're doing to those boys."

"I told you to get out," his fury seemed barely under control.

Shae turned away and slowly started walking towards the door.

I could feel her presence the closer to the door she got.

Shae turned back at the door, "Do you even care about them anymore?"

"Of course I care," Craig huffed. "I wouldn't have to do any of this if I didn't care. Everything I do is to care for this household, including them."

"Is it? Is it really?" Shae turned and took a step towards him. "Randy spends every waking hour as far away from here as possible. It used to be the two of you were inseparable." She took another step. "When was the last time you sat down with them? When was the last time you actually talked to them?"

"I—" Craig stuttered.

"I mean REALLY talk. Not given an order or command. When did you last check on Sean and David to see how they were getting along?"

"They're fine," Craig said.

"If you're going to lead this place, you must know your people." Shae's eyes were hard.

"Don't go there," he spat. "I lived with them longer than you have!"

"You can live with someone a hundred years and never know them. Others you can spend five minutes in their company and know them as you know yourself. Which are you?" Shae asked.

"Don't you condescend to me. I was chosen to run this place!" Craig said.

"True, but think about this. Ever since you were put under that madman's heel, has every action been yours or that of Pagoda's slave?" Shae offered.

"Why you..." He came around the desk in a flash and was in her face.

I tensed, pulling my concealed pistol.

No James. Shae's voice caused me to freeze in place, keeping me from bursting into the room.

"You, of all people, shouldn't talk," Craig roared.

"You're right, but you have no idea what that man did. You had to deal with him for a few days; I had to deal with him for 14 years," Shae said quietly.

"Then you should understand why I did what I did," Craig said calmly.

"No one should put a collar on another person, no matter how righteous they feel. You should know that. You've been free of his influence for months. You could rescind your bond anytime you want," Shae said.

I suddenly felt the ghost of something around my neck. Something old and cold but strangely familiar due to years of use. The feeling was gone as quickly as Shae's memory had appeared, but my throat still felt the tightness of it.

"But we're safer now. Everything I've done has made this place safer for everyone," Craig countered.

"Be that as it may, when does it end? When are you safe enough to give them back their freedom?" Shae asked.

He closed his mouth and turned away from her after a moment. "They wouldn't stay."

"I'm not saying it will be easy. I can see where you think you were in the right, but I wasn't one of the ones you put a collar on. I can pretty much guarantee they won't see it your way." She reached out and touched his shoulder. "You were all brothers once; you may be again with time. But if you want to earn back their trust, you have to trust them first."

"I don't know," Craig hesitated.

"You need to make a choice. You need to either release them from all bonds and try to put your family back together, or you need to understand why you refuse to let go of that power. Because it's never been about the safety of this place, and you know it," Shae said quietly, but firmly.

He was quiet for a long time. "If I release them...will you...help me restore the peace?"

She gently turned him around to face her. "I'll stay as long as it takes." She searched his eyes and found what she was looking for. "We can work through this together. I promise."

His face was troubled, and he had a hard time coming to meet her eyes, but eventually, he did. "Then I'll release them of all bonds. What do I have to do to make that happen?"

"You've already done it. If you meant it, then they're free. They just don't know it yet," Shae whispered.

I had been so focused on what Shae was seeing I'd lost track of myself. So, it wasn't until I heard the crash of the door being kicked in that I realized I wasn't holding my gun anymore. I blinked back into my body just in time to see Billy raising my pistol and firing as he entered the room.

By the time I'd pulled myself together enough to react, Billy had emptied the pistol and was still pulling the trigger. The hammer repeatedly fell on an empty chamber until I reached up and took the pistol from Billy's hands.

Billy's eyes were empty as he stood and stared at what he'd done.

Shae had managed to throw herself to the side as Billy opened fire. Luckily, she'd been fast enough to get out of the way. Craig, the intended target, wasn't so lucky.

Billy had never been much in the way of firearms. But what he lacked in marksmanship, the power of the anti-vampire "jewel" rounds more than made up for. Five of the eight rounds he'd fired had struck with catastrophic results.

Craig lay in pieces on the floor, very much dead.

When I heard we were going into a vampire estate and weren't sure of the status, I'd broken out two magazines worth of jewels from the Dilla. I had hoped I wouldn't need to use them, but I didn't want to be caught short, just in case. Now I wish I'd left them in the truck.

Rhi stood just behind Billy now, holding his arms. He didn't resist; he just stood there in shock.

"You OK?" I asked as I helped Shae up off the floor.

"I'm fine." She glanced from what was left of Craig's corpse to Billy. "He's not." She closed her eyes for a long moment. "I knew you and Rhi were out there. I didn't know Billy was."

"I didn't expect him to do something like that," I said.

"I guess he still resented Craig for turning him," Shae said. "When Craig released all bonds, I guess that included the whole not killing your maker restraint." Shae glanced at Craig's remains again, "Goddess...I thought I'd gotten through to him, too."

"Don't blame yourself; I should have maintained control of my pistol," I said.

"No, there's no blame here that doesn't fall on Billy." Shae sighed. "Even if it wasn't today, he would have found a way, if he really wanted to."

Just then, the others began to arrive, having been summoned by the sound of the gunshots. David had to lead Sean away as he became violently ill. The others just stood around in shock until Randy showed up.

Randy surveyed the scene and then came to Shae, who gave him a quick rundown on what had transpired. "OK," was all he'd said before getting Thomas to help him remove Billy from the scene.

We waited a few days for the family to adjust to what had happened. After the truth of what had transpired came out and the shock had worn off, things seemed to return to some semblance of normal.

Billy continued to be non-responsive, in an almost zombie-like state. Someone had to always be with him to feed and care for him. If you tried to talk to him, he just looked through you as if you weren't there. If you led him by the hand, he'd follow. But if you let him be, he'd simply stop.

Rhi had tried several times to get through to Billy, both

verbally and mentally. But not even with a bloodtouch could she reach him.

"He's simply folded in on himself, I can't get through to him," Rhi said. "He might come out of it eventually, but it'll have to be his choice. Regardless, it'll probably be a long road."

While the group was relieved to no longer be under someone's mind control, they soon found they actually needed someone to be in charge. They hadn't realized how much Craig had been managing the house behind the scenes. They eventually appointed Randy to be de facto-in-charge. He didn't want the job as it restricted his freedom. But now that Craig was gone, he didn't have a reason to run away anymore.

I ensured Randy had the information he needed to contact the Austin compound before we packed everything up and got back on the road.

The goodbyes were solemn ones. Shae teared up when she told Billy goodbye and made Randy promise to keep her informed on how he was doing.

No one felt much like talking once we were back on the road as a gloom had descended on the group. I could only hope it would lift once we reached Baytown.

The Bay Comes to Baytown

JAMES

"Holy God," Rhi gasped.

"That about sums it up," I said as I scanned what was left of the town known as Baytown. Roofs had been torn off houses, building rubble was strewn everywhere, and at least three fires were still burning out of control. You could also see where water had come in, flooding the town from the gulf.

I lowered the binoculars. "Can you see anything?" I asked.

Shae was using the tablet to scan the city with the Dilla's optics suite. "I'm not getting any movement, alive or dead," she said, still scanning. "Looks like that hurricane hit the city pretty hard."

The city itself wasn't that big. It sat on the inner edge of the bay, right up against the waterline. From our vantage point at the crest of the large bridge over the mouth of the bay, we could see everything for kilometers around.

Climbing back into the Dilla, I pulled up the computer interface. I hated using the military's computer system. Whoever had designed their software had made the simplest task take about 12 times longer than its civilian counterpart. But then again, it was intended to link up with other military units and track battlefield data in real-time, not Google addresses.

A few minutes later, I was focusing on the part of town

where Liam's family lived. There was obvious damage, even from this distance, but it looked like mostly wind, not fire. There was a chance someone might still be there.

I knew I was probably kidding myself. There's no way someone would still be there after all this time. But if I didn't check, I'd always wonder.

"Anyone ever heard of JTF Steel?" Rhi called out, looking through the binoculars to the East, not the West where Baytown was.

"Never heard of it, why?" Shae said.

"Check out 2 o'clock, about 15 kilometers," Rhi said.

Shae zoomed the suite in and was shocked by what she saw. "Woah."

I leaned over, and Shae turned the tablet towards me. "Goowah!" I choked.

JTF Steel was apparently a prominent steel manufacturing plant consisting of several long buildings that had to stretch for a good three kilometers. I could see train cars lined up along the far side, along with a large water tower.

There didn't appear to be any damage to the buildings, even though they looked old and weathered. Someone had the forethought to reinforce the fence line with large steel plates that had to be nearly four meters high. They'd been lined up, overlapping each other the entire perimeter of the complex.

It was a good thing, too, as there looked to be a couple hundred shamblers surrounding the place.

"Why are they all just hanging out around that place?" Rhi said when she stuck her head into the Dilla.

"Probably attracted to the noise of the mill if it's still going," I said.

"Someone's still alive," Shae said as she pointed at several people who appeared to be walking inside the perimeter.

"Zoom in on that." I pointed towards the screen. "Looks like they're trying to expand the fence to take in more land."

A large crane was in the middle of a field outside the metal walls. It was surrounded on three sides by unfinished steel walls.

"There's nothing there. Why would they want it?" Rhi

asked.

"Farmland," Shae supplied.

"Farmland? This close to the ocean?" I asked.

"If you're careful, several crops can survive in the salty conditions." Shae shrugged.

"Huh," I said. "Learn something new every day." I looked at the mill again. "I don't know anything about metal mills, but with the size of those buildings, you could easily house five or six hundred people."

"Try a grand," Rhi chimed in.

"Yeah, remember the conditions at Ellington," Shae added.

"No idea how you could feed and water that many, though." I shook my head. "Anyway, let's go take a look at why we're here."

"James..." Shae said.

"I know, Shae. There's probably no point, but I still have to check," I said somberly.

$$\infty\infty\Omega\infty\infty$$

JAMES

As we entered the densely packed suburban area, the streets quickly became impassable, and we had to continue on foot. The neighborhood was a lower high class with large houses packed close together since land was at a premium. Baytown was known for its oil industry, and there was a lot of money here.

What were once well-maintained and manicured lawns were now overgrown with weeds and broken tree limbs. Nearly every window in the neighborhood was broken, allowing the elements inside homes that once had full-time maids to keep them spotless.

At one point, a pack of dogs who'd returned to their most basic instincts had approached us but thought better of it and went in search of easier prey. It would have been funny to see toy purse dogs running in a pack if it weren't for their blood-stained muzzles.

I wondered if any of the pretend "service animals" had turned on their owners. I'd had friends with legitimate service animals trained to help them in everyday life. Not these people who carried their Chihuahuas in their purses in Walmart and said they were service animals just because they had a little red vest on.

We soon found Liam's family home in the same condition as the others. No one was home when we entered. We took a while searching the premises, looking for any clues or remains of what might have happened.

Expensive paintings hung on the walls next to child school photos and Little League pictures. All of them hung crooked, reminding me of how much "normal" life had been turned on its head.

"What was the name of that steel place?" Shae asked.

"JVC?" I offered.

"JTC," Rhi corrected. "JVC..." She shook her head at me.

"What?" I shrugged.

Shae handed over the envelope she was reading. When I turned it over, the bright red letters of "JTC Steel" were on the return address, and it was addressed to "Shareholder Henry Ellas."

"Seems your friend's father had a major stake in the steel mill's revitalization project." Shae handed me the letter that had been in the envelope. It outlined where the revamp project currently sat, estimated completion dates, etc.

"You think they might have gone there?" Rhi asked.

"Worth a shot, I guess." I folded the letter up and put it and the envelope down.

"Good, I wanted to check that place out anyway," Rhi said.

"Why?" Shae asked.

"Why? Are you kidding me? Of all the places we've come across so far, these guys look like they have a serious plan for staying alive. We might be able to get some ideas we can incorporate back in Austin," Rhi said.

We planned to return to Austin after this. It seemed like we'd been gone six months already. Of course, Rhi had been gone longer, but that was a whole different story.

We didn't run into any shamblers returning to the Dilla. Being so close to a major city was weird. We'd only run into one zombie on the way to the house and it had been trapped under a fallen tree. It looked like it had broken its back but was still trying to move. Rhi had put it down quickly and quietly before moving on.

The land around the steel mill was flat with only a few trees for concealment. We were a short distance away, not wanting to get too close as to disturb the horde around the place.

"How are we going to get in there?" I mumbled to myself.

"The better question is, will they let us in?" Rhi added.

"Well, aren't you just a ray of sunshine?" I retorted.

"Gotta be honest. No matter what we do, they may not open the gates," Rhi said.

Shae's snapping fingers drew our attention. "Give me a pen, paper, something," Shae said, her eyes fixed on the mill.

Rhi handed up the tablet, and Shae removed the stylus before opening a note program.

There was a flashing light coming from the mill. Someone was on one of the walls, using a mirror or something to signal us.

"Morse?" I asked and was immediately "shushed" by Shae, who was rapidly scribbling. We all remained silent as the minutes ticked away. Finally, she sighed and looked down at her scribbling. She then glanced about for the handle that operated the external spotlight. She swiveled it towards the mill and began to click it on and off for a few seconds.

"Well, we can talk to them," Shae started.

"What'd they say?" Rhi asked.

"You don't know Morse?" Shae asked. "I thought that was taught to the military?"

"Not the Army," Rhi said.

"Nor the Air Force," I added.

"Well, that's dumb." Shae frowned. "They want to know who we are and what we want," Shae said. "Of course, my morse is so rusty I could be wrong."

"Could have guessed that without the Morse," I started, but Shae's flat stare brought me up short. "Sorry."

"So, what do we want to say?" Shae asked.

"Tell them," I thought about it. "Tell them we're separated military searching for missing family."

"That's technically true." Rhi smiled as Shae began clicking.

"They want to know what family," Shae said.

"Tell them, Ellas," I spelled it out.

After a minute, "They're telling us to wait," Shae reported.

It was probably ten minutes before they came back. "They say they can't open a gate because their 'moat' is too big," Shae said, looking down at the tablet.

"We could scale the thing." Rhi eyed the metal walls.

"Or we could go through and wipe them out." Shae looked around the area.

"That," I started, "Would be a lot of work."

"Which one?" Rhi asked.

"I could do it," Tara spoke up. She didn't talk very often, so when she did, all eyes turned to her.

"Tara, that's a lot of zombies. The amount of metal you'd have to control...this isn't an enclosed space like Drakes," Rhi said cautiously.

"Exactly. All I'd need would be one bullet," she said.

"One bullet?" Shae asked.

"Just the one. If I can see them, I can move the bullet from one to the next until they're all gone," Tara said confidently.

"I could be with her in the turret," Rhi offered. "We haven't seen a rotter who could climb the Dilla yet."

"Yeah, and I didn't know they could climb stairs until Drakes," I added.

We were quiet for a moment. "It's not a bad plan," Shae conceded.

"But they would see the whole thing," I said.

"I could use the suppressor and pretend I was sniping," Rhi countered.

"You sure you can do it? It's going to take a while," I said.

"Piece of pie," Tara said.

"Cake honey, piece of cake," Rhi corrected.

"Whatever," Tara shrugged happily.

After signaling the mill, we maneuvered to the other side

near the makeshift gate. A massive slab of steel was attached to a crane. Two people were standing to either side of the entrance now, looking out over the top of the wall.

Rhi was screwing the suppressor onto the M4 while Tara popped the turret hatch.

"Why the suppressor?" Shae asked.

"That way, they won't know I'm not actually shooting," Rhi winked.

"Good luck," I said.

Rhi waggled her eyebrows and stood up in the turret with Tara.

When the girls signaled they were ready, I moved us forward until we were close enough to draw attention.

Locking down the brake, I said, "Have at it, Tara."

"Ready?" Rhi aimed her rifle at the first approaching shambler.

"Yes," Tara said.

The rifle cycled as the suppressor absorbed nearly all the muzzle blast. The round went through the zombie's skull before continuing its impossible flight towards the next target. What followed was the most bizarre game of pinball I'd ever seen. Rhi continued to aim her rifle in the general area where the bodies were falling as she couldn't keep track of the bullet. She'd had to fire three more times because either Tara had lost the bullet or the bullet had disintegrated to the point she couldn't use it anymore.

After twenty minutes, Tara was exhausted. The sweat had made her clothes stick to her skin, and her head was hurting so bad she said she was having a hard time seeing straight. She slumped back into the Dilla as the last one fell around us.

"Great job, Tara. You OK?" Shae asked as I moved us toward the now-opening gate.

A weak thumbs up was all Shae got in reply.

Rhi stayed in the turret, scanning the area as we entered the compound.

"Fast mover!" Rhi called before dropping it with a neat headshot just as the gate began to close behind us.

"I can't believe there are still fast movers out there," Shae shook her head.

"Not all safe havens stay safe," I said.

"Pleasant thought," Rhi said, dropping down and securing the turret.

A ring of seven armed guards met us, all dressed in run-of-the-mill casual clothes. The guns they sported were an assortment of hunting rifles and shotguns with a few pistols sprinkled in; nothing military in sight. None of the guards said a word as we dismounted.

A tall man with gray hair and a salt-and-pepper beard approached us from the building. I thought he looked familiar but couldn't place him. When he got close enough, he held out his hand.

"Henry Ellas. I must say it's good to see any military presence after this long."

"You're Liam's father!" I said.

Henry looked surprised. "You know my son?"

"Yes, I'm James Sable. Liam and I were friends when I was back in school in Austin. I believe you and I have met once or twice before, but don't ask me when. My memory's not what it used to be," I smiled.

"James," Henry seemed to ponder the name. "It's familiar, but I'm afraid I don't remember it. Time's not been too kind to my memory either."

"That's alright. Is Liam here? We came up from Austin, and I was trying to check on family in the area."

"Um," Henry looked over my shoulder. "Not to be rude, but what's with her? Is she contagious?"

I didn't have to look to know he was referring to Tara. "Oh, chemical burns. Nothing to worry about." I tried to sound casual.

"And the tail?" Henry asked.

"Cosplay," I said.

"Cos-what?"

"She likes to play dress up. It's her...coping mechanism for everything that's happened." I was getting better at my BSing.

Henry nodded, "Well, it's not the strangest thing I've seen so far. We had a man wander in here a few weeks ago who thought he was a dog. He used to sleep in one of the box cars out back. Then, one day, he was just gone."

I nodded as he finished. "Wow, takes all types, I guess. What about Liam? Is he OK?"

Henry's face was pained, "I don't know. He went out with a group to gather supplies, and they never came back."

"How long overdue?" I asked.

"Two days," Henry grimaced.

I hissed. Two days was a long time. I was still lost in thought when Henry cleared his throat.

"Hmm? Oh, I'm sorry." I made introductions all around, my mind still on Liam.

"You said you were separated military?" Henry asked.

"We're currently a detached unit operating out of Austin. There's not a lot of military left; we're spread pretty thin," I said.

"I can imagine. But I'm sure your people are tired. We don't have much, but we can offer food and a bed," Henry said.

"Thank you," I hesitated. *Shae, Rhi?*

I'll stay here with Tara; you two go. I want to get a good look around, Rhi said.

Shae nodded.

"Sir, CAPT Rhiannon and Tara here would like to talk to you about your defensive designs. She's looking to make improvements to our compound in Austin and will take any advice your people could offer," I said.

"We'd be more than happy to help in any way we can," Henry said. "Nowadays, we need to help each other as much as possible."

"I, on the other hand, would like to head out to find Liam. Can you tell me where to start?" I asked.

"Of course. Come this way," Henry said and led us inside.

My Spidey sense is tingling, Rhi chimed in.

Yeah, mine too, Shae agreed.

You still want to stay? I asked.

Of course, Rhi smiled. *Since when did I let common sense stop me?*

It turned out that Liam had gone out on a supply run with

four other people. Liam had the only military training and had overseen the run. Their objective was a nursery several kilometers away. The mill was attempting to start gardening and needed a lot of supplies to make it work. The party took two vehicles, and what should have taken a couple of hours was already into day three. Henry showed me where the nursery was on a map as well as the route Liam was supposed to have taken.

Watch your back, I said to Rhi as Shae and I mounted up in the Dilla.

Always, Rhi smiled. *Don't go getting yourself bit again.*

I thought chicks dug scars, I said.

Not zombie scars. Be safe, Rhi turned serious at the end.

Always, Shae replied.

Rhi snorted in disbelief and turned away as we departed the mill.

Several zombies had already started to appear from the woods surrounding the place. The mill constantly ran, pumping out more steel plates for the walls. The sounds were appropriately loud, drawing all sorts of unwanted attention.

I easily avoided the few shamblers and turned the Dilla toward the nursery.

∞∞Ω∞∞

JAMES

We left the Dilla a good way from the nursery and approached on foot. The only other building aside from the nursery was a small strip mall on the other side of the road, which we were currently crouched atop.

You see anything? I asked, but Shae only shook her head.

The nursery looked relatively intact, somehow the hurricane had spared it. It sprawled probably a good acre or so back and had covered greenhouses with opaque siding. The two vehicles Liam's crew used were parked out front, empty and doors open.

Looks like they got out in a hurry, Shae observed.

Or they were getting back in when something happened. Looks like they might have been loading up. I could just make out some plastic bags lying in the back of the truck.

Only one way to find out. She looked at me, and we both silently slipped off the roof and across the street.

They were definitely loading up. I ran my hand across the plastic fertilizer bags stacked in the back of the truck.

Keys are still in the ignition, Shae said.

Must have been in a hurry if they forgot those, I said.

Well, it's not like a rotter is going to drive off with it, Shae said.

True, I said.

Blood, Shae pointed at the ground beside the van, where several dried blood stains were in the dirt.

Leading inside, I knelt and looked at the stained soil. *Drag marks heading inside as well.*

Someone bit? Shae suggested.

Could be, I adjusted my AUG in its shoulder sling. *Keep your eyes open.*

We moved towards the front doors. They were simple swinging doors and were unlocked. The room inside was filled with tools, hoses and other assorted gardening implements. Almost everything was untouched.

Have you noticed how much Tara looks like Rhi? Shae suddenly sent.

What?

It's just that I keep catching them standing together, and they have so many similarities it's freaky, Shae said, looking behind a counter.

I...they...now's not the time Shae, I said as my brain grinded gears trying to shift between combat and personal thoughts.

That way, Shae said without missing a beat. Apparently, she kept her trains of thought on separate tracks and somehow easily jumped between the two. I was jealous.

Shae was pointing past the checkout registers and toward another set of double doors on our left. The blood trail led up to and through them.

Beyond was a long, hot house. Here, there were signs of a struggle. Overturned tables, uprooted plants and broken pots littered the ground.

Are those bullet holes? Shae pointed at the wall.

Looks like it, I glanced at her. *Good eye. You're getting better at this.*

You're a bad influence. Shae smiled, trying to break the tension.

I chuckled nervously as we moved on and into another hot house. This one was full of baby trees and shrubbery.

Careful, lots of hiding spots in here. I flexed my hands as I caught myself tensing up on the grip of my rifle. I double-checked my rifle's scope was at zero magnification. If something started in here, it would be real close quarters.

As if on cue, the bushes burst apart as the fast mover sprang at us with a growl.

Shae's rifle barked twice as I rolled out of the way and came up just as Shae put a third bullet through the zombie's head as it was trying to get up off the ground.

Thanks, I swiveled my rifle, looking for more targets.

Well, if they didn't know we were here before, they do now, Shae said, looking at the body. *You think this might be one of the group from the mill?*

Probably a good guess. It would explain why they didn't come back. I didn't take my eyes off our surroundings. I'd already been caught off guard once. I wasn't about to let it happen again.

We paused at the doors to the next hot house. We could hear movement beyond the doors.

How many you think? Shae asked.

I don't know, at least five, I guessed.

The sounds were getting louder, slowly shambling towards us. We started to back away from the door with the intention of letting the shamblers come to us when something latched onto my leg and tripped me.

I felt the heat of the muzzle blast from Shae's rifle as she dispatched what was left of a shambler who'd drug himself through the bushes toward me.

That's two I owe you, I didn't hear her reply as a crowd of rotters pushed through the swinging doors and headed toward us.

I had only fired from my back a few times, mainly when using a modified areal gunner position for the M60 machine gun. It was dangerous to do as the possibility of shooting your toes off was pretty good. With this in mind, I flattened out and spread my feet as I began shooting towards the door.

Bodies fell in the doorway, lodging the doors open as we both opened fire.

My rifle locked open, the magazine empty. I was reaching for a replacement when Shae's voice called to me, *Fast mover!*

Shae forgot her current target and shifted her fire toward the figure sprinting towards her from the other side of the room. She pulled the trigger, and nothing happened; the rifle had jammed.

The thing cleared a table, knocking bushes to the floor and leaped on top of another as it advanced.

Shae fumbled, not experienced with clearing a jammed rifle. She glanced down to try and see what was wrong with the rifle, taking her eyes off her target. Looking back up, she found the thing in mid-air, just a meter away. As if in slow motion, she watched as its head exploded. Shae tried to spin out of the way but still caught a glancing blow from the body.

The fast mover hit the ground unmoving as I downed the last of the zombies.

*You OK?" I asked.

Yeah, just flustered.

Next time, transition, I said, picking myself up off the ground, my pistol still smoking in my hand.

Transition? Shae asked.

If your gun jams or you're out of ammo, sometimes switching weapons is faster. I picked up the magazine I'd dropped and finished reloading my rifle before putting the pistol back in its holster.

I'll remember that, thanks, Shae said, finally clearing the rifle's jam. *Maybe next time, we should use the whole knock-and-wait method?*

You're right. I made a mistake...again. Got worried about Liam and wasn't thinking. I sighed, trying to shake off the embarrassment. *Shall we?* I motioned towards the pile of bodies holding the door open for us.

The next hothouse had row after row of flower pots full of every colored flower imaginable. The flowers were wilted but still held their color. On the other side was a metal door. A door with blood smeared across it.

We looked at one another before slowly approaching the door. I tried the door but found it locked.

"Anyone in there?" My voice sounded unusually loud in the eerie silence of the nursery. I banged on the door and tried to see through the glass into the dark room beyond

Shae glanced around the room to make sure we hadn't picked up any unwanted attention.

I was about to bang on the door again when a bloodied face slammed against the glass, causing me to jump back and bring my rifle up. Before I could fire, a barely audible voice escaped from the bloodied visage.

"Is someone there?" The voice was weak, almost a croak.

"Yes, we're US military. The people at the mill sent us, open the door," I said.

"Sorry, can't do that," The face said.

"You need medical attention; open the door and let us help you," I said.

"There's no help for me; I'm protecting you," the face said.

"Are you bit?" Shae cut in.

"Oh, I'm way past bit, little lady," the voice had just a bit more life to it than before.

"Liam?" I finally recognized his voice.

There was a pause. "Who are you?"

"Liam, it's James. Your father sent us, open the door."

"James," the face against the glass shifted, trying to bring its other eye up to the window. "What are you doing here?"

"Looking for you, now open up," I was losing patience. If Liam was hurt, there wasn't much time.

"Can't do it, amigo. No telling when I'm going to turn into one of those things," Liam said.

The words stabbed into my chest, causing my throat to tighten up. "Liam, I'm not going to leave you in that metal box."

"That's just what you're going to do," Liam coughed and spat. "The van is packed with the fertilizer the mill needs. The truck's only half full, but better than nothing," he growled in pain.

"Don't be stupid, Liam, open the door," I had both hands flat on the door and was staring through the window into my friend's good eye.

"By the time you need more fertilizer," Liam began. "I'll be one of the slow ones, easy to deal with."

Liam's voice told me he meant it. Liam had always been way too calm and collected about things. I'd only seen him upset a handful of times, and even then, most people would only consider it as being "put out." If he said he wouldn't open the door, he meant it.

"What about your father, Liam?" Shae tried.

"Who is that?" Liam strained to see Shae.

"Open the door, and I'll introduce you," I offered.

"Nah," the humor in Liam's voice was interrupted with a racking cough. When he could speak again, he said, "It shouldn't be too long. You should get going."

Shae, help me. I took hold of the edge of the door and began to pull, the metal immediately beginning to strain.

Shae slung her rifle and grabbed the lip of the door as well. Our combined strength caused the metal to protest loudly.

I felt the metal biting into my hand as a sudden warmth marked my skin breaking, but I wasn't about to stop now. With blood now seeping into my palm, I almost lost my grip just as a tearing sound announced the door popping open.

Liam's battered and bloodied body fell towards us and I caught him out of reflex. I could see multiple bite marks on his arms, and his face was white as a sheet.

I knelt and helped prop Liam up against the metal door, using part of his shirt to wipe away some of the blood from his face. I couldn't exactly see where the blood was coming from as Liam was covered nearly head to toe.

"Well, hi," Liam gave what I guessed had to be a smile, but it quickly turned to a grimace as his body shook.

"What happened?" I asked.

"Everything was great. No problem getting here, no zombies. It wasn't until we were almost done loading that Skylar yelled out. We didn't see them coming. I have no idea where they had been, but the next thing I see is Skylar, Rhet and Benji being chewed on. They fought them off, but there were more all around us suddenly. We ran back inside, but there were more in there, too. Just don't know where they came from.

"Next, everyone's shooting and things are crazy. Something slams me in the side of the head, and I go down like a sack of potatoes. Next, I wake up, and Herbert is dragging me towards the back. I couldn't move but could see the bite marks; I knew what that meant. He puts me in here and tells me he's going for help.

"Just stay put and lock the door; I'll be back," he says. So, I managed to get the door locked and proceeded to pass back out. Next thing I know, you're banging on the door." Liam tried to raise his head, "Did Herbert send you?"

"No, I don't think Herbert made it," I said.

"You sure?" Liam asked.

"Pretty sure, both vehicles are still out front," I said.

"Well shit," Liam shook his head.

James, Shae said. *They said they left three days ago. Which means he was probably bit two days ago.*

So? I said. *So what?*

He's been infected for more than 24 hours, probably 48. That's the longest I've ever heard of anyone being infected and still alive. Let alone alive and coherent, Shae said.

What are you trying to say? I asked.

That's just it, she started. *I don't know what to make of it, but he shouldn't be alive.*

I looked at Liam, this time assessing his wounds. The bite wounds had scabbed over; they weren't pretty, but they weren't bleeding. There was a huge lump on the back of his head, probably from whatever had hit him and knocked him out. I felt Liam's skin. It was warm to the touch, warmer than it should be, possibly fever from infection?

Shae, call in the Dilla, I said.

What are you doing? Shae said as she pulled the tablet from her pocket.

I'm taking him back, I reached for the medkit on my back.

Taking him back? She looked up at me from the tablet. *You think that's a good idea?*

I don't know, I said. *All I know is that I've seen more impossible things in the last four months than I could have imagined. Why can't this be another one of those impossibilities?*

Shae shook her head and turned back to the tablet.

One of the many features of the Dilla was the ability to drive it remotely. We'd never used it before; we'd never had a reason. The controls on the tablet were similar to most modern console video games; the designers had known their target audience. It was practically intuitive. Luckily, I'd gotten around to teaching Shae how to drive the Dilla on one of the spare days we'd had at Drakes.

"What are you doing?" Liam said, rousing from the unconsciousness he'd slipped into after his long story.

"Patching you up," I said.

"Don't bother; you're just wasting supplies," Liam said, making it seem like he was going to push my hands away, but his arms wouldn't move.

"I just ripped a metal door off its hinges, don't try to fight me," I started wrapping the wounds with gauze.

"You did, didn't you?" Liam mumbled.

You think I can risk morphine? I glanced at Shae, who didn't look up from the tablet.

I have no idea, she said.

"Are you allergic to morphine?" I asked Liam.

"Never had it before," Liam said.

"We'll risk it," I started to reach for one of the precious vials I had and instead pulled my pistol. Before anyone could react, I fired over Shae's shoulder and dropped the shambler behind her.

Thanks, Shae risked a glance over her shoulder at the body.

No problem, I noticed Liam barely flinched at the noise. I broke the ampoule and pressed it into Liam's thigh before returning to the bandages.

I carried Liam to the Dilla and belted him into the front passenger seat.

What if he— Shae started.

Do what you must, Shae, I nodded and climbed into the overloaded van.

I left Liam with Shae because I wasn't sure if I could put him down if he turned while en route.

We convoyed back towards the mill at a slow pace, and I tried to baby the van as much as I could. Once we were close enough, I reached out.

Rhi, I included Shae in the link.

What's up, puddin'? Rhi responded.

She does that on purpose, you know, Shae whispered privately.

What? I asked.

Comes up with as many pet names for you as she can. It's endearing, Shae smiled.

Shaking my head, *Rhi, I need you to get a hold of Henry. Let him know he's got a decision to make.*

∞∞Ω∞∞

JAMES

"Well, he's definitely got a fever," The older gentleman said as he washed his hands with hand sanitizer. "I've got him on a drip and drugs that will keep him out of it for a while. The wounds themselves show signs of a serious infection, but not in the same way as the zombie infection looks. The normal human mouth is a breeding ground for disease, let alone the mouth on one of those things. I'm hoping the drugs I'm giving him knock it out. I'd say we'll know in 24 hours, but remember, I'm just a vet."

"That's better than I could have asked for, doctor, thank you," Henry shook the man's hand and turned back to the group. "Thank you again for bringing my son back. The fertilizer is great, but having him back in relatively one piece is a miracle."

I nodded, looking around the small infirmary. They had converted a tiny nurse's office into a clinic using scrounged supplies.

"Since his mother passed and his brother is still missing, Liam is all I have. I know it's selfish, but I need him," Henry said.

"There's nothing selfish in wanting your family safe," Shae said.

"Anything you need, you let me know," Henry said as he turned back to the chair beside his son's bed.

Do You think he'd be able to do it if Liam changes? Shae asked.

Maybe, I replied. *But if he did, I'm pretty sure he'd follow right behind.*

"You find what you need, Rhi?" I asked her once we were out of the clinic.

"Did I? What I'd give to have this place near our compound. Did you know they're building modified steel walls that have moving slits that allow you to take out rotters safely from the other side? It's really an impressive setup," Rhi said.

"Where are they getting their raw materials?" Shae asked.

"There's an old railroad yard behind the place. They used to pull the train cars right up to the back dock and load them up. Well, there are a lot of unused train cars out there that are perfect for melting down. It may not be the best steel, but it's more than up to the job of holding back a few hundred rotters," Rhi said.

"Is there anything we can use back at the compound?" Shae asked.

Frowning, Rhi replied, "Not really. But if we find a shit-ton of steel plating, I know exactly what to do with it now."

I managed to refuel the Dilla after scrounging from a few vehicles. We spent the night intending to leave once we had word on Liam, one way or the other. Unfortunately, we didn't have to wait long.

The doc guessed Liam had gone into septic shock, resulting in cardiac failure. Even if the doctor had known, Liam had gone septic, and they didn't have the drugs needed to treat it. The doctor tried to revive Liam, but he never came back.

There had been a short service before Henry had burned the body.

I didn't feel right leaving, but there was nothing more we could do. Henry thanked us again for bringing Liam home before retreating to his office.

In Behemoth's Shadow

TARA

Hello Father: I apologize for the poor handwriting but I'm writing to you from the backseat of a motor vehicle. I think I mentioned it before, it's like a wagon but without horses as it moves under its own magic power.

We're currently heading back to Rhi's hometown, a place called Austin. Let me catch you up on the last few days.

After the loss of James's friend at the large foundry, we returned to Drakes.

Rhi had the idea to pull the flying armor that attacked me back in Krodon from her storage at Drakes and bring it to the people at NASA. Rhi says if anyone can do something with it, they can. Plus it "beats having it sitting around in a box collecting dust." Rhi says the NASA people create flying ships that take people to the stars. If this is true, they shouldn't have any trouble making use of this.

I have to admit, seeing the thing that caused me such harm gave me mixed feelings. While I was happy it was dead, something else in me stirred at the close proximity.

James's melancholy deepened as he told his friend, Trent, of Liam's demise. Apparently, they were all childhood friends. While sad, Trent seemed grateful for the knowing of Liam's fate, as he had wondered himself. He said he would look in on Liam's father if he could.

Shae has taken over driving as I feel she doesn't trust James's current frame of mind, not that I can blame her. The man seems to enjoy being crotchety.

To make matters worse, we stopped at several houses to check on the family of a man named Mark. I've not met this man yet but he seems of some importance in Austin. We couldn't find his sisters at their houses and James says there's no information on them in something he calls a survivor infobase. I guess they are lost. Hopefully they still live as this world seems to have more than enough woe to go around.

Our journey to Austin is a quiet one. Everyone seems to be feeding on James's foul humor. Rhi tried on several occasions to lift his spirits, but to no avail. Eventually, she gave up and settled into the silence.

Even though we travel at amazing speeds, it's still taking the better part of a day to reach Austin. Along the way is a war-torn landscape full of burnt villages and the remnants of lost battles. While the dead are prominent, we've seen no signs of the living. I fear these are portents of the future for all of us.

So far, this world has been a mixture of wonder and terror. The constant state of excited horror can be draining at times. But it's a price I'm more than willing to pay if it keeps my wife and I together. If not for Rhi, I fear I would retreat to my village regardless of the marvels this world offers.

*Now, I must stop writing for I begin to feel what Rhi calls "car sick." While she says it's harmless, I feel as if my meal is trying to return to the plate from which it came. As a result, I must say goodbye for now, Father. My love, --
Tara*

∞∞Ω∞∞

<u>JAMES</u>

The drive back to Austin was relatively quiet. I wished I could have driven; it would have given me something to think about instead of dwelling on what happened to Liam. I kept replaying what happened over and over in my head, trying to find if there was something I could have done better that might have saved Liam. While I couldn't think of anything, it didn't stop me from torturing myself.

By the time we hit Austin city limits, I'd recovered from my funk enough to speak.

"Rhi?" I started, remembering something.

"Yuppers?" Rhi said.

"Why are you still with us?" I asked.

"What do you mean?" Rhi leaned forward to see my face.

"I mean, I'm not complaining. It's just that you had this whole other world you could have stayed in; you didn't have to come back here. Even if you did, you didn't have to stick with us. You could have gone off and done your own thing, the two of you, I mean," I indicated Tara.

Rhi looked at me with the most peculiar look I'd ever seen from her. She kept that look for quite some time before finally speaking. "Y'all are my battle buddies, idiot. I'd go AWOL for you two."

Rhi's words and her look had me at a loss for words. I could only stare at her as I came to the realization of how much these three woman actually mattered to me. Even though I'd only known Tara a short while, she'd fought beside us and loved with us. She was one of "us." She'd just stepped into the group as if she'd always been here, as natural as could be. I had to look away as my eyes started to blur.

Rhi grinned while patting my shoulder and leaned back.

The Alamo compound didn't appear to have changed, aside from the fact there were more people on guard now. We were met in the courtyard by Mark, Becca, and Adira (Mark's vampire second-in-command.)

Before we could start talking, Trish came tearing out of the main building and made a beeline straight for Rhi.

Crap, Rhi said.

Uh oh, Shae added.

This should be good, I finished, the first bit of humor bubbling to the surface since Houston.

Just before Trish reached Rhi, Tara stepped in front of Rhi, causing Trish to skid to a halt.

"Hello," Tara said, smiling widely, her fangs showing.

Knock it off, she's harmless, Rhi said, stepping around Tara and embracing Trish.

Not as harmless as you think, Tara countered.

Trish never took her eyes off Tara as the two girls stared each other down.

Uh, I started. *I heard that,* I sent to our group, including Tara apparently.

So did I, Shae said.

I should hope so, Tara said glancing over her shoulder at me with eyes I didn't recognize.

How—

"INCOMING, INCOMING, INCOMING," The warning blared from the Dilla, cutting me off mid-sentence. A whooshing sound marked the arrival of an energy disc that hit the ground and exploded, showering everyone with dirt.

The roaring sound of CWIS assaulted our ears as 20mm rounds began shooting into the sky, tracking the flying target.

Everyone scattered for whatever cover they could find.

I realized all our weapons were still in the Dilla and was about to make a break for it when the CWIS, on top of the

Dilla, exploded under a rain of energy discs.

Tara, can you grab that thing? I yelled over the roar of the flames now coming from the Dilla.

It's not metal! Tara yelled back.

Some sort of ceramic composite, Rhi said as another disc burst near her and Tara.

The discs stopped coming, and an eerie silence filled the yard only broken by the cracking flames of the burning Dilla.

The roar of a jet engine broke the silence as the armor came to rest on top of the perimeter wall, overlooking the area.

"Bring me the Daemon, and no one else has to die," the pilot's modified electronic voice blared. The sun reflected off the dented and chipped white armor, sending a cascade of reflections bouncing off the walls.

Tara started to stand up, but Rhi's grip held her firmly in place. When Tara looked, Rhi shook her head violently.

"I've destroyed your areal defenses. You are powerless to stop me. Give me the Daemon and—"

The report of a rifle sounded, followed by the *ting* of a bullet bouncing harmlessly off the white armor.

Before a second shot could be fired, the armor swung its cannon towards the sniper and, seemingly without effort, sent an energy disc flying that tore the man apart.

"You see," The voice continued triumphantly. "There's nothing you can do to me. I—"

The entire area around the armor erupted as lances of blue light rained down. Everywhere the light touched erupted in blue fire.

The wall beneath the armor crumbled, sending the flying armor crashing backward to the ground. The pilot recovered quickly, the armor leaping back in the air. Aside from a thin stream of smoke trailing it, the armor appeared undamaged.

Just as the armor cleared the treetops, a dozen tiny smoke trails darted toward it. The armor tried to dodge but the damage seemed to cause it to stutter. A dozen explosions erupted, enveloping the armor in a rolling fireball before an ear-ringing secondary explosion burst outward, and the armor was no more.

As bits of the armor rained down on the compound, people

reluctantly emerged from their cover, looking skyward and trying to locate their would-be savior.

*Everybody OK?" I asked and received a thumbs-up all around. *Anyone see it—*

A massive blue mech landed in the spot where the ruined wall had been. It was larger than the white armor, looked sleeker and more maintained and had a swirling green dragon design snaking about the armor. As we watched, the armor knelt, and it looked like the dragon design shifted, moving away from the knee to avoid being knelt on.

The blue armor design was similar to the white one, but this one stood a good seven meters tall and was more heavily armed. Four large cargo boxes were attached to the sides of the armor. At a glance it was obvious they didn't belong there. Each box was the ominous size of a coffin.

The armor secured the two smaller hand cannons to its sides. Everyone flinched as the sound of escaping gasses emerged from the chest compartment.

"Good, you're all here," a woman's voice came through the external speakers of the armor. "There's not much time; more will be following me once they realize what's happened," the voice continued.

"Who are you?" Shae asked, taking a cautious step forward.

The gas escaping from the chest compartment finally subsided. Multiple panels swiveled outwards from the suit's chest, revealing the pilot within. She was easily ten years older than the last time we'd seen her. Her head was shaved, revealing several scars that raked across the top of her scalp.

"You're coming with me, all of you," Beth indicated to Shae, Rhi, Tara and myself. "Behemoth commands it!"

65 6e 64 – Book 2

Bio-Habitat 00117 Observation Post 36211

CR'EON

I looked around me to see if anyone was watching. They weren't, they were still glued to the monitors. I subtly ended the recording of the battle and moved it to my personal storage. I sighed with relief when the transfer completed and disappeared from my screen before my supervisor turned to me.

"Cr'eon," my supervisor started, "I know this is your first Chosen Army retrieval. The admitting team will need all the information they can get about the incident. Ensure you get this report filed right away."

"Of course, right away," I echoed before watching her depart. The only other personnel in the recently expanded room were a handful of techs who were too busy chattering about the battle to pay me any attention.

I waited until DC9001 gated back to Behemoth before starting my report.

AFTER-ACTION
ANGEL GUARD ALERT
BIO-HABITAT 00117
Observation Post 36211, Cr'eon reporting.

An Angel Guard Mark 72 (designated AG2, see incident 8346Ag866) appeared at attached coordinates and time. No evidence of gating was recorded and sensors did not detect AG2 until it fired. Possibility of new stealth protocol annotated for further investigation, possibly in remains of AG1 (see incident 8346Ag866.)

AG2 destroyed local land vehicle from previous incident via a Tach 12 hand-held weapon. AG2 then landed and demanded custody of a DAEMON(a resident of Bio-Habitat 20343), designated D1.

DC9001, assigned to patrol area 47821, arrived on scene and engaged AG2. After a brief areal battle, AG2 was destroyed by DC9001 via MM212 sub-munitions.

See attachment 2 for AG2's debris field location.

DC9001 proceeded to land and acquire Chosen Army candidates: D1, and three (3) sanguivore-types: one (1) v.3.1, one (1) v.5.9, and one (1) v.2.6. DC9001 then departed the area before gating to Behemoth, bay 00117-J16.

Chosen Army candidates are believed to have operated within system fluctuation area (see report J78Fie8) for an extended period of time. Additional examination is recommended.

See attachment 4 for Chosen Army candidate information.

A pinch in my shoulder flared as I finished the report and forwarded it. I tried to keep my observations professional and short as my supervisor had already disciplined me for "guiding" my findings last time. She told me one more slip-up and I'd be transferred to a consequences assignment. I guess I wasn't as clever as I thought.

Turning back to my sensors I watched the aftermath unfold. As if the culling hadn't been enough, the presence of the AG now marked the Bio-Hab as contaminated. Any subsequent stock pulled from it would be tagged the same.

This Bio-Hab just couldn't catch a break.

I wondered what would destroy the Bio-Hab first, the culling or the AG? It didn't make a difference to me as long as I got to record it.

Epilogue

RHI

Yeah...not really much to say here, especially since I'm currently unconscious. As Nat would say, spoilers and all that. But how about that cliffhanger, right? Yeah, so anyway, I know Book 3 is half done, but I don't know where he's going with it. There's some weird shit going on that I can't get into, but let's just say even I'm scratching my head. If you thought the end of Empire was a downer, hold my beer...

ABOUT THE AUTHOR

Yeah, I'm from Texas, and retired military, and I inflicted my zombie nuttiness on my troops, and yeah I was an extra in WWZ, and yeah I'm in Colorado with my family.

But what really matters is that whiny Maine Coon. I swear, I don't know why he's so whiny, but it's ridiculous. The vet says he's fine. It's a good thing the noises he makes are cute. If you don't have one, adopt one. Then we can swap stories.

ABOUT THE AUTHOR'S CAT

ATEV"INP op[/m\]/[utvync 'p9mu4QW# U6KER
12   rtp9mu4QW# U6KER 12 rt

INTERESTED IN MORE OF THIS UNIVERSE'S INSANITY? CHECK US OUT ON FACEBOOK AT
"MUGZ INK BOOKS"